TWO TRUTHS AND A MURDER

Kensington Books by Colleen Cambridge

The Phyllida Bright Mysteries

Murder at Mallowan Hall

A Trace of Poison

Murder by Invitation Only

Murder Takes the Stage

Two Truths & A Murder

The American in Paris Mysteries

Mastering the Art of French Murder

A Murder Most French

A Fashionably French Murder

In the Spirit of French Murder

TWO TRUTHS AND A MURDER

Colleen Cambridge

KENSINGTON PUBLISHING CORP.

kensingtonbooks.com

This book is a work of fiction. Names, characters, businesses, organizations, places, events, and incidents either are the product of the author's imagination or are used fictitiously. Any resemblance to actual persons, living or dead, events, or locales is entirely coincidental.

To the extent that the image or images on the cover of this book depict a person or persons, such person or persons are merely models, and are not intended to portray any character or characters featured in the book.

KENSINGTON BOOKS are published by

Kensington Publishing Corp.
900 Third Avenue
New York, NY 10022

Copyright © 2025 by Colleen Gleason

All rights reserved. No part of this book may be reproduced in any form or by any means without the prior written consent of the Publisher, excepting brief quotes used in reviews.

Without limiting the author's and publisher's exclusive rights, any unauthorized use of this publication to train generative artificial intelligence (AI) technologies is expressly prohibited.

All Kensington titles, imprints and distributed lines are available at special quantity discounts for bulk purchases for sales promotion, premiums, fund-raising, educational or institutional use. Special book excerpts or customized printings can also be created to fit specific needs. For details, write or phone the office of the Kensington Special Sales Manager: Kensington Publishing Corp., 900 Third Avenue, New York, NY, 10022. Attn. Special Sales Department. Phone: 1-800-221-2647.

KENSINGTON and the K with book logo Reg. US Pat & TM Off.

Library of Congress Control Number: 2025937860

ISBN: 978-1-4967-4278-0

First Kensington Hardcover Edition: November 2025

ISBN: 978-1-4967-4280-3 (ebook)

10 9 8 7 6 5 4 3 2 1

Printed in the United States of America

The authorized representative in the EU for product safety and compliance
is eucomply OU, Parnu mnt 139b-14, Apt 123
Tallinn, Berlin 11317, hello@eucompliancepartner.com

*"A child boasts of having witnessed a murder.
Only a few hours later, that child is dead.
You must admit that there are grounds for believing that it might—
it's a far-fetched idea perhaps—but it might have been cause and
effect. If so, somebody lost no time."*
—Hercule Poirot, *Hallowe'en Party* by Agatha Christie

LISTLEIGH VILLAGE

LISTLEIGH RIVER

AVONLEA'S COTTAGE

CEMETERY

BOGGY MEADOW

IVYGATE COTTAGE

WOODS

FOOTPATH

WILDING HALL

PLOUGHMAN'S CLOSE ROAD

MERTON ROAD

CRESTWORTHY MANOR

GARAGE

MALLOWAN HALL

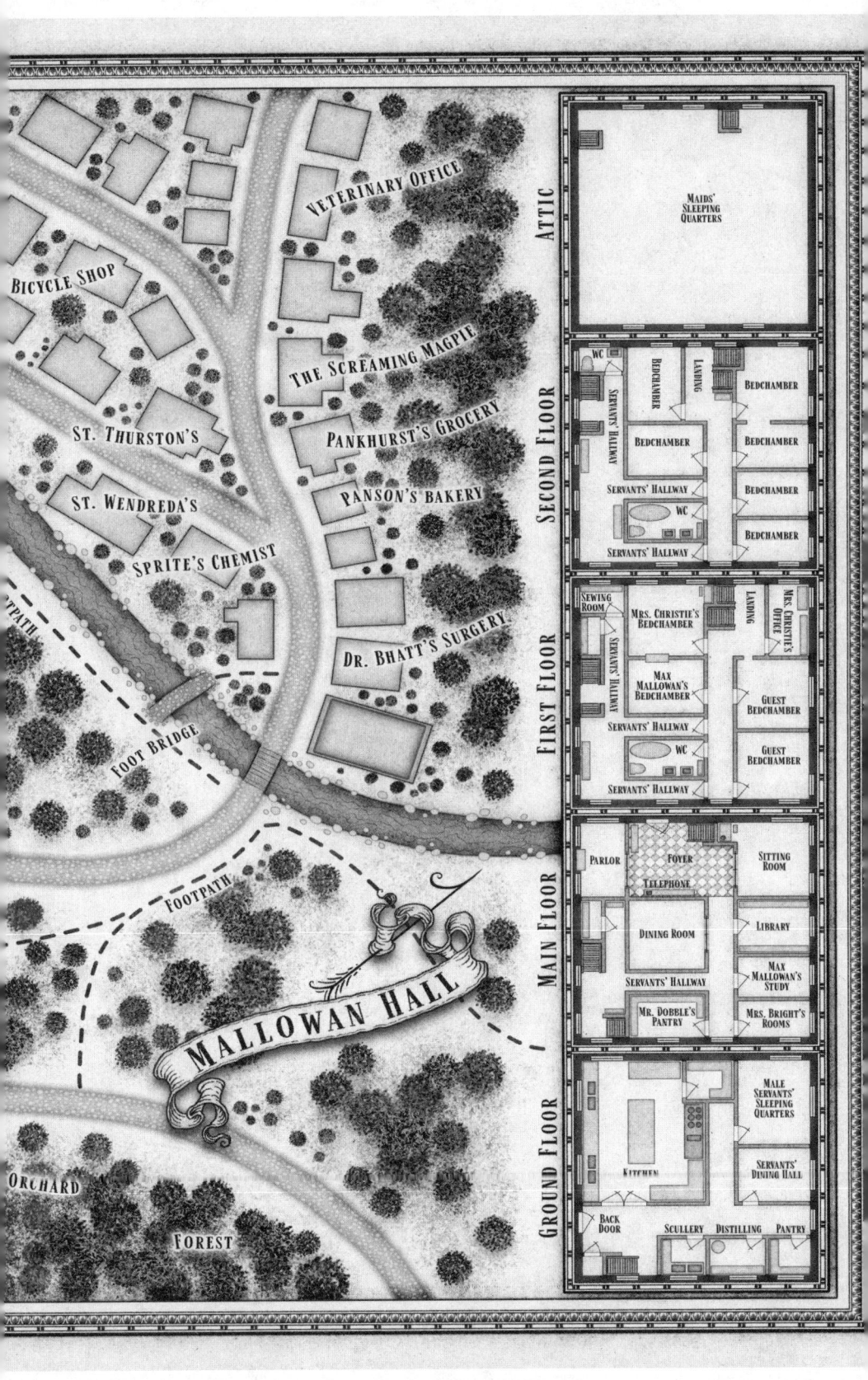

Mallowan Hall

Village Map (left side)
- Bicycle Shop
- St. Thurston's
- St. Wendreda's
- Sprite's Chemist
- Foot Bridge
- Footpath
- Orchard
- Forest
- Veterinary Office
- The Screaming Magpie
- Pankhurst's Grocery
- Panson's Bakery
- Dr. Bhatt's Surgery

Mallowan Hall Floor Plans (right side)

Attic
- Maids' Sleeping Quarters

Second Floor
- WC
- Bedchamber
- Landing
- Bedchamber
- Servants' Hallway
- Bedchamber
- Bedchamber
- Servants' Hallway
- Bedchamber
- WC
- Servants' Hallway
- Bedchamber

First Floor
- Sewing Room
- Mrs. Christie's Bedchamber
- Landing
- Mrs. Christie's Office
- Servants' Hallway
- Max Mallowan's Bedchamber
- Guest Bedchamber
- Servants' Hallway
- WC
- Guest Bedchamber
- Servants' Hallway

Main Floor
- Parlor
- Foyer
- Telephone
- Sitting Room
- Dining Room
- Library
- Servants' Hallway
- Max Mallowan's Study
- Mr. Dobble's Pantry
- Mrs. Bright's Rooms

Ground Floor
- Male Servants' Sleeping Quarters
- Kitchen
- Servants' Dining Hall
- Back Door
- Scullery
- Distilling
- Pantry

CHAPTER 1

*P*HYLLIDA BRIGHT WAS NOT AN ORDINARY HOUSEKEEPER.

She happily and deftly managed Mallowan Hall—the large home of Agatha Christie and her husband, Max Mallowan, located outside the village of Listleigh, in Devon—but she also had a number of hidden talents, including the ability to pick locks, climb into a second (or third, when necessary) story window, and sense from two floors below when her housemaids were holding up the wall and gossiping instead of holding up their feather dusters and employing their mops.

And she had lately come to realize she had a knack for solving murders.

Aside from this recently discovered penchant to follow in the footsteps of the fictional Tuppence Beresford, Bundle Brent, and others, Phyllida, who'd been friends with Agatha since the Great War, was also the recipient and keeper of a number of secrets. Not only her own secrets—and there were many—and those of her employer, but also those of a number of other people—both famous and infamous, in the highest levels of government, of the wealthiest of the wealthy, and even of the lowliest servant in the grandest of homes.

For some reason, people tended to think of Phyllida as a sort of impervious cistern of information and confidences . . . as well as a sage of wisdom for advice and pragmatism.

And that, Phyllida could only conjecture, was why she was currently sitting in the front parlor at Mallowan Hall with Mrs. Vera Rollingbroke—who was married to the wealthy and affable Sir Paulson Rollingbroke, better known as Sir Rolly.

Mrs. Rollingbroke was an attractive woman in her early thirties with an air that sometimes bordered on birdbrained. Yet Phyllida had come to discern a subtle layer of shrewdness in the younger woman's mien. And, she knew, the woman's skill in writing detective stories seemed to have improved over the last two months... possibly because Mrs. Rollingbroke had been involved—on the periphery at least—with some of Phyllida's murder investigations.

But the two of them had been sitting here for more than ten minutes discussing the weather and little else, and Phyllida was still mystified as to specifically why Mrs. Rollingbroke would have requested a private meeting with her at Mallowan Hall. Although Phyllida was a high-ranking servant who had an unusually familiar and egalitarian relationship with her employer, she was still, after all, a servant in the eyes of everyone else.

"I do appreciate your meeting with me, Mrs. Bright. May I call you Phyllida?" said Mrs. Rollingbroke as she leaned forward, her voice low as if in confidence. "I feel as if we've become friends over the last several months, you see."

"Of course," replied Phyllida encouragingly.

Mrs. Rollingbroke was wearing one of her extremely fetching hats. This one was dark red with a swath of netting over one eye and a jaunty bright red feather arching toward the back. Silk roses in shades of crimson, pink, and other similar hues were tucked in along the brim. As usual, Phyllida admired and mildly coveted the woman's chapeau. Mrs. Rollingbroke, whose figure was slender and lithe, was always dressed in the most flattering and newest of fashions.

She had dark blond hair and vibrant blue eyes. Her features were nothing less than patrician, enhanced by the subtle employment of cosmetics. Her fingers were long and elegant, and studded with bejeweled rings. But today, they trembled ever so slightly.

"What can I do to help you, Mrs. Rollingbroke?" Phyllida asked in an effort to get the woman to come to the point. She might have an excellent group of maids in the kitchen and working in the parlors and upstairs chambers, but they still needed overseeing and supervision. And there were menus to finish so that Agatha could review and approve them, along with placing orders with the merchants for supplies and tending to the distillations in the back room—currently those of elderflower syrup and chamomile tincture. She had some cheque drafts to write for suppliers and other vendors, as well as some correspondence to complete.

Aside from that, it was a lovely day, and there was no need to avoid going outside to have her tea in the rose garden. Myrtle was gone with her master and would not be barking, leaping, or otherwise expressing her pleasure at seeing Phyllida.

"Please *do* call me Vera," replied the other woman with a warm smile. Her eyes sparkled cornflower blue from beneath slender, carefully plucked brows. "After all, Phyllida, we got to know each other quite well during the terrible events of the Murder Fête." The other woman gave her a meaningful look. "And at Mr. Wokesley's . . . erm . . . Murder Party."

"Ye-es," Phyllida said, drawing out the word in an effort to encourage her to go on.

Mrs. Rollingbroke—Vera—gave her a little, uncomfortable smile and settled back into her chair. She was holding a cup of tea that, so far, remained untouched by her lips, as evidenced by the lack of red lipstick on its rim. The cup rattled a little in its saucer and a bit of pale, cream-laden liquid splashed over the top.

Then Vera leaned forward again. "I'd like to engage your services," she said quickly, as if she'd had to force out the words before she lost her courage.

Phyllida blinked, hiding her surprise. "Why, Mrs. Rollingbroke, I'm quite humbled and honored by your interest in employing me, but I'm very happy here at Mallowan Hall with Mrs. Christie. I truly have no intention—"

"Oh, no, not at all. Not *those* services, dear Phyllida. But the other . . . erm . . . I mean to say, your *investigative* services. You see"—Vera leaned forward even further, her voice dropping lower, her wan smile fading—"I . . . I need you to find out something for me. To—to investigate s-something."

"And what is that?" Phyllida replied, intrigued in spite of herself. As much as she did enjoy her position here at Mallowan Hall—despite Mr. Dobble and his persnickety, nosy ways—she also found crime scene investigation quite stimulating and a trifle more challenging than overseeing a passel of well-trained servants.

Here Vera's courage wilted. "It's simply . . . oh, dear, I can't . . . why, I-I . . ." To Phyllida's surprise, the other woman's eyes suddenly filled with tears and she blinked rapidly, setting down the teacup with an alarming clatter as she moved to fish a handkerchief from her pocketbook.

"What is it, Mrs. Rollingbroke?" Phyllida's impatience with nonsensical babbling ebbed in the face of such emotion. "What's wrong?"

"It's—it's Rolly," she said tearfully, barely above a whisper. "I think . . . I'm afraid . . . I b-believe . . . oh, Phyllida, I'm quite certain he's h-having an affair." Mrs. Rollingbroke dissolved into quiet sobs as Phyllida took in this shocking information.

Her immediate reaction was to flatly decry such a possibility. She'd witnessed Sir Rolly's affection and and regard for his wife many times. Even during Mrs. Rollingbroke's silliest and most vapid moments, he'd doted on her without being impatient or, more importantly, condescending. It was obvious at least to Phyllida that Sir Rolly loved his wife.

That didn't mean, of course, that he hadn't strayed from his marriage vows. Many men were of the belief they could have a wife *and* a mistress, in some cases having deep regard for both of them. Still. Sir Rolly simply didn't seem the type.

"Tell me why you think this, Vera," she said, using the woman's familiar name even though it felt odd to do so.

"He's—well, I've caught him speaking on the telephone and his voice suddenly goes very quiet when I walk into the room. Or he hangs up abruptly. And I . . . well, he got all queer the other day when I mentioned Genevra and Ethel coming to my dinner party." Vera's face had acquired a slight greenish cast. "You see, I—I think it's Genevra. The other woman."

"Genevra? Do you mean Miss Blastwick?" Phyllida said, successfully hiding her surprise.

She didn't know Genevra Blastwick—or her sister Ethel for that matter—all that well, but she'd certainly encountered her at some of the social events in Listleigh. The daughters of a retired professor of anthropology, they were in their late twenties and unmarried. They spent much of the year at their family's small manor house called Ivygate Cottage, just a few miles outside of Listleigh. The cottage was conveniently located near a significant earthen depression, where Dr. Blastwick apparently spent many happy hours digging in the dirt, hoping to find the next Stonehenge. Apparently, an old Roman coin had been unearthed in a plow furrow some years ago, leading Dr. Blastwick to believe there was more to uncover.

While Genevra was the more attractive of the sisters, as well as the more outgoing and friendly of the pair, she struck Phyllida as a sort of self-involved braggart. Unlike Vera Rollingbroke, who could be scatterbrained and chatty, but was also warm and kind, Genevra had a desperate edge to her personality—as if she was always trying to steal the scene or to one-up those around her.

All that was to say, if Sir Rolly was indeed enamored with Genevra Blastwick, Phyllida could not imagine what was the attraction other than her obvious physical attributes.

"I think it's her," said Mrs. Rollingbroke, clearly unconcerned by the rules of proper grammar. Fortunately, she took more care with those rules during her story writing.

"I see." Phyllida lifted her own teacup and took a sip as she collected her thoughts. "And you would like me to . . . do what, precisely, Mrs. Rollingbroke?"

"*Vera*. Oh, do call me Vera. I simply can't abide knowing that someone who calls me Mrs. Rollingbroke knows that I'm a—a *cuckold*! It's the sort of thing one would prefer to keep between friends, you see, Phyllida. You do see, don't you?"

Phyllida nodded. "Yes, of course." Having never been a cuckold herself, she had to take the other woman's word for it.

"Right, then. What I want you to do is to find out whether . . . well, whether I'm correct. Whether Rolly"—her voice broke momentarily—"is—is having an affair with Genevra Blastwick."

"Do you want me to find out whether he is having an affair with Genevra Blastwick, or do you want me to find out whether he is having an affair . . . at all?" Phyllida asked.

"I want to know," Mrs. Rollingbroke—Vera—said, looking at her with blazing but sad blue eyes, "I want to know all of it. If it's her or someone else. But I'm certain it's her."

"Why are you certain it's Miss Blastwick?"

"Because she is always giving him those looks. Those languishing, 'take me away' looks. And she laughs so very hard at all of his jokes." She dabbed at her eyes. "I love Rolly, Phyllida, I truly do—there is no other man for me—but the truth is, his jokes are often not very funny. In fact, sometimes they are quite painful. I do chuckle at them most times, and I tell him how amusing he is—but I'm his *wife*. You see?"

"Quite," Phyllida replied, for she did see. In her experience, men required efficient and careful handling.

"And I was in Pankhurst's last week, it was, giving Myrna Crestworthy my condolences—tragic, that, about the poor chap; he was Rutherford's secretary I believe—and Genevra came into the shop. She was ever so polite, but when she stopped to speak to us, she had this—well, this *smile*. Like she had a secret and she was daring me to guess what it was." She gave a little shudder, her lips quivering, her eyes blinking rapidly. "I think that is when I became certain, you see, Phyllida. It was the way she looked at me. That catlike, sly way."

Phyllida made a quiet sound of consolation. It certainly sounded as if Mrs. Rollingbroke had reason to wonder.

"I want you to attend a little dinner party I'm giving on Monday night," Vera went on, suddenly the brisk society lady. "Genevra and Rolly will be there, of course, and I want you to observe them and see what you can find out."

Phyllida's brows rose. "Monday night?"

"I've invited Mrs. Christie as well," Vera explained. "She hasn't said whether she'll attend, but I do hope you will, at least. It'll be the perfect opportunity for you to observe them. Rolly and Genevra. And I'll be so busy playing hostess that it'll give you the chance to . . . well . . . to see what happens when—when they think I'm busy and not paying a-attention." Her voice choked up and she lifted the handkerchief to her eyes again.

"I'll have to speak with Mrs. Christie about the situation," Phyllida said. "Monday is not my usual night out. But I'm certain I can arrange to be there considering the circumstances, even if Mrs. Christie is not. She's rather soft-hearted when it comes to my investigations."

"Oh, thank you, Phyllida! And I shall thank her too, of course." Vera reached over and took up Phyllida's hands in hers, squeezing them tightly. "Thank you so much. I do hope . . . I do hope I am proven wrong," she said unsteadily. "But if I must learn the worst, then I shall have to gird myself and buck up. Stiff upper lip and all of that. I can put the pain into my writing, I suppose," she said, dabbing at her eyes. "That's what writers do, isn't it? They inject the pain and sorrow from their lives into their work. It makes the stories more authentic."

Phyllida could only nod, knowing it was best if she held her tongue. Vera Rollingbroke wrote short crime stories featuring a young and wealthy society woman nicknamed Biscuit—whose original nickname, Bunty, had been noted as too similar to Mrs. Christie's intrepid "Bundle" Brent, so it was changed. Biscuit solved mysteries and conducted investigations with the help of a long-haired cat named Mrs. Cuddlesworthy. A cat who, apparently, *talked*.

Phyllida was uncertain what sort of sorrow and pain would be included in such fanciful stories. She expected she would never have the courage to read them, as the inauthenticity of a talking cat was a cause of great agitation for her.

"I do appreciate it, dear Phyllida," Mrs. Rollingbroke said, releasing her hands and rising. "Oh, heavens! I almost forgot to tell you." The tension disappeared and her eyes sparkled once more as she clasped her hands to her breast. "I've just heard from an editor at *The Queen*. He's interested in reading some of my Biscuit stories!"

"Why, that's wonderful!" Phyllida said with genuine enthusiasm and, to be honest, a flare of surprise. "Congratulations!"

The Queen was a women's society magazine that had been started by the husband of the great Mrs. Beeton, whose tome on household management was the bible for any wife or housekeeper. Phyllida had the latest edition of the book—which was five inches thick—sitting on her desk at this very moment, for she was reviewing the process for distilling elderflowers into a sweet liqueur.

Mrs. Rollingbroke's smile faltered a little. "It's only that I'm so *nervous* about it. I have to send three of them, and what if he doesn't like any of them? I haven't even told Rolly about it, you see, because . . . well, because." Now the smile fled.

"Quite understandable," Phyllida replied, patting the other woman's hand. "I do hope you have good news from the editor. It would be quite a success to have one's stories printed in *The Queen*."

"It's not about the money," Mrs. Rollingbroke went on. "I mean to say, I feel that receiving money for one's writing is at least some measure of success . . . but it's only that I just hope for Biscuit and Mrs. Cuddlesworthy to find an audience. You see?"

"Indeed. I hope they find an appreciative audience" (whoever it was) "as well."

"Thank you. Your encouragement means quite a bit to me." She stood, giving Phyllida a hopeful yet sad look. "I'm so very glad you are willing to help me about this . . . the problem with Rolly. The truth is, I'm placing all of my trust in you. You're just *ever* so capable. Thank you once again."

Phyllida walked with her to the door and waved her off as she went down the steps. Just as Mrs. Rollingbroke climbed into her sporty Excelsior, another motorcar trundled up the drive.

It was not the Mallowans' Daimler, Phyllida noted, squelching what was absolutely not a tiny flicker of disappointment. Not at all. It was relief that had caused her belly to give that subtle lurch.

TWO TRUTHS AND A MURDER

Bradford—the Mallowans' chauffeur—and his impertinent dog, Myrtle, had not driven back to Listleigh with the rest of the household staff when they returned from London several weeks ago. Man and dog had merely dropped them at the railway station in London and not been heard from since.

Therefore, Phyllida had had several weeks of calm and quiet, uninterrupted by barking and leaping and soulful canine gazes, not to mention unwanted verbal masculine commentary and all-too-knowing sidewise looks.

She had no idea where Myrtle was and why she hadn't yet returned and she certainly hadn't asked the whereabouts of the dog and her master. Although Agatha had returned a few days after Phyllida, Mr. Max had remained in the city due to some arrangement with the British Museum whereby he was cataloging a small collection of pottery fragments or whatnot from some recent bequest, but it wasn't necessary for him to have the Daimler or a driver in the city. He hadn't even kept Elton, his valet, with him—to the delight of the housemaids, who were all sweet on the handsome valet.

Phyllida might not know where Myrtle was, but she certainly knew what the wild little beast was doing: attempting to ingratiate herself with the cook at whatever locale she and her master were staying, barking at every leaf, squirrel, wheeled conveyance, or bee that happened by, panting loudly and damply whenever possible, and attempting to climb into the laps of anyone who might be sitting.

The canine seemed to prefer the laps of females, if her attention to Phyllida was any indication. Phyllida suspected that was due to the fact that skirts provided a more comfortable hammock than trousers, which was certainly understandable.

The arriving vehicle came to a stop and Phyllida noted that it was a basic, elderly lorry that probably didn't go any faster than five miles per hour. On the side of one of the doors were painted the words HATTEN'S DELIVERY SERVICE. The person who climbed out wore the cap of a courier but moved with the deliberateness of one who was aging as he went around to the boot of the vehicle that still rumbled quietly in place.

Phyllida waited at the entrance as he opened the back of the lorry and extracted a crate.

It appeared to be a rather weighty object, not to mention ungainly, for the container was large enough that the delivery person couldn't see around it as he carefully walked toward the steps leading to the front door.

Phyllida wasn't aware of any delivery being expected for the household, but it was possible Mr. Mallowan had ordered some archaeological tool or had purchased an antiquity for his collection. Even so, it was a bit surprising that the crate was being taken to the front entrance and not to the rear where the staff and most deliveries went.

Noting the creaky sort of movements of the delivery person, she ducked back inside the house and quickly rang for one of the footmen. Mr. Dobble, who most often answered the door, would be useless in such a situation; he was very nearly as rickety as the deliveryman. Aside from his questionable ability to do so, the butler would never lower himself to conduct any sort of task that required physical exertion.

But to her surprise, Mr. Dobble followed Stanley, the head footman, when he came out of the front door.

"Do be careful," snapped Mr. Dobble when Stanley hurried to wrest the crate from the deliveryman.

Phyllida looked at the butler, whose attention was fastened on the box with the same unwavering attention Myrtle's would be on a ham bone being dangled in front of her.

"Inside, and *take care* I said!" Mr. Dobble gestured sharply toward the door, watching Stanley like a hawk.

It was only then that Mr. Dobble saw Phyllida standing at one side of the wide porch; his attention had been so focused on the delivery that she'd escaped his notice.

"Mrs. Bright," he said stiffly as he stepped inside. "I suppose you find it necessary to greet every delivery person now, do you?"

Phyllida lifted her brows, following him into the foyer. "Not at all, Mr. Dobble." And because she sensed he absolutely did not want to acknowledge the fact that he had rushed to the door to greet Mr. Hatten's delivery, she went on. "But what a very large and intriguing package that is. And heavy—not to mention fragile—if your reaction is any indication. A person might begin to wonder what's inside."

Mr. Dobble's eyes narrowed. "One might wonder if one had a habit of sticking one's pointy nose where it didn't belong."

As Phyllida's nose was indeed a trifle pointed, charmingly so (as she'd been told), she had no doubt to whom he was referring. "I suppose it must be for Mr. Mallowan. A collection of bones or skulls or pottery, perhaps. Surely Stanley can manage to deliver it to Mr. Max's office without supervision."

She smiled pleasantly at the footman, who stood there holding the cumbersome crate as he watched the two of them uncertainly.

Mr. Dobble looked as if he'd just swallowed a very tart lemon. "The delivery is not for Mr. Max."

"For Mrs. Agatha, then? Copies of her new book, perhaps. Stanley, if you would please take it up—"

"The package is *mine*." Mr. Dobble's voice was so cold she practically felt her nose go icy at the tip. "This way." He whipped out an imperious hand, pointing down the hall toward his pantry.

Phyllida watched the two of them go, with Stanley nearly staggering down the hall with his burden and coming far too close to a candelabrum on one of the side tables as he did so. The poor boy couldn't see around the crate, and—

Crash!

There went the tall blue and white vase Mr. Chesterton had given Agatha after the Murder Fête. Ginny, the parlourmaid, rushed from the study, feather duster in hand, but Mr. Dobble didn't even give Phyllida a glance of apology over the mess of shattered pottery, water, and strewn roses as he ushered Stanley into his pantry.

A mere second or two later, the footman rushed out and the door slammed shut so closely it bumped his heels.

"I'm sorry, Mrs. Bright," Stanley said, looking abashed. "I'll get it cleaned up right away."

"Right then, of course you will. Ginny has already gone for a broom and mop. Thank you, Stanley." She decided for now not to ask him any questions about what might have been in the crate. It wouldn't do for Mr. Dobble to get even a suggestion that she was interested.

Because of course she *was*.

What on earth could the butler have had delivered that was so heavy and fragile and large?

Ah well. She'd find out soon enough.

CHAPTER 2

"*How* pretty you look! And what a splendid frock that is!" said Agatha when Phyllida came into the front hall on Monday evening. "Did you get it in London?"

"I did," Phyllida replied.

She had fallen in love with the material the moment she laid eyes on the dress. It was a soft, buttery yellow that looked well with her unusual rosy-reddish-blond hair. The fabric, which had splashes of large white and cream flowers over it, was light and airy. The skirt was cut on the bias, its hem rippling delicately about her ankles. It was perfect for a summer dinner party.

"I'm not the least bit ashamed to say that I spent some of the money from the Satterwaits on this dress, along with a tiny bottle of Chanel No. 5," Phyllida said.

"And well you should have," said Agatha with a fond smile. "I see no need for you to dress like a frumpy housekeeper when you are far much more than that. Incidentally, I did just receive the nicest letter from Mrs. Satterwait expressing her pleasure and relief over how you handled the incident in London, despite the delays with my new stage play."

"That was very kind of her," Phyllida replied. The last time she'd seen Mrs. Satterwait, the woman hadn't been completely pleased with her. Phyllida had managed to expose her nephew's killer, but her tactics had left Mrs. Satterwait a bit irritated. Still, she'd been paid a surprisingly handsome sum for her investigative work—even though Phyllida had mostly done it to help Agatha, who was friends with the Satterwaits.

"And now Vera Rollingbroke needs your help as well," Agatha went on, giving her a knowing look. "I told you that your reputation would grow. I only hope I won't lose you to full-time crime-solving, dear Phyllida."

"Of course not," she replied.

But Agatha looked at her closely, her head tilted. "Are you quite certain? Now that you no longer have the need to avoid London, you wouldn't be required to stay tucked away here any longer . . . like me."

"Not at all," Phyllida replied firmly, feeling a wave of empathy for Agatha. Both of them had their reasons to want to be "tucked away," as she put it—and not only due to Agatha's shyness. Agatha was still subjected to gossip and impertinent questions from reporters about her disappearance during the early stages of her divorce from Archie Christie.

And, yes, whilst Phyllida's visit to London had certainly changed some things, it had not lessened her contentment working at Mallowan Hall. "I have no intention of going anywhere. I'm perfectly happy here in Listleigh." Then she made a gesture to her friend. "But you don't look at all as if you're ready to leave for Wilding Hall."

"Quite so. You know me, Phyllie—I simply prefer to stay home and noodle about with my books and writing. And with Max gone, it's even easier for me to decline social engagements." She smiled. "But of course you must go and see what you can do for Vera. She didn't tell me all of it, but I'm not a crime writer for nothing. I suspect I know what's bothering her, and I hope you can set things to rights as soon as possible. Meanwhile, I've simply got to get back to Poirot. He's having quite a time on the train."

"Oh?" Phyllida knew Agatha was working on a book that took place on a train called the Orient Express, but not much else about it.

Agatha smiled. "There's been a snow drift, you see, and the dratted train is stuck in the mountains outside of Vinkovci. And of course there is a murderer about." Her eyes danced, then the levity faded. "But it's the victim who is quite terrible. Utterly wicked. He certainly deserved to die. I'm not even certain Poirot would *want* the killer to be brought to justice after what he did. The victim, I mean. Such a monstrous person. I've already sent word to Vera. I'm certain she'll understand. It's truly you she wants to see anyhow."

"Very well," Phyllida said. She wasn't terribly surprised that her friend had chosen to stay home. She even understood it, and would have done the same if she hadn't been implored so strongly to attend.

"It's too bad Bradford isn't here to drive you over," Agatha said as she studied her closely.

"As you well know, I'm perfectly capable of driving a motor myself," Phyllida replied firmly, giving her a quelling look.

"Of course. There isn't much you can't do, is there? And my little MG is just perfect for short trips around the shire. Easier to handle than the Daimler. Incidentally, he's only asked for a bit of time away to attend to some personal matters," Agatha went on, still eyeing her without trying to be obvious about it—and not really succeeding. "And the Daimler is having some repairs done whilst he is gone. I expect he'll drive back when Max is finished with his job. Or perhaps sooner."

"Quite," Phyllida replied, not allowing herself to be curious about what those personal matters of Bradford's might be and how much longer Mr. Max's engagement would be in London. It was, after all, rather quiet without Myrtle yapping and yipping about.

With this conversation, her contentment in working for Agatha and her husband was renewed. Phyllida felt safe in the knowledge that they'd given Bradford leave to do what he needed to do—whatever it was. Other employers mightn't be so accommodating. Heaven knew Agatha had been more than generous with Phyllida's time during multiple murder investigations over the last few months.

"I suppose I should be off, then," Phyllida said. She was quite looking forward to getting behind the wheel of a motorcar again.

The last time she'd done so, it had been at the gunpoint of a killer.

She expected the drive to be much less harrowing tonight.

"Do give my best to Vera," said Agatha, but her eyes had gone vague and Phyllida knew that her boss's mind was already returning to Poirot and his case. "And do try to avoid dead bodies, will you, Phyllida?"

They both laughed, albeit a little uneasily. After all, the last time Phyllida had attended a local social event without Agatha, someone had, in fact, been murdered.

It was a pleasant summer evening to be driving through the green and rolling hills of Devon. Phyllida actually preferred to be behind the wheel through these twisting, narrow roads because oftentimes as a passenger she became a little queasy during such rides. Bradford usually insisted she sit in the front with him for that reason, for the motion sickness didn't bother her quite as much when she did.

Just as quickly as the thought of him breeched her mind, Phyllida dismissed it. What had happened between them in London had been . . .

Well, it had been quite a new development in their relationship, such as it was. Phyllida didn't particularly like to use the word "relationship" even in her personal thoughts, but she had to admit in this case it was accurate.

A relationship was the connection or association of two things—according to the *Oxford English Dictionary* (Phyllida had looked it up in order to assuage her discomfort using the term, even in her own mind).

Such a bland, unassuming syntax—and one she could accept. They were connected and associated by virtue of their employment status. They were *connected* and *associated* because his dratted dog insisted on expressing her boisterous affections toward Phyllida whenever possible. They were also connected and associated because he had assisted—in his own sardonic way—in some of Phyllida's murder investigations.

And then there had been the interlude in the garden one night, back in London.

Well, two nights... and then there had been that early morning incident...

Phyllida was grateful she was alone, for her cheeks heated at the reminder, and since she had rather fair skin to go with her red hair, it would be visibly noticeable.

Fortunately, none of the other staff were aware of this... development... and by the time Bradford returned to Mallowan Hall—if he even did—it was just as likely things would have burned out.

So to speak.

Phyllida was grateful when she saw the tall, pointed gates of Wilding Hall, for her arrival gave her something else to think about other than chauffeurs and garden interludes.

The brick and stone edifice was a large and sprawling one, a hodge-podge of wings, balconies, chimneys, and turrets. It was clear to Phyllida that an array of different architects, each with ambitious styles and fancies, had contributed to the design over the centuries. Despite its appearance of being several chunks of architectural tone simply stacked upon or next to the other, there was a welcoming aspect to Wilding Hall.

Hot pink roses climbed up the brick front on either side of the main entrance, which was situated at the top of a long, narrow, covered porch. Boxwood hedges lined the drive, opening to the broad steps of the porch. Large pots of cascading ivies and neat lavender topiaries flanked the doorway. Beaming gas lanterns sat on poles at either end of the porch, and one hung from the ceiling overhead, lighting the entrance.

Phyllida left Agatha's little coupe parked in the drive with several other motorcars. They were all lined up neatly, their hoods and tops gleaming in the low light. She didn't know all that much about motorcars, but she did recognize the Hispano-Suiza next to hers with its sleek, sharp-beaked stork mascot perched atop the hood—mainly because Agatha had given Bundle the same motorcar in *The Secret of Chimneys* after she and Phyllida had admired a similar vehicle in London. She walked past a shiny, stately Bentley, unmistakable because of the elegant, winged mascot on the hood, and three other more inexpensive and common motors—perhaps a Crossley, a Morris, and an Austin—or maybe one was a Buick. A bicycle leaned against the stone fence that opened to the stairs leading to the entrance.

But it was the Bugatti that had Phyllida pausing with a sly, nostalgic smile just before she started up the steps to the house. It was a gorgeous vehicle, and one that not only caught her eye because of its long, finely tuned race-car body, but because she'd once known someone who owned a Bugatti. Those had been delightful, exciting days, driving around at high speeds in a motor that had such sex appeal. (Its owner had had his own S.A. as well; hence her pleasant reminiscence.)

Still smiling, she patted the Bugatti's hood and its shiny ornament gently as she passed by and started up the steps to Wilding Hall.

As a servant, Phyllida usually went to the rear entrance of any home she visited—a habit she'd had to develop, having *not* been in service most of her life. But in this case, she was an invited guest and was welcomed at the main entrance.

The Rollingbrokes' butler, Mr. Whalley, swept the door open and ushered her in. "Sir and madame are in the drawing room with the other guests, Mrs. Bright," he said, gesturing to a short hall that opened into a double-doored room.

Phyllida caught the subtle hitch in his expression as he welcomed her—another servant—as a guest. She had become somewhat renowned amongst the downstairs folk throughout Listleigh, as her reputation for being a fair-minded boss preceded her. Not to mention the fact that during her crime-solving escapades, Phyllida had not only employed the gossip chain of servants to assist in gathering information and clues, but she'd also proven the innocence of more than one of them who'd been accused of murder. And when a low-ranking maid at Mallowan Hall had been murdered, Phyllida had given her death as much attention and certainly more empathy than that of any other victim.

So, despite the fact that Mr. Whalley might feel strange welcoming her in a position above her station, he surely also appreciated her reputation.

And, Phyllida thought dryly as she went into the drawing room, if Sir Rolly was having an affair, Mr. Whalley surely knew about it. And he likely even knew that Mrs. Rollingbroke—Vera—had engaged Phyllida's assistance.

Servants simply knew everything.

"Oh, dear Phyllida!" Vera Rollingbroke was carrying a glass with half a martini as she glided over to greet her. When she offered two quick kisses in the air above each of Phyllida's cheeks—a startling expression of informality and equality—Phyllida caught the distinct whiff of spirits.

When Vera stepped back, Phyllida's suspicions were confirmed: her hostess was filled with tension and anxiety, poorly masked by a brittle smile and too-bright eyes.

The poor woman. Phyllida squeezed Vera's hand and gave her a reassuring smile. "Thank you for having me. What a delightful drawing room. And what a splendid Gainsborough!" She admired the pastoral painting that hung above the fireplace. It looked exactly like a place she would like to relegate Myrtle to—a hilly, forested location distant from any structure or road that would keep the beast far from her skirt and stockings.

"Why, thank you. It's one of Rolly's favorites," Vera replied. Phyllida detected the slightest quaver in her voice, but that was only because she was paying strict attention.

"Mrs. Bright!" boomed a voice in Phyllida's ear. "What a nice surprise! Eh . . . say you ain't hunting down any murderers here tonight, won't you?" Sir Rolly said with a jovial smile and twinkling eyes.

He was in his mid-forties, almost a decade older than his attractive and stylish wife. While Vera Rollingbroke was smooth, elegant, and slender, Paulson Rollingbroke was slightly round in every aspect: his chin, his nose, his deeply dimpled cheeks—which curved above a magnificent blond mustache that looked like a well-groomed horse's mane—and his abdomen. His entire mien was one of affability with an underlying sense of pragmatism. He knew how to enjoy himself, but he was particular about how and when—and with whom—to let his hair down, so to speak. He held a glass of something dark amber in a hand that sported an ebony signet ring on one chunky finger.

"Of course not, Sir Rolly," Phyllida replied, smiling back. She liked the man quite a bit, even though he'd skirted legality a while back during the Murder Fête. She didn't hold that little incident against him since he hadn't really done anything wrong—although the intention had been there. Besides, it had been done in the name of love, and as much as she might try and hide it, Phyllida was more of a romantic than she liked to admit.

"Didn't know you'd invited Mrs. Bright, old girl," said Sir Rolly, sliding an arm around his wife's slim waist. "What a splendid idea! She can tell us what she thinks of Mrs. Paddington's veal roast."

"Of course, darling," said Vera, then added to Phyllida, "Rolly seems to think Paddington can't cook a roast properly, but I think she does quite well. Now, let me get you something to drink while you say hallo to our other guests. Surely you know most of them." She pulled away from her husband's easy embrace, casting a sad little smile downward as she did so.

Phyllida caught the reaction in Sir Rolly's eyes as Vera pulled away—surprise, hurt, and something she thought was a flash of fear. *Interesting.*

"I'll have a tonic with lemon for now," Phyllida said, thinking she'd like to keep her mind clear. Besides, there would be wine served at dinner. She smiled and turned dutifully to greet the other guests—specifically Genevra Blastwick.

Genevra and her older sister, Ethel, sat on a sofa together. In their late twenties and only a year apart in age, the sisters bore more than a passing resemblance to each other—both had brown hair, light golden skin, and pretty, delicate features. If Mr. Dobble wanted to see a truly pointy nose, he could look at those of the Blastwick sisters. Tonight, they were both dressed in blue, although Genevra's frock was a brilliant cornflower hue, while Ethel's was a more subdued hazy-sky color.

Although they sat on the same divan, each was angled slightly away from the other. With their resemblance and similar clothing, and positioned in this way, the sisters seemed to be a sort of reflection of the other.

Phyllida was struck by the impression that it was as if one—Genevra—was the true, vibrant image, while the other sister—Ethel—was the murkier, more faded one, as if one was seeing Genevra reflected in a murky pool of water in the figure of Ethel. Their personalities, voices, and even coloring were similar, yet next to her sister, Ethel seemed muted.

"And I was simply aghast that he should say so." Genevra's face was tipped up as she spoke to a short, lithe man with a full head of unruly brown hair and a broad, wax-tipped mustache that stretched nearly to his ears. "After all, *I* already knew all about it, and if he had simply listened to me—"

"Quite so, quite so," the man replied, then, as he spied Phyllida, turned his attention with obvious gratitude to her. "Why, Mrs. Bright! What a pleasure to see you."

"Good evening, Mr. Sprite," said Phyllida, giving him a sympathetic smile. Bartholomew Sprite—who was aptly named considering his slight figure and energetic movements—owned the chemist shop in Listleigh. "And Genevra! How nice that you and your sister were able to attend tonight. Did I hear that you were in London for a visit?"

"Only a short one," replied Genevra with a sly smile curving bright red lips, "Papa simply wouldn't have it with us spending the summer in the City. Or the autumn. Or the spring, for that matter. He much prefers to be here, digging about in those old holes. I like the summers here myself because it's just so much cooler than in the city, and far more relaxed. I'm simply so busy when I'm in London—because I only visit there for a short time, you see.

"Invitations every day, of course, and people wanting me to go to the races or watch a tennis match or visit a museum. Of course we never stay in the city so very long, so people need to catch up with me. And, I really need to have a rest after such a busy spring. I simply can't continue to go on at such a frantic pace."

Genevra *would* have gone on if Phyllida hadn't stepped in. "I'm sure you're quite in demand, especially with the young men—in London and hereabouts as well." As an investigative strategy, her implied question was rather heavy-handed, but Phyllida suspected Genevra was too self-involved to notice.

"Oh, well, one does get asked out quite a bit—to the cinema or the dance clubs—but there are people who can't seem to appreciate that when one is . . . shall we say . . . *enamored* with a special someone, that one simply can't always announce it from the rooftops because of . . . well . . . propriety . . . and so one simply has to accept other invitations in order to keep up appearances, you know. So that people aren't assuming you've not got anything happening."

She lifted her glass to her lips and sipped as her eyes danced with glee that bordered on maliciousness. "You understand that sometimes, one simply can't let on when there's someone special. At least, right away. But secrets can be quite delightful to keep," she added. "And I have ever so many of them."

Phyllida couldn't tell exactly whom Genevra was looking at when she made that statement, but the woman's speech had certainly given her cause for concern on behalf of Vera Rollingbroke. Even through Genevra's roundabout, provocative soliloquy, Phyllida had managed to extract one indubitable fact: Genevra was involved with a man she couldn't publicly identify.

Just then, the dinner gong sounded.

Phyllida accepted Mr. Sprite's arm, which he'd offered so quickly she assumed it was so he'd not be left escorting Genevra Blastwick.

They followed their hostess, who was being escorted by Mr. Varney, the area's veterinarian. Behind followed Ethel Blastwick on—interestingly—Sir Rolly's arm, and behind them were Genevra and Mr. Rutherford Crestworthy, a distinguished man of forty who'd taken over his wife's family business of making some sort of mechanical part. Apparently, there were several factories and all were doing quite well, considering the economy.

Next was Mr. Pete Heathers escorting Mrs. Myrna Crestworthy, who was laughing in a high-pitched trill at something he'd said. Mr. Heathers was a friendly sort who was always accompanied by the aura of pipe smoke, even when one didn't appear to be in his hand. He and his wife had moved to Listleigh a year ago to take over his brother's tobacco shop. Phyllida glanced around and noticed that Mrs. Heathers was not present this evening.

Bringing up the rear of the parade into the dining room were Miss Winnie Pankhurst, the town's grocer, and Professor Wilfred Avonlea, a retired literature professor from Eton who'd bought a small cottage in order to raise bees at the outskirts of the village. He wore a set of pince-nez that gave him a studious look and had a bright red handkerchief protruding from his breast pocket.

Phyllida was not surprised to discover she'd been seated across the table and down one from Genevra, and she sighed internally. She'd known this evening would be trying, but until she'd greeted her in the drawing room, she hadn't been prepared for *how* tiresome Genevra's constant stream of one-sided conversation would be. It was childish, the way the woman seemed to crave attention and praise. As if she couldn't bear to have anyone share the limelight—or conversation—other than herself.

Phyllida pitied Mr. Varney, who'd been seated to Genevra's left, and Mr. Crestworthy, who was on the other side. They would have no escape. At least Phyllida could turn her attention to Mr. Sprite, who'd been seated on her right.

Sir Rolly was on Phyllida's left at the head of the table—presumably to make it easier for her to observe any interactions between him and Genevra.

Ethel Blastwick sat on the other side of Mr. Sprite, and only two seats across from him was Miss Pankhurst. Phyllida mentally lifted her brows at this seating decision by Vera. Everyone in Listleigh knew the chemist and grocer had an ongoing feud because each of them believed *they* should be the sole proprietor in the village to stock items like Epsom salts and bicarbonate of soda . . . and so both of them offered those products for sale amidst ongoing price wars, special offers, and other incentives. Generally it was safer to place the two as far apart as possible.

Vera was at the foot of the table, with Mr. Heathers on one side and Mrs. Crestworthy on the other. Professor Avonlea was between Mrs. Crestworthy and Ethel Blastwick.

As they all settled into their places and Mr. Whalley, with help from an obviously new footman, began to serve soup from a large, porcelain tureen, Phyllida realized that everyone present lived in Listleigh or its environs.

In a way, it was a strange collection of people for a dinner party. The Rollingbrokes most often entertained friends from London, many of them titled and wealthy. The fact that everyone here was not of the upper class—except for Sir Rolly and Vera—was curious. Even the Crestworthys' wealth had come from a family business rather than land and title.

And then Phyllida thought she understood why. Vera Rollingbroke had not wanted any of her friends or family to be witness to any interactions between Sir Rolly and Genevra that might cause gossip, but at the same time, she needed an excuse for Phyllida to see them together.

Dinner was less tedious than Phyllida expected, for it turned out that Mr. Sprite was a charming conversationalist, amusing them all with anecdotes about his work dispensing medicines and health aids. He might have been trying to keep the conversation from drifting toward his feud with the grocer, and for the most part, he succeeded. Winnie Pankhurst actually tee-heed at one of his stories about a mild explosion when he'd accidentally mixed vinegar and baking soda.

"I thought it was flour, you see," he said with a self-deprecating chuckle.

"Did I tell you—my motor has been repaired and returned to me at last," said Miss Pankhurst, glancing at Phyllida. She was a tall, angular woman in the neighborhood of fifty. Her prominent nose had a high, slender bump on its bridge, giving her the look of a condescending parrot. Tonight, she wore a bright green frock that added to the impression. "That was a most unfortunate incident."

Phyllida, who'd nearly been killed when a killer conscripted Miss Pankhurst's little Austin Seven and tried to run her down one night in the village, nodded. "Indeed."

"If one didn't leave one's start-up keys in the motor, it wouldn't be available to thieves," commented Mr. Sprite to Phyllida, but loud enough for Miss Pankhurst to hear.

Phyllida forestalled the sharp comment from the grocer that surely would have followed by saying brightly, "I understand you have a new feline at the shop, Miss Pankhurst?"

"Oh, yes," replied the woman, her eyes going gooey with affection. "He's simply the smartest cat one has ever met."

"Even smarter than Mrs. Cuddlesworthy?" said Sir Rolly, his voice booming over everyone else's low chatter. "My dear Vera's literary cat is splendidly charming *and* intelligent. I do hope some smart publisher realizes it someday, old bean." He smiled at his wife from down the length of the table. "She's really quite extraordinary and so is her creator."

"Thank you, Rolly," Vera replied with a flicker of that same sad smile Phyllida had noticed earlier. "Professor Avonlea, I must thank you for the honey you sent over—"

"*My* cat is so smart, he plays fetch," said Genevra, drowning out any response the professor might have made. "If I throw a ball for him, he'll bring it right back. I taught him how to do that. And he has figured out how to open the cupboard doors—I'm certain it's because of the way I showed him how to bat at a stuffed animal!" She seemed particularly gauche and frenetic tonight; or perhaps it was simply Phyllida's irritable mood.

"Why, one day I found him sitting inside Papa's bookshelf—and the door had been closed! You see, Boots opened the door and got himself in! It's really just a matter of working with them, to use their natural instincts, you see. I've been studying up on it, you know. It's not terribly difficult if one has the time and determination."

Phyllida gritted her teeth and kept her smile bland with interest. She watched Sir Rolly's expression of barely disguised distaste and incredulity as Genevra continued to lecture and thought, *There is no possible way that man is sleeping with that woman.*

No matter what Vera thought, if Sir Rolly was having an affair, it wasn't with Genevra Blastwick.

CHAPTER 3

With that inescapable conclusion, Phyllida relaxed a trifle. She would have more investigative work to do to determine whether Sir Rolly was cheating on his wife, but the prime suspect had been marked off the list.

Dinner—with an excellent veal Wellington, which prompted praise from Phyllida to Paddington the cook by way of Mr. Whalley—finally concluded. The end of the evening was in sight and Phyllida allowed herself to accept a martini as the group filtered from the dining room into the parlor for cards or other games.

She'd finish her drink and then take her leave. Bridge or whist didn't interest her tonight and she certainly wasn't going to play charades.

"I only just learned about this game when I was in London," Genevra was saying to Mr. Varney and Professor Avonlea—but in a loud enough voice for all to hear—as the guests flowed their way into the parlor. "It's absolutely brilliant and very clever and ever so intriguing."

The parlor was a large and charming space with plenty of seating on chairs or divans. Two card tables boasted bridge decks and scoring pads with pencils. A grand piano adorned one corner, and a massive fireplace was closed up for the summer with an ornate metal peacock sitting in front of it. Large vases spilling with fresh roses, peonies, and artistically arranged branches of boxwood sat on the large coffee table and a credenza laden with spirits and glasses. The delicate floral scents mingled with that from cigarettes as the diners lit up for their after-dinner smokes.

"The game is called Two Truths and a Lie, and we simply must play it. I *insist*," Genevra said, swiftly co-opting Vera Rollingbroke's role as hostess and anything she might have planned for after-dinner socializing. "Everyone sit down, now—pull the seats into a circle so we can all see and hear each other."

She stood watching like a sergeant as the men—Mr. Varney, Mr. Crestworthy, Mr. Heathers, Professor Avonlea, and Mr. Sprite—did as she directed.

Phyllida glanced at Vera Rollingbroke, but the woman's expression was studiously blank. She was surprised Vera wasn't putting a stop to this appropriation of her party; Phyllida certainly would have done if it were her house and her gathering. But there was something different about Vera tonight. She seemed uncharacteristically subdued and even uncertain. Perhaps it was her goal to simply allow things to play out, for Phyllida's sake in the investigation.

Phyllida was certainly looking forward to putting the woman's fears about Genevra and Sir Rolly to rest.

Sir Rolly walked into the parlor at that moment, puffing on a cigar. Vera looked at him, then swiftly away and so she missed the same way he glanced at her, with the same morose look. Phyllida resisted the urge to snap at them for being so foolish.

The Rollingbrokes were clearly at odds over something, but she suspected it was for quite a different reason than Sir Rolly having an affair. She was certain they merely needed to talk.

"Oh there you are, Sir Rolly!" cried Genevra, gliding to his side. "You simply must join us! This is the most fun and intriguing game I've ever played." She took his arm and beamed up at him as she tossed her head. As she did so, her gaze went slyly to the side as if to confirm whether someone in particular was watching.

Phyllida glanced in that direction and saw her hostess, who was contending with the unpleasantness by loudly offering a glass of whisky to Mr. Crestworthy and turning to pour it with mechanical movements. Ethel Blastwick gripped a gin and tonic as if she were afraid it would escape as she made her way behind the sofa. Professor Avonlea was moving his chair in order to be closer to a table that offered after-dinner chocolates.

The faces of the other guests mirrored Phyllida's disinterest and mild horror, but everyone gamely took a seat, for it seemed Genevra would have it no other way.

Even her sister Ethel appeared reluctant.

Phyllida eyed the quieter, more muted Blastwick sister. Ethel hadn't said more than five words at dinner, and she looked as if she was supremely uncomfortable even now. She wondered why Ethel had bothered to come tonight if she was so miserable.

Her eyeglasses hung from a beaded chain over the front of her pale blue frock. Her hair was pinned to the sides with plain combs, and her makeup was subtle if it even existed. Whatever lipstick she might have worn had not been reapplied after dinner. She leaned over and made a quiet, intense comment to her younger sister that could very well have been a plea for restraint, but if it was, Genevra ignored it in favor of directing everyone where to sit.

Thus rebuffed, Ethel took her place in a chair behind one of the sofas, which put her at a little distance from everyone else. Both of the Blastwick sisters were of delicate build, and when Ethel settled into the large armchair, it looked as if she were being swallowed by its dark green upholstery. Perhaps she thought if she sat away from everyone and allowed the furniture to envelop her, people would forget she was there and not force her to participate.

Phyllida rather liked that idea and eyed another chair that was tucked in the corner near Ethel's.

"And you're right there, Phyllida dear," Genevra said, taking her by the arm as she pointed to a large and comfortable chair surprisingly centrally located. "You're such a celebrated detective, I'm certain you'll find this game right up your street!" Her words were complimentary, but Phyllida heard the subtle bite in them.

She extracted her forearm from the other woman's grip and said, "I'm feeling a headache coming on, Genevra. I'll sit over there."

And she moved swiftly away and to the chair she'd originally decided upon.

"How do we play?" said Winnie Pankhurst, obviously wanting to get things over with as quickly as possible. She was sitting on a small brocade divan next to Bartholomew Sprite. Phyllida noticed that the two of them were doing their best to avoid looking at each other. What were they arguing about *now*?

Sir Rolly, who'd been bullied into the seat next to Genevra, puffed on his cigar so that the smoke came out in great clouds like a railway engine. He appeared supremely uncomfortable, as if he were a cornered rat.

"Right, then. Attention everyone!" Genevra raised her voice needlessly and clapped her hands sharply, also needlessly, as everyone was sitting quietly and with obvious impatience to get things moving. Sooner started, sooner ended.

"Here's how the game works. Everyone has to say three things about themselves—nothing obvious. I mean to say, Ethel, you can't say something like, 'I wear glasses' or 'I like to ramble about the countryside' because we already all know that. It has to be things people don't know about you."

"Why is it called Two Truths and a Lie?" asked Professor Avonlea, who, of everyone there, seemed to be taking it the most seriously. Probably because he was a college professor and liked to keep his class in order. He adjusted his pince-nez and peered closely at Genevra.

"Becauuuuse," she replied, drawing out the word with a sly smile, "two of the things you tell us have to be true, but one of them has to be a lie. And everyone has to guess which is the lie!"

Phyllida saw the mild stir of interest that rippled over the people in the room. At least it wasn't charades or anything where a person had to wear a blindfold. She sipped her martini and immediately decided to tell three lies. She'd make them as outrageous as possible.

"You go first, Ethel," said Genevra once everyone had gotten drinks and settled into their seats.

Her sister's face froze into a stunned mask. "Oh, no, no, I don't want to go first," she said, gripping her dangling spectacles with the hand not holding her drink. "You go ahead, Genevra. You know how the game is played. I'd probably mess it all up."

Nice deflection, Phyllida thought.

"All right, then," Genevra said, smiling around at all of them in a manner that suggested things had worked out just as she'd planned. "Two truths and a lie . . . now, let me think."

Phyllida managed to hide her cynicism. As if Genevra hadn't already planned out what she was going to say.

"All right, I've got it all figured. Are you ready?" Genevra looked around expectantly.

Phyllida took a very generous sip of her martini. The sooner it was gone, the sooner she could make her excuses and bolt.

"Right, then. Here we go." Genevra paused, trying to heighten the suspense (which only served to annoy Phyllida and cause Mr. Sprite to mutter something unflattering under his breath). Ethel shifted in her seat.

"All right. Two truths and a lie. Number one: I speak three languages. Two: I was arrested for indecent exposure. Three: I once saw a *murder*."

Several people gasped but more of them chuckled. Ethel lost the grip on her drink and the glass fell from her hand. It landed on the floor in a tinkle of glass.

"Don't bother yourself, Ethel, dear," Vera said quickly. "I'll ring for the footman."

Ethel nodded, but Phyllida noticed her face had gone pale and she had shrunk even further into the large armchair.

"Why, that's too easy, my dear," said Mr. Crestworthy, waving a cigarette about. "Of course you didn't see a *murder*."

But Genevra merely lifted a brow and looked around, still with that arch expression. "Didn't I? Are you so certain of that, Mr. Crestworthy?" Her voice was almost a purr.

"That's ridiculous. If you'd seen a murder, we'd all know about it," said Mr. Sprite—quite accurately. "You would have told us—and you would have told the police, too, of course."

"Maybe I didn't realize it was a murder when I first saw it,"

Genevra said, still with a sly smile and shrug. "And maybe I *will* report it to the police."

"What sort of murder isn't obviously a murder when you see it?" demanded Sir Rolly, who was clearly at the end of his patience. "That's ridiculous."

"So do you all give up?" Genevra said, her eyes dancing.

"Well, now wait a minute," said Professor Avonlea, sitting upright in his chair. "Let's approach this logically. Miss Ethel, do you know how many languages your sister speaks?"

Ethel squeaked when she realized everyone was looking at her expectantly. Her cheeks darkened slightly. "Oh, er, yes. Papa insisted that we each learn Latin. He said it would come in handy, you know."

"And so she knows Latin and English . . . does your sister know any other language?"

"Oh. Um. N-no, I don't believe so." Ethel's eyes darted around and Phyllida was afraid the poor thing was going to vomit in front of everyone. Was she simply that painfully shy?

"But she might have learnt another one and you don't know about it," said Mr. Varney in the kind voice he used when soothing an injured feline.

"I-I suppose that's possible. Away at university maybe." Ethel managed a shaky smile.

"So that *could* be the lie—that she knows three languages," said Mrs. Crestworthy.

"Which would make the other two true? That she's seen a murder and that she's been arrested for indecent exposure?" said Miss Pankhurst incredulously. "Balderdash!"

"I'd certainly believe the latter," Phyllida heard Mr. Crestworthy mutter under his breath.

"Let's suppose she does know three languages," said Mr. Sprite, glancing at Miss Pankhurst. "Just for devil's advocate. That would make either the arrest or the murder a lie. I can't imagine someone seeing a murder and mistaking it for something else, so that has to be the lie. So she must have been arrested for indecent exposure. Very simple."

Everyone looked at Genevra, who was still gazing about her with a sly, feline smile, then turned their attention to Ethel, who'd made a quiet noise.

"What is it, Miss Ethel?" said Mr. Sprite kindly.

"It's . . . only . . . it *is* true. The part about being arrested."

A little murmur—and a stifled cough from Mr. Crestworthy—spread through the group as the looks toward Genevra turned speculative.

"So she *was* arrested?"

"Yes," murmured Ethel.

"For indecent exposure," Genevra clarified, her eyes seeming to tip up at the corners in delight. "I was sunbathing at the beach, you see, and I'd unbuttoned my blouse, and—"

Sir Rolly harrumphed loudly and Miss Pankhurst and Mrs. Crestworthy began talking over her in loud voices. Mr. Crestworthy seemed amused as he drew on his cigarette, then exhaled. Professor Avonlea lost his pince-nez and Mr. Heathers merely gaped silently.

"Very good, very well," said Mr. Varney, whose attention seemed to bounce everywhere but toward Genevra. His cheeks had gone a bit pinker.

"So either she does know three languages or she thinks she saw a murder," said Professor Avonlea as he replaced his glasses. "One of those statements is a lie."

"A murder that wasn't really a murder when she saw it but became one later?" Mr. Sprite scoffed. Miss Pankhurst scoffed in solidarity.

Everyone looked at Genevra. She folded her hands in her lap, trained her gaze around the circle of guests, and said, "I didn't take any languages at university. Which makes that I speak three languages the lie."

Soon after Genevra's revelation, Phyllida made her excuses and prepared to leave. The young woman's claim that she'd seen a murder had put an unexpected pall on the evening.

The other guests also began making noises about calling it a night—likely due to their disinterest in the game in the first place. They had reacted as expected to Genevra's provocative statement: Surely she wasn't playing the game properly, surely she'd been teasing them. Surely she only wanted attention—and to win the game. Perhaps the truth was that she hadn't seen a homicide, but some other sort of death.

No one believed she'd actually seen the murder of a real person. And when pressed about it, Genevra merely smirked, shrugged, and shook her head, clearly reveling in the attention and intrigue. Although Phyllida wasn't completely ready to dismiss the young woman's claim—perhaps she was speaking of the murder of a chicken for dinner, or the squashing of a spider, or even the editing of some words out of a letter or story—she decided not to expend any further energy from her little gray cells on the tiresome woman.

Phyllida was just donning her hat and gloves in the foyer when she saw Sir Rolly hurrying toward her, the smoke from his cigar making a wild eddy behind him.

"Ahem, er, Mrs. Bright . . . if I could have a moment?"

He seemed ill at ease, a fact which piqued Phyllida's interest. She suspected she was about to learn why he'd been casting mooning glances at his pensive and remote wife all evening.

"Of course, Sir Rolly," she replied.

He glanced around. Then, when he saw some of the other guests making their way toward them from the corridor, he reached for the front doorknob, turned it, and pushed out into the pleasant summer night.

Mr. Whalley fairly leaped over to assist, clearly horrified that his employer would lower himself to open his own door.

"Go buttle something somewhere else, Whalley," Sir Rolly said irritably, and ushered Phyllida outside, slamming the door behind them.

"What can I do for you, Sir Rolly?"

"Well, it's—er—I—well, I mean to say that . . . well, dash it all, Mrs. Bright, *you're* the detective!"

Phyllida lifted her brows and waited, looking up at him from under the brim of her hat. It was a lovely evening, she noted. A light breeze just barely stirred the air and a swath of stars glittered in the sky. The guests' motorcars were still lined up in their neat row, their bumpers and hoods gleaming in the starlight.

"It's just that—well, devil take it, Vera's simply not—she's not quite the thing right now, you see, and I'm . . . well, I'm worried about her, you see." He scrubbed a hand over his brow and glared out into the night as his cigar trailed smoke around them. "Something is off about her lately, you see, and . . . well, dash it all, Mrs. Bright, can't you *see?*"

He was clearly miserable and utterly ignorant about how to handle his wife. As that was not an unusual condition for a husband, Phyllida decided to take pity on him. "I certainly do see," she replied.

"Well, what's a chap to do about it then?" he demanded.

"A chap ought to not hang up the telephone suddenly when his wife walks into the room. And a chap ought to not drop his voice very low when he is on a call as if afraid she might hear. Or otherwise act as if he has something to hide. And then perhaps his wife won't think he's stepping out on her."

"S-stepping out? On Vera? Me?" He dropped his cigar. "Why, that's *preposterous!*"

"She's quite convinced you are, because of the way you've been acting so secretively," Phyllida told him severely.

"But I—of *course* I'm not! Would never do that! It's only that . . . well, dash it all . . . talk about *secrets!*"

The door behind Sir Rolly began to open and he snatched at the handle, yanking it closed before anyone could breech the threshold. Phyllida heard a yelp of surprise from inside and stifled a smile.

"My suggestion, Sir Rolly, is for the two of you to have a frank conversation. I am quite confident that once you do so, you will both realize neither of you have any cause for concern relative to the other's secrets."

He looked down at her with great skepticism, then after a moment, nodded briskly. "Very well, then, Mrs. Bright."

"One more thing you ought to know," Phyllida said as she began to descend the steps to leave. "Mrs. Rollingbroke was under the impression that it was Genevra Blastwick."

His sound of astonishment and abject horror was vehement enough to have Phyllida still chuckling to herself as she climbed into the tidy little MG. It was nice to have her conclusion so stridently confirmed.

She suspected the Rollingbrokes would have a very good evening tonight, once they talked everything through and revealed the secrets each of them had been keeping. To that end, she expected the guests would be sent on their way the moment Sir Rolly went inside.

Having accomplished what she'd set out to do, Phyllida started back to Mallowan Hall with the smile still on her face. She really did enjoy being behind the wheel of a motorcar. She even rolled one of the windows down—something she wouldn't do on her way *to* somewhere, but now she could afford a little buffeting of her hat and hair.

But her smile faded as her little gray cells decided, of their own stubborn volition, to return to the curiosity of Genevra Blastwick and her two truths and a lie. The whole event niggled unpleasantly at Phyllida, leaving her feeling nettled without comprehending why.

Could Genevra actually have witnessed a murder? If Genevra had actually seen a homicide, why hadn't she reported it?

Or had she?

And if she had reported it, why hadn't people heard about it? Bartholomew Sprite was correct: Heaven knew Genevra's self-importance would have made it impossible for her to keep anything like that prudently under wraps.

However, the murder might not have happened here in Listleigh. But the fact that Genevra had fairly bragged about witnessing something awful left an ugly taste in Phyllida's mouth. It was almost as if she were taunting someone . . .

A terrible thought crashed into Phyllida's mind so suddenly that she nearly slammed on the brakes. Her eyes bulged as she stared into the nighttime, cut by the two beams of the motor's headlights.

Surely even Genevra wouldn't be so foolish as to taunt a killer by crowing about having seen them do the deed and hoping they would hear about it.

Or be *present* to witness her statement.

Certainly not.

That was a ridiculous, dramatic, absurd thought and Phyllida shoved it away. Most likely, Genevra had seen something that was not actually a homicide and had decided to use the idea as a way to attract attention and to try and fool everyone.

At least, Phyllida seriously hoped that was the case.

When she trundled in the roadster up the drive to Mallowan Hall, Phyllida couldn't help but glance toward the garage. It was an automatic gesture, and she was, after all, driving a motorcar, which belonged in the garage, so it was the natural thing to do, she told herself.

The building was dark and quiet. Not that she'd expected Myrtle and her master to have returned during the few hours she was gone. It was simply habit, to make certain she wasn't taken by surprise by the unruly beast . . . or worse, to run her under the tires of the roadster.

Elton would open the heavy garage door to move the motorcar inside tomorrow morning, so Phyllida left it parked under the starlight. She hurried inside without another glance at the garage, unwilling to contemplate why she felt a tightness in her chest.

"Good morning, Mrs. Bright."

"Good morning, Opal," Phyllida greeted the scullery maid as she brought in a tea tray for her at eight o'clock sharp the next morning. "How are you this morning?"

As usual, the thirteen-year-old maid was neat as a pin, her uniform crisply pressed and apron fairly glowing white despite the fact that one of her first chores in the morning was to start the fire in the kitchen hearth, as well as light the gas oven's pilot light. There was not a speck of soot or ash anywhere on the uniform. Her hair was braided tightly into two plaits and pinned neatly around her head.

"I'm right fine, Mrs. Bright," replied Opal. "Only, Mrs. Puffley's all atwitter today because the const'ble has invited her to a *to-do* and she hasn't got a thing to wear, she hasn't." She nodded, her gray eyes wide with concern for her boss's conundrum.

"That's very exciting for Mrs. Puffley," Phyllida replied, pouring her tea—a favorite, floral Darjeeling, which she had purchased from Harrods during her recent days in London. "And I'm quite certain she'll rise to the occasion and find something to wear. Mrs. Puffley is a very resourceful sort. Do you know what sort of to-do it is?"

Mrs. Puffley, the cook at Mallowan Hall, had recently begun to be visited on the regular by Constable Greensticks, a policeman who was not at all young or inexperienced, despite what his name might imply. Phyllida had found it mildly disconcerting to come into the kitchen and discover the constable present—usually ingesting something delicious baked, roasted, or stewed by Mrs. Puffley—when there was no dead body or other illegality to be seen.

"Only, she didn't say, mu'um," Opal replied. "Only that she ain't got nothing—I mean doesn't have anything—to wear. And that it come on a very fancy piece of paper, the invitation, I mean."

"Quite so. That sounds very exciting," Phyllida replied quite sincerely. She was confident she would soon learn every detail about this to-do. "And is everything else fine with you, then, Opal?"

"Oh, yes, mu'um," the scullion replied with a grin that revealed her too-big front teeth she had yet to grow into. "It was ever so 'citing to be in London, but I'm glad to be back here where it ain't so loud and crowded."

Phyllida was about to ask Opal whether any of the downstairs folk had been talking about Mr. Dobble's mysterious package from yesterday, when the telephone jangled in the hall.

"I wonder who'd be ringing so early," she said, rising to stop the sound before it disturbed Agatha, who liked to write early in the morning. "Thank you for bringing my tea, Opal," she said as she slipped past the maid, who gave the quick bob of a curtsy.

"Yes, mu'um," she replied.

"Mallowan Hall," Phyllida said when she picked up the receiver. She cast Mr. Dobble a complacent smile, for he'd been approximately three steps too slow to answer the call.

"Oh dear, Phyllida! Thank heavens it's you! It *is* you, isn't it?" It was Vera Rollingbroke.

"Yes," Phyllida replied as her heart sank a little. Surely nothing bad had happened last night between the Rollingbrokes . . .

"Did you hear? Did you *hear?*"

"I don't believe so," she replied crisply. "What is it?"

"It's Ethel Blastwick. *She's been killed.*"

"Good heavens," Phyllida said, not feeling quite as surprised as she might have done. Then she frowned. "*Ethel* Blastwick? Not Genevra?"

"No! It was Ethel. She—they found her *on the road*. She was hit by a motorcar! And whoever it was *didn't stop* or even report it!"

"Dear God. How horrendous!" Phyllida sent up a little prayer of godspeed for the poor young woman. What a terrible way to die. "That's simply awful. Surely it was an accident?"

"Surely it was. Oh, I don't know. Do you think . . . do you think it's possible they mistook her for Genevra?" Mrs. Rollingbroke's voice dropped. "I mean to say, after last night . . ."

Obviously, she had the mind of a crime writer even if her stories did feature a talking cat. Phyllida's thoughts had gone in that direction as well. After all, she, too, lived in a world of both fiction and reality where any unexpected death often turned out to be murder.

"You're suggesting that Genevra was the target because of her boasting about seeing a murder," she said, more to herself than to Mrs. Rollingbroke. "And that would imply—"

"That someone at the party last night is a killer because they knew she was talking about *them!*" Vera's voice rose in pitch, her words coming faster. "I can't believe I had a *murderer* at my table for dinner . . . although, good heavens, that wouldn't be the first time, would it?"

"No," Phyllida replied. She wondered if Constable Greensticks was in the kitchen with Mrs. Puffley and if she could badger any information out of him, although she suspected he would be absent (at least she hoped he would be) if there was a dead body to be seen to. "Thank you for telephoning, Mrs. Rollingbroke—"

"Please, I insist you call me Vera," she said firmly. "I know it's quite irregular, but after what you did for me last night, Phyllida, I simply cannot think of you as anything but a friend."

"Of course. Er . . . am I to understand that you and Sir Rolly have talked things over?"

"Quite so and *very* much to my satisfaction," replied Vera with a little purr in her voice. "There is no longer any question as to Rolly's devotion to me and only me. It turns out he was being all secretive because he was working on a surprise. He's going to have some of my stories printed and bound in a beautiful red leather volume! Even if the editor at *The Queen* doesn't want them, at least I'll have them. And he's even found an illustrator so that they can do little drawings of Mrs. Cuddlesworthy. That was why he was so secretive on the telephone—so I wouldn't hear!"

Phyllida smiled. "Why, that's a lovely idea. I'm very pleased to learn that you've talked things over. Thank you very much for ringing. I'm certain I'll be speaking to Inspector Cork soon enough. He'll want to talk to everyone who was there last night in case it wasn't an accident."

And she wanted to make certain he understood the severity of the situation. That, if it wasn't an accident, that meant Genevra Blastwick was in danger. And even if it was an accident, it was still a crime to run down a person and leave the scene.

Vera made a sound that expressed her lack of confidence in the inspector—a perspective shared by Phyllida—then rang off.

Phyllida replaced the telephone receiver and went to find out whether Constable Greensticks was, in fact, in the kitchen.

CHAPTER 4

CONSTABLE GREENSTICKS WAS NOT IN THE KITCHEN AT MALLOWAN Hall.

But he clearly had been.

"Good heavens, Mrs. Bright, did you hear about the accident?" Mrs. Puffley said by way of greeting. "What a terrible thing to have happened."

She was a woman in her mid-forties, built like a steam engine, with a perpetually flushed, shiny face—all of which suited her chosen trade. Today, her dark hair, mottled with gray, was tucked into a net to keep stray curls from seasoning a soup or filtering into a pie filling. Her muscular hands were in the process of trussing the first of a pair of chickens that were to be roasted for tonight's dinner.

"About what happened to Ethel Blastwick? Mrs. Rollingbroke telephoned from Wilding Hall to tell me. How did you hear about it?" Phyllida asked pointedly.

"Well, now, of course, it was Barney who told me," Mrs. Puffley replied without a flicker of her surprisingly thick and dark eyelashes. "He stopped by on his way to the office to . . . er . . . warsh his hands," she added quickly.

It made Phyllida's eyelid want to twitch when Mrs. Puffley referred to the constable as Barney, because of the implied intimacy.

The two were an unlikely couple and Phyllida wasn't delighted with the knowledge that he seemed to find every excuse to stop by the kitchen and potentially interrupt the work being done there. Nonetheless, she had to acknowledge that Mrs. Puffley's performance as household cook had not been the least bit compromised by this developing relationship (there was that word again) over the last few months. If anything, she seemed to be less volatile with the rest of the kitchen staff than she had been in the past. So Phyllida had kept her thoughts to herself.

"Is it another murder, Mrs. Bright?" asked Molly, the first kitchen maid. She'd worked with Phyllida longer than anyone else. Since she seemed to feel more familiar with their boss than the other maids, she often acted as a sort of spokesperson for the staff, asking the questions no one else had the courage to ask.

Phyllida didn't mind. Molly was an excellent worker and she knew her place and her job—at least when she wasn't competing with the other maids for the attention of Mr. Max's handsome valet, Elton, who actually rarely acted in that capacity. If Phyllida should ever be required to enumerate her favorites among the staff, Molly would be at the top of the list.

Emboldened by her colleague's question, the second kitchen maid, Benita, asked, a trifle more bashfully, "Are you going to investigate, then, Mrs. Bright?"

"It's quite too early to be discussing murder," Phyllida said crisply, knowing that this demurring nonetheless would evoke winks and giggles and gossip the moment she left the room. "It could very well have been an accident." Although she simply couldn't push away the niggling thought that it was more than an unfortunate incident.

"Oh, it 'tweren't no accident," Mrs. Puffley said sagely. "'Ccording to Barn—I mean, Constable Greensticks."

Phyllida looked at her. "Is that so? How does he know?"

"Well, I mean to say, it's police work, ain't it?" Mrs. Puffley replied, then, uncharacteristically, clamped her lips shut and returned to her work, humming quietly to herself.

Phyllida tucked that bit of information away. She was not the least bit surprised that Ethel Blastwick's death appeared to be purposeful, but she did find it surprising that Inspector Cork and the constable had come to the conclusion so quickly. It would certainly bear some further investigation on her part. "Regardless, since I was at the dinner party last night, I'm certain Constable Greensticks or Inspector Cork will want to speak with me. Now, how is that syrup of chamomile coming along in the distilling room, Molly? And Benita, did you prepare Mrs. Agatha's morning tray yet? I'll take it up to her myself."

"I did tell you to stay away from dead bodies," Agatha said when Phyllida apprised her of the news upon the delivery of her tea tray. "But I suppose you can't be blamed for a death that happened *after* the party was over." Her eyes twinkled, then the levity disappeared and she sobered. "The poor, *poor* girl. I'd only met her once. Ethel was the quiet one, wasn't she? Far more pleasant than her tiresome sister, as I recall. She seemed a lovely young woman. A horrific way to die."

"Quite," Phyllida replied soberly. "And it is especially upsetting after her sister made a very brash statement at dinner last night. She claimed she'd seen a murder."

"She claimed she'd seen a murder? In front of everyone? Why, what an absolutely foolish thing to do," Agatha said, outraged. "That's very nearly asking for oneself to be done away with, isn't it? I mean to say, if the killer was present."

"Quite right. Or even if the killer wasn't present, certainly that sort of statement would be the fodder of wildfire gossip and most likely come to his or her ears."

"Indeed," Agatha said, still clearly upset.

"But it wasn't Genevra who was killed," Phyllida said. "And so if the death *was* deliberate—as the police seem to believe, and, frankly, I tend to agree—one could surmise that the driver mistook Ethel for Genevra."

"Yes, they do resemble each other, don't they? Very interesting. It is certainly one way to get oneself killed—to announce that one knows about a murder they've witnessed or whatnot. I think a person ought to be able to craft an interesting story around that idea . . ." Her eyes went a little vague, so Phyllida fished a notebook and pencil out of her dress pocket and handed them to Agatha.

"Right, then, thank you, Phyllida," said Agatha, turning away to jot some notes on a side table near the window. She was always using random notebooks or notepads on which to write down her thoughts.

Even here in her office she didn't always have one at hand, so Phyllida had taken to carrying extra ones with her or tucking them away in drawers throughout the house for this very purpose. It was more convenient than having one's grocery list being conscripted in order to write down clues or suspects or malicious means of murder.

"I mean to say, if a person blasts out to everyone that one's seen a murder, it very much puts a target on one's head. But what sort of person does that? And why?" Agatha was tall, and bent uncomfortably over the low table while she murmured to herself and jotted some more lines, as Phyllida waited patiently for her to return to the moment. "I can think of several reasons, can't I.

"Right, then," Agatha said at last, looking up with owlish eyes as if surprised to see that her friend was still standing there. "Now what was I saying? Oh, yes . . . I'm certain you'll determine precisely what happened to the poor girl. And why. One could hope it was an accident . . ."

"Indeed."

"But you aren't convinced."

Phyllida shook her head. "No . . . and neither are the police. It's simply too convenient. The timing, I mean to say. And if it were an accident, surely whoever it was would have stopped to help. Or at least reported it, even anonymously. But . . . do you think I'm jumping to conclusions?"

"Not at all," said Agatha. "But then again, I rather have a mind that tends toward murder. That does mean someone ought to be watching over the other Miss Blastwick."

"Precisely my thought—and one I'll be sharing with the authorities as soon as possible. I already rang over to Ivygate Cottage, but no one answered. I only hope I'm wrong about it all . . ."

"But I don't think you are. You'll take the MG if you'd like, Phyllida. Unless you'd rather Elton drive you around?"

"Good heavens, no." Phyllida did not want the young and handsome Elton to conduct her around during a murder investigation. He would certainly begin to get ideas.

He already *had* ideas, to be sure.

Agatha looked at her in surprise. "Very well, then, Phyllie. But do take my motor. I won't be using it today." Thankfully, Agatha didn't seem to be aware that the valet was so besotted with Phyllida that at one time he'd lost his senses and actually *referred to her by her given name.*

Fortunately, he and Stanley, the first footman, had been fully engaged over the last few days of bringing out all of the draperies, curtains, and heavy brocade bed coverings in order to beat the dust out of them.

"Thank you. Are you certain you don't mind?" Phyllida asked.

"Not at all. Besides, it will force me to stay here in my office with dear Peter and write all day. Poirot is getting closer to determining who the killer is, and I'm not shy about saying he's rather more sympathetic toward the killer than the victim. Do you know I patterned the victim—he's a horrible man, he truly is—after that wicked person who kidnapped the Lindbergh baby? What a terrible tragedy that was." She bent over to pat her wire-haired spaniel as if she needed comfort because of the topic. Phyllida actually almost liked Peter because he didn't jump, sniff, or slather—even when he was offered a biscuit. He just slept in his basket all day long.

"Besides," Agatha went on after a moment, "someone has to attend to investigating the dead bodies that seem to keep cropping up here in Listleigh and all about. It's really quite extraordinary, isn't it? How they keep turning up?"

"Quite," Phyllida replied with great feeling.

"You don't suppose . . . well, you don't suppose it's because of me, do you?" Agatha said with a sudden, startled look. "That I'm rather . . . well . . . *attracting* murders? Because that's quite all I think about—how to kill people?"

"Nonsense," Phyllida replied sharply. "That's absolutely nonsensical."

She sighed. "Sometimes I do wonder."

"Don't give it another thought, Agatha," Phyllida said firmly. "There are murders happening all over the world every day, and you certainly have nothing to do with any of them."

"I suppose you're correct, Phyllie. You always are."

Phyllida rang over to Ivygate Cottage a second time in order to express her sympathy for the tragedy of Ethel Blastwick's accident. This time, the housekeeper answered and informed her that Miss Genevra was "taken terribly over her sister's death" and had finally lain down to rest after having a sleeping draught. Dr. Blastwick was also ensconced in his room, just as devastated by the loss of his elder daughter.

Feeling as though sleeping in her own bedroom was likely the safest place for Genevra Blastwick at the moment, Phyllida left word with her condolences and asked for the woman or her father to telephone when they awoke.

Then she set to the tasks that absolutely required her attention before she could turn her attention to crime solving, which, first and foremost, included speaking with Inspector Cork.

A short time later—after having approved some slight changes to menus for the week and reviewed the books and the merchants' bills (the fishmonger's account seemed a bit high this month and would need some closer attention)—Phyllida was just putting on her hat and gloves in front of the mirror when there was a knock on her office door. It was ajar as it usually was, and she looked over to see Ginny, the first parlourmaid, poking her head in.

"Yes, Ginny. Come," she said with a wave.

"Is it true, Mrs. Bright? You're off to investigate another murder?" Ginny was, as always, fresh and pretty as a daisy, with her shiny honey-golden hair tucked neatly beneath her cap. Her uniform and apron were spotless and starched, and she carried a feather duster. The new vacuum cleaner—Ginny's nemesis—was likely languishing in the front parlor in hopes that Mary, the other parlourmaid, would use it. Ginny tended to be a bit excitable and high-pitched, and as she and the vacuum did not get along, it was often a rather loud experience when they were together.

"Well, I'm certainly going to speak with the inspector about what happened to poor Ethel Blastwick," Phyllida said, knowing that the staff would already be aware of all the details of the death. "He'll certainly want my observations of the evening. Whether it becomes a murder investigation remains to be seen, but if it does, of course I will be there to assist."

Assist was a kind word in Phyllida's mind; in her experience, Inspector Cork tended to need direction and close supervision rather than mere assistance.

"Now, is there something you wished to speak to me about? Is the vacuum acting up?"

"No—I mean to say, I don't know. I haven't—Mary's been using it, Mrs. Bright. I'm sure she'll be telling you if there's a problem. Only, it's Mr. Dobble, you see. He won't let me in to dust his pantry."

"Indeed?" Phyllida's brows rose.

"And he wouldn't yesterday, neither, ma'am, and I just wanted you to know so that . . . well, you ought to know that I can't get all my work done because he won't be letting me in."

"What happened, precisely?"

"Well, ma'am, when I knocked on the door like I usually do, he didn't call me to come in like he always does. And the door was closed, you see, not even open like usual. Like yours. He came to the door and poked his head out and said, 'I don't need any dusting today, Ginny,' and then shut the door real quick-like. And he did the same thing today when I knocked again."

"You couldn't see inside, into the room, then?"

"No, ma'am. He was standing there in the way and he only opened the door a smidge. Only, I didn't want you to get mad that I didn't do all my work," Ginny said earnestly.

"Quite so. I assure you, I won't get mad if you are prohibited from gaining entrance to the room to clean it."

"Thank you, ma'am. Oh, and he won't let Mary in neither with the vacuum. And I heard him say to Stanley not to be poking his nose in there either." Now that she was assured she wasn't going to be in trouble, Ginny was clearly enthusiastic and intrigued about the situation.

"I see," Phyllida said. She kept her tone modulated; there was no need to feed the gossip that would spread through the staff—or probably already had.

"What do you think it is he's hiding, Mrs. Bright?" said Ginny, her eyes dancing with interest. "Did he make a big mess and don't want anyone to see it? Surely it ain't a dead body." Her words were certain, but her eyes sparkled with hope.

Obviously, the plethora of murders in the shire had been taking its toll on the maid's imagination.

"I'm certain Mr. Dobble has his reasons and I'm quite certain it's not because there is a dead body in his pantry," Phyllida replied, knowing that, were the situations reversed, the butler would certainly not be as circumspect as she was being. "I'll speak to him and ask when he thinks he might want to have his pantry cleaned. Until then, you needn't bother with it."

Clearly disappointed, Ginny gave a quick curtsy and said, "Yes, ma'am. Thank you, ma'am."

Phyllida finished adjusting her hat: a fetching dark-colored straw confection with a sassy little curled-up brim all the way around. Bright blue feathers danced at the back (but not too many; Phyllida was of the opinion that less was more), moored by a wide strip of ribbon in blue, yellow, and white. It certainly wasn't as stylish as Vera Rollingbroke's headwear, but it would more than do.

She drew on her gloves and retrieved her handbag, within which she'd begun to carry several accoutrements helpful in crime scene investigation—including a petite torch that would fit into the palm of her hand. It was made by a company called Bond and it took two batteries. The batteries were dear to purchase, so she intended only to use the torch when completely necessary.

"Well, what do you make of that?" she said to Stilton and Rye, pausing at the door. "What's Dobble hiding?"

Her two cats—named for the cheese and the whisky respectively—gave her assessing looks, but declined to answer. Instead, Stilton went back to sleep and Rye pointedly turned his attention to the view out of the window.

Phyllida huffed a laugh, then left her office with its door slightly ajar, as was her habit. There was nothing valuable or private in there—her personal items were locked away in a secret place under the floorboards in her bedroom—and even if there was, she trusted her staff implicitly.

Just then, Mr. Dobble appeared, materializing like a tall, colorless wraith. It was almost as if he'd been waiting for her to emerge.

"Mrs. Bright," he said, not bothering to hide his sneer. He was a slender, almost skeletal man who seemed to always be in a snit about something. He was very fair and very bald, which revealed the fact that he had a dent in his head just above the left ear, contributing to the staff's nickname for him: Old Dent, which was never used in her hearing. Despite the lack of hair on his head, he sported a pair of very robust gray eyebrows. "I see you're off again today and leaving your staff to their own devices."

She didn't bother to acknowledge his snarky comment. Instead, she smiled beatifically at him. "Shall I provide you with your own feather duster, Mr. Dobble?"

"What?" He drew himself upright, taken by surprise. Of course a *butler* would never even take up a feather duster, let alone employ one. "To what purpose, Mrs. Bright?"

"Surely your pantry will need dusting at some point," she said.

He sputtered for a moment as she looked at him, keeping her expression benign. "You needn't be impertinent, Mrs. Bright," he finally said.

"Impertinent? Of course not, Mr. Dobble. I was only offering to assist you in maintaining the privacy you are so clearly demanding."

He snarled something under his breath, but obviously had no real response to her very reasonable statement.

Phyllida smiled at him and ended the conversation by saying, "Good day, Mr. Dobble."

She swore she could hear the grinding of his teeth as she

walked off, heading to the downstairs. She'd make one last stop in the kitchen to ensure everything was going along as planned, and then intended to drive into town to the constabulary and offer up her observations.

But to her surprise, Phyllida discovered Constable Greensticks *and* Inspector Cork in the kitchen with Mrs. Puffley. She hadn't seen their serviceable black Austin parked in the front, so they must have driven round to the rear. Perhaps so she wouldn't notice?

They were sitting at the worktable, each with a cup of coffee in front of them, as well as a plate of oatmeal muffins and some slices of ham. Molly and Benita were not present; presumably they were off on other tasks. Opal was peeling potatoes at the corner of the table.

Phyllida cleared her throat loudly. "Back to wash your hands again, Constable?"

"Oh, Mrs. Bright," said Mrs. Puffley quickly, her cheeks going dark red. "We were just about to ring up to you. The inspector would like to speak to you."

"And the constable as well?" Phyllida said pointedly as the inspector stood, holding his cup of coffee.

Constable Greensticks flushed and rose so fast he bumped the worktable with his knee. It was a heavy, solid walnut thing, so the only result was a dull thud and the constable's suppressed groan of pain. "Of course, Mrs. Bright."

"It was only that they'd been up since very early this morning with the finding of Miss Blastwick and all, and the poor dears were desperate for a cup of coffee, they were," said Mrs. Puffley.

"I see," Phyllida replied. "And a muffin." She didn't begrudge the civil servants respite—they did work hard, or, at least, they worked long hours—but she suspected they'd been sitting there far longer than any of them wanted to let on. In fact, they must have arrived shortly after she'd left to drop off Agatha's tray, and took care to park round back.

"Shall we speak in the dining hall, then, Inspector? I certainly don't want to keep you any longer than necessary."

"Of course, Mrs. Bright," replied Inspector Cork. He was in his late thirties and wore a brown, bristly sort of mustache that always seemed to need a trim. Today was no exception. As far as Phyllida knew, he was unmarried, and this supposition was supported by the thread that trailed from his coat and the coffee stain that had been there since last she'd seen him.

This was not the first time she'd met with the inspector and constable in the servants' dining room, which was tucked just next to the kitchen and around the corner. A long, heavy table of the same style as the worktable in the kitchen lined the room. Twelve chairs were neatly pushed in and the floor was recently swept—a testament to Opal's efficiency. There were plates and flatware set up at places for each servant for the midday meal. Bradford's usual spot remained devoid of a place setting.

She sat and waited for the two men to do the same. Mrs. Puffley brought in a pot of coffee, a cup of tea for Phyllida, (a canny decision on the cook's part, to be sure) and the plate of muffins, then hurried back to her kitchen.

"You've heard about Ethel Blastwick, then, Mrs. Bright," said the inspector.

"Only that she was found run down," Phyllida replied. "But there seems no question that it was deliberate."

She and the inspector had butted heads during previous murder investigations. And, apparently, the inspector had not suppressed the urge to complain about her (although what there was to complain about when she was the one identifying the killers for him, she didn't know) at Scotland Yard. That had become known to Phyllida during her investigation of Mrs. Satterwait's nephew in London, when the detective on the case there had been aware of her reputation, due to Inspector Cork.

"Oi, now, Mrs. Bright, that's for us to decide, isn't it," said the inspector. "We're not here for your opinions about anything. We're just here to get your statement about what went on last night at the Rollingbrokes'." He nodded at the constable, who quickly abandoned his muffin to fish a notepad and pencil from his pocket.

"Indeed," Phyllida replied. "But since I'm certain you've already heard about what happened at the dinner party—what Miss Genevra Blastwick said—then you must have come to the proper conclusion that Miss Ethel Blastwick was mistaken for her sister and purposely driven over."

"Let's stick to your statement if you please, Mrs. Bright." He had a pair of eyes that always seemed to be bulging slightly from their sockets, giving him a perpetual expression of surprise. This time, his expression appeared more fishlike and condescending than surprised.

Phyllida suppressed a sigh and glanced at the constable. The constable prudently did not meet her gaze. It had been so much easier when she'd been investigating the Murder Game death a few months ago and Inspector Cork was delayed in London due to a bridge being out. The constable had welcomed her insight and assistance, and the two of them had worked together quite well—mainly because *she* had run the investigation and he had been properly grateful for her direction.

"Very well, then, Inspector. I arrived at Wilding Hall at precisely half seven. I joined the other guests and the Rollingbrokes in the drawing room for drinks before dinner. Then—"

Inspector Cork held up a hand. "Am I to understand that you were in attendance at the dinner party as a *guest*, Mrs. Bright? Not in any—er—other capacity?"

"Precisely," Phyllida replied, declining to give any explanation for this apparent anomaly. It wasn't any of his business.

The inspector gave her a curious look but remained silent, gesturing for her to continue.

"Dinner was a pleasant affair except for the tendency of Genevra Blastwick to dominate the conversation about inane topics." She described where everyone was seated, although she doubted that was terribly relevant, as the motive for murder hadn't been introduced until afterward. Still, she intended to be thorough.

"After dinner, as I'm certain you know, Genevra Blastwick insisted we play a game called Two Truths and a Lie. She strongly urged her sister to take the first turn. Ethel, of course, demurred—as suited her retiring personality—and so Genevra took the inaugural turn. I'm quite confident that was the woman's intention to begin with. Genevra made three statements, two of them quite dramatic—surely you already have them written down, Constable, so I don't need to repeat them—and her sister reacted by dropping her drink in what could have been shock or surprise, or simply bad timing.

"Through the ensuing discussion—which was part of the so-called game—it became clear that Genevra wasn't lying about having seen a murder. Or, at least, claimed she wasn't lying about it. So one could conclude that she had seen a murder—although what precisely constituted 'murder' was, at the time, unclear."

Inspector Cork nodded. "Go on, Mrs. Bright."

"However, it seems apparent that either a killer was present at the dinner party last night, or he or she somehow found out about Genevra Blastwick's boasting and feared theirs was the murder to which she was referring.

"The murderer obviously decided to silence her before she exposed them . . . but instead, drove down her sister in error. Where was Miss Ethel Blastwick found? Do you have any idea when she was killed? Is there any indication that it *was* deliberate? Have you spoken to Miss Genevra to find out more about the murder she witnessed?"

The inspector gave her a dark look. "Mrs. Bright, leave the investigating to me. I'm more interested in anything you might have observed from the other members of the dinner party, as well as when you left. I understand you drove yourself in Mrs. Christie's motorcar?" His protuberant eyes seemed to bulge a little more.

Mrs. Puffley must have divulged that bit of intrigue. "I did, yes. I was the last one to arrive and thus the first one to leave. If you've been to Ivygate Cottage, you understand why. The drive is narrow and the motorcars are required to park next to each other, one by one, so one cannot maneuver one's vehicle until the one behind them has gone."

Inspector Cork nodded again but remained silent as any good detective knew to do whilst his or her subject was speaking. Phyllida was mildly surprised by this improved form of his technique. Perhaps he'd been taking classes at Scotland Yard.

"I didn't see the order in which the others left. I had been outside speaking with Sir Rolly when the rest of the guests began to filter out. I got in the motorcar and drove away."

"You were outside speaking to Sir Rolly?" Inspector Cork was unable to hide his surprise and suspicion. "About what?"

Phyllida kept her smile in place. It was a valid question and one she would have asked during a murder investigation. But she didn't like having to answer it. "About a misunderstanding between him and Mrs. Rollingbroke. I advised him how to clear it up."

Inspector Cork eyed her with continued misgivings. She returned his look with a bland one of her own.

"Is there anything else I should know? Did you notice any reactions among the guests when Miss Genevra made her statement that she'd seen a murder?"

"I did not, unfortunately." Phyllida was irritated with herself for having to answer in that manner. She simply should have known to look around and notice whether anyone appeared taken aback and stunned by this announcement—besides Ethel Blastwick.

"The line of your questioning suggests that Miss Ethel was run down last night after the dinner party," Phyllida said. "Rather than early this morning. And that whoever did it left the party with the intention of silencing Genevra Blastwick, likely mistaking Ethel for her in their agitation. That does make sense, for the sisters do resemble each other. Incidentally, they were both wearing blue last night, although the shades were quite different." She was watching the constable, not the inspector, as she spoke. His reaction—an absent nod of affirmation—was all she needed. "One does wonder why Ethel Blastwick was walking along the road at half ten last night, however."

Inspector Cork's mustache shifted as he clamped his lips together behind it. "Is there anything else you wish to add to your statement, Mrs. Bright?"

He might not be willing to tell her what she wanted to know, but she could certainly find out on her own. And the fact that the authorities were interviewing everyone who'd been at dinner suggested there was evidence Ethel's death was no accident.

She stood, requiring the men to do the same. "No, Inspector Cork. I'm certain you have many other people to interview. But more importantly, I hope that the first thing you'll do—if you haven't done already—is to interview Genevra Blastwick about this murder she's witnessed before the killer does away with her too. And to keep her safe. We don't need another tragedy."

CHAPTER 5

*P*HYLLIDA RANG OVER TO IVYGATE COTTAGE FOR A THIRD TIME, BUT, as she'd expected, neither Genevra nor her father were willing to come to the telephone. She hesitated but ultimately decided not to leave word of her belief that Genevra was in danger. After all, the woman was cloistered in her own home and thus as safe as one could be. Surely the police had taken measures—although of course, Inspector Cork hadn't deigned to confirm.

Phyllida would get the information to her soon, but she didn't want to take the chance of the message being garbled.

She decided to begin her own interviews of last night's dinner guests with the Rollingbrokes since they were the closest to Mallowan Hall. She didn't seriously suspect either Vera or Sir Rolly, but Phyllida was also a reader of Agatha Christie stories and she knew that sometimes the least likely suspect was the killer (even if that wasn't the case in real life). Everyone was considered a suspect until they could be eliminated.

Aside from that, she wanted Mrs. Rollingbroke's and Sir Rolly's impressions of the evening.

"Oh, Phyllida, I'm so glad you've come," said Vera with a wan smile as she joined her in the front parlor.

Mr. Whalley had given Phyllida another inscrutable look as he showed her in. He was clearly having a difficult time coming to terms with the idea of a servant—and one of a lower ranking than himself—being treated as a guest. Nonetheless, he kept whatever thoughts he had to himself (something Phyllida suspected Mr. Dobble would be unable to do were he in the same situation).

"Thank you, Vera," she replied. Phyllida had finally decided to refer to her hostess by her given name after so much insistence that she do so. It felt strange, but she also appreciated the verbal efficiency of being able to say "Vera" instead of "Mrs. Rollingbroke."

"Have you spoken to Genevra?" asked Vera, gesturing for the footman to set the tea tray on the table. She winced a little as it tipped and nearly went over, but finally settled with an alarming but benign rattle. She grimaced at Phyllida and mouthed, *He's new.*

Phyllida, whose purview did not include having to train new footman, nonetheless sympathized. "I haven't spoken to Genevra. Not yet. I rang over, but the housekeeper said that she was inconsolable and had taken a sleeping draught. Oh, good morning, Sir Rolly," Phyllida said as he came into the room.

"I've told Rolly to join us, of course," Vera said as her husband took a seat next to her on the sofa. He took one of his wife's hands in his two larger ones and gave Phyllida a subtle wink of thanks. "I knew you'd want to talk to both of us. We both slept in late this morning," she added with a blushing look at her husband, whose cheeks had also gone a bit ruddy. "And only came down after the inspector called. Why, we were both still in our dressing gowns, having breakfast in bed!"

"Yes, of course, thank you," said Phyllida. There was no reason to beat around the bush. "It seems that someone either took Genevra Blastwick seriously last night, or had direct reason to believe her, and decided to silence her before she could divulge what she'd seen. Unfortunately, poor Ethel was mistaken for her. Which means that Genevra must be in danger."

"I told Rolly the same thing," Vera said, sitting upright. "The very same thing! Why, we finished our breakfast after the inspector left, and I told him that had to be the case."

"Indeed. The inspector wouldn't give me any information about the accident when we spoke, but his demeanor suggests that the death was intentional. Which means—"

"Which means the killer had to be here last night," Vera said. "Oh, Rolly! I simply can't believe it's happening *again!*"

Sir Rolly's horse's-mane mustache curved downward as he patted her hand. "Now, Vera, old girl, it's simply *not* your fault you . . . er . . . continue to consort with murderers."

He cleared his throat as if he'd realized he might have said something wrong and went on with a bit of a harrumph. "Now, Mrs. Bright, you're going to attend to all of this, aren't you? My darling Vera needs to get back to her writing. She can't have this sort of distraction going on. Not good for the writer's noggin, is it, old girl? And what about poor Biscuit and the housemaid who was stabbed in the throat? Rather bloody sort of scene, it was, but—"

"Oh, Rolly, I'm not worried about my writing! I'm worried about poor Ethel Blastwick, and Genevra, and the fact that *a killer was sitting at our table last night!*"

"Of course, darling, of course, terrible tragedy it is. Poor girl. Terrible way to go. And dash it all, didn't mean to imply it wasn't because it's a most tragic—"

Phyllida decided it was time to intervene. "Pursuant to that," she said firmly, "I wonder if either of you noticed anything that might be helpful. For example, when Genevra was boasting about seeing a murder, did you happen to notice whether anyone else had a strange reaction?"

"Ethel dropped her drink," Vera said thoughtfully. "Do you think she might have known what Genevra was talking about?"

"That is possible," Phyllida said. "Or perhaps she simply was clumsy.

"It's likely that the killer knew—or perhaps suspected—Genevra might have seen what they'd done, but perhaps they believed—as Genevra seemed to have done—she hadn't realized what was happening or what the killer had done when he or she committed the murder.

"And since Genevra hadn't said anything to anyone—the killer or the police—then the killer must have assumed that Genevra wasn't suspicious at all and hadn't realized what she'd really seen. Because, of course, no one would expect Genevra Blastwick to keep something like *seeing a murder* to herself.

"Sadly for the killer, that assumption was quashed last night when she boasted about it."

"By Jove, you're *right*, Mrs. Bright," said Sir Rolly, his eyes bright with interest. "Bit confusing, of course, but it makes sense now you say it."

"Quite," Phyllida replied. "But something must have happened recently to cause Genevra to realize what she had seen *was* a murder."

"Do you think someone said or did something last night that clued her in?" said Vera. "Something that made her realize?"

"It's quite possible it happened last night, whatever it was. That would make sense as to why Genevra was suddenly talking about seeing a murder," Phyllida replied thoughtfully. "An offhand comment, perhaps, that suddenly made her realize what she'd seen. Yes, I like that, Vera. That bears following up. And she was acting rather . . . well, almost feverish, last night."

Sir Rolly beamed as if he'd come up with the idea himself and patted his wife's hand. "Brilliant, old girl, only just brilliant of you."

"Oh, Rolly, *stop*," she said. "A girl's been killed!"

"Quite so. Sad thing too. Terribly tragic. Wicked thing to do. Anyone see the motorcar who done it?"

"Inspector Cork was unusually tight-lipped about the details of the accident," Phyllida said grimly. "But I'll find out. In the meantime, did either of you happen to be looking at anyone other than Genevra when she announced she'd seen a murder? I mean to say, to notice any unusual reactions?"

"Can't say I was . . . well, now you say it, I did notice Mr. Varney. He seemed to sit right up when that all happened, eyes going wide and such. Could've been because Ethel dropped her glass, o' course, but he did seem rather shocked about it all," said Sir Rolly.

"I was . . . well, I was rather distracted last night, you see, and I didn't notice anything," said Vera. "I was almost glad when Ethel dropped her drink because it gave me something to do—to call in the footman. I'm sorry, Phyllida, but I didn't see anyone reacting strangely."

"That isn't surprising," Phyllida said. "Everyone was so shocked by what Genevra was saying, they were looking at her and not at each other. I certainly was. And then when Ethel broke the glass, we all turned our attention to her."

Vera leaned forward to pour a cup of tea. "Yes. And I'm ever so glad you were able to . . . erm . . . clear things up, dear Phyllida," she said, giving her an uncharacteristically shy smile. "I should have thanked you straightaway."

Phyllida smiled complacently to herself. It might not be for her, but a true, long-term, loving relationship was beautiful to see and she was glad she'd been able to help smooth over the bumps and misunderstandings between the Rollingbrokes. But now she had a murder on which to concentrate.

"You've already thanked me, Vera. Anyhow, the inspector seemed very interested in the order in which people left here last night, which suggests—"

"Do you mean to say she was killed last night? On her way home from *here*? I thought it must have been this morning! Oh, Rolly! Last night? It might have been on our very driveway!"

"I'm certain it wasn't, old girl," said Sir Rolly. "Odd thing, though, the girl to be walking home in the dark at half ten at night, don't you think?"

"Quite. But Ethel Blastwick was quite a rambler. Perhaps she only wanted a bit of air," said Phyllida. And a break from her loud and irksome sister.

"And Ivygate Cottage isn't all that far from here," said Vera, a note of hope in her voice.

"The killer must have seen Ethel walking along the road and thought she was Genevra. Do you remember in what order the guests left and whose motorcars would have gone after the Blastwick sisters'? I believe I was the last one to arrive, and their motor was right next to mine."

"I haven't the foggiest idea," Vera said, stirring a lump of sugar into her milky tea. "Quite honestly, I was glad to see them all leave. I wasn't feeling quite the thing, you know, and I was just happy they were going home early. That was before . . . erm . . . well, before. You walked out with Mr. Heathers, though, Rolly, didn't you? And stood for a while?"

"Did indeed," replied Sir Rolly. "And Avonlea too. Were talking about cigars, of course, and stood there a few moments whilst everyone else was climbing into their motors. Well, now, wasn't there one or perhaps two bicycles, now I think about it? What about Avonlea? He likes to cycle. And Sprite, too. Might have seen his there."

"Bicycles," Phyllida replied thoughtfully. "Professor Avonlea rode in on a bicycle?"

"Why, yes, as I recall. Not even sure he owns a motor, at that. Didn't pay much attention to them, quite frankly. *I* wouldn't cycle to a dinner party."

If Professor Avonlea bicycled home, he couldn't have driven over Ethel Blastwick. Same with Bartholomew Sprite.

"Do you remember anything else about what order people left?" Phyllida said.

"Heathers and Avonlea were the last to go, as I recall, but I didn't watch them down the drive and wasn't paying any attention to them all leaving. Wanted to get back inside soonest"—he harrumphed awkwardly—"and would've been sooner but Avonlea don't know how to stop blabbing." He gave his wife an endearing look. "Got back inside soon as I could, now, didn't I?"

Vera blushed and reached for his hand. "Not soon enough, dear Rolly, for I was simply tortured, worrying that you were—well, that something else was happening, you were outside so very long. But then you were there, and . . ." She gazed up at him adoringly.

Phyllida decided it was time to leave. She rose. "Thank you very much for all of your information. If you think of anything else that might be important, please ring me up."

The Rollingbrokes bid her a proper farewell, Sir Rolly standing, but neither saw her to the front door (Mr. Whalley did that) and Phyllida watched the door close to the parlor behind her.

Smiling a little to herself, she went back out to Agatha's motor.

As she did so, she glanced over and saw the Bugatti she'd admired. It didn't surprise her that was the vehicle Sir Rolly drove; for she couldn't imagine him in Vera's little two-seater, which was parked behind it. It appeared to have been moved, for it wasn't as perfectly aligned in the drive as it had been last evening.

Phyllida paused and turned toward the pair of motorcars. "One must be thorough," she muttered to herself, and went over to look at the two Rollingbroke vehicles. "And eliminate all suspects."

Neither of the motors had any sort of scrape, dent, or other indication of a collision; although she wasn't certain that a woman's body hitting the ground would leave any sign of impact, or even any blood.

Phyllida was just turning to be on her way when she thought of something else. The only thing she did know was that Ethel Blastwick had been found at the side of the road, according to Mrs. Puffley.

She bent and looked under each of the motorcars.

In the front of the low-riding Bugatti, tangled up beneath the bumper and the underside of the inner workings of the motor, were several clumps of grass and some splashes of mud.

The village of Listleigh was charming and compact, filled with stone and brick cottages contained by a retaining wall on the east side. A small river trundled happily through the town center, bordering one side of the plot of St. Wendreda's—where a priest had been poisoned during the Murder Fête a few months ago—while many oaks and maples dotted its shoreline.

There were gardens filled with a profusion of colorful flowers—dahlias, daisies, roses, clematis, pelargonium, and more. Some climbed walls, others spilled from pots, still others danced and swayed in the breeze against low brick fences or white picket ones. Lavender, thyme, rosemary, parsley, and other aromatic plants thrived in clumps and raised beds. The air was filled with summer floral and herbal scents, along with woodsmoke, coal, and the occasional burp of motorcar exhaust.

The main street, which bisected the village with the two churches—St. Wendreda's and the C.O.E. parish of St. Thurston's—and a small village green on one side and residences on the other, was lined with shops and businesses.

Phyllida parked in front of Panson's bakery, tempted by the scents of scones and muffins. She hadn't had the opportunity to even eat her toast, let alone finish her tea this morning.

"Why, good morning, Mrs. Bright," said Mrs. Panson, coming right to the door when she saw her. "I suppose you're investigating what happened to poor Ethel Blastwick?"

News certainly traveled fast.

"Quite so," Phyllida replied. "It's a terrible tragedy."

"Certainly is," said Mrs. Panson knowledgeably. She stood there with the door open and gestured her inside. "Now, what can I get for you today, Mrs. Bright? I'll box it all up and you can tell me everything you know whilst I do so."

Submerging a flicker of impatience, Phyllida smiled and went inside. She hadn't planned to stop at the bakery, as delicious as things smelled, but she didn't want to appear rude. Listleigh was a small village, and a person had to take care how they interacted with people. Especially those who were part of the gossip grapevine and could potentially provide information to help solve a murder.

"*Milton!*" Mrs. Panson hollered toward the back, making Phyllida's ears ring because she'd barely turned away. "Bring up one of those blueberry oat muffins Mrs. Bright likes so much. She's here investigating poor Ethel's murder!"

"An oat muffin sounds wonderful, thank you," replied Phyllida, wincing a little that Mrs. Panson had announced her intention so loudly the entire village must have heard (not that they didn't already know). And apparently, it was a foregone conclusion that it was, in fact, murder. "And for up at the house, I'll have a dozen lemon lavender biscuits, a half dozen crullers, and one of the white sponge cakes with fresh strawberries."

"And so you will, won't you," said Mrs. Panson, beaming as she reached for the flat bakery boxes. She reminded Phyllida of an apple, for she was the shape of one and her cheeks were perpetually a flushed and shiny red—even when she wasn't yelling back to her husband, who was the baker. "Now they're saying it was murder—is that true?"

"The circumstances are suspicious and so I, at least, am treating it as one," said Phyllida as Mr. Panson came up from the back of the shop. In his huge hand, he carried a small plate with an oat muffin on it.

"Hullo there, Mrs. Bright! Be hoping you catch that killer soon," he said, giving her the plate. Mr. Panson was a tall, large man who was also perpetually shiny and flushed due to his work with hot ovens. "It's on the house," he said, giving his wife a meaningful look. "Can't have killers just running people down, now, can we? Mrs. Bright will set things to rights."

"All right then, you said your piece—now off with you! Them pie crusts ain't gonna roll themselves out!" Mrs. Panson watched him lumber away with an affectionate smile. "Now, tell me what you know, Mrs. Bright. Is it true that Genevra Blastwick said she saw a *murder*?"

Phyllida was regretting her decision to be guilted into the bakery. As delicious as the muffin was—as well as the other treats that were being boxed up—she didn't really have the time or inclination to tell Mrs. Panson about her investigation. After all, it had hardly just begun and she couldn't spend all day away from Mallowan Hall. She had a household to run.

Nonetheless, she'd had time to think while driving into the village and she'd come to the conclusion that this was going to be an investigation of two parts. She would obviously look closely into the death of Ethel Blastwick. But at the same time, there was clearly a previous murder that had occurred—the one that Genevra had witnessed. Which meant Phyllida needed to uncover what exactly that murder was as well. It would certainly help when she could speak with Genevra about it.

But in the meantime, since the crime hadn't been reported—as far as she knew—that meant she'd have to do some digging.

So she swallowed her impatience and said, "Yes. She did say that last night, and I suspect that the death of Ethel was caused by the killer, who mistook her for her sister—"

"Because he—it has to be a man, of course, to *drive over* someone, doesn't it? And not stay to help?" Mrs. Panson gave a little shudder, even though her eyes were bright with interest. "It's because he didn't want her to tell everyone what he'd done."

"Quite so," said Phyllida, not necessarily in agreement with Mrs. Panson about the sex of the killer. But she did agree that someone who didn't stop to help after they'd run over someone implied murder, not accident. "And so that means—"

"Why, that means someone kilt someone, it does," said Mrs. Panson, nodding as she slid the strawberry sponge cake into its box. "I mean to say, besides poor Ethel. They must've thought she was Genevra, walking down the road.

"But who'd have thought Genevra Blastwick had seen a murder and kept quiet about it anyhow? That young woman could really learn to think before she speaks, she could. And no one would think it was *Genevra* walking down the road, now would they?"

"Apparently they did. It was dark and late, of course."

"I suppose they do look alike," Mrs. Panson said as if making a concession. "Both such pretty girls. It's only their personalities make them seem so different."

"Indeed." Phyllida nodded. "I haven't spoken to Genevra yet to find out more about what she saw, but someone recently died in a way that perhaps didn't seem to be a murder, but really was. Can you think of anyone who died suddenly or unexpectedly here in Listleigh in the last, oh, probably year? Or someone who disappeared?"

Mrs. Panson paused, her hands on the lid of the cake box. "Why, that's right smart of you to think of that, Mrs. Bright." She beamed as if she'd thought of it herself. "Why, if there was a murder that ain't a murder—but it really *was* a murder after all—then there had to be a dead body somewheres, there did."

Phyllida had broken off a piece of muffin. It tasted so good, with the blueberries bursting in her mouth and just the right touch of honey, she broke off another piece to nibble. "Indeed.

Perhaps you ought to think about that and when I come back to pick up my boxes—I don't think I ought to carry them during my investigations, do you?—you can tell me what you've remembered."

"Right then. Too bad you ain't got that handsome driver with you to carry them now, ain't it?" Mrs. Panson peered through the bakery window as if expecting Bradford to appear at any moment.

"I'm certain I can manage," Phyllida replied. Even though she was perfectly capable of carrying her own bakery boxes, she didn't want to get into any discussion with the baker's wife about the benefits and drawbacks of Bradford's presence. "I will be back for them shortly. Thank you, Mrs. Panson."

She slipped out of the bakery before the other woman could delay her any further. The small clock on the steeple of St. Thurston's was just striking half ten as Phyllida walked into Pankhurst's Grocery.

She was delighted, and, considering the events of the last evening, surprised to find the shop was empty of customers.

"Good morning, Miss Pankhurst," she said.

"Oh, good heavens, Mrs. Bright! Can you believe it? I simply can't wrap my head around it all!"

Winnie Pankhurst was clutching a calico cat to her chest, her long, slender nose buried into its fur. The feline did not appear pleased at being imprisoned by his underling's embrace, for his eyes were narrowed and his tail swished alarmingly. One paw had its claws extended, ready to swipe.

Phyllida decided intervention was necessary. "What a handsome cat! Do put him down so I can see his markings, won't you, Miss Pankhurst?"

Once released, the beleaguered creature streaked away without even a nod of appreciation to Phyllida. Being experienced in feline manners, she could not be offended.

Today, Miss Pankhurst wasn't dressed in a bright-colored, parrot-like frock as she had been last night. For her work days, she donned a sober uniform of soft gray with white lace cuffs and collar. No apron, but her skirts had pockets—as any reasonable woman's dress ought. Today the soft gray was relieved by blue pinstripes and the white cuffs were narrow and simple.

She was a tall woman made of all right angles except for her eyes, which were round and a soft gray that matched her frock. Miss Pankhurst was notorious for managing to keep in her head not only the shopping preferences of every villager in Listleigh and the inventory in her shop, but also the balance on each shopper's account.

For those reasons and more, Phyllida had always been quite impressed with the woman.

"Why, that was quite rude of you, Xerxes!" Miss Pankhurst said to the cat, who'd taken a safe perch on the highest shelf above the cash register. His tail still twitched and his golden eyes watched unblinkingly. "She only wanted to admire you."

Having accomplished her goal of freeing Xerxes, Phyllida chose not to comment further on the feline, and instead quickly moved on to the reason for her visit. "You've obviously heard about poor Ethel Blastwick, Miss Pankhurst. It's such terrible news. It seems someone ran her down last night after they left Wilding Hall."

"They must have thought she was Genevra. What a stupid thing for that girl to do," said Miss Pankhurst. "Say she'd seen a *murder*. Of course that's all bunk. Who could see a murder and not know it was a murder? Still, I'm sure she feels terrible about her sister. At least, I hope she does."

"I'm certain she does," Phyllida replied. "I haven't been able to offer my condolences because she and Dr. Blastwick have secluded themselves. But the horror of Ethel's death does imply that there was, in fact, a murder that might not have been obviously a murder. And whoever ran down Ethel must have been at dinner last night. Do you have any idea who might have done it?"

"Someone from last night?" Miss Pankhurst shuddered, then she heaved a sigh. "I suppose it has to be, hasn't it? That's a terrible thought. Absolutely terrible."

"Did you see Ethel Blastwick walking along the road when you left Wilding Hall?"

"Why, I don't believe I did. It was rather dark and I was quite irritated. That Bartholomew Sprite, you know. He said that the bumper on my motor didn't look as if it was straight and it could fall off again, or catch on something—as if I'd asked his opinion. I told him his job was to sell medicines, and not to fix motorcars.

"Did you know that he offered a buy-one-get-one-half-off sale on bags of Epsom salts? Why, who needs that much Epsom salt?" She crossed her arms over her chest and glared out the window, presumably at the shop of the offending chemist, which was directly across the road. She huffed and sniffed as she continued to glare out the window. "Much as I dislike the man, I have to say, I do know Bartholomew Sprite wasn't the one to drive over Ethel Blastwick. He insisted on stowing his bicycle in the back of *my* car and suggested *I* ought to drive him back! The nerve of that man. I did it, but I had to listen to him complain all the way back about the bumper being crooked.

"Anyhow, that Mr. Sprite might be underhanded when it comes to competition and impinging on a person's right to make a living—and now he's planning to carry witch hazel rub!

"Then he had the gall to complain that I have chamomile tea and ginger root extract—excellent for nausea, you know. That nice Dr. Bhatt told me about that. But he—Mr. Sprite, I mean to say—well, he wouldn't have taken his motorcar and driven up over Miss Ethel. I must say that."

"Quite," Phyllida said in an effort to stem the tide. "Miss Pankhurst, do you remember anyone acting strangely last night after Genevra did her two truths and a lie and Ethel dropped her glass? Did anyone seem upset or did they seem particularly shocked when all that happened?"

"Can't say I did," said Miss Pankhurst, tearing her attention from Mr. Sprite's chemist shop. "I was doing my best to avoid having to speak to him very much. Sitting right next to me on the divan made it quite difficult to ignore him. *I* sat down first. Can't think why he had to be right next to me. The man wears too much cologne, if you ask me. Now my motorcar smells like it too. Pleasant enough scent, but he could have a lighter hand with it."

"Whose motorcar was ahead of you and behind you when you left last night?"

"Why . . . I don't quite recall. As I said, I was quite irritated—"

"Yes, yes, I see," Phyllida said, keeping her smile pleasant with effort. "If someone did see a murder that wasn't obviously a murder, it had to have been either a sudden death or that someone disappeared and the body hasn't been found. Can you think of any sudden deaths that happened in, perhaps, the last year or so? Or do you know of anyone who went away unexpectedly or otherwise disappeared?" Phyllida had no reason to home in on the time frame of a year, but one had to start somewhere.

Miss Pankhurst had been looking at Phyllida during this speech, her head tilting from one side to the other like an inquisitive bird. "Why . . . that makes quite a bit of sense, Mrs. Bright. You are very clever, aren't you? The police didn't ask me a thing about that."

Phyllida smiled complacently. "Can you think of anything?"

"Well . . . there was Randolph Greenhouse. He had a terrible reaction to bees—made his throat close up when he got stung once. Can you imagine? Why, bees are everywhere! But somehow he got stung—whilst driving, right inside his own motorcar!" She shrugged, her expression sober. "By the time Mrs. Greenhouse found him, it was too late. He'd suffocated to death—his throat all tight and everything. Poor chap. Terrible way to go.

"And such a terrible time it was, so close after that terrible accident with their dog. Poor Mrs. Greenhouse. She was beside herself, you know, because it *was* an accident—Mr. Greenhouse driving over her old hound. And then to lose her husband not long after. Such a terrible—"

"Yes, I can see that she would be. Are there any other deaths you can think of?" Phyllida interjected, having heard the word "terrible" enough times for the moment.

After a moment of considered thought, Miss Pankhurst shook her head slowly. "I can't quite think of anything—well, there was that motorcar crash off Hiller Hill Road. Ellie Mayhew drove right into a stone fence. But I don't know how that or someone drowning or whatnot could have been a murder, no matter how you slice it up. The bee sting thing . . . well, all one would have to do is release a bee right in his motorcar or whatnot, and Bob's your uncle." She drew back suddenly, a hand going to her throat. "I mean to say, if a person were intent on murdering someone."

"Quite," Phyllida murmured. "All right then, thank you very much. Oh, and where is your motorcar parked? I'd like to see how fine it looks now that the repairs have been finished."

Miss Pankhurst was quite eager to show Phyllida the repairs on her automobile. They were on the street admiring the Austin (as Phyllida searched for grass clumps or any sign of a recent impact) when Bartholomew Sprite came out of his chemist shop.

His thick, dark hair was combed back neatly, gleaming a little in the sunlight with whatever product he'd used on it. His broad mustache also shined a little. He was wearing a white chemist's coat and an air of officious concern.

"I told you the bumper was crooked," he said, pointing to the offending piece of metal. "Do you see it, Mrs. Bright? Can't rely on anyone these days to do a job right, now, can you? It'll fall right off again, and then where will you be?"

Miss Pankhurst drew herself upright. She towered over Mr. Sprite by a full head and the bridge of her sharp-edged nose caught the sunlight. "It certainly drives well enough, crooked bumper or no. And *I* can't see that it's crooked, Mr. Sprite, so please keep your thoughts to yourself.

"And did you know that Mrs. Bright is investigating the murder of Ethel Blastwick? Anyway, *I* told her that you've started carrying witch hazel extract even though it's been on *my* shelves for twenty years, but even so, I told her, that Mr. Sprite ain't going to be the sort of person to do something like running someone down. Stealing a person's livelihood, yes, but murdering someone—*no.*" She huffed and folded her arms in front of her middle.

Mr. Sprite gave her a sidewise look, then turned his attention to Phyllida. "Of course I didn't run down Miss Blastwick. I rode my bicycle to the dinner and Miss Pankhurst graciously drove me back last night."

"Quite," Phyllida replied, believing him—at least for the time being. That didn't mean he couldn't have gotten in his vehicle once he returned to the village and drove back to do the deed. Still, that would take quite some time. "So this is your motorcar, is it?" She pointed to the one Miss Pankhurst had indicated—another sedate, boxy little Austin. Almost the twin of Miss Pankhurst's. There was no sign of grass clumps on its bumper under-hang.

"Yes, of course it is. I said to Miss Pankhurst here that we could have driven there together last night, but she wouldn't hear of it." His gave his rival a frown. She huffed again and tightened her folded arms over an angular bosom.

"I see. I understand Professor Avonlea also rode his bicycle. Did you see him along the road at all?"

"Oh, I might have done. Seems like I did notice someone. He would have gone round the cemetery on that trail that cuts through the edge of the woods—brave one to try it during the night, but I suppose he's used to it. Always talking about how it's good for the lungs to be cycling." Mr. Sprite didn't seem terribly convinced on that topic, even being a cycler himself.

"Did you notice anyone reacting strangely to Genevra Blastwick's statement last night that she'd seen a murder?"

Mr. Sprite peered at Phyllida from behind perfectly round glasses, his eyes magnified like large dark marbles. "At the time, I thought it was quite silly of Miss Blastwick to say such a thing. But now . . ."

"Now Miss Ethel is dead," snapped Miss Pankhurst, as if Mr. Sprite was to blame.

"It seems likely that whoever killed Ethel Blastwick mistook her for her sister," Phyllida said.

"What she's saying is that *someone* must have killed *someone* here!" Miss Pankhurst told him impatiently. "And so we need to think of all of the people who died suddenly or went away—"

"Or who disappeared," said Mr. Sprite, his eyes narrowing in thought.

"Precisely," said Phyllida.

"I already told her about Mr. Greenhouse and the bee stings. And Ellie Mayhew, poor girl. Wasn't there another sudden demise? Surely you remember." Miss Pankhurst turned to Phyllida. "He still nags me about the time I accidentally ordered bicarbonate instead of bleach."

"There was that lorry driver with Betchler's," said Mr. Sprite. "He was here no more than a month, and then all at once he was gone."

"Oh, he surely just ran back to the city," said Miss Pankhurst, making a *pish* sound. "Didn't want to work very hard, you see. Such a handsome young man, but he was certainly worthless when it came to working.

"I had him unloading crates into my back room and I came in one day and found him smoking a cigarette! With all the linens! I told him there was to be no smoking—why, there's ash and soot and the *smell* and I can't have that on my sheets and tablecloths, now can I? Who'd buy them if they were streaked or smelt like smoke?"

"What was his name?" asked Phyllida.

"Was it Claude? Or Clement?" asked Miss Pankhurst.

"It was Clement Dowdy," said Mr. Sprite smoothly, obviously pleased to be of assistance. "Hard to say—maybe he ran off to the city."

"Do you know where he lived? Did he have any friends or family here?" Phyllida asked. "Anyone who might have known where he went?"

"He rented a room over top of the Screaming Magpie," Mr. Sprite said as Miss Pankhurst opened her mouth to reply. The grocer glared at him. "He was employed by Betchler's, but he said as how his family was from Smithfield. Maybe he returned there, maybe someone did away with him." He shrugged affably.

"All right, then, thank you," Phyllida said. "If you think of anything else, ring me up at Mallowan Hall."

"Of course," said Miss Pankhurst as Mr. Sprite said, "I certainly will."

She left the two of them glaring at each other and discussing the proximity of their motorcars to each other along with the benefits of witch hazel extract and why chemists should carry it but grocers should not (the latter was Mr. Sprite's position).

It was approaching eleven o'clock and Phyllida knew she needed to return to the house, but she wanted to speak to Mr. Varney before she did so. He had a small animal surgery just down the road from Mr. Sprite's. Hopefully he was in, and not out delivering a small horse or whatnot.

She was just about to turn up the walkway of the veterinary establishment when she heard someone call her name.

Phyllida, not Mrs. Bright.

CHAPTER 6

"John!" Phyllida turned and waved at Dr. Bhatt, who'd seen her from across the street and was already making his way toward her.

John Bhatt was the town's general practitioner doctor, and he and Phyllida had become good friends since the first time he'd been called to a murder investigation. He had made overtures that suggested he was interested in being more than friends, but she had forestalled him every time. Nonetheless, she considered him a friend and a stimulating companion and conversationalist.

The possessor of a magnificent blue-black mustache that even Poirot would covet, Dr. Bhatt was a thoughtful man who lived to treat people, but nevertheless had a strong interest in poisons. He wrote as-yet-unpublished detective stories about a doctor who solved crimes, and he had his very own arsenic testing setup in a workroom behind his surgery.

"I'm very glad you've returned," Phyllida said, taking his hand in hers in a form of greeting that was less intimate than the kiss he pressed to her cheek before she could step back. "How was your trip?"

He'd traveled to visit aging family members in India and had been gone for over a month. She hadn't seen him since before she'd gone to London.

"It was very long and arduous, but I am happy to be returned. I have missed you, dear Phyllida." His smile was warm and she smiled back, putting a little space between them. "Tell me, how many murders have you solved in my absence?"

"Two," she replied promptly, for he had still been here when she was involved in the Murder Party affair.

"They rang me to see about Ethel Blastwick this morning," he said, his smile fading. "There was nothing I could do for her. I suppose you've heard about that?"

"Yes, of course. What a terrible tragedy. You were called to the scene?"

"I was. Unfortunately, as I say, there was nothing to be done for the poor girl. She'd been dead for quite some time."

"For how long?"

"I arrived at half seven this morning. She was stiff and there was dew on her body and clothing as well," he replied. "I told the inspector the time of death was most likely before midnight. Of course there will be a full postmortem and an inquest, but I'm certain I'm correct."

"Where was she found?"

"On the side of Ploughman's Close, the road between Ivygate Cottage and Wilding Hall. Indications are that she had been walking home, likely from the dinner party last night. I understand you were present."

"I was. Everyone was shocked when Genevra Blastwick announced that she'd seen a murder. No one believed her."

"But now everyone does," said John with a small, sad smile beneath his mustache. "I expect you are looking into it."

"Of course. Where on the road—do you remember?"

He explained, describing the location. "You will readily be able to find it. The grass is flattened with tire tracks. Several of them." His expression sobered.

"So there's no doubt it was intentional," Phyllida said.

"Not the least bit of doubt. It appears the person . . . drove over—her—several times." He swallowed hard and Phyllida's stomach lurched unpleasantly.

"How awful," she managed to say, her mouth dry. "How terribly wicked and awful."

"Indeed. Sometimes people are terribly wicked." He heaved a sigh. "I suppose you have spoken to Miss Genevra Blastwick? Surely she must be warned."

"Not yet," she replied. "But I will. She's been in isolation, and so has her father. I intend to find out as quickly as possible what she actually witnessed, murder or not. But clearly it was a murder, and that brings me to another point. Someone died suddenly or unexpectedly in the last year or so, I would imagine." Phyllida quickly filled him in on the second "trail" of her investigation, knowing that as the town physician, he could be in a position to know of unexpected deaths. Especially suspicious ones.

He was a very intelligent and educated man, but not necessarily an imaginative one (a fact that was eminently apparent in his short detective stories, which were very good but stopped short of being excellent, in Phyllida's opinion), and so she was required to explain why she needed to know about any sudden deaths.

"Ah," he said, his eyes lighting up when he comprehended. "Now, I will have to think about that, Phyllida. Perhaps we can meet for dinner on your night out this week? We have many things to talk about."

"I will appreciate any assistance you can give me, John, but I don't know that I'll have a night out for merely social engagements in the near future. This murder investigation is going to take up quite some time, and I do still have a position to fulfill. I simply can't take advantage of Mrs. Christie's goodwill. She's so very understanding about these things. I could stop by your surgery tomorrow morning if that suits you." She smiled, but saw the tick of disappointment in his eyes.

"Of course. Anytime you would like to come in tomorrow morning. That will give me time to look through my files from—last year?"

"I should say within the last year. I don't know that something of that nature would have gone unremarked for that long. But after I talk to Genevra, I hope to know more."

"Very well. Good day, Phyllida." He tipped his hat to her and smiled.

She waved, tucking away a little splinter of guilt that penetrated her mood as she entered the veterinary surgery office. At one time, she might have been more interested in getting to know John better, but since the events in a certain garden courtyard in London . . .

"Is Mr. Varney in?" Phyllida said to the woman who answered the door to her, shoving away thoughts that weren't the least bit constructive or relevant to the task at hand.

"He's taking his luncheon right now, Mrs. Bright. Please come in," said the woman, gesturing her inside. "He had a difficult morning, you see. Poor thing. Had to put down an old cat. He hates doing that, you know."

The sounds of barking and the yowl of a very annoyed feline filtered from the back of the building. The place smelled faintly, as one would expect, of cat, dog, and other creatures, along with antiseptic and tobacco.

Mrs. Buckwhile was the veterinarian's housekeeper who also did some office work for him. She was fairly new in the position, having taken over for a different housekeeper who'd moved to Bath last year.

Phyllida had met Mrs. Buckwhile a few months ago when she was required to bring Stilton in for a shot, but she was mildly surprised that the woman so readily remembered her name from that brief visit—especially since she had no cat with her at the moment. "Would he be willing to speak with me for a moment whilst he's finishing up?"

"I'm certain he would. I do hope there's nothing wrong with Stilton. Or . . . you do have another cat, don't you?"

"I do. His name is Rye. They're both quite healthy and perhaps a *trifle* thick, due to a small rodent infestation in the pantry. Needless to say, the rodents have been eliminated but Stilton and Rye look a little rounder. I shall have to cut back on their fish skin treats." Phyllida smiled as they walked into the waiting area for the surgery. "Do you live in here at Mr. Varney's, Mrs. Buckwhile?"

"Oh, yes I do," she replied. "He needs a live-in because of the telephone calls that might come in with emergencies. Someone should be here all of the time, you see. One never knows when a patient might come in. We had an emergency surgery yesterday just before he was to leave to go out last night, in fact. Poor little dog got kicked by a horse! Nice gash in front had to be all sewed up."

"He was leaving to attend the dinner party at Wilding Hall," Phyllida said, and Mrs. Buckwhile nodded. "Were you here when Mr. Varney came home last night from the gathering?"

"Of course I was," she replied. "I like to sit up and read with a cup of tea after the day is done, you see. With Jenny—the char-girl—coming in to see to things right off in the morning, I don't have to get up too early, you see. I'm reading Mrs. Christie's Roger Ackroyd book and it's quite keeping me guessing!"

Phyllida smiled. "It's very clever. One of her best, I think. Do you remember what time Mr. Varney returned last night? And what sort of mood he was in?"

Mrs. Buckwhile opened her mouth to reply, then closed it and gave Phyllida an assessing look. "Is this about poor Miss Blastwick?"

"She was run down last night on her way home from the dinner," Phyllida replied.

"So I heard. How terrible that the person didn't stop to help her! Surely you don't think Mr. Varney had anything to do with that," Mrs. Buckwhile said, even as her eyes shifted nervously toward the recesses of the house.

"I'm simply attempting to find out whether anyone had seen anything," replied Phyllida. "Do you remember what time it was when he arrived home?"

"Well, it was just past half ten, I do believe. He came in rather quickly and loudly, now that I think about it. I was in my bedroom in the back, sitting in my rocking chair, and I could hear him clumping around. Normally, I leave him a pot of coffee on the stove, you see, and any messages that came in by the telephone, but he told me last night not to bother about the coffee because he would be at the dinner."

"Is he not normally loud when he comes in?" Phyllida asked.

"Not at all," replied Mrs. Buckwhile. "He doesn't like to upset the patients, you see, and we usually do have some overnight. If they get woken up, you can't imagine the yowling and yipping! But he didn't seem to care last night. In fact, he didn't take much care at all. I thought perhaps he was a bit soused, you see, he was making such a din."

Just then, the veterinarian emerged from one of the doorways down the short hall.

"Why, good morning, Mrs. Bright," he said, smiling at her. He had a few crumbs, presumably from his luncheon, on the front of his jacket, along with a collection of animal hair. Phyllida wondered how much of that hair had found its way into his sandwich and suppressed a shudder.

"What can I do for you today, Mrs. Bright?" He looked around as if searching for something such as a cat carrier. "Everyone else is healthy back at Mallowan Hall, I hope?"

"Stilton and Rye are sleek and happy," Phyllida told him. "I was hoping to talk with you about last night at the dinner party."

"The dinner party? Do you mean that ridiculous game?" His eyes narrowed and he made a scoffing sound. He was a slender man with knobby knuckles and, usually, a calm demeanor. But now a glint of ire showed in his eyes. "Genevra Blastwick should have known better. And now she's got her sister run down because she said something very stupid."

"Why do you think someone would purposely run down Ethel Blastwick?" Phyllida asked.

"They must have mistaken her for her sister, of course. And Genevra Blastwick had to go off telling people she'd seen a *murder*." He shook his head sadly. "The poor girl. I suppose if I were Genevra Blastwick, I'd start watching behind me to make sure whoever it was don't come after me next." He nodded.

"Did you notice anyone reacting strangely when Genevra said last night that she'd seen a murder?"

"Besides Miss Ethel dropping her drink?" Mr. Varney replied. "Poor girl. She was probably just as shocked as the rest of us."

"Did anyone else react unusually?"

He thought for a moment, then said, "I was sitting next to Avonlea. As I recall, he made a very surprised sound. His pince-nez fell off his nose."

"Anyone else?" Phyllida asked.

Mr. Varney shook his head. "Not that I noticed."

"When the dinner party was over, with whom did you leave?" Phyllida said.

"Why, I suppose we all walked outside together," said Mr. Varney, frowning. "Didn't really pay much attention to it all. I suppose I followed the Crestworthys, as their Bentley was parked after mine, so I couldn't leave until they did. Sir Rolly and Heathers were standing on the porch talking about something as I recall. Didn't hear what it was."

"What about Professor Avonlea? I understand he rode his bicycle."

Mr. Varney shrugged. "Didn't really notice. He's rather a bore, you know. If it's not his bees, it's his garden or Shakespeare or what. I try to avoid getting caught up in conversation with him. It's impossible to escape. Should put him and that Genevra Blastwick together and let them duke it out who can talk the most."

Phyllida ignored this comment. "Did you drive away when the Crestworthys did?"

"I followed their motor down the lane, of course. Why are you asking all of these questions? You don't think *I* had something to do with Miss Blastwick's death?" He gave Phyllida a dark look. "It's my practice to help and heal, not to run down and maim," he added frostily. "I loathe to put down a sick animal, even when I must. I'm certainly not going to *kill* someone."

"Someone ran down Ethel Blastwick last night after the dinner party, and it seems likely the driver was one of the people who heard her sister announce that she'd seen a murder. As you suggested, the killer must have thought she was Genevra."

"Terrible tragedy to be sure, but I certainly didn't do it, and I didn't see anyone else who could have done. Got in my motor and drove home and that was it."

"Did you see Ethel Blastwick walking along the road?" If Mr. Varney had left after the Blastwick sisters, then he probably would have passed Ethel on the road.

"Now you mention it, I might have done. It was dark and I wasn't paying much attention—I was in a hurry to get home, and it was dark—but I did think I saw someone along the side, near the end of the drive. Walking. Don't know why she would have done that," he said, shaking his head. "Though I suppose Miss Ethel *was* a sort of rambler, wasn't she? Seen her out and about more than once when I'm driving to a patient. One time even up a tree, if you can believe it. Outdoorsy sort, wasn't she?"

"You say the Crestworthys' motor was in front of yours, then. Did you see which way it turned at the end of the drive?"

"Do you mean did I see whether they turned to go home or turned to run down Ethel Blastwick?" Mr. Varney said angrily. "Of course they went home. Rather impudent of you to suggest that one of us drove over Miss Blastwick, you know."

"Well, someone did," Phyllida replied evenly. "Do you remember whose motorcar was behind you? And who was still behind at Wilding Hall?" Phyllida asked.

He frowned, his spike of anger fading. "Don't really recall. A smaller one, perhaps. But I do remember Heathers and Avonlea talking to Sir Rolly on the porch. He walked down the steps with them and they were standing there when I left. Oh, and Miss Pankhurst and Mr. Sprite were arguing as they got into her motor. They drove off after the Crestworthys. Wasn't Avonlea on a bicycle?"

"You said you were behind the Crestworthys," Phyllida reminded him.

He shrugged impatiently. "I don't recall exactly, Mrs. Bright. The Crestworthys drove away, then Miss Pankhurst and then I went off and then Heathers, maybe . . . I don't remember every bit of it. Had had a drink or two and was tired and I didn't know I was going to be questioned about it all."

"But you did see what might have been Ethel Blastwick walking along."

"I don't know. Maybe I did. Maybe it was just a–a shadow or a deer or something. I told you, I wasn't paying much attention. Didn't matter to me at the time."

Phyllida suppressed a sigh. She was going to get no further help from him. "Very well, then, thank you, Mr. Varney."

She'd spared all the time she could for now. It was time to return to Mallowan Hall.

Phyllida didn't glance toward the garage this time when she drove up to the house.

Pleased with herself for this restraint, she alighted from Agatha's little MG and gathered up the bakery boxes from Panson's.

Delicious smells of roasting chicken and baking bread wafted from the kitchen window—a sort of transom at ground-level—reminding Phyllida that she hadn't eaten anything but a few bites of the muffin. She'd also managed to keep her visit to retrieve the bakery boxes brief, as Mrs. Panson had been waiting on two other customers when she came in and been too distracted to converse with her.

When she dropped off the boxes of pastries in the kitchen, she noticed that the maids and Mrs. Puffley seemed unusually quiet, going about their tasks with silent industry. They each barely glanced up as she came in, and their greetings were suspiciously bright. She got the impression they'd just been all atwitter over something gossipy and had gone suddenly silent.

"Is everything well, Mrs. Puffley?" Phyllida asked, wondering if she'd just missed encountering the constable coming by for another visit.

"Of course, ma'am. And how has your day gone on?"

"Fine, thank you," Phyllida said, faintly mystified by the congenial question. Normally Mrs. Puffley had little time for such niceties; she usually launched into some speech about a problem with the menu, the supplies, the maids, or the oven. Phyllida caught Molly exchanging glances with Benita and Opal, but when the girls saw her look at them, they returned their attention to their work.

"Has Mr. Dobble been down here?" Phyllida asked, stifling a mild sense of disquiet. Something was definitely on.

"No, ma'am," said Mrs. Puffley. "Ain't seen hide nor hair of him—"

"And when I tried to deliver his tray, he chased me away from his pantry!" said Molly. "Told me to stop snooping around. He took the tray from me, though."

"Yes," Phyllida said. "He's been rather dithery about his office as of late."

"Ever since that crate come yesterday," said Benita.

"Indeed," said Phyllida.

"Ginny said she thought she heard some strange noises coming from inside there, ma'am," Opal said. "A sort of rattling and such."

"I thought we ought to ask Amsi if he could peek inside Old Dent's office window and see what's what in there," said Molly, her eyes dancing, speaking of the gardener.

"Stanley said as he could get a ladder and put it by the side and we could all take a gander," said Benita, her cheeks flushed with enthusiasm. "But I told him I didn't think that was a good idea, Mrs. Bright," she added quickly when she saw Phyllida's expression.

Molly rolled her eyes and muttered something under her breath. Phyllida got the impression that she, at least, would have gladly peeked from a ladder, and that she wasn't pleased that Benita had ratted out the idea to their boss.

"Mr. Dobble is welcome to his privacy," was all Phyllida said. "And I'm quite certain when his pantry becomes dirty enough, or he becomes hungry enough, he will allow service to continue as usual. In the meantime, I don't want to hear about anyone trying to peek through windows or sneak into his pantry whilst he is out. Understood?"

Not that Mr. Dobble went out all that often. He used to play chess with the vicar every Wednesday night and their weekly game had been as sacrosanct as the Catholic mass on a Sunday. But something had happened and the two seemed to have had some sort of falling-out. And then when Mr. Dobble was in London, he began playing chess with the cook at the house Mrs. Agatha and Mr. Max had leased.

Since they'd all returned from London, Phyllida was not aware of Mr. Dobble reinstating his weekly chess games with Mr. Billdop, although she hadn't spent any time wondering why. That was his business, and unlike the butler, she had no interest in sticking her nose into anyone else's private life.

"Yes, ma'am," said Molly.

"Yes, ma'am," echoed Benita and Opal.

Mrs. Puffley scoffed under her breath, but Phyllida didn't press her. She couldn't imagine the woman, who was as agile as a barge, having the desire or the ability to climb a ladder stuck in the ground in order to peer into a window.

"Very well then," Phyllida said. "I shall take a luncheon tray up to Mrs. Agatha, as she is working through a difficult story with Poirot and doesn't want to be disturbed. Until then, I shall be in my office. Ring up when the tray is ready."

Phyllida took the stairs up from the below-ground level to the main floor. As she came down the short hall that led to her office and Mr. Dobble's pantry, she noticed that his door was slightly ajar.

A little wave of interest prickled over the back of her neck. This would be the perfect opportunity to take a peek and see what he had hidden inside there. Either he would be sitting at his desk and she could get a glimpse inside before he could stop her, or he'd left the office and the door hadn't closed tightly behind him.

The hall was silent and empty. In the distance she could hear the vacuum cleaner—in the study at the far end of the house—but there were no other sounds of activity.

She took two steps past her office toward Dobble's, then stopped. No...

She wasn't going to give him the satisfaction of expending any of her little gray cells' energy about his secret. For all she knew he was creating this air of mystery just to disturb her.

She turned and took one step back to her own office. Just as she pushed the door open, she saw Dobble come out of his pantry.

She was very glad she hadn't gone down there to take a peek, for he would have seen her and there would have been no end of his condescension and arrogant remarks. He'd probably left the door open as a lure in an effort to see if he could catch her. After all, he'd surely seen her return in the roadster. It was his business to pay attention to all the comings and goings.

"Ah, Mrs. Bright. I see you've decided to rejoin we of the lowly," he said.

Was there an air of disappointment in his eyes? Had he anticipated catching her trying to take a peek, but she'd stymied him? Phyllida smothered a grin.

"Are you ready for a feather duster yet? You'll also want to do a good mopping in there too, Mr. Dobble. I can have Mary bring a pail for you—"

"You received a telephone call whilst you were gallivanting about the countryside."

Instead of asking for the information, she waited for him to continue, a tactic Phyllida knew made him want to grind his teeth. She smiled.

"It was a Dr. Robert Blastwick. He asks that you return his telephone call straightaway—"

"Yes, thank you, Mr. Dobble," she said, not caring that she'd interrupted him (something she generally avoided doing simply because waiting him out was much more preferable because he usually ran out of sarcastic things to say). But this was the message she'd been waiting for.

His eyes widened and his thin lips clamped tightly, but he said nothing more.

She hurried to the telephone and asked the operator to connect her with Ivygate Cottage.

"Dr. Blastwick, please," she said crisply when the call was put through to the other end. "This is Mrs. Bright speaking."

"Oh, Mrs. Bright! Oh, it's me, Genevra." The voice on the other end of the line wailed and was followed by the sound of someone bursting into tears. "Oh, could you come? I need your help!"

CHAPTER 7

After assuring Genevra that she would come as soon as possible—and urging the woman to stay at home and not to admit anyone to the cottage—Phyllida hurried down to the kitchen.

Mrs. Puffley was standing at the stove stirring something, and the three maids were arranged at the worktable.

"Mrs. Agatha's luncheon tray, please, Molly," she said. She'd take it up to her boss early and make certain it was permissible for her to leave again.

"Yes, of course, Mrs. Bright. Only, is . . . er . . . everything all right?" Molly—along with Benita and Opal—were all eyeing her with unusual interest. Even Mrs. Puffley had turned from the stove and was stirring while looking at her.

"Yes, of course. It's only that I'm required to leave again and—what in heaven's name is wrong with the lot of you?"

"What do you mean, Mrs. Bright?" said Opal. She was always filled with innocence and guile, but now she had such an exaggerated air of ingenuousness that Phyllida felt even more suspicious. Especially when each of the maids returned their attention to their respective tasks—slicing potatoes, pitting cherries, and chopping wonderfully pungent rosemary and thyme from the garden, all with that same sense of industriousness they'd had earlier.

"Never mind," she replied. She had no time to waste with whatever gossip on which the maids were fixated. "The tray, if you please, Molly."

Molly scurried over to finish putting together the tray while Phyllida continued to eye the maids mistrustfully. Something was definitely going on.

A sudden whirlwind of activity caught her attention when Ginny flew into the kitchen.

"Well? Did she see h—*oh!* Mrs. Bright." The girl's face turned scarlet as she came to an abrupt halt. "There you are, Mrs. Bright."

"Yes, Ginny. Here I am. Were you looking for me?" Phyllida was aware that the maids and the cook had all studiously returned to their tasks after this new arrival, even as Ginny and Molly exchanged peeks at each other. What on earth was going *on*?

"Um . . . well, you see, I n-needed to t-talk to you about, um, Mr. Dobble," said Ginny.

"Yes?"

"H-he . . . well, he still won't let me in there," she said miserably, clearly aware that she'd backed herself into a corner.

"Yes, Ginny, I believe we discussed this previously. Mr. Dobble is . . ."

Phyllida had caught sight of the shadow of a figure in the hallway outside the kitchen. Her words dried up as the figure moved into the doorway.

"Hallo there, Mrs. Bright," said Bradford as he stepped into the kitchen and removed his cap.

Through the sudden rushing in her ears, Phyllida *swore* she heard a squeak from Ginny and a little sigh from Molly, but she was too focused on the way the room seemed to tilt and her bloody knees went weak.

"Bradford," she managed to say in a voice she hoped and prayed was steady and nonchalant. "You've returned." Her heart was thudding wildly in her chest, drat it all, and of course he'd returned—he was *standing there*. What an inane thing to say. Of course anyone's heart would be racing if they'd been taken by surprise as she had. She frowned, looking around suspiciously. "But where's Myrtle?"

Normally, the excitable canine was the first indication of Bradford's proximity, a reliable and unmistakable sort of warning. But that had clearly not occurred today.

Had something happened to the wild beast? Had she been caught beneath the wheels of a motorcar in London? She'd had the propensity for wanting to run after them . . . Phyllida was shocked that she felt a true wave of concern by the thought.

"Myrtle's taking a bit of a snooze," said Bradford. His attention had not moved from her person, and Phyllida felt the weight of his gaze on her. When their eyes met, she couldn't seem to look away either. "Myrt's been to see the veterinarian, you see, and now she's sleeping a bit."

"Mr. Varney?" Phyllida heard herself say inanely. Again. Good heavens, what on earth was the matter with her?

"Aye, of course. She'll be fine, he says. He stitched her right up."

"I see. I'm . . . glad to hear that." Phyllida still felt as if she was underwater, and that infuriated her. She gave herself a mental shake and said briskly, "Well, I ought to take up Mrs. Agatha's tray soonest. Molly, if you haven't put it together by now—"

"Yes, ma'am, it's right here," Molly said.

There was a spring in the kitchen maid's step and a wide grin on her face, and Phyllida couldn't ignore the fact that she and Ginny had been exchanging what they obviously thought were covert glances. Benita had been openly staring at her and Bradford ever since his appearance, and Opal seemed to be biting her lip as she forced herself to look steadily at the large pot of sliced potatoes to which she was adding.

Phyllida very nearly blushed, but she managed by great force of will to keep her face from turning hot.

Good heavens, what had the maids thought would happen when Bradford returned? That there would have been some sort of altercation or snappy exchange of mild rebukes regarding the jumping dog?

Not that that would be a surprise or cause for such interest—she and Bradford had always had a sort of . . . well, salty . . . type of interaction. Their tart conversations likely served as great entertainment for the staff—usually with Phyllida expressing her extreme dislike for Myrtle and her slathering ways, whilst Bradford seeming to egg on the little canine to cavort beneath Phyllida's feet and encourage the beast to run pell-mell through the kitchen and yard. Not to mention all of his dry, sardonic comments about her investigations.

Thank heavens the staff didn't know about . . . well, about . . . *things*. The two nights in the garden (and the single early morning) . . .

Phyllida snatched up the tray from Molly and said, quite needlessly, "Mrs. Puffley, I'll expect dinner to be on time tonight." She sailed out of the room, the dishes on the tray clinking gently.

Her knees were still a trifle weak as she climbed the two flights of stairs to the first floor, where Agatha's office had been set up adjacent to her bedchamber, and now the questions came.

When had Bradford returned? Why had no one mentioned it? How had she not seen him, or noticed the Daimler? And if he had taken Myrtle to Mr. Varney's surgery, how had she not seen him when she was there only a short while ago? *Was* Myrtle going to be all right? So that was what Mr. Varney had meant when he said "Is everyone else at Mallowan Hall all right?"

Obviously, Phyllida didn't herself care so much whether the exasperating, mop-like canine was going to heal properly (Stitching her up? Had Mr. Varney needed to do surgery? Was that the surgery Mrs. Buckwhile had mentioned?), but she knew Bradford would be greatly affected if something happened to his dog.

The tread of rapidly ascending footsteps from behind and below had her pausing just before she opened the green baize door that led from the servants' staircase into the main hall of the first floor.

"I would have carried the tray for you," said Bradford as he climbed the last two steps.

"Nonsense. A chauffeur carrying a tr—"

Before she could stop him, or step back, or even think, he'd taken her face gently in his large, warm hands and covered her mouth with his.

It was a brief kiss, but, she had to admit, a welcome and very pleasurable, very thorough, one. Even better than those from the Bugatti driver, if one cared to compare. It was a wonder the tea tray remained intact, for all the attention she paid to it—but fortunately, it had been trapped between their bodies.

"Well now," he muttered as he stepped back. He wore a half smile and his eyes were dark and deep and warm. "It's sure good to see you again, Mrs. Bright."

She knew he found it highly amusing to refer to her in such a formal manner despite the intimacy of their interactions.

"When did you get back?" she said, trying to settle her heart rate back into its normal pace even as she leveled out the tray. Thankfully nothing had gone over or spilled.

Bradford relieved her of her burden, and she thought better of trying to fight with him over it. She was a little shakier than she liked to admit. *Drat it.*

"Late last night," he replied. "I understand you've been tooling about the countryside in Mrs. Agatha's coupe investigating another murder."

"I've found it's quite convenient to have a motorcar at my disposal whilst—"

She heard the footsteps and clunking of a mop inside its pail seconds before the door opened, and fairly leapt away, putting herself at a distance from Bradford.

"Oh, my saints and angels, Mrs. Bright!" Bess, one of the chambermaids, nearly dropped the pail. "And Bradford!" (He refused to answer to "mister" from anyone except Opal.) "You gave me a turn!" But her surprise faded quickly into sly interest.

"I was just bringing this tray to Mrs. Agatha," said Phyllida, taking it from Bradford. The china clinked and the sugar spoon fell from its dish, but she was mostly annoyed because she'd lowered herself to explain her presence to one of her maids.

Bradford didn't say a word. He merely pushed open the door and held it as she went through.

"Bess, I expect you to bring the vacuum up and use it," she said, pausing in the hallway to turn back. "Ask Elton or Stanley to carry it up if you need, but there'll be no avoiding it."

"Yes, mu'um," said the maid grimly.

"I don't understand why they're so terrified of that machine,"

Phyllida said as, for some reason, Bradford walked along the hall with her to Agatha's office. What was he doing? Why was he sticking to her like a burr?

"Well, now, it's loud and heavy, and it feels alive, I suppose," he said. "It's a bit disconcerting to some."

Phyllida shrugged and was just about to set the tray on a table so she could knock at Agatha's door when Bradford stepped forward and rapped.

"What are you doing?" she said in a low voice.

"Why, I'm coming to speak with Mrs. Mallowan," he replied just as the voice from within said, "Come."

Phyllida gave him a suspicious look and marched past with the tray when he opened the door.

"Oh, Phyllie, thank you. How did you know I was famished so early? And Joshua! Do tell me how poor, dear Myrtle is! I've been so worried about the little thing. A horse's hoof in the chest, was it? How tragic! And frightening for the little luvvie!"

Phyllida busied setting up the tray as Agatha and Bradford launched into a discussion that expressed their mutual adoration and concern for canines. That was one thing she and Agatha didn't see eye to eye on.

"Poor, darling Myrtle," said Agatha. "I'm so relieved Mr. Varney was able to see her so quickly. And he stitched her up nice and tight?"

"Yesterday afternoon." Bradford's eyes flickered toward Phyllida, then returned to Agatha. "I waited until the operation was over and she came out of it, you see."

"Of course you did," said Agatha with a gentle smile. "Anyone would do."

Phyllida wasn't quite certain about that, but she supposed in Bradford's case it was to be expected. He was more than a little taken with that canine. But she was still thinking about the fact that he'd been returned to Listleigh since yesterday afternoon and she hadn't known about it.

Not that she had to know all of his comings and goings, but she rather didn't like surprises and he had certainly surprised her this morning. She liked even less that he had surprised her in front of the witnesses of her staff.

"Mr. Varney says she'll be right as rain in a fortnight, but she needs to be kept quiet for another week at least," replied Bradford. "And keeping her from licking at the wound once the bandage is off will be another problem entirely."

"Oh, yes, it would be," replied Agatha, reaching over to pat her own dog. "When Peter had his surgery—for a completely different matter, of course—that was the most difficult thing. But he was such a good boy. He's been a very, very good dog—and so has Myrtle. I think it's time to induct her into the Order of the Faithful Dog," she added, beaming. "Only the best dogs get invited, and I'm inviting her." Agatha was so fond of dogs, for she felt they were far more steadfast than most humans, she'd created her own fictional and imaginary Order of the Faithful Dog.

"She would be quite honored to accept, Mrs. Mallowan," Bradford replied, smiling back at her. He always referred to Agatha as Mrs. Mallowan because he'd come to the household via a connection with Mr. Mallowan's brother Cecil, and so of course thought of her in that way, whereas most other people thought of her by her previous name because of her fame as a writer.

Phyllida realized she was standing there uselessly as they spoke about something she was hardly interested in. Normally, she would excuse herself and allow them to finish their mutual mooning over the canines, but she wanted to get permission from Agatha to leave the house again.

"I'm quite relieved to hear that Myrtle is expected to be her normal boisterous self in a fortnight," Phyllida said, actually meaning it. She certainly didn't celebrate or wish illness or injury on any creature; she simply didn't like them jumping on her. She and Myrtle would likely get along fine if the canine would learn that. "And in the meantime, I can't deny I'll enjoy the lack of her enthusiastic greetings. Erm . . . Mrs. Agatha, I did just receive a telephone call from Genevra Blastwick."

"Oh, that is splendid," replied Agatha, as if the matter was settled. "If she wants you to find out what happened—which of course she does—then Inspector Cork certainly can't stymie your investigation, now, can he? If you've been privately engaged by the family to look into the matter, I mean to say."

"I wouldn't be too certain of that," Phyllida replied grimly, but with an uptick of pleasure that her friend and employer was so quick to understand the situation and encourage her participation.

"I suppose you'll need to speak with her soonest," Agatha said. "Do impress upon Genevra the danger she herself is in, but I suppose once she tells you all she knows, then there won't be any sense in the killer coming after her, now will there?"

"Precisely," Phyllida replied.

Before she could go on, Agatha said, "Joshua, you'll drive Mrs. Bright over to Ivygate Cottage, won't you now? Myrtle can stay in here with me if she needs company whilst she recuperates. Dear Peter would be delighted to have a friend, and you know how gentle he is."

"Of course, Mrs. Mallowan," replied Bradford. Phyllida wasn't certain how she felt about the relish in his voice. "Mrs. Bright will be thrilled not to have an invalid canine joining us in the Daimler."

"She certainly will be," Phyllida replied tartly, not at all thrilled that she'd been neatly removed from the position of being her own chauffeur to having to be accompanied by Bradford.

Things were simply so complicated, and she had enough to contend with in this murder investigation. She didn't need to be in close proximity to Bradford. The dratted man distracted her.

"All right then. I've got to get back to Poirot," Agatha said, moving to her desk, her eyes going vague.

Phyllida knew the signs—and presumed Bradford did as well—and left the room. He was on her heels.

"How soon do you want to leave, Mrs. Bright?" he asked in a very smooth voice.

"As soon as you can prepare the Daimler," she replied in a similar tone. "Or do you wish to deliver Myrtle to Mrs. Agatha's office first?"

"Oi, Myrts will be fine settled on her bed in the back hall by the kitchen," Bradford told her as they began to descend.

"But not *in* the kitchen," Phyllida said firmly.

"Of course not, Mrs. Bright."

"And not in the pantry either. Or the dairy. Or the storeroom. Heaven knows what she could get into in there."

"Quite so, Mrs. Bright."

She gratefully left the stairwell at the ground floor while he continued to the downstairs. She didn't see Mr. Dobble when she slipped into her office, and this time his pantry door was closed tightly.

Phyllida took her time setting her hat into place and checking her hair, refusing to dwell on the fact that she could still feel Bradford's large, warm hands cupping her face. They hadn't left any motorcar grease or oil on her skin, thankfully; she'd noticed they were devoid of both today, which was unusual because he rarely wore gloves.

However, what little of her lipstick that was left from this morning had smeared. She was optimistic that Agatha hadn't noticed since it was a subtle color, and there had hardly been any left to smear, but it was possible Bess might have noticed. It seemed the sort of thing any of the maids would notice—something about their boss being even slightly mussed. She hoped their interaction had been brief enough and that the stairwell was shadowy enough that the smear wasn't noticeable.

When she came downstairs to leave, she discovered Benita and Opal in the back hallway, fussing over Myrtle—who'd been ensconced in a wicker basket filled with an old blanket and . . . was that one of Bradford's shirts?

"I'm certain the creature will recuperate faster if she's left to sleep," Phyllida said crisply, eyeing the dark brown mop of a dog.

The maids jumped, startled by their boss's sudden appearance, and hustled back to the kitchen.

Myrtle looked up at Phyllida and gave a short little bark of recognition and thumped her tail twice. Her beady black eyes, usually bright with mischief, were dull and droopy. Her mouth was closed, with no sign of her wet, pink tongue lolling. The fact that the beast didn't even try to climb from the basket to launch herself at Phyllida was testament to her condition.

The silky-haired canine was wrapped in a white bandage around part of her trunk and down along a front paw. Phyllida admired Mr. Varney's work, approving of the neatness of the way the thick, curling dark fur had been shaved from most of the leg—even the part not covered by the bandage.

"I suppose you'll be milking this recovery for all its worth," she said to the canine. She found herself lowering to a half crouch—merely in order to make certain the beast fully comprehended what she was saying. "But don't expect me to bring you a biscuit every time I walk by. Perhaps *once*, but I certainly don't approve of canines in the house, as you well know. This is an extenuating circumstance and as soon as you've recovered sufficiently, you'll be remanded to the garage. I simply don't wish to contend with Stilton and Rye's sulking over your presence. Do you understand?"

Myrtle thumped her tail again and gave a ladylike yip.

"Excellent. I'm delighted you see my point of view," Phyllida told her, and reached out to pat her gently on the head, simply as a way to emphasize their agreement. Certainly not because she intended to show affection. She'd learned that any sign of even absent interest caused the beast to go into raptures, which often resulted in torn stockings or wet slatherings on her hand or the back of her knee.

As always, she was surprised by how soft and springy the hair felt. Not so very different from that of her master's.

Phyllida rose swiftly, feeling the heat in her cheeks. Drat and blast, she did not like the way that man continued to intrude upon her thoughts. It was no wonder Poirot hadn't had a woman in his life.

Exasperated with the entire situation, Phyllida marched into the kitchen. "I will be leaving for a short while."

"Are you taking Mrs. Agatha's motor?" asked Molly.

Phyllida turned a jaundiced eye onto her. "As you likely already are aware, Bradford is driving me in the Daimler."

"Yes, ma'am," said Molly, not appearing the least bit chastised.

"I want to make it clear that whilst Myrtle is allowed to be in the hallway in her basket as she recuperates—and only when Bradford is not present to care for her—that canine is not to even sniff in the direction of this kitchen. I refuse to permit even a single canine hair to be incorporated into any food prepared in this kitchen. Do you all understand?"

The chorus of "yes, ma'ams" were dutiful, yet Phyllida had the nagging sensation that the moment she climbed into the Daimler, the wicker basket would be brought into the kitchen and tucked into a corner. "Very well. I anticipate returning in time to serve tea."

Bradford was waiting next to the Daimler. He had the front passenger door open for her and he certainly took his time noticing her legs as she climbed in. Her cheeks were warm as she settled into her seat.

"Ivygate Cottage, then, Mrs. Bright?" he said as he began to navigate the motor down the drive.

"Yes," she replied. "Miss Ethel Blastwick was killed late last night. A motorcar ran her over. It was no accident. There were multiple tire tracks."

Bradford made a quiet sound of horror, and said, "Bloke who did such a thing ought to be hanged." After that, he remained silent. He likely expected that if he did so, Phyllida would fill him in on the details of the situation.

Normally, she would keep her own counsel. However, she'd discovered that it often helped to talk about a case with Bradford. He, on occasion, offered up sensible ideas and logical thoughts, and he had actually assisted her in proving her case against the killer when they were in London.

"There was a dinner party last night at Wilding Hall," she said. "Mr. Varney was in attendance, in fact. He must have tended to Myrtle before coming to the dinner."

"Aye, he did say he was going to a dinner party. That was why I stayed with Myrts until she woke up, because he was leaving."

"I didn't realize you'd returned," Phyllida said, knowing her words sounded a little stiff.

"I ate dinner at the Screaming Magpie after and then arrived to

Mallowan Hall late. The MG was in the drive, so you'd already returned, I suppose."

Phyllida nodded, and didn't react as he reached over to curl his ungloved fingers over hers. But she didn't move her hand away either, and she even tucked her fingers a little tighter over his, feeling the warmth of his hand through her gloves.

"I rang thrice over the last few weeks," Bradford went on. "To speak to Mrs. Mallowan. But Dobble answered each time."

Phyllida nodded. "I see." It was best that he hadn't tried to leave word for her, or to ring her, or to write to her. The staff would have heard about it.

He had to shift gears, so was required to release her fingers. "Now, as we've nearly arrived, I suppose you'd best tell me about this murder, Mrs. Bright," he said.

She gave an organized, detailed, yet succinct description of the situation.

"And you're saying the person who ran over this Miss Blastwick must have mistaken her for her sister," Bradford said when she finished. He sounded skeptical. "Is that likely? Do they look that much alike?"

"They certainly bear a resemblance," Phyllida replied a trifle sharply. Was he already questioning her suppositions? "And it was in the dark."

He made a thoughtful sound but said nothing as he wheeled the Daimler onto the drive at Ivygate Cottage.

At the Blastwicks' home—a compact, plaster-covered brick block of an edifice—there was no grand porch with broad steps and a roof. There was, however, a climbing yellow rose that emitted a heady fragrance as it rambled up the bricks exposed where the plaster had broken off or chipped away. The walkway to the front door was made from the same uneven cobblestones as the drive. A small garage, its door closed, was tucked behind a short stretch of fence, where two chickens were enclosed, pecking about.

There was no sign of a motor parked in front of the cottage, and Phyllida was relieved not to be encountering Inspector Cork. Presumably, he'd come and gone, which would leave her free to converse unhampered with the Blastwicks.

"I'll wait here if you like, Mrs. Bright," said Bradford as he opened the Daimler's door for her.

"Thank you. I shan't be long, I'm certain."

Phyllida didn't even have the opportunity to employ the knocker before the door swung open to reveal Genevra Blastwick. Behind her hovered the housekeeper—likely the person who'd taken Phyllida's telephone calls.

"Oh, Mrs. Bright, thank you for coming. Papa and I . . ." Genevra's eyes and nose were swollen and red and she clutched a handkerchief. Her brown hair appeared unbrushed and straggly. "It's just *awful.* I simply can't believe . . . I can't believe she's gone."

"I'm so very sorry for your loss," Phyllida said, taking the young woman's hands and squeezing them gently. No matter how bombastic the young woman had been last night, Phyllida could hold no reserve toward the poor thing. She'd lost her sister in a terribly violent way.

"P-please, come to the study. Papa's still lying down. He was—we were both—quite upset after the police came, and Mrs. Gilbody gave us both a sleeping draught to help us rest. It was she who suggested we ring you, and Papa insisted. I—I hope it's not too much trouble. I need to speak to you, Mrs. Bright. I need your help."

"Quite," Phyllida replied, following Genevra into a small room crowded with bookshelves, glassed curio cabinets, and the sorts of display cases one usually saw in museums. She glanced in one of them and saw a jumble of pottery shards. Mr. Max would be in his glory in this place.

The study smelled of pipe smoke and strong coffee. The curtains had been opened, but the windows were closed to the summer's day. An ancient dog of indeterminate breed lay on a rug before the cold and empty fireplace. To Phyllida's relief, he barely cocked an ear in her direction as she took a seat in one of two armchairs in the corner. A cat, presumably the famous Boots from Genevra's conversation last evening, was curled up on a rocking chair in the corner. He glanced up, then went back to sleep.

"Mrs. Gilbody will bring some tea," Genevra said, obviously attempting to keep up the niceties of a social call. But Phyllida knew this was nothing resembling a social call.

"Again, I'm so very sorry about Ethel. I'll do whatever I can to help, Genevra. Now, please tell me what you can. I know only that she was struck by a motorcar last night."

Genevra gulped and sniffled and nodded. Her expression was one of wretchedness. "Yes. And it's my fault. It's all *all* my fault. All of it!"

"Tell me."

"You see, it wasn't *me* who saw a murder, Mrs. Bright. It was Ethel who saw the murder. And now I've gone and got her killed."

CHAPTER 8

GENEVRA EXPLODED INTO SOBS THAT WERE AS FLORID AS HER PERsonality.

"*Ethel* saw the murder." Phyllida had not expected this turn of events, and she immediately had to stop the whirlwind of thoughts that had spun through her mind since she'd had the news about the death. "Not you."

"Y-yes. She told me, and I pooh-poohed her—just like everyone pooh-poohed me last night. Only, you see, Ethel doesn't lie. She never exaggerates. She's the most mousy, honest, uninteresting person I've ever met... and she was my sister! And I've killed her." She swiped at her nose with a handkerchief that was so damp it was hardly up to the job.

From her handbag, Phyllida fished out one of her own handkerchiefs—she'd started carrying extras now that she kept attracting murder cases—and offered it to the distraught young woman.

"They must have thought it was me walking down the road," Genevra sobbed. "And they ran her down... just like she was nothing!"

At that moment, Mrs. Gilbody came in with a tea tray and set it on the table. Phyllida had met her once before and remembered her as a calm and smiling woman. Now, her face was drawn and her eyes encircled by puffy, shadowed skin.

"I'll pour, Mrs. Gilbody," said Phyllida, realizing the woman likely needed some time to herself just as much as Dr. Blastwick did. Servants grieved too.

"And so Ethel was walking down the road and she was run over by a motorcar," Phyllida said after the housekeeper left. "How did she come to be walking down the road so late at night?"

Genevra looked down, her tears dripping heedlessly into the handkerchief she held in her lap. "Y-you see, Ethel and I got into a row just when we were leaving Wilding Hall. She was *furious* with me for teasing everyone about seeing a murder.

"'Now you've really put the fat into the fire,' she said. And then she called me some terrible names and said she was going to have to think about what to do about it all. And so she told me she was going to walk home. She couldn't even stand to be in the motorcar with me, she was so upset."

"Did she seem frightened about the situation? Or angry?" Phyllida contemplated the topic as she poured tea for both of them.

Why would Ethel leave the relative safety of the motorcar to walk home if she knew the killer had just witnessed her sister's bragging? Perhaps she hadn't realized the killer was present . . . But how could that be? If she'd witnessed a murder, surely she'd at least seen the person who'd done it.

"She was angry, and, yes, a little frightened. She was just walking h-home when th-they ran her down. There in the dark—they just drove right over h-her like they didn't care at all." Genevra drew in a shaky breath. She appeared nauseated.

"No one realized it until this morning when the milkman came along and saw her in the grass by the side of the road. Just lying there. Right there, on the way home from Mrs. Rollingbroke's. It was . . . it was terrible."

"You weren't aware she didn't come home last night?" Phyllida tried not to sound accusatory. The poor young woman was miserable enough as it was—and well she should be. What a stupid, foolish thing for her to have done.

"N-no. We don't share a bedroom and I went to sleep right away. I'd had quite a few martinis last night." Genevra swabbed her eyes and nose, but kept her face averted. "And Papa sleeps like the dead in the back of the house."

"And the dog?" Phyllida gestured to the canine. "Wouldn't it have barked when she came in?"

Genevra shook her head. "No. Jarvis knows us all. Besides, he can't hear very well anymore."

Phyllida nodded. "All right, then. It seems likely that whoever ran Ethel down was coming from Wilding Hall and had been at the dinner party. Do you remember who, if anyone, was still at the party when you two left? Was anyone around to hear you arguing and who could have seen Ethel get out of the motor when she decided to walk?"

Genevra shrugged. "I don't know. I wasn't really paying attention—we were arguing and I was driving. All of the rest of the guests left at about the same time, but I'd parked the motor off to the side, as we were late arriving to the dinner. I don't think anyone could have gotten past us—except for you, Mrs. Bright, because you were the last one there and you left first. Ethel—she didn't get out of the motorcar until we were just to the end of the drive, you see, because that was when she said she couldn't even bear to be in the vehicle with me."

So anyone could have heard the argument and even seen Ethel get out of the motorcar to tromp angrily down the road.

Whoever it was could have either driven past Ethel and then come back around, or even turned in the wrong direction and returned when it was certain there was no one around to see. The killer would also know which way Ethel was going—back to Ivygate Cottage—and could plan their route accordingly.

It would be instructive to know from which direction the tire tracks had come. John hadn't given that detail.

Phyllida lifted her teacup and sipped. Surely the killer had realized it was Ethel who'd seen the murder, not Genevra. It seemed that a person who'd killed someone knew where and when they'd done so and who might have had the opportunity to witness their crime. Maybe he or she had suspected or feared someone (Ethel) had seen them, and now knew for certain. Perhaps the incident had taken place outdoors somewhere—an environment Genevra wasn't known to frequent. Aside from that, it was also far more likely that Ethel would be walking than Genevra, for, as her sister had pointed out during the party, Ethel liked to hike.

"How long does it take to walk from Wilding Hall to here? Is it a road all the way, or are there any walking shortcuts she might turn off on? And where was your sister found on the road? Closer to which property?"

"It would take close to three quarters of an hour because she wouldn't take the short cut through the field in the dark," said Genevra. She finally seemed to have gotten her emotions under control. "Ethel was a good rambler—she's out and about wandering the woods and meadows all the time. She'd rather walk than ride anyhow, which is why I didn't really think too much about it when she got angry and wanted to walk. It's—it's happened before," she admitted.

"And was she closer to home or to Wilding Hall when she was found?"

"She was about halfway between the two."

"So she'd been walking perhaps twenty minutes or so."

Genevra nodded and rapidly scooped four large spoonfuls of sugar into her tea, then stirred vigorously. Phyllida approved. Sugar was good for a shock.

"What precisely did Ethel tell you about the murder she witnessed?" Phyllida said, deciding it was time to get to the nitty-gritty of the matter.

"Only, that's the thing . . . n-nothing. I've been trying to remember," said Genevra in a more controlled voice than she'd yet used. "I'm afraid, as I said, I found it rather ridiculous that she should have seen a murder but not realized it was a murder. She did say that—that she'd seen something and only later realized it must have been a murder. How could that be? But she wouldn't say more, and so I thought she might have been exaggerating.

"Then I thought it would be amusing to needle her a bit about it by pretending *I'd* been the one to see it." Her voice trailed off. "I can't believe what I've done."

"Genevra, if you want justice for your sister, you'll need to collect your thoughts and stop wallowing in your mistakes. Nothing will change that now. I need you to tell me everything Ethel told you regarding the murder. Any little detail you remember."

Genevra's cheeks turned dark pink under Phyllida's reprimand, but she kept her eyes lowered. "She didn't say very much," she said, shifting her shoulders.

Phyllida spoke in a steely voice. "She must have said something."

"All right. I remember her saying that she thought she might have seen a murder once. But that she hadn't realized it at the time. It wasn't until later that she began to wonder if it *was* a murder." Genevra looked up at last.

"Where was she? When did she see it? Anything about the victim?" Phyllida had to work to control her frustration.

"I'm sorry. She didn't say very much and I suppose I didn't let her. I was too busy talking about . . . other things. I thought maybe she was just trying to shut me up. But . . . maybe she just wanted to talk to someone about it. To help decide what to do." Misery shone in Genevra's face.

"She gave you no details? No information about what she saw? How the person died? Anything at all?"

"The only thing . . . I expect she must have been out walking when she saw . . . whatever it was."

"So it happened here in Listleigh."

Genevra nodded. "Yes. I'm certain of that at least. She doesn't like to go about in London the way she does here. And . . . maybe it was late last summer or autumn. August, perhaps. September? Oh, now I remember . . . she'd said she'd had her bicycle in for repairs, that's why she was walking. She'd only got it late last summer, July it was, I think, so it couldn't have been before then."

Phyllida nodded. That was helpful. At least now she had a time frame for the witnessed murder. "Did she say why she didn't report it to the police?"

Genevra sighed. "Mrs. Bright, you'd have to understand my sister. She's—she was—a shrinking violet. She doesn't like to be the center of attention. She doesn't like any sort of confrontation—which is why it was easy for me to needle her.

"Ethel doesn't—didn't—like to rock the boat, you see, and I think she only thought if she forgot about it, the problem would go away. She might have hoped that what she saw she'd only imagined to be far worse than it was. But I don't really know why she wouldn't have come forward if she thought someone had actually *killed* someone."

"Or maybe she did and no one took her seriously . . ." Phyllida mused.

"Yes. And whoever did it was there last night." Genevra sniffled and sipped her tea. "Can you help, Mrs. Bright? Can you help find out who did this to Ethel?" Her eyes glittered with tears.

"I'll do my very best," Phyllida promised. "Now, I'll go and examine the place where it happened."

Genevra shuddered and looked away, clutching the handkerchief tightly. "P-please don't ask me to–to go with you, Mrs. Bright. I don't think I could bear it."

"Of course not," Phyllida replied. She wondered whether this radical change of personality and self-censure would be a permanent improvement in Genevra Blastwick's character, or whether, like for so many other people, such an intended improvement would wane with time.

"There is one more thing I must impress upon you, Genevra," Phyllida said as she stood. "You may not know anything about what your sister witnessed, but the killer doesn't realize that."

Genevra froze, then gasped, a hand going to her throat. "A-are you saying th-they might come after *me*? B-but I don't know anything! I told you, I don't know anything!"

"I understand that, but the killer might not realize this—or he or she might believe you are lying about what you know."

"But—but I'm not!" Genevra said, loudly and angrily. "I'm not lying! I don't know anything! Do you think I wouldn't tell you if I knew?"

"Quite so. But a killer is not always logical. Oftentimes he—or she—is impelled by emotion and fear. Which is why they always get caught.

"I tell you this not to frighten you, but to impress upon you that you might be in danger. I suggest you stay near home and don't . . . well, you must be suspicious and take great care around anyone who was at the dinner last night."

"Even Mrs. Rollingbroke? And—and Sir Rolly?"

"Everyone is a suspect, Genevra. However, I concur that it's unlikely either of the Rollingbrokes left their house after the dinner party to run down your sister. How would they even know she was on foot?" Phyllida said, even as she remembered the tufts of grass and splotches of mud caught up in the underside of Sir Rolly's Bugatti.

And hadn't Vera commented that she'd "waited ever so long for him" to come inside?

And there was the fact that the motorcar had definitely been moved since she arrived at the dinner party.

She would ask Bradford what he thought, and he would certainly have an opinion. Perhaps grass tufts got caught up under motorcars quite regularly. Mud certainly must get splashed up, and there had been quite a lot of rain as of late.

"V-very well, Mrs. Bright," said Genevra. Then suddenly she bolted to her feet. "Papa. He's not in danger too?"

"I wouldn't think so, but, as I said, logic may be lost on the killer. He or she might think Ethel spoke to both of you about what she'd seen. I should like to speak with your fath—"

"I simply can't believe it," Genevra said, shaking her head as she buried her face in the handkerchief again. "I can't believe it all."

There was nothing more Phyllida could say to alleviate the girl's shock and grief; spending her energies and exercising her little gray cells to find the killer would be more beneficial than holding the girl's hand and listening to her wail and sob her regrets.

Still, she felt a rush of sympathy. Genevra Blastwick was a shallow, impetuous person, and she had brought about her sister's death because of her actions . . . but she had lost her sister. Phyllida reached over and patted the girl's hand.

"I'll do whatever I can to help, Genevra. You can rely on me."

As she took her leave, the sounds of heartbroken sobs followed her out of the room.

"You were correct to challenge my assumptions, Bradford," Phyllida said in a clear voice as she climbed into the Daimler.

He looked at her in shocked amazement. "Why, Mrs. Bright, I don't know what to say."

"You needn't be cheeky about it," she replied, fighting to control a smile at the sight of his expression. In that moment, he looked so young and carefree ... and handsome. She did have a weakness for a rugged, handsome face, didn't she? Even if it was an inconvenient weakness.

"Well," he said after a moment, "are you going to tell me what—ah, I know. About Miss Ethel being mistaken for Miss Genevra. She wasn't, was she?"

"Correct," she said, relieved that he'd returned most of his attention to maneuvering the motorcar down the short drive. "It turns out that it was Ethel who'd seen the murder, not Genevra."

"But the younger Miss Blastwick decided to take credit for it," he said grimly. "And thus put her sister's life in danger."

"Quite, and tragically so," Phyllida replied. "Oh, and I should like to see the place where the accident happened. It's on the road between here and Wilding Hall. John Bhatt said it would be obvious to locate."

Bradford nodded, his eyes fixed on the road. "And so have you been seeing quite a bit of Dr. Bhatt, then, Mrs. Bright?"

She felt her cheeks heat, *drat it*. This was simply not the least bit convenient, this ... whatever it was with Bradford. "Not at all. He's only just returned from India. I encountered him this morning when I was in the village and he told me about the accident—and that it was definitely no accident."

"But you would like to see for yourself."

"Of course. I do think it's always best to examine the scene of a crime for oneself, don't you think, Bradford?"

"I certainly don't have the experience in investigating crime scenes that you have, Inspector Bright."

"That brings me to a question that does involve your expertise," Phyllida said, ignoring his little barb. "It seems one might expect to find pieces of grass and perhaps some clumps of mud up beneath a motorcar that drove off the road in order to run someone down. Perhaps some other evidence as well?"

He gave a short nod. "One might expect the grass or brush, certainly, Mrs. Bright. Mud, too. I suppose you've been looking under all of the motorcars from last night, then."

"Certainly as many as I've been able to," she said. "But... would there be any other reason to have grass or brush caught up under there?"

Now he glanced at her. "Someone's motor has grass in the undercarriage and you don't think they did it. Or you don't *want* them to have done it."

"I'm merely collecting information," she replied. "It's far too early to make assumptions and to draw conclusions. Ah, it looks as if we've found it."

But Bradford had seen it too, the site of the accident, and he brought the Daimler to a halt on the side of the country road.

The road was not quite wide enough for two vehicles to pass each other without one going off the pathway. There was a narrow strip of mid-calf-height grass on either side to allow for such a passage, but beyond were taller grasses leading into brush-filled and wooded areas. A number of tire tracks had flattened the grass in one particular area, testament to the tragic violence that had happened late last night. John had been correct: It was hard to miss.

Phyllida found herself moving slowly as she approached the place where Ethel Blastwick had been killed. She'd seen far too many deaths in her lifetime—from the war, as well as other, more deliberate demises—but there was something forlorn and awful about the flattened strips of grass and the larger one where the body had rested. There was only the slightest bit of blood—a small sprinkling over the ruined grass.

She imagined Ethel, walking home in her light blue frock and black Mary Janes, fueled by anger and shock—and perhaps a little fear, too—over what her sister had done.

Could Ethel have realized at that time—just a little too late—that she'd become a target? Had she regretted getting out of the motorcar almost as soon as she'd done so? She wasn't impetuous like her sister was, but perhaps her anger had spurred her to do something risky for once.

Phyllida pictured the young woman, walking along the road in the balmy summer evening, angry, perhaps frightened . . . certainly upset. The night was lit by a swath of stars and a partial moon. It was silent but for the hoot of an owl, perhaps the scream of a fox, the bark of a dog, a rustle of wind through the leaves . . . It wouldn't be terribly dark due to the night's celestial bodies, but there'd be shadows cast by the trees and bushes and the grasses. But Ethel would surely feel comfortable, having walked this road often during her lifetime.

It had been a relatively quiet, calm night with the lights from the motorcars of her fellow diners trundling past on their way home. Ethel would stay off to the side, of course, for it was late at night and the diners had been imbibing, and the grass wasn't terribly tall . . .

And then all at once, there were headlights that didn't slow . . . that didn't move to the side in order to make room for her. A set of headlights that came closer . . . *faster* . . . and that didn't stop or slow or veer or swerve . . . and there was nothing to do, nowhere to go—

Phyllida realized her fingers had begun to tremble and her breathing had gone shallow.

"All right there, Mrs. Bright?" Bradford stood next to her. His arm brushed against hers and the back of his hand nudged the back of hers—just a light brush of knuckle over gloved knuckle. He must have heard her shaky breath, for he said, in a more sober tone, "A little close to home, is it, Phyllida?" The utterance of her given name—which he used on very rare occasions, usually ones involving intense emotion—told her he understood why all at once this scene had such a profound effect on her.

"Yes," she said. He'd been the one—well, it had actually been Myrtle—to find her after she'd nearly been run down by a killer in Winnie Pankhurst's Austin. It was only the indentations between crenelations in the brick wall that saved her from a fate similar to that of Ethel Blastwick.

She gave herself a mental shake. "Right, then. Now, let us see if there is anything to learn from this sad scene."

She stepped away from him, as much to investigate as to prove to herself that she didn't need support, and began to move around the area taking care to avoid the tire tracks. She didn't know what she expected or hoped to find; it was just that she needed to become familiar with the scene of the crime. To put herself there, so to speak. To put herself inside the mind of this cold-blooded killer.

"They came from this direction," Bradford said, drawing her attention from the large, irregular depression in the grass where, she realized, Ethel Blastwick had breathed her last. No blood. No trace of a person. Only the large, flat area.

Phyllida joined him where he was standing. "From there?" She pointed in the vicinity of Ivygate Cottage. Wilding Hall was behind her.

"Aye."

"So the killer left the Rollingbrokes', drove past Ethel, then turned around and *came back*," she said. "So he or she must have seen her, then went on down the road—perhaps to make certain no one was around to see, and in order to make it look as if they were going home—then doubled back and . . . killed her."

"Aye," he said again.

Phyllida looked down at the tracks and saw that he was correct—although she probably wouldn't have realized it if he hadn't pointed it out. The bottommost track would have been the first one, and it was definitely flattened in the direction of a vehicle that had been turned around after passing by Ethel's route and come back. She shivered a little.

So instead of roaring up from behind her, the motorcar had borne down on the poor woman from the front. She would have seen those headlights coming at her before she realized they were actually coming *upon* her.

"The poor thing," she murmured, her eyes prickling with tears. "I do hope . . . I do hope it was quick."

"Aye," said Bradford quietly.

"Is there anything else you've noticed?" she said after a long moment.

"The type of grass," he said, showing her a few strands in his hand. "To compare, if you like, with any that might be caught up underside a motor."

"Excellent thought," she said. "Are there that many varieties of grass, then?"

He shrugged. "Blimey, I don't know. I'm no naturalist. But we—er, you—have it to compare if necessary."

She nodded. "Very well. Thank you."

"Where to now, Mrs. Bright?" he said as she walked over to the Daimler.

"I confess, I'm not certain," she said, then readied herself for him to make a sardonic comment about her investigative abilities.

"Well, then, what are your options?" He'd come to stand next to her by the passenger door of the motor. There was no one about. The road was empty and the air silent but for the sounds of birds twittering and the far-off bark of a dog. Gray clouds hung overhead, suggesting a bit of precipitation in the future.

"You see, it's rather awkward. I haven't an excuse, really, to simply present myself to Professor Avonlea or Mr. Heathers and demand they answer my questions," Phyllida confessed. "And while I could justify a social call on Mrs. Crestworthy, I'm not certain— well, she was with her husband in the motorcar."

"You're suggesting it would be unlikely that a husband and wife decided together to murder Miss Ethel," Bradford said. He didn't sound ironic or skeptical; he was merely putting her unspoken thoughts into words.

"I'm not discounting them, of course, but it seems less likely. And there is the fact that Professor Avonlea was on a bicycle, so in order for him to have done the deed, he would have had to cycle home, get his motor—if he even has one—then drive back."

"Possible, but less likely," Bradford said in an agreeable tone. "Did he have the time to do such a thing?"

"Ethel had been walking for perhaps fifteen or twenty minutes," she replied.

He made a thoughtful sound. "I suppose it might have been possible, depending how fast he cycled home."

She went on. "It was simple to speak to Mr. Varney, for I know him and merely walked into his surgery. And of course Mr. Sprite and Miss Pankhurst are always willing to talk. But for the others..."

"Right," he replied. "Well, then, Mrs. Bright, this could be your lucky day."

"And why is that?" She looked up at him, the brim of her hat helping to shield her eyes from the bright sun.

"Because of the poker game at the Screaming Magpie tonight," he replied. "Avonlea will be there I believe, as will Crestworthy and perhaps even Heathers, though I can't say for certain about him."

"Why, that's... but, no, even I cannot invade a man's card game," Phyllida said candidly. "I mean to say, I *could*, but I would expect my presence to be so off-putting that it would deter any information I might glean from them."

"You needn't play poker," he replied, a little smile twitching his mouth. "But I certainly can."

"That is an excellent solution," she said with great enthusiasm. "And I shall come along and ... erm ... perhaps ..." She stopped short of suggesting they have dinner together. It would cause too much gossip amongst the villagers—especially if her maids heard about it. And they would, because everyone gathered at Heathers's sweet and tobacco shop on their days out and gossiped and flirted.

"You could sit at the bar counter and chat at Guinevere whilst I join the game. Perhaps Dr. Bhatt would sit with you," Bradford suggested. "That would ensure no one get the wrong idea about the two of us."

Phyllida started to speak, then closed her mouth. She didn't know what to say to that. Although his words were easy, there was a subtle warning note to them.

"And what precisely would the wrong idea be?" she finally said, suddenly feeling rash and impulsive. She moved closer, putting her hands on his chest and tilting her head back in order to meet his eyes.

No one was around to see them, and, drat it all, she *had* missed him. The man was—besides being arrogant and surly and sardonic—solid, intelligent, amusing, and, quite often, a useful assistant in her crime investigations.

His arms slid around her waist as he demonstrated another admirable talent: splendid kissing skills.

"I truly did miss you, Bradford," she murmured when she remembered to breathe again. "I simply..." Her words trailed off into a sigh as he kissed the corner of her mouth, slid his lips gently to the curve of her jaw, and gave the sensitive spot on her neck a little nibble because he knew how much she liked it. She shivered pleasantly and wished they were somewhere other than a deserted country road where another motorcar could happen upon them at any moment. Although the back seat of the Daimler was very roomy...

"You simply don't want to be perceived as human by your staff," he said, pulling back a bit to look down at her. His words were mild and she didn't see even a hint of reproach in his eyes. Perhaps he did understand.

"I simply don't wish to provide them a topic of gossip or any form of entertainment," she said, reaching up to touch his face. He'd obviously shaved late this morning, for his cheek and jaw were silky smooth.

"And if they already knew?"

She stepped back, horrified. "You haven't told anyone!"

"Of course not," he replied easily. "But your maids are quite able to ferret out gossip on their own."

She brushed that aside. "Not at all. They simply know I cannot abide Myrtle jumping all over me and I certainly don't want her in the house, and so they like to watch me reprimand her—"

"And me—"

"*And* to hear you and me go back and forth about it all," she replied. Her attention trailed to the Daimler's back seat. It was *quite* roomy.

Bradford must have noticed, for his eyes darkened and a little smile twitched his mouth. "Tempting, isn't it, Mrs. Bright? But if you're not wanting to cause gossip . . ."

"Yes, of course," she said briskly, flustered that he'd so easily read her mind. "Anyhow, I appreciate your offering to play cards tonight with some of my suspects. I shall attend as well, and I suppose we shall see what we shall see."

CHAPTER 9

*T*HE SCREAMING MAGPIE WAS THE ONLY PUBLIC HOUSE IN THE VILlage of Listleigh, and aside from serving a proprietary nutty brown ale, it had the added advantage of offering several rooms to let on its upper floor.

Not very many months ago, a killer had been one of the tenants.

Bradford had gotten an earful more than once from Mrs. Bright about the misnaming of the public house. She'd point to the sign with a withering look. "That bird is *not* screaming—do you see, its beak is quite closed. And I'm certain it isn't even a magpie," she'd inform him primly.

"Well, it looks like a magpie to me," he'd drawl, just so he could watch her get that schoolmarmish look in her eye as she went on to enumerate all the reasons that it probably wasn't.

He sure liked it when she got all prim and proper, because he liked even more to watch her get all ruffled up when he made comments meant to rile her. Her eyes would flash, her prim lips would become full and soft, and her entire figure (and what a figure it was!) would vibrate with energy.

Myrtle, the love, was an excellent instigator for ruffling up the housekeeper's feathers, and early on, Bradford had made certain to reward the smart little mutt every time she did so. It had actually been a good thing that he'd trained Myrtle to sniff out Mrs. Bright—although he'd certainly never admit to her that he'd done such a thing—because the feisty pup had tracked her down one night after a killer tried to run her over. Bradford admitted only to himself how his heart had stopped beating and the ground seemed to fall away from beneath his feet when he saw a slumped-over, unmoving Mrs. Bright pinned to the wall by Winnie Pankhurst's Austin.

Despite the recent and radical change in their relationship and interactions, Bradford found himself continuing to refer to the housekeeper as Mrs. Bright, both verbally and in his head. He found if he allowed himself the familiarity of thinking of her in informal terms that he thought of little else *other* than her in informal (that is, intimate) terms, and that was certainly not a prudent thing to do.

Aside from that, while the name *Phyllida* suited her exceedingly well as a proper, pedantic, and pragmatic housekeeper, it did *not* suit her as the passionate, thoughtful, and amusing woman he'd come to know—if only during a few brief interludes.

Tonight, Mrs. Bright had actually agreed to remain at Mallowan Hall whilst he joined the poker game at the pub. They'd had a heated discussion about whether her presence was necessary in order to make certain he'd properly conduct what she called "interviews with the suspects," but in the end, he'd convinced her that it would be less suspicious if she wasn't hovering about, giving him direction. Still, he wasn't completely certain she'd acquiesced because of his logical argument or because she had a different plan that she didn't wish to divulge.

He sighed. He'd surely find out either way.

Although he could have driven the Daimler, Bradford rode a bicycle into town from Mallowan Hall. It was a beautiful evening and he craved the exercise. Driving about in a motorcar was all good and well, but a bloke needed to move, didn't he? Have the wind ruffling through his hair and on his face . . .

He really ought to get a basket for Myrts to ride in, once she'd recovered and perhaps even before. She'd love it.

The inside of the pub was dim and dingy with a low ceiling lined by heavy wooden beams and a layer of dirt on the floor.

Mrs. Bright believed there were actually planks of wood that made up said floor beneath said dirt, but Bradford knew that wasn't the case. He hadn't the heart to tell her because he suspected she'd never set foot inside again if she learned the truth.

The electric lighting in the pub was a new development—likely having been installed whilst Bradford was off attending to those matters in and around London—but the bulbs in the fixtures gave off illumination that was anemic and yellowish. If Mrs. Bright was there, she'd surely suggest that it was a deliberate decision on the part of the proprietress in order to keep from shedding too much light, so to speak, on her housekeeping skills.

The proprietress of the Screaming Magpie was the sort of person a man approached like one approached a cornered tiger that was in possession of both a gun and a keg of ale. One wrong word—or even the wrong, sidewise slant of a glance—and the woman would take the head off a bloke instead of pulling him an ale.

Somewhere in her mid to late fifties, Guinevere had deep grooves in her sallow cheeks and a definite sagging about her square, mannish chin that often sported a small cluster of wiry hair. The graying hair atop her head was cropped so short its curls were hardly more than wings springing from beneath the scrap of a mobcap that sagged from the back of her crown. Along with a scowl, the proprietress wore trousers and a loose shirt with a full apron over her spare, lean figure. Guinevere's perpetual disgruntlement was so notorious that a recent travel guide about inns in Devonshire had praised the Screaming Magpie's hearty brown bread and nutty ale, but forewarned travelers about its cantankerous proprietress.

The card game was already in progress when Bradford came in. He made his way directly to the table in the corner, aware of Guinevere's assessing gaze on him.

"A draft of your finest if you please," he called to her with a careful smile. A fellow had to make sure the smile wasn't too big, too small, too happy, and certainly *not* flirty.

She mumbled something derogatory, but Bradford saw her snag a glass off the shelf and turn to the keg. Whether it was a clean glass was uncertain, but at least the beer would destroy whatever germs lingered inside.

"Deal me in?" he said easily, taking one of the two empty seats at the table.

As he'd expected, the players included several of Mrs. Bright's suspects: Wilfred Avonlea, Rutherford Crestworthy, and Peter Heathers, along with the baker, Milton Panson, and Fred Stiller, who owned the cycle shop and was a friend of Bradford's.

"Nice to see you back, Josh," said Stiller, who was shuffling the cards. He was a good bloke, maybe thirty-five, and had a wife and two adorable children who called Bradford "Uncle Dotsu" because they couldn't say "Joshua." "Five card stud, draw three, two of clubs wild. A crown'll see you in."

Bradford grunted his assent and fished out the coin and a cigar from his coat pocket as he sat. "Heard there was an accident last night," he said, tossing the crown onto the table. "Someone died?"

"Girl by the name of Ethel Blastwick," said Stiller as he began to deal. "Quiet thing. Nothing like her sister."

"That's for certain," said Avonlea, drawing on his pipe.

"Need a light, there, Bradford, is it? You're the driver up to Mallowan Hall?" said Crestworthy, who held a cigarette trailing smoke.

"That I am," Bradford replied, leaning in so the man could light his cigar with the expensive silver lighter he offered.

"How you getting on up there?" Crestworthy went on. "Up at the detective writer's place?" The man was quite flush due to his wife's family's factory business. Yet, he obviously didn't mind slumming it with a chauffeur, a bicycle repairman, a tobacconist, a professor, and a baker in a dank pub for a bi-weekly card game. The chap had a distinguished look to him; the type that seemed to attract the ladies: smooth, sleek hair glistening with too much pomade, a neat, slender mustache, and a square chin.

"Can't complain," Bradford replied, settling back into his seat as he drew deeply on the cigar a few times to get it going. It just seemed like a cigar and a brown ale had to go along with a card game.

"Seems like it'd be a bit off-putting, being around a woman always writing about doing away with people," said Crestworthy with a wry smile.

"Speaking of doing away with people . . . that girl who got hit last night—what happened? They know who did it? Surely it was an accident. She was walking along the road at night, I hear." Bradford picked up his cards and scanned them even as he kept an eye on the three suspects, waiting for their reactions to his question.

"Oi, it wasn't no accident," Milton Panson said, reordering the cards in his hand. "Not like what happened to that bloke what drownt a fortnight ago. He were yourn, weren't he, Crestworthy?"

"Yes, my secretary. Sad thing. Very tragic. Didn't know he couldn't swim. Don't know what a fellow was doing by the river when he can't swim," said Crestworthy, making a tsking noise. "And all the rain, making the current go faster. But this one last night—someone is saying it wasn't an accident?"

"That Mrs. Bright—you're knowing her, right, then, Bradford?—she was in the bakery today asking questions about it all," said Panson. "Said it weren't no accident. Was done deliberate."

Professor Avonlea scoffed. "Balderdash. Isn't any way to *tell* if it was done deliberately. The chit was walking home in the *dark*, wasn't she? What's she expect? At least a cycle has a reflector on it." He set the pince-nez on the bridge of his nose so he could inspect his cards.

Avonlea was a man in his fifties who looked exactly like the professor he was: he wore tweeds, smoked a pipe, and had a pince-nez tucked into his pocket. His mustache looked like a horse brush had been affixed to his upper lip, and his eyes were pale gray and must have been a little watery, for he had a habit of blinking often. Instead of an air of absentmindedness, Avonlea came across as a man who knew everything there was to know because no one else knew anything.

"I should think she'd expect a motorcar driver would see her in the headlights and not run her down," said Bradford evenly.

"She was hit way over on the grass, off'n the road," said Panson. He was a tall, red-faced man who tended to make every chair he sat in creak whenever he moved. "My Mildred, she hears it all, you know. Everyone comes into the bakery and they all talk."

"Oi, now, what are you saying? The bloke—he ran off the road and hit her?" said Stiller, staring at him with a shocked look. "On purpose?"

"Seems that way. That's why that Mrs. Bright was in. You know she's being like a detective or something. Asking questions around and all," Panson said, looking up from his cards. "Check," he said, confirming he wasn't going to raise the bet.

Avonlea scoffed again and said, "Check. Nosy woman."

"Half crown," said Bradford, liking his chances with his hand so far and not truly able to disagree with Avonlea's description of Mrs. Bright. Still, he didn't like the tone of the man's voice. He tossed in his money and said, "Why would someone run down this Ethel Blastwick?"

"Call," said Crestworthy reluctantly, putting in his half crown to match Bradford's bet raise. "They thought it was her sister. What's her name, Genevieve?"

"Genevra," said Peter Heathers.

Well into his fifties, Heathers was the oldest cardplayer at the table, and he'd moved on to his second cigarette since Bradford had joined them. He seemed a pleasant enough sort of bloke with a methodical frame of mind, as evidenced by the amount of time he perused his cards. Had a dry sense of humor too. Bradford knew that he and his wife had moved to Listleigh to run his brother's tobacco shop.

In the year since, Bradford had noticed the little shop had become quite popular with the housemaids and other young women due to the additional offerings of sweets like hard candies, chocolates, and carbonated sodas—not to mention the Heatherses' handsome young son who worked the soda and sweets counter.

"Call," Heathers said, pushing his coins into the pot.

"You're saying someone killed this Ethel Blastwick because they thought she was her sister? Why would they want to kill her sister?" Bradford puffed on his cigar as he looked around at all of them.

Just then, Guinevere swept up. She put his ale down with a thump that sent a good gulp or two slopping over the top. Bloody waste of beer, but he sure wasn't going to say that to her or he'd likely end up with the rest of it on his head. Instead, Bradford thanked her and picked up the drink to take a taste. He sighed happily. It was indeed worth navigating the hazards of Guinevere for the dark, rich, caramelly brew she served.

"Could be lots of reasons," said Avonlea. "That younger sister . . . she seems a bloody loudmouth. That type always wants to be center of attention, you see. Probably someone got tired of hearing her."

"But it's got to be from what she said," Panson said. "Fold." He closed up his cards and set them down, his chair creaking as he adjust his seat.

"What was it she said?" Stiller then looked at Avonlea and added, "You gonna call?"

"Yes, yes, and give me two," said the professor as he pushed two of his cards, facedown, toward the center. Stiller waited until he added his half crown to the pot before dealing him two replacements.

Bradford drew thoughtfully on his cigar. He couldn't have asked for a better situation. Stiller and Panson were driving the conversation, and all he had to do was observe the others.

"She said she'd *seen a murder*," Panson replied, lighting a handmade cigarette with hands big enough to wrap around a motorcar axle. They were powerful from all of the kneading and rolling he did. "She was at a dinner party and she told everyone she'd seen a murder."

"Balderdash! What murder?" demanded Avonlea. "That girl is delusional."

"She said she saw a murder and then someone tried to kill her after?" Stiller said incredulously, then gestured toward Bradford with the deck of cards, his brow raised in question.

"Two," Bradford responded, shoving his pair of discards away.

"You were there," said Panson, gesturing to Avonlea and Crestworthy, and Bradford decided he owed the baker a beer for putting the suspects on the spot and sticking with the topic. He didn't need to do a thing but listen.

Avonlea harrumphed and shrugged. "So what if I was? Can't blame me for it all. He was there too." He gestured with a sharp thumb to Heathers, who shrugged in acknowledgment.

Bradford scratched his head, making it look as if he was just putting the pieces together. "You're saying this woman was at a dinner and she told everyone she saw a murder, and then someone ran down her sister thinking it was her? Why would they do that? Did they really believe her?"

"Why, to shut her up, of course," said Avonlea, seeming to have forgotten his statement that no one could tell whether the death had been an accident or not. His pince-nez was crooked, but it didn't seem to affect his ability to read his cards. He grimaced and pushed them together, setting them down. "Fold."

"Then that would mean . . . the *killer* must have heard her say it," Bradford replied.

"Are you suggesting the killer was at the dinner? Sitting at the table with us all?" snapped Crestworthy, sloshing his glass of whisky. "That's preposterous. There was no murder. It was only that Genevra Blastwick going on as she is wont to do."

"Bloody hell, man, there *was* a murder, Crestworthy. *Ethel Blastwick* was killed," Bradford reminded him coolly. "Begs the question, doesn't it, who there at the dinner saw her walking down the road and decided to silence her?"

"Sure does," said Panson. His chair creaked quietly. "Coulda been any'a you who were there."

"If you're accusing me of something, say it right out there, Panson," said Crestworthy, half rising from his chair. "For God's sake, my wife was with me!"

"Ain't accusing anyone. I only reckon it's the truth, though—and so does that Mrs. Bright." Panson glanced at Bradford, then back to the group. "She's a smart lady, she is, just like her name. Remember how she found out who it was that poisoned Father

Tooley? That someone used *my* cake box from *my* bakery, and tried to point the finger at *us*."

Crestworthy sat back down but he sent a cool look at Panson, who ignored him.

"Woman ought to just stay back at the house," muttered Avonlea. "No need to be running about the countryside, poking her nose into things. Let the police do their job."

"Did any of you see Ethel Blastwick walking home after the dinner?" Bradford asked, changing the subject before he allowed himself the luxury of telling the professor precisely what he thought about his opinions. Not that he hadn't suggested the same to Mrs. Bright in the past . . .

"Of course I didn't see her," said Avonlea, puffing rapidly on his pipe. "It was dark and late and I wanted to get home. I rode my bicycle, you see, so I couldn't have run anyone down anyhow. Don't even have a motor."

"I might have seen someone," ventured Peter Heathers. He tossed three cards away and waited for replacements. He wore a neat, grizzled beard, but beneath it one could make out the same handsome features he'd passed on to his son. "I thought I saw someone, I mean to say. It could have been Miss Blastwick."

"We were right behind your motorcar," said Crestworthy, "and I didn't see anyone. But then, I wasn't looking, was I?" His expression was disgruntled.

Bradford took another healthy swallow of the ale and considered his next move. He didn't want to press too hard for information. The best thing would be to speak to each of the men separately and ask whether they'd noticed anything about the others at dinner, and whose automobile they'd followed when leaving Wilding Hall.

And as for Professor Avonlea and his bicycle . . . It seemed he could be eliminated from consideration, although Bradford decided he'd best let Mrs. Bright make that determination. Him being correct once in a day was probably all she would allow. His lips twitched at the thought.

He also wanted to examine each of the motorcars of the suspects for any sign of damage or impact, but he wasn't certain who drove what. That would bear some further investigation and conversation as well. He supposed he'd best sit in for another hand or two.

All in all, thus far, he didn't feel as if he'd obtained much relevant information, and Mrs. Bright would surely have something to say about *that*. He stifled another grin. He'd have to soothe those ruffled feathers and distract her, and he had a few ideas how to do that.

After all, an apartment in a garage was much more comfortable—not to mention private—than the back of a Daimler ... or a garden bench.

But just as he was tossing in money for the next hand, the door to the pub opened and none other than Mrs. Bright burst in.

A wry smile started over his face—of course he'd been expecting her to show up—then faded when he saw that she appeared to be in distress. He bolted to his feet.

Was that blood all over the front of her? And streaked on her face?

CHAPTER 10

DESPITE THE APPEARANCE OF ACQUIESCENCE TO BRADFORD'S SUGgestion that she need not be present at the Screaming Magpie and the ensuing card game, Phyllida had had no intention of staying in at Mallowan Hall for the evening.

She encountered Agatha in the front hall late in the afternoon, several hours before the card game was to begin and shortly after her tacit agreement to let Bradford handle that without her supervision. To her surprise, Agatha was dressed in traveling clothes. The portable case for her typewriter was sitting on the floor next to a valise with an umbrella leaning next to the cases.

"I simply have to get away," Agatha told her as Elton appeared to pick up the luggage. "I'm driving up to London, and Max and I will come home together now that Joshua is back. There's no need for him to go back to London."

"You're going to drive yourself?" Phyllida was mildly surprised. Normally, Agatha preferred the train and would have someone drop her at the railway station in Listleigh if she and Mr. Max didn't drive together. But it certainly wasn't unheard of for her boss to drive herself.

"Yes," she replied, heaving a sigh as she grimaced. "I simply need to—to drive a bit, Phyllida. I need to think, you see, and a little road trip is just the ticket, I believe. Two or three hours of solitude behind the windshield with nothing but my thoughts.

I've simply got to figure out this situation for Poirot and the snowbound train. It's quite difficult to be horrified by a killer when they've done away with someone so terribly wicked."

"I'm certain you'll come to the best decision," Phyllida told her, patting her friend on the arm since no one was around to witness the familiarity. "I have faith in you, and I expect because you're having such a difficult time with this book, it'll be one of your best and most famous stories."

Agatha gave her a wry smile. "I do hope you're right, Phyllida. Anyhow, with both Max and myself gone, that should free you up a bit more to find out who did such a terrible thing and killed Ethel Blastwick."

"Quite," Phyllida replied, "but of course you know that taking care of your household is always my first priority."

"Yes, yes, of course. But you manage to handle both with great aplomb and efficiency." Agatha's eyes lit up. "And whilst I'm in London, I should love to play your Hastings again, Phyllida, if there is anything you can think I could do to help. I so enjoyed doing so during the Wokesley incident.

"I've learnt I love to have a reason to poke about at the newspaper or even the police office. People always adore speaking to a murder writer, you know. They think they might appear in a book or something. Besides, one can't sit at a typewriter all day long you know." Agatha chuckled.

Phyllida smiled. "What a splendid idea! Thank you for thinking of it. It would be most helpful for you to find out what you could learn about a young man named Clement Dowdy. He was driving a delivery lorry here in the area for an outfit called Betchler's and he went away last summer without a word to anyone. Miss Pankhurst claims he just up and went back to his family in Smithfield, but Mr. Sprite doesn't seem to think he was quite that irresponsible and is afraid he might have been met with foul play."

"Why, that's a splendid trail for me to sniff along," Agatha said, her eyes still sparkling. "I shall speak to my friends at Scotland Yard about whether they've had any news about him—a missing person, a dead person, you know what I mean to say—and also poke around a bit with the newspapers and in Smithfield. Dowdy is the family name, you say? Clement?"

"Yes." Phyllida gave her as much information as she had about the missing man. "That would be quite helpful. If I can strike him from my list as the murder Miss Ethel saw, then I can concentrate on the only other option: Mr. Greenhouse and the bees."

"I do love a good bee or wasp story," Agatha said. "Poor Poirot—he's still fuming over the murder that happened right in front of him on the aeroplane," she added with a satisfied chuckle. She often acted as if Hercule Poirot was a real person who existed outside the bounds of her novels—even when she found him tiresome or annoying. "I suppose if someone could bring a wasp on board in a matchbox, someone could hide a box or jar of bees in a person's motorcar." She made a little humming sound. "One does wonder whether the killer—if there is one, I mean to say—might have been inspired by my story."

"It remains to be seen whether it was an accident or a murder," Phyllida replied. "Even so you shouldn't feel the least bit of blame over it. *You* only kill people on the page!"

The front door opened and Elton returned.

"Everything's all packed up in the MG, ma'am," he said. As usual, his hair was combed neatly and he was clean-shaven and looked as fresh as a well-shined shoe. "And I checked all the air in the tires and cleaned off the windshield for you."

"Oh, thank you, Elton," said Agatha with a smile. "How very competent of you."

Phyllida noticed that Mr. Dobble hadn't poked his long nose from out of his pantry during these interactions, which was uncharacteristic of him. She resisted the urge to ask Agatha whether she knew what was in the large crate that had been delivered to the butler. She fully intended to use her investigative skills to find out without him or anyone else knowing of her curiosity.

"I'll be off then," Agatha was saying. "Please do ring me in London if you need anything, and certainly to give me all the news about your investigation, Phyllida. I'll telephone once I have any information about this Clement Dowdy."

"Thank you very much. And give my best to Mr. Max," Phyllida replied as her friend went out the front door. Then, seeing a look in Elton's eyes that was very near that of a mooning calf, she gave him a cool one in return that was meant to quell any fantasies he might have. "Have you and Stanley brought all the rugs back inside?"

"Yes, Mrs. Bright," he said, flushing a little. He always blushed when she spoke to him, and, sadly, it made him look even more attractive. He was broad-shouldered, lithe, and tall enough that most everyone needed to look up when they spoke to him. Everyone except Dobble and Bradford.

"Is there anything else you need, ma'am?" His eagerness might have been endearing if it wasn't so predictable.

"Not at this time. Perhaps you ought to check with Mr. Dobble," she said as a gentle reminder that, since he was mostly acting in the capacity of footman when Mr. Max was away, the butler was technically his boss—even though Phyllida was certainly able to make use of the footmen when needed.

"Only, he's told us not to bother him," Elton replied. His flush had subsided. "He's been awfully strange lately, Mrs. Bright."

Lately? The butler was always a bit strange. Of course she kept her thoughts to herself in the spirit of solidarity—although she suspected, were the positions reversed, Dobble wouldn't give a whit about solidarity with her.

"Quite," she murmured. "Yes, well, then, thank you, Elton." She turned to go.

"Erm . . . Mrs. Bright," he said, his voice faltering a bit.

"Yes, Elton?" She turned back. He was blushing again.

"Only, it's just that if you need someone to drive you about whilst you're investigating the murder, you see, I would be happy to do it," he said. "Bradford is so busy with his—with Myrtle—and I thought—"

"Yes, quite, thank you, Elton," Phyllida replied. Oh dear . . . this *was* becoming irksome. Why he couldn't redirect his attentions to one of the housemaids . . . although that could cause even more dramatics should he choose one over another. She sighed internally and went on. "I shall take that under advisement. Should I need your driving skills, I'll certainly call upon you."

"I'm quite strong, too, Mrs. Bright," he said quickly, as if to forestall her leaving (which she desperately wanted to do before he said or did something imprudent or overt that she'd have no choice but to address). "And fast. I mean to say, hunting a killer can be awfully dangerous, and I could help protect you, ma'am. Like I did when that all happened at the Wokesleys' and—"

"Yes, of course, Elton," she said. "I appreciate your thoughtfulness and your offer—"

"And Bradford, well, if you don't mind my saying, he's quite not so very conscientious about it all, is he, Mrs. Bright, what with him training Myrtle to hunt you up and always encouraging her to sniff at you, instead of him being gentlemanly and civil like, you see," he rattled on earnestly, as if he'd memorized lines. "I guess he's more concerned with that dog than he is about anything else, including your safety."

Phyllida blinked. She almost said, *Pardon me?* but she stopped herself from expressing her shock at this information.

"Yes, thank you very much, Elton. I do appreciate your sentiments. Now, if you will excuse me, I have some accounts that need reviewing."

She ducked into her office, which fortunately was only several steps away, before he could say another word.

She closed the door behind her and let his words sink in.

. . . What with him training Myrtle to hunt you up and always encouraging her to sniff at you . . . ?

"Why, that *infuriating man*," she hissed, folding her arms over her middle even as she fought off the exasperated huff of a chuckle.

But this was no laughing matter! Bradford had *trained* Myrtle to accost her?

"That absolutely sneaky, *cunning*, arrogant . . ." For once, she didn't have the words.

So he'd been rewarding Myrtle for slathering all over her, had he? He'd been teaching her to find Phyllida and sniff and pant in her direction? That certainly explained why the beast always seemed to make a beeline toward her whenever they came into proximity. And why she always wanted to sit by Phyllida or even curl up on her feet and pant adoringly up at her.

"Can you believe it?" she demanded of Stilton and Rye; neither of whom seemed to comprehend the severity of the situation. "Well, how would *you* like it if that creature was always sniffing at *you*? If she was being *rewarded* for going near you?"

If cats would deign to roll their eyes, she suspected Rye would have done so, with the message of "As if it would dare try." Instead, he gave her a disgusted look and settled back into his nap, a definite sneer twitching his whiskers.

She gathered up Stilton, who was closer and less likely to protest affection, and buried her face in the soft white fur mottled with blue-gray.

"Well, I'm certainly going to have to decide how to respond to this information, aren't I?" she said, sinking into the chair she normally reserved for reading. It was tucked in the corner with a small lamp on a table that was just large enough for a cup of tea and a small plate of biscuits.

She sat there for a while, enjoying the warm weight of a purring cat on her lap, stroking along Stilton's spine as she contemplated . . . oh, many things. Not the least which was how she was going to ring Bradford's ears about this little game he'd been playing . . . but also about Ethel and Genevra Blastwick, and the difficulty of identifying who from the dinner party had turned around and driven back last night in order to murder Ethel.

"Yet, I simply don't think that's the most logical and efficient tactic," she said to Stilton. "Trying to determine if anyone saw anyone else's automobile motoring back toward Wilding Hall or driving over Ethel. Whoever did it would have made certain no one was around to see.

"No, Stilton, I believe the best way to approach this entire puzzle is to identify what murder it was that Ethel Blastwick saw last summer. Once I do that, I'll better be able to identify motives and opportunity for her own death. Still," she mused as the cat lifted her pink nose in order to offer a brief, scratchy kiss on Phyllida's hand (feline kisses were much more polite than those of canines, and not at all sloppy and wet), "attempting to solve a murder that took place almost a year ago certainly has its challenges."

But of course she was up to it.

Just then, she heard the chime of the doorbell at the main door.

"How curious." She stood, allowing Stilton to ooze back onto the chair in a pile of fur, bones, and a cute pink nose. "I don't believe Agatha was expecting anyone." And she well knew the constable and inspector would go to the back door where they would need to pass by the kitchen and its amenities if they wanted to speak with her.

Phyllida stepped out of her office to find Stanley, the first footman, ushering in none other than Mr. Billdop, the vicar at the Anglican parish, St. Thurston's.

"Why, Mr. Billdop," said Phyllida with a smile. "What a pleasure to see you. Please come in. I'm sorry to say that Mrs. Christie has only just left for London some time ago."

"Oh, yes, of course, but it was actually, erm, you that I was hoping to speak with, Mrs. Bright," he replied.

It was impossible to miss the way he glanced furtively down the corridor in the direction of Mr. Dobble's pantry. It was also impossible to miss the disappointment that flashed in his eyes, but was quickly obscured.

"Yes, of course. Please do come into the front parlor, Mr. Billdop. I shall be right with you," Phyllida said, her mind working quickly.

She didn't know why Digby Billdop had come to call. She also didn't know why the weekly chess games between him and Mr. Dobble had abruptly ceased. But she couldn't help but suspect that this lack of social engagement, close friendship, and, one assumed, intellectual—and perhaps other—stimulation, was part of the cause of Mr. Dobble's particularly short temper as of late.

Yes, he'd been playing chess with the temporary cook whilst they were in London, but that was in London and now they were back in Listleigh. Phyllida was of the opinion that intellectual stimulation, as well as limited societal interactions, was an imperative element in a person's life.

She gestured Mr. Billdop into the parlor, noting automatically and with approval that it was neat, dusted, hoovered, and that the pillows had been plumped and arranged perfectly on the divan and one of the armchairs. A fire was laid in the fireplace, which had recently been swept out after a dreary, rainy day last week that had necessitated a small blaze, and a decorative metal fan stood on the hearth, ready to be removed should another rainy day come upon them and the fire needed to be lit. Cheery yellow roses and boxwood were fresh in their vases, and the curtains were closed halfway against the blaze of late afternoon sun.

"I'll be with you in one moment, Mr. Billdop," she said again, coming back out of the parlor. "Stanley."

She caught the footman just as he was walking back to the dining room where, she expected, he had been putting away the silver and china since Agatha wouldn't be eating in tonight.

"Yes, ma'am?"

"You and Elton are needed in the orchard for . . . perhaps the next hour or so," she said, calculating swiftly. "You are not to respond to any calls or ringing until at least an hour has passed. Do you understand?"

Stanley blinked, appearing utterly flummoxed. "The orchard? But what should we be doing? But, ma'am, Mr. Dobble—"

"I shall attend to Mr. Dobble," she said firmly. "If he even bothers to stick his nose out of his pantry. Now, find Elton and the two of you make yourselves scarce. If I see either of the lot of you in the next sixty minutes—check the time, now, so you know—I'll send you up to the attic to go through and catalog all of those old trunks of Mr. Max's. Do you hear me?"

"Yes, *ma'am*," he said, giving a soldierly bow. Absolutely no one wanted to dig through the dozen or so trunks that likely had dusty archaeological books, pottery pieces, or sheaf upon sheaf of notes, journals, and exams from Mr. Max's university days—and, quite possibly, even old bones.

"And on your way outside, please send Molly up to me immediately. I need her at once," she said, still calculating. She couldn't leave Mr. Billdop in the parlor for too long, but she had to account for all possibilities.

Throughout all of this, Dobble's pantry door had remained tightly closed. Whatever he had going on in there must be exceedingly important, private, or—she thought with a sudden grim smile—incredibly mortifying. For him not to have ventured out during all of the comings and goings was wildly uncharacteristic.

She certainly hoped he wasn't *dead*.

(She truly did.)

"Yes, Mrs. Bright?" Molly was out of breath when she came up from the lower floor. Her eyes were bright with worry and concern.

"I want you to bring up a tea tray for two right away and put it on the table outside the front parlor. Under no circumstances are you to take it *into* the room, nor are you to be seen by anyone—especially Mr. Dobble. Not that I expect he will venture out, but just in case."

"Yes, Mrs. Bright?" Molly appeared confused. "Just put it on the table there?"

"That is what I said. Just leave it there. Don't knock or open the door. And make certain there is that black Assam tea on the tray, if you will," she added, knowing that it was Dobble's favorite.

"All—all right, then, Mrs. Bright." Molly looked as utterly confused as Stanley had done.

"And then I want you to stay downstairs. You and every one of the maids. Do you hear me? No one is to come up here until I say otherwise—no matter what, no matter how many times the bell rings. Ginny, Mary, Bessie, Opal, Benita—the lot of you. Is that understood?"

Molly was gaping at her with wide brown eyes. "But Mrs. Bright—" She must have seen the fierce look in her boss's gaze, for she cut herself off and swallowed. "Yes, ma'am. I'll tell them all. No one is to come up or to answer a bell until you say."

"After you bring up the tea tray," Phyllida reminded her.

"Yes, ma'am." Molly fled, most likely fueled more by the idea of gossiping about the strange doings up on the main floor than the urgency of Phyllida's request. That was to be expected, however, and in this case, Phyllida was willing to risk it in order to ensure her plans went off.

"Mr. Billdop," she said as she went into the parlor.

He jumped a little and turned from where he'd been pacing the room. "Yes, yes, Mrs. Bright." He was a compact, fluttery sort of man with a bit of extra around the waist and a dimpled chin that always put Phyllida in mind of a ripe apricot.

"Let me ring for tea. Please take a seat," she said, putting words to action and ringing a bell she knew would not be answered. "What can I do for you? Is this about poor Ethel Blastwick?"

"Yes, I'm sorry to say. What a terrible tragedy."

"It was. A horrific action on the part of some wicked person," Phyllida said with great emotion.

"I knew the Blastwicks—I mean to say, I *know* them," said Mr. Billdop, looking a little flustered. "Quite well, in fact. Miss Ethel was a very nice young woman. Quiet. A little shy. What a shame what happened to her. What a *shame*. Her father is a bit of an unusual sort, isn't he, but I suppose many of us are unusual in our own ways. Such a tragic thing to have happened."

Phyllida nodded in agreement. She couldn't help but notice that the vicar hadn't mentioned anything about Genevra. He was, by nature, a kind and truthful person, so that was to be expected. "Yes, indeed," she replied, then lapsed into silence in order to encourage him to tell her why he'd come.

"I hope you're investigating, Mrs. Bright," he went on. "It's just that these police officers . . . well, they don't always get it right, do they?" He had the right to be concerned; after all, Inspector Cork had once arrested him for murder. Phyllida had set the inspector straight, but the event—as short-lived as it was—had still been very upsetting to the gentle vicar.

"Quite so," she agreed, reaching over to ring the bell a second time. "I was at the dinner party where Genevra made her very bold and impetuous statement."

"Yes, yes, I heard about that. Terrible. Absolutely terrible! Why would she do such a thing? And now her sister is dead because of her bragging." He shook his head sadly. "Even so, I am relieved to hear that you are looking into it. Very relieved. That is why I've called. I want to implore you to investigate. Poor Dr. Blastwick has had quite a difficult time of it, losing his wife and now his daughter."

Phyllida inclined her head in acknowledgment. "Thank you. And, as it turns out, there is a bit of a plot twist, if you'll forgive the phrase. Genevra has told me that Ethel was the person who saw the murder. Genevra did not."

"*Miss Ethel* saw the murder?" Mr. Billdop's eyes goggled. "But . . . but . . ." His pudgy hands flailed.

"Quite. And that leads me to the conclusion that whoever conducted the murder witnessed by Ethel Blastwick had to have been present last night in order to realize Genevra was lying—and then went on to silence the actual witness, who was, of course, Ethel."

"Good Lord," breathed the vicar. "Then that makes what I have to tell you even more important. Good heavens." He appeared almost faint.

"And what is that?"

"I was motoring home last night rather late. Just after ten. I had a visit to the Melvilles' out on Cutberth Hill—old Rudolph is in his last days, you see, and his daughter wanted comfort and for me to sit with Rudolph for a bit. On my return, I happened to be driving along the Ploughman's Close back into the village, and I saw Miss Ethel walking along the side of the road."

Phyllida, who never slouched anyhow, straightened her spine even more and leaned forward. "Indeed."

"Yes. Of course I stopped and asked her if she wanted a ride. She very firmly declined, but she was in quite distress, you see. Quite distress. I urged her to climb into the motor but she was determined that she would walk. 'It's not very far, Mr. Billdop, and I truly do not make good company right now. It's only I have to decide what to do. It's only just the worst thing possible,' she said, her eyes filled with tears." He looked miserable. "I should have insisted, Mrs. Bright. I should have *insisted* she climb into my motor and then this would not have happened."

"You did everything you could have done," she said. "Who could have anticipated such a thing would happen? And it is only the killer to blame, Mr. Billdop. They are the evil one."

"I know you're correct, but I simply can't assuage my guilt. It's simply terrible." He withdrew a handkerchief from his pocket and dabbed at his shiny forehead and cheeks. "But the most important thing is that I very well might have passed by the killer's motorcar."

"You passed a vehicle coming along the road?" Phyllida sat up even straighter again.

"I did," he said. "There were no other motors behind or in front of me but this one—it was dark and I would have seen the lights. And I was just about to where Miss Ethel would have turned off to take the little lane to Ivygate Cottage. I understand she was—was found not far from there."

"She was. And we know the motorcar that hit her was coming from the direction of the village," she told him as he nodded.

"You know that for certain? Why, then . . . it *must* have been the killer I saw. I didn't pass any other motor after that one, all the way into the village."

"What do you remember about the vehicle?"

"That's just it . . . I have only a passing memory of it. I'm afraid I was still thinking about poor Miss Ethel. But I've been racking my brain to remember everything I can. The two headlights . . . coming toward me. A trifle fast, I thought, for nighttime driving. I had to pull close to the side of the road so we could pass by each other. If only I had looked more closely!" he said in disgust.

"Did you get any impression at all about the motorcar or the driver? Anything at all? How many headlights?"

"The headlights . . . well, there were two, with perhaps a lower one in front. Yes, I think there was a third one down low. And one of them up top was a bit brighter than the other. The—the one on the left, I think."

"That is very helpful. What color was the motor? Could you tell what type or style it was?"

He shook his head. "I'm afraid I'm not very qualified to talk about motorcars, Mrs. Bright. I only know that it was a dark color and that it was not a small one. Not like a roadster. A sedan or the like."

"But one of the headlights was dimmer. That could be very helpful," Phyllida said. "Now, what about the driver? Did you see *anything*? Anything at all?"

"It happened rather quickly; as I said, he was driving along at a rather fast clip. I never take my motor above five miles per hour, you see, and he was going much faster. And it was dark, of course. I pulled over and he rumbled past. I might have seen a hat, but that was all. I'm so sorry, Mrs. Bright."

"Not at all," she replied. "This is very helpful. I'm ... er ... assuming you have shared this information with the inspector?"

He grimaced. "Not yet. I will do so. I simply don't see how a person can place their trust in a policeman after he's made such *serious* mistakes in the past."

"Quite. Now, let us talk a bit further about this investigation. You may have other information that is helpful." Phyllida went on to explain why her attention would be directed toward investigating any unusual deaths that had occurred last summer. She also unobtrusively rang the bell again. "Can you think of any unexpected deaths, Mr. Billdop?"

"Oh. My. My goodness ... well, I suppose ..." His face scrunched up as he contemplated. "Unexpected deaths. Well, there was Mr. Greenhouse. That was surely an accident, but one never knows."

"Yes ... the bee sting. It seems an accident, but it *could* be arranged, I suppose," Phyllida said. "To that end ... can you think of anyone who might have had reason to murder Mr. Greenhouse by putting bees in his motorcar?" Her eyes narrowed when she suddenly recalled that Professor Avonlea kept bees.

"Well, my goodness. I ... oh, good heavens, it's simply not ..." He heaved a sigh. "May I speak frankly, Mrs. Bright? After all, I am a man of the cloth ..." He appeared pained as he struggled with his conscience.

"I think it's incumbent upon you to speak frankly," she told him. "*Particularly* as a man of the cloth. Identifying a killer is far more important than worrying about a bit of gossip."

"Yes, yes, I suppose you're right. Well, when it comes to murder, one always has to look at the spouse, don't they?" replied Mr. Billdop, obviously quoting from his extensive experience reading detective fiction. "And Mrs. Greenhouse has always struck me as the sort of person who's rather . . . well, a bit *obsessive*, I suppose is the word. Very much enamored with her pets—she had a dog and several cats. She was quite upset over what happened to her dog, I recall. It was some time ago Ralph accidentally drove over it. It was terrible.

"And I do believe she inherited a bit of family money after her husband died, too, if the gossip is true. He was one of the Yorkshire Greenhouses, you know. Quite a bit of money in bricks, I understand."

Phyllida made a thoughtful noise. "Even so, Mrs. Greenhouse wasn't at the dinner party last night, so how would she have known what Genevra said?"

"Do you know whether she's taken up with anyone else since her husband died?" She rang the bell a fourth time. In this household, a bell would *never* go unanswered after a second ringing—if it even got to a second ringing, which, when Phyllida was in charge, it certainly did not.

"Do you mean a man?" He flushed a little. "I don't know about that. But . . . as I said, Mrs. Greenhouse does have several cats, I believe," he added, giving her a meaningful look. "And one of them was quite ill recently."

Phyllida nodded again. "Is there anyone else who might have had it in for Mr. Greenhouse?"

He shook his head.

"And what about Ellie Mayhew?" Phyllida went on. "I understand she was in a motorcar accident. Since we are confronted by a murderer who has used an automobile to kill, it isn't out of the realm that they might have employed a motorcar in the past for such a purpose. Did you hear anything about how it happened?"

"Do you mean, did someone cut her brakes?" he replied with a flicker of a smile. "As I recall, the accident wasn't on a hill or around a bend where her brakes going out would have caused it. She went off the road and hit a stone wall, as I recall. It was at night. But you ought to speak to Fred Stiller about it. I think he took a look at the automobile afterward."

Fred Stiller owned a bicycle sales and repair shop in the village, but in the absence of an automobile mechanic in Listleigh, he often looked at motorcar problems as well. Bradford had mentioned he might be playing cards tonight at the Screaming Magpie with the others.

"Excellent idea, Mr. Billdop. Thank you. Can you think of anything else? Any other disappearance or unexpected death?"

He paused for a moment then shook his head. "Last summer, you say?"

"Sometime in July or August. Perhaps September, I suppose."

"Well, there was Arthur Grainger who passed on unexpectedly. Found dead in his bed, I heard. The chap was only fifty-five. Rather young to just go off in his sleep, you ask me."

Phyllida agreed with that sentiment. "Arthur Grainger. Did John Bhatt attend him?"

"Yes, I do believe he did."

"That is all very helpful, Mr. Billdop," Phyllida said. "I shall speak to Dr. Bhatt."

The interview was at its end, but he wouldn't know that Phyllida wasn't finished with her agenda. "Good heavens, Vicar, I cannot fathom why no one has come with the tea tray yet."

She rang the bell once more, long and hard and quite violently. If that didn't get Dobble out of his pantry, nothing short of yelling "Fire!" would—a tactic she wasn't about to dismiss.

"If you'll excuse me, Mr. Billdop, I'll see what is happening down in the kitchen to explain the delay."

Just as she got to the door of the parlor—which was partway ajar—it came fully open to reveal a tray swiftly making its way into the room. The tray was suspended in the air by a pair of slender, pale, and shockingly *gloveless* fingers, which were attached to a tall, almost skeletal figure moving quickly but smoothly.

Excellent, Phyllida thought to herself.

She dodged behind the opening door as Dobble glided in with the tray, apologies forming on his thin lips. He was in such a state that he didn't seem to notice her as he breezed by toward the seating arrangement. Phyllida recognized the moment he realized that Mr. Billdop was the room's singular occupant, for the tray made a sudden rattle-clink when the butler's step hitched. Fortunately, he corrected course and the contents of the tray remained upright and intact.

"Digby," was all he said. Two bright patches of red had appeared on his pale cheeks.

The vicar's reply was inaudible, but Phyllida saw that he'd stood to greet Dobble. The two men stared at each other.

Phyllida slipped out the door. As she closed it behind her, she heard the alarming clink and rattle as the tray was placed unsteadily on the table. A low murmur of voices, stilted, reached her ears.

She leaned against the door and smiled complacently.

Now then. She'd certainly accomplished her good deed for the day.

CHAPTER 11

With the parlor door closed behind her, Phyllida glanced down the corridor.

Dobble's pantry was obviously unoccupied, and if her instincts were correct, it would be unoccupied for some time.

She stood there, considering. It had been her plan to get Dobble and Mr. Billdop together in a private location, for clearly there was unfinished business between them. But she hadn't decided whether she'd succumb to the temptation of sneaking a peek inside the butler's pantry.

Still. It was the perfect opportunity to assuage her curiosity.

Phyllida was just beginning to edge down the hall when the telephone rang. Its *brrringgg* was so sharp and unexpected, she nearly jumped. Then she did jump—toward the telephone—in order to pick it up before Dobble used needing to answer it as an excuse to vacate the parlor.

"Mallowan Hall," she said. "Mrs. Bright speaking."

"Oh, Mrs. Bright. This is me, George Chockley, ringing you back about the accounts."

Mr. Chockley was the fishmonger, and he was very apologetic about the error over an order of fresh sardines and sole being charged incorrectly. He was also extremely verbose in his apologies, unnecessarily detailed in his explanation, and filled with questions about poor Ethel Blastwick. By the time Phyllida was able to extricate herself from the telephone call, it was far too many minutes later.

TWO TRUTHS AND A MURDER 143

She glanced toward the parlor door, which had remained closed—an indication that things were going as she'd planned. Still, she wasn't certain she ought to take the chance of peeking into Mr. Dobble's pantry.

But this was the perfect opportunity...

She considered the situation, and had just made the decision to take a quick look when the parlor door opened. Moving swiftly, she ducked into her own office, which was right at hand, as Mr. Dobble and Mr. Billdop came into the corridor. With her door cracked she could hear just a bit of their conversation.

"... plenty of space at my rectory," the vicar was saying. "Must be quite cramped..."

Dobble murmured something like, "... most appreciative..." as they walked past, and moments later, he opened the door to the pantry. Both of them went inside and Phyllida had lost her opportunity to snoop.

Drat it.

She left the door to her office ajar and focused her attention on fixing the account book based on Mr. Chockley's corrections. This led to making another note about the butcher's account, and then the linen service, and adding another line to the ledger of supplies, and then another, and she hadn't noticed how much time had passed when she heard voices in the corridor.

But when one of them became raised and she recognized the tense and terrible voice as that of Mr. Dobble, she set aside the account books and reluctantly emerged from her office.

"... don't know where the lot of you had gone off to, but the lapse in attention is *unacceptable*." Mr. Dobble was standing over Stanley, Elton, Molly, and Ginny. They were goggling at him helplessly and he was holding the tea tray he'd ended up delivering and was using it to emphasize his words. *Clink, clink, clinkety clink.*

"Is there a problem, Mr. Dobble?" Phyllida said in a clear and calm voice. It was obvious Mr. Billdop had taken his leave and now the butler was taking his own bile out on the staff.

"And where were *you*, Mrs. Bright? I'll have you know I was interrupted in my pantry by the ringing of the service bell for the fifth time," he said in what was meant to be a terribly affronted and furious voice, but had no effect on Phyllida. "I had to take it on *myself.*"

"Why, I was visiting with the vicar," she replied smoothly, giving him a very steady look. "And then I went down to the kitchen to speak to Mrs. Puffley and left him alone in the parlor for a short while. Whatever has happened? Did you see Mr. Billdop out, then? He appears to have gone."

This last was her way of indicating that she was very well aware of their tête-à-tête in the parlor, and even admitting that she had arranged it, while daring him to make a further scene about it all—which would prompt her to fill in even more details she was certain he wouldn't want divulged.

Mr. Dobble's face went pale with comprehension, then his cheeks flared with two bright pink splotches. He looked as if he'd just swallowed a fish. Then, his eyes narrowed, focusing on her with acute dislike. "See to your staff, Mrs. Bright. And ensure that all of the service bells are working properly."

He turned abruptly and started to walk away, then spun back. "Stanley," he barked. The footman jumped.

"Yes, sir?" The young man's Adam's apple bobbed wildly.

"Fetch the crate from the package that was delivered yesterday." Then he turned again, and this time he stalked all the way to his pantry without pause, flung open the door, and went inside. The door closed firmly.

Molly, Ginny, Stanley, and Elton swung to look at Phyllida.

"Never mind him," she said. "Stanley, do as he says and fetch the crate. Molly, Ginny, back to work. Thank you, Elton," she said, since she had no task to which she could set him.

Back in her office, she returned to her work and reviewing a section in *Mrs. Beeton's*. She became so absorbed in the details of making elderflower—and, later, once the remaining flowers turned to berries, elder*berry*—liqueurs that she was startled when Opal arrived with a small pot of tea and a neat dinner tray. Generally speaking, Phyllida did not eat in the servants' dining room, although she did make an exception on occasion. Mr. Dobble did so even more rarely.

"Why, thank you, Opal," Phyllida told her. "I hadn't realized the time."

"Yes, ma'am," said the scullion with a little curtsy.

"Is all well in the kitchen?"

"Yes, mu'um. Only, Mrs. Puffley is still going on over what to wear to this fancy shindig the const'ble is taking her to. She says it's the policeman's *ball*," Opal went on, her eyes wide. "Why, I never knew anyone who went to a ball before. I ain't even sure what it is besides a bunch of ladies in big, fancy frocks, and dancing. Sounds uncomf'table to me."

"That about sums it up," Phyllida said with a wry laugh. "Thank you for bringing this. I'll ring when I've finished."

It was several hours later when Phyllida realized the afternoon light had given way to the setting sun, for the pages of her ledger and the household book were becoming dim.

A glance at the clock told her that Bradford had surely left for the Screaming Magpie by now and she had missed her opportunity to ride with him.

It occurred to her then that her plans to go into Listleigh regardless of her tacit agreement to stay home might be stymied if he'd taken the Daimler—what with Agatha having gone off in the roadster. That would leave her with limited transportation options. She certainly wasn't going to *cycle* into town, although a brisk walk on the shortcut footpath along the river would be pleasant on such a pretty summer's night.

She rang for her dinner tray to be removed and went into the adjoining bedroom to freshen up her hair and reapply her lipstick and a bit of mascara. Phyllida never painted her fingernails, but they were kept buffed and the tips filed into neat half-moons. After a moment of contemplation, she selected a frock in blue with tiny white flowers—a darker color than she normally would wear for an evening out, due to the questionable housekeeping and sanitary measures taken at the pub. The darker color would hide any stains she might acquire. But her cuffs and collar were pretty white eyelet lace, and she cinched a white belt around her waist.

When she went downstairs, she found most of the staff sitting in the servants' dining hall. Mrs. Puffley was knitting something. Elton, Stanley, Amsi, Bessie, and Molly were playing cards, arguing loudly and amicably about something or other. Ginny was writing letters in her big, loopy handwriting. Opal was reading Agatha's *The Man in the Brown Suit*, her mouth forming the words as she worked laboriously through the page.

It was a characteristic scene for the staff on an evening in which their employers were not in residence and dinner was finished. Friendly arguments, jokes, laughter—all were being exchanged. It was a time of camaraderie, and one that Phyllida appreciated, for it was far easier to have a staff who got on than one who didn't. Even the maids, who were in constant competition for Elton's attention, weren't giving each other glowers.

No one noticed her peeking inside, and Phyllida had no qualms about that. She wasn't interested in joining their fellowship at the moment. She turned to walk down the hall, intending to go outside to determine whether the Daimler was still available or whether she would be walking when she noticed that Myrtle's recuperation basket was empty.

Surely no one had taken her into the dining hall . . . no, she certainly would have seen the little beast. Or, more likely, the beast would have seen *her* and made a vocal commentary about it.

Stifling an exasperated sigh, she started toward the basket, noticing the bedding—the blanket and Bradford's shirt—had been dragged down the hall in the opposite direction. There were bits and pieces of what appeared to be bandages (heaven knew Phyllida had seen enough bandages during the war) strewn about.

And then she saw the blood staining one of the largest pieces. Bright red. Fresh. And the amount of it was quite alarming.

Her heart leaped into her throat and she rushed forward, seeing more blood trailing down the hallway.

"Myrtle?" she called, following the splatters, smears, and paw prints. "Myrtle! Where are you?" she demanded, fear creeping into her voice as she rounded the corner into the scullery.

"Good *heavens!* What has happened?" she exclaimed when

she discovered the dog huddled in a corner. There was blood everywhere and Myrtle was panting heavily. Her eyes were glassy and even without touching it, Phyllida could see that her nose wasn't wet.

Without thinking, Phyllida surged toward the beast and gathered it up into her arms. "What have you done, you foolish little thing? And why didn't you go the other way, for help?"

But it was clear what had happened—the canine had torn off her bandages, and quite possibly torn or nibbled away at the stitches Mr. Varney had installed. The suture on her leg and the front of her torso was open and blood was streaming everywhere. And, from the looks of it, Myrtle was shocked and weakened by the results of her actions. She'd likely gone toward the exterior door in search of Bradford, and became tired and frightened.

Phyllida rushed down the hall, clutching the dog to her chest. "Elton! Molly! I need help!"

"What has happened? Oh, Mrs. Bright!" cried Molly when she saw the situation. She reached to pat the canine on its head. "What's happened to Myrtle?"

"Elton, is the Daimler here? We need to take this dog to Mr. Varney's immediately."

"Yes, ma'am!" Elton bolted out of the house, then came rushing back. "Yes, it's here. I'll drive you, Mrs. Bright."

"I've got a towel for her," Opal said, hurrying forward.

"Bring another one," Phyllida said as Opal draped Myrtle with the towel, but she didn't wait for her to finish tucking it around or for the other towel to arrive. She strode outside to find Elton with the passenger door of the Daimler open and waiting. The motorcar was already running.

"Oh, Mrs. Bright, is she going to be all right?" said Opal tearfully as Molly and Ginny crowded with her, arms around each other. "There's an awful lot of blood for such a bitty thing!"

Phyllida didn't consider Myrtle "bitty"—she had to weigh more than two stone—but she sympathized with Opal's sentiments.

"I'm certain Mr. Varney will fix her up," said Phyllida as Elton closed the door. She still held the dog close to her, but now she allowed her burden to settle onto her lap, partially wrapped in the towel.

Benita came running up and thrust a towel through the open window to Phyllida, then she joined the other staff, who stood, watching in silent dismay.

Phyllida took the second piece of cloth and pressed it tightly to the worst part of the open wound, wrapping the end around Myrtle's leg in a tourniquet as Elton eased into the driver's seat and closed his door.

He pressed on the accelerator and with a roar and a great lurch, the Daimler leapt forward into the twilit night.

"Good heavens, Elton, I should like to arrive at Mr. Varney's in one piece," Phyllida told him sharply as she gripped the side of her seat.

"Yes, ma'am," he said, but if he eased up his foot from the accelerator, Phyllida couldn't tell the difference.

It was a good thing she had Myrtle to attend to, for if she hadn't, Phyllida surely would have been in fear for her life or nauseated from the speed at which he took the turns and roared up and down the little hills—or both. As it was, she found herself crooning quietly to the creature that panted in her lap, holding it close and secure as Elton navigated the curving road, heedless of the gloaming light. She was forced to close her eyes at least twice, and she never released her grip on the edge of the seat.

One thing was certain: *Bradford* would be driving on the return to Mallowan Hall.

By the time they arrived at Mr. Varney's surgery, Phyllida didn't feel anymore wetness coming through the towel she'd pressed firmly to the wound. Myrtle had stopped panting quite so hard, but, having very little experience or knowledge about canines, Phyllida wasn't certain whether that was a positive development or not.

As Elton helped her out of the motor with her burden, the door of Mr. Varney's office opened and the veterinarian came out, walking rapidly.

"Mrs. Puffley telephoned from Mallowan Hall and said you

were coming," he explained, carefully extricating Myrtle from Phyllida's secure grip. "Looks like the little thing couldn't resist taking off that bandage. *Tsk, tsk,* little one," he said, "let me see what you've done."

As before, Phyllida could not condone any description of Myrtle as "little" but she said nothing as she and Elton followed Mr. Varney into the building.

Mrs. Buckwhile appeared, firmly blocking Phyllida's intention to follow the vet into a back room.

"We'll just leave Mr. Varney to handle things, won't we now, Mrs. Bright," she said pleasantly, gesturing to a chair obviously meant for Phyllida to sit. "He'll set things to rights."

Feeling a strange sense of disquiet now that Myrtle was no longer under her supervision and care, Phyllida hesitated. Then she realized what she must do.

"Yes, of course," she said, and turned away.

"Mrs. Bright?" Elton was hot on her heels.

"Someone needs to inform Bradford, of course," she said, walking at a brisk pace.

"But—"

"I suggest you straighten that parking job of the Daimler if you ever want the opportunity to drive it again."

She left Elton to it and continued down the road. It was past dusk and well into twilight, so the streetlamps had been lit but most of the shops were closed. A glance at Mr. Sprite's establishment confirmed that his lights had been extinguished for the night, and across the street, Pankhurst's Grocery was also closed.

Phyllida walked into the Screaming Magpie, stepping into a place filled with heavy cigarette and pipe smoke, the stale aroma of spilled beer and whisky, and the low buzz of conversation, argument, and laughter. She spotted the table of card-players and started toward it immediately, waving off Guinevere's imperious glance (an action which she knew she might later come to regret).

Bradford had seen her come in, and he must have recognized that something was wrong, for he got to his feet and started toward her, his eyes wide with concern.

"She's going to be quite all right," Phyllida said, holding up her hands in an effort to stave off his worry. "I'm certain of it."

"What's happened?"

"Mr. Varney has things well in hand with Myrtle," she told him.

"Myrtle!" he exclaimed. "What's happened to Myrtle?"

"Why, the foolish little thing pulled off her bandages and chewed away her stitches, is what's happened," she said. "The suture opened and there was quite a bit of blood."

"I can see that," he said grimly, gesturing to her person. She looked down. Despite her practical choice of the blue frock, bloodstains had colored the white flowers of its pattern, her lace cuffs, and part of her belt. "When I saw the blood, I thought it was *yours*—but then you said 'she' and so I was—but Mr. Varney has her, you say? Myrtle?"

"Yes. He's attending to her as we speak. Mrs. Buckwhile wouldn't allow me to supervise, but one must assume the man knows what he is about," Phyllida replied. "After all, he did stitch her up the first time. Although one might question the efficacy of his work if it was so simple for Myrtle to tear it out. Nonetheless."

"Shall we go to Mr. Varney's and wait together?" she suggested.

"Yes." To her surprise, he took her hand firmly in his as they walked out of the pub.

Because she'd been in such a rush to leave Mallowan Hall, Phyllida hadn't had the chance to don gloves—or to get her handbag—and so the feel of his large, warm, rough hand curled around hers was steadying. She hadn't realized until that moment that she'd *needed* steadying. Not because of Myrtle. It must have been due to that harrowing motorcar ride.

"What happened?" he asked, slowing his longer stride to match hers.

"I discovered that Myrtle had vacated her basket, and in doing so, left quite the trail of blood along the corridor," she told him. "I followed the spatters and streaks and found her in the corner of the scullery. I surmise she was attempting to locate you once she realized the gravity of her situation."

"And so you gathered her up and drove her to Mr. Varney's like an army ambulance driver?" Bradford gave her hand a little squeeze as he glanced down with a wry smile. "At the cost of your frock, I see. That was very kind of you, Mrs. Bright, considering your feelings toward Myrts."

"Well, I certainly wasn't going to allow her to lie there and *bleed* to death," she retorted with a half-hearted attempt to free her hand from his. But he tightened his grip and she ceased resisting. "She appeared quite dazed and forlorn. It's rather a wonder she wasn't searching for *me*, considering the reward that would likely be in her future had she located me."

Bradford glanced at her and even in the low light, he must have read the spark of ire in her eyes. "Oi. So you've figured that out, have you?"

"It wasn't terribly difficult to do so. And, incidentally, it wasn't me who drove. I was holding Myrtle and attempting to stanch the bleeding. It was Elton who commandeered the Daimler. And I implore you, Bradford, to please *not* allow him behind the driver's wheel of that vehicle ever again when I am riding."

He gave a choked laugh. "Very well, Mrs. Bright. I shall relieve the earnest speedster Elton of that duty. I can stow my bicycle in the back for the return trip."

"I'll have you know, Elton has offered to drive me about for my murder investigations," she went on. "He claims he's very strong and rather quick, and that he would be extremely useful in protecting me from angry murderers—unlike yourself, who, according to Elton, is more concerned with Myrtle's well-being than my own."

Bradford snorted, but by now, they were turning up the short walkway to the surgery, and he didn't comment. Just as they approached, the door opened and Elton emerged. His attention went immediately to the joined hands of Phyllida and Bradford, then his eyes lifted to meet hers in a shocked and horrified look.

"Now, now, Bradford," said Phyllida, thinking quickly as she dropped his hand like a hot potato. "I'm certain Myrtle will be just fine and you won't need to grip my hand *quite* so tightly any longer." She gestured for him to precede her into the veterinary office.

"Mrs. Bright," Elton began, his attention swiveling between her and Bradford, who was hurrying into the building, and then back at her again. He was holding his cap, twisting it in his hands.

"Did you correct the Daimler's parking job?" she asked.

"Yes, ma'am, of course I did. Only, I was wondering, since we're here, you see, and Mr. Varney is seeing to Myrtle, if maybe we could—you and I, I mean, could have a—a sherry, I mean to say, at the Screaming Magpie. You and I. Together." A sconce lit the entrance to the veterinary office, and she could see that his cheeks were slightly pink and his gaze was determined.

A number of thoughts rushed through Phyllida's mind, along with several different verbal reactions—including expressing her disappointment that he should think she was the type to settle for a namby-pamby drink like sherry. (Not that the Screaming Magpie would offer such a temperate libation anyhow.)

She corralled the stampede of reactions in favor of the simplest and most prudent.

"While that is a very kind gesture, Elton, I do not believe it would be the wisest of choices."

"But, Mrs. Bright—Phyllida, if I may be so bold—"

"You may not," she said tartly.

Instead of being put off by her remonstration, he merely seemed more infatuated. "Right, then, of course, Mrs. Bright. One must keep up appearances. But surely a simple glass of sherry wouldn't be amiss, considering the fact that you have investigating to do."

The young man did have a lovely pair of blue eyes. With ridiculously long lashes. And broad shoulders.

If she weren't his boss—after a fashion anyhow—*and* if her affections weren't at least somewhat engaged elsewhere—she might have considered accepting his offer. He was, after all, very earnest and sincere. And young. Quite young.

But . . . not *that* young.

"Elton, I'm not the sort of woman who drinks sherry. I prefer a civilized martini, or, if unavailable, a rye whisky. The darker the better."

"Of course, Mrs. Bright, I understand—"

"Aside from that," she went on, speaking over whatever new

tactic he was surely about to try, "I don't believe I am presentable enough to be seen at a public house." She gestured to the bloodstains on the front of her frock and, sadly, on the white patent leather belt.

Elton's attention skimmed over her figure, and his cheeks flushed a dark red as he jerked his gaze back up to hers. "Yes, of course, Mrs. Bright. I-I hadn't—"

"Besides, I simply don't feel able to leave Myrtle and her master here without supervision. You saw the state poor Mr. Bradford was in! And over a mere canine, who, I predict, will rebound with even more energy than before."

"In spite of those assurances, I believe it is my responsibility to ensure both Mr. Bradford and Myrtle are safely returned to Mallowan Hall this evening. And therefore, it's incumbent upon me to remain nearby for supervisory purposes."

"I—I see, Mrs. Bright." He seemed at a loss at how to proceed—a development for which Phyllida was quite grateful.

"Elton, I quite appreciate your offer of assistance"—not that it was precisely *assistance* he was offering—"but perhaps you could be of help to me in a different way."

This suggestion had the desired effect, for Elton seemed to adjust himself to ramrod straight, with an earnestness that was quite adorable. "Yes, Mrs. Bright. What is it? What can I do to assist?"

"I should very much like to learn whether Fred Stiller is still present at the Screaming Magpie, and if he is, I wonder if he might be willing to speak with me whilst I wait here in order to . . . er . . . provide support and supervision to Bradford." She rather hoped Bradford never heard of her intent to "supervise" him. She was certain he would protest vociferously.

"I'll find out straight away, Mrs. Bright."

Having dispatched him off on an errand she certainly could have done herself, Phyllida was relieved to have the opportunity to enter the veterinary surgery and assess Bradford's state of mind.

She found him standing in the center of the empty waiting room, his hands clasped behind his back.

"Mr. Varney hasn't come out yet," he told her.

Stating the obvious was something Bradford didn't generally do, which suggested he was more upset than he appeared.

Phyllida glanced toward the desk, which was currently unmanned (or, more accurately, unwomanned) by Mrs. Buckwhile. It beckoned to her, for her curiosity and investigative instincts had been aroused by her conversation with Mr. Billdop.

"Where is Mrs. Buckwhile?" she asked, edging toward the desk.

"Don't know. Said she had something to do with some . . . chickens, I believe it was." Bradford fixed her with a narrow look. "Why?"

"It's only that it was suggested Mr. Varney had been seeing Mrs. Greenhouse quite a bit due to her cat—or perhaps it was multiple felines; Mr. Billdop wasn't clear on that point—having medical problems."

Bradford's eyes narrowed thoughtfully. "And you're wondering if that interaction became a motive for murder and caused Mr. Greenhouse's untimely death?"

"That, or was, perhaps, a result of it," Phyllida said, pleased that she seemed to have momentarily distracted him from Myrtle's fate. "I thought I might . . . well . . ." She gestured to the desk.

"I highly doubt Varney would leave any sort of incriminating love letters in his file, but have at it, Mrs. Bright. I'll stand watch for Mrs. Buckwhile whilst you snoop."

Although Phyllida tended to agree with Bradford's assessment, she still felt it necessary to take the opportunity to snoop—as he put it. Who knew what else she might find?

It wasn't difficult to locate the file for the Greenhouse pets. There were three felines, and the now-deceased canine, as she learned from flipping through the file. Two cats had recently been treated for fleas, and the third for worms. There were other visits as well for dental assessments, loss of appetite, and a strange fatty deposit under the skin near the belly of one of the patients.

It seemed Mr. Varney made house calls to the Greenhouse residence, which Phyllida found *quite* interesting. He'd never offered to come up to Mallowan Hall to examine Stilton or Rye.

She went to retrieve the small notepad from her pocketbook

and realized in her anxiousness to get Myrtle to the veterinarian's, she'd gone off without her bag. *Blast.*

She tore a piece of paper from a notepad on the desk and jotted down the dates—seven of them in total—where Mr. Varney had made house calls to the Greenhouse residence. She would compare them to the date Ralph Greenhouse had died and see if anything was interesting.

"*Hssst.*"

Bradford's warning had Phyllida darting from the desk and sliding into a waiting chair just as Mrs. Buckwhile appeared.

"Is everything going well with Myrtle?" Phyllida asked immediately in an effort to keep the woman from wondering what she'd been doing during her absence. She slipped the note with the dates into the pocket of her frock.

Phyllida never had dresses made without pockets.

"Oh, yes, Mrs. Bright," replied Mrs. Buckwhile. "Mr. Varney ought to be out any time now to give a report."

As if summoned by her words, Mr. Varney materialized. He had an excellent prognosis for Myrtle, to Bradford's obvious relief, and suggested it would be best if the canine continued her recuperation at the surgery, at least overnight, where the veterinarian could keep a closer watch on her.

Bradford seemed mildly disconcerted by the idea of leaving his pet, but he acquiesced nonetheless.

"You can retrieve her first thing in the morning," Phyllida said soothingly. She stopped short of sliding her arm through the crook of his elbow in order to brace him up. She didn't want to cause any gossip about the housekeeper and chauffeur from Mallowan Hall.

Just as she and Bradford were walking away from the veterinary surgery, Elton arrived. A tall, spindly man in his mid-thirties was in tow. "Mrs. Bright, I've brought Mr. Stiller," said Elton unnecessarily.

Bradford cast a curious glance at Phyllida, but remained silent. They stopped under one of the streetlamps.

"Ah, yes, Mr. Stiller. I'm Mrs. Bright from up at Mallowan Hall.

Thank you for coming to speak with me. There was a bit of a mishap with a bleeding canine—I mean that literally, not in the profane sense—and I thought it best if I refrained from being seen in public." She gestured to the blood on her lace cuffs and the front of her dress.

Fred Stiller looked from Phyllida to Bradford. His brows twitched upward and a flare of comprehension lit his eyes. "It's a pleasure to meet you at last, Mrs. Bright," he said gravely. He possessed a shock of carrot-red hair that seemed to have a mind of its own, sweeping high and smooth over his forehead, and an Adam's apple that protruded in the same way the knuckles did on his long, gangly fingers. "I understand you are investigating the death of Miss Ethel Blastwick."

"Quite right. Now, I should like to know whether you took a look at the motorcar Miss Ellie Mayhew was driving when she died in the crash last summer."

A trace of surprise and confusion flitted over his face, but he didn't comment. "Oi, yes I did, Mrs. Bright."

"And was there anything suggestive or strange about the motorcar? That is to say, was there anything that seemed wrong or out of place?"

"She is asking whether someone cut the brake line," Bradford said, obviously feeling the need to translate what Phyllida knew had been a perfectly clear question. "Or sabotaged it in any way."

"Oi, right then." Stiller scratched his forehead, which was furrowed in thought. "I can't say as I did. I mean to say, the brake lines were fine and the tires were inflated. No flats. Everything looked in order to me, innit. There was no damage to the vehicle except the front, where she rammed into the wall.

"Seemed the girl just lost control of the steering wheel and ran into the wall. It was at night. Coulda been a hart or fox run out in front of her, you see, and she turned the wheel too hard and was going too fast. Some of those young drivers do that, they do. That stone fence is awfully close to the road."

Phyllida nodded, but glanced at Bradford to see whether he agreed or had any other questions to ask. After all, he was more mechanically inclined than she.

"Sad thing," Bradford replied, "but it happens. Nearly crashed into a deer once myself. Came right from nowhere. Appreciate it, Fred."

"My pleasure. Mrs. Bright," he added with a grave smile. "I hope you find out who done it. To Miss Blastwick, I mean."

"I shall do my very best," Phyllida replied. "Now, I suppose we ought to return to Mallowan Hall. It is getting rather late." Then another thought struck her. "But, is the card game breaking up anytime soon, Mr. Stiller?"

"Oi, I don't know, Mrs. Bright. I'm, er, not certain whether they would—er—agree to—er—"

"I don't want to *play*," she said impatiently. "I want to see the headlights on the motorcars of the suspects when they drive off." She went on to explain how a witness—she chose not to share that it was the vicar—had seen the auto that had run down Ethel Blastwick. "I want to determine whether any of the right-side headlights are dimmer than the left-side ones. And which ones might have three headlamps."

"Excellent thought, Mrs. Bright," said Elton—whom she'd forgotten was standing there. "Shall we return to the Screaming Magpie and wait for them to leave?"

"I see Crestworthy coming out now," replied Fred Stiller. "And Avonlea is behind him."

The small party of Phyllida, Bradford, Stiller, and Elton started down the block toward the pub. The two men, Crestworthy and the professor, were saying their farewells. Mr. Heathers and Milton Panson trailed out after them, and Phyllida congratulated herself on having perfectly timed her quest. She suspected the game might have broken up because Stiller and Bradford had left.

"Now, we'll just stand here and—Bradford? What are you doing?" Phyllida frowned.

He'd gone off at a slightly faster pace, and it became clear he was intending to speak to Crestworthy and Avonlea. She suppressed a sigh and ignored the way Elton edged closer to her as they walked. If he tried to take up her hand as he'd seen Bradford do, she was going to box his ears.

"Mrs. Bright," said Mr. Crestworthy as she approached. He did not sound particularly pleased to see her. "Good evening."

"Good evening. And to you too, Professor Avonlea." She smiled. "How did the card game finish up?"

"I was down," grumbled Avonlea. "Stiller always deals me terrible cards. I must be on my way now. Have things to attend to at home. My bees, you know." He rushed off without another word.

"Sore loser," muttered Crestworthy. "You were saying you wanted to see my motorcar?" This was directed at Bradford, and Phyllida's eyes widened. How dare he give away the game!

Bradford ignored her glare. "Mr. Mallowan mentioned he was interested in a new automobile, and I recalled that you have a Bentley—an eight-litre, is it? And thought you might let me take a look. Under the hood, perhaps the chassis as well."

"Right, then, but I have only a minute. I've—er—got a meet-up," said Mr. Crestworthy.

Realizing Bradford's game, Phyllida followed the two men over to the sleek Bentley. It was a fine-looking motorcar to be sure.

Bradford wasted no time in looking under the chassis, and he somehow encouraged Mr. Crestworthy to turn on the engine and the headlights.

Phyllida was quite delighted to see that one of them was fainter than the other.

CHAPTER 12

"It's not at all uncommon for one headlight to be dimmer than the other," Bradford informed Phyllida. "They wear out at different rates, you see, or one could be newer than the other."

They had just climbed into the Daimler—Phyllida in front, Elton in the back, having had his driving role usurped by Bradford.

"It's also a simple problem to fix," Bradford went on. "By simply replacing the bulb. But you'll be pleased to know, Mrs. Bright, that when I inspected the underside of the Bentley, I did find some grass and mud caught up in there."

"What about Mr. Heathers's motor?" Phyllida said.

"Mr. Heathers walked home," said Elton, his voice from the back perhaps a trifle louder than it needed to be. "He lives only a short walk from the pub."

"Do you happen to know what sort of motorcar he has?" Phyllida asked.

"No, Mrs. Bright, but I'm certain I can find out for you."

"Right then. That would be helpful. Nonetheless, it seems that the clue of the dimmer headlight might not be as conclusive as I'd hoped," Phyllida said.

"Perhaps you could get more information from your witness. Such as how much dimmer the light was, and confirm that it was the left headlamp and not the right," Bradford said in a mild voice. "And he or she might recall some detail they hadn't done previously. Also, it would be instructive to learn whether any sort of unusual bruising was found on Miss Ethel's body."

"Unusual bruising? Such as from a tire tread?"

"As gruesome as it might sound, the front of a motorcar can leave an imprint—the headlamps perhaps or even decorative ornaments. That was another reason I wanted to see Crestworthy's Bentley."

Phyllida realized she was sulking a bit over his easy tone. The man was being entirely too reasonable. Far too helpful and logical. Much too accepting of her investigating this murder, when usually he contented himself by making snide comments and gently poking at her.

The real problem, she had to admit, was that her insides were in a bit of a flutter. It was exceedingly annoying. What would happen when they returned to Mallowan Hall? Would she simply go into the house (as she certainly *should* do), or would she . . . not?

As they trundled along the narrow, winding road in a much less harrowing ride than on the way into the village, she lapsed into silence, consumed by these thoughts, and feeling uncharacteristically indecisive about her actions once they arrived home. She was furious with herself for this internal dithering. For heaven's sake, she was a grown woman who'd faced down any number of threats and discomfiting situations over the years.

It was due to this distraction that she didn't hear the motorcar coming up from behind until it was nearly upon them.

Bradford was aware, however, and he cursed as he spun the steering wheel sharply to the side. The Daimler leaped and twisted, bounding wildly off the road, spurting dirt and stone as the other vehicle roared past.

Phyllida saw the shadowy shapes of trees weave and slide in her vision as she was tossed to the side, crashing into Bradford's shoulder then being thrown against the door next to her. The Daimler shuddered to a bumpy halt as the shadowy shape of a motorcar—no taillights—disappeared hastily into the distance.

"Blimey, Phyllida, are you all right?" said Bradford, immediately feeling for her. His voice was low and tense as he found her arm and curled his fingers around it and gently tugged. "*Phyllida.*"

"Yes, yes, I'm all right," she replied, experimentally touching the part of her forehead that had banged into his shoulder. That side hurt more than the bump into the window, which was not surprising as sometimes Bradford could be as implacable as stone.

"Elton?" Bradford said, turning in his seat even as he continued to hold Phyllida's arm, as if afraid she'd evaporate. "Elton, are you all right?"

"Oi, yes," came a voice from the back seat. "Mrs. Bright? Are you hurt?" There was fumbling in the back and the door opened. Elton all but tumbled out of the motorcar into the tall grasses where they'd come to a halt, and was yanking on the door next to Phyllida.

"I'm *fine*," she said crossly, as the thudding in her temple became a pounding and the passenger side door opened. She was also feeling a little woozy from the spinning and bumping about, and she was absolutely *not* going to be sick in front of either of these two men. "I should like to know who the bloody hell that driver thought they were, driving like a mad person on these roads at night!" She was pleased that her voice came out rather steadily.

"Do you want to get out for a moment, Mrs. Bright?" Elton said, holding out a hand to assist her to climb from the motor.

"N-no, I . . . well, yes, I think perhaps I . . . I might want to . . ." She swallowed hard as the nausea surged alarmingly in her belly. Goodness. She hadn't been this shaken up or wobbly since someone had tried to run her down with Winnie Pankhurst's motorcar.

Bradford released her arm and Elton helped her out of the motor. She stood unsteadily, but for some reason, the wooziness evaporated once she was upright.

Elton gave a cry when he caught sight of her face. "Oh, Mrs. Bright, you're bleeding!" he said, fishing in his pocket, presumably for a handkerchief.

"As are you," she replied, giving him a visual once-over. "I should apply that to the cut on my own forehead, Elton, if I were you. I have my own handkerchief, thank you." She extracted it from her pocket, and turned to discover that Bradford had also alighted from the Daimler. He was inspecting the exterior of the vehicle.

"To answer your question, Mrs. Bright," said Bradford, "I expect it was a murderer driving that motorcar."

"A murderer, you say," she said crisply, going to stand next to him as she dabbed at the blood from a small cut at her temple. Bradford's hair was even more disheveled than usual, but he seemed uninjured. Likely he'd been able to anticipate the impact of the side-swiping motor and brace himself from being tossed about as she had been.

There really ought to be some sort of personal restraints installed in a motor vehicle for situations like that.

"Aye. I suspect you've done it again, Mrs. Bright," Bradford said as he rose from his examination. His eyes flickered over the spot where she held the handkerchief, then came to rest intently on hers. It was far too dark to read the emotion in them, but she could feel the weight of his gaze.

"And what is that?"

"You've upset a killer, and they've attempted to silence you," he replied.

"That's rather a leap, don't you think," she said, even as she thought to herself, *Ah, here's the Bradford I know, with his crusty, snide comments about my investigations.* "You know how reckless some drivers can be."

"That automobile did not slow down and it did not swerve or even attempt to overtake us with care. In fact, it accelerated as it came up behind us. Most importantly, its headlamps were off. It didn't want to be seen until it was too late.

"The sideswiping was deliberate, Phyllida, and you and I both know why. You've upset someone, as you always do when you start snooping around and poking your nose into dangerous matters."

Phyllida did not care for the tone of his voice. She cared even less for the sense his words made.

"If you are correct, then that merely means I've come close enough to the truth to upset someone," she retorted, stuffing the handkerchief back into her pocket. "Which means they are worried they shall be exposed. Now, let us examine the situation and see what information we can glean from this incident."

Bradford made a sound that was a cross between a growl and a keen of frustration. Really, he could learn to control his emotions better.

"What did you notice about the vehicle?" she asked.

"Aside from the fact that it was about to ram into the rear bumper of Mr. Max's motorcar? As it forced us off the road?" Bradford still sounded growly. "If we had been near a stone fence or a tree, we could have been pushed into it and killed."

"Bradford. You're not being helpful."

"It was dark," Elton said. Phyllida had almost forgotten he was present. "The motorcar I mean. Its color. And it was the size of a sedan. Not low to the ground, I mean to say."

"That's not much help at all, is it," Phyllida said in frustration.

"I'm quite certain that was the point," Bradford retorted.

She gritted her teeth. "Whoever it was came from the direction of the village. What about tire markings? They might have left marks on the road."

This time the noise Bradford made was more positive; even agreeable. "There's a torch in the glovebox."

Phyllida had a moment of renewed irritation that she'd forgotten her pocketbook with its compact, portable light in it, but, since it didn't matter in this case, she pushed it aside.

The beam from the torch illuminated the road, which was constructed of tar-covered gravel, random cobblestones, and even some interspersed pieces of wood. Of course, that surface wasn't malleable enough for a tire to leave an imprint, but Phyllida hoped there might be some tracks on the edge of the road. After all, the side-swiping motorcar hadn't actually hit them, so it must have gone off the road itself.

Bradford seemed to have the same thought, for he trained the light along the edge of the road.

"There," Phyllida said.

He paused the beam at the spot where she pointed. There was

a bit of dirt exposed where grass wasn't growing, and the short length of a tire imprint showed. It appeared fresh.

She and Bradford, along with Elton, peered down at it for a long moment. Phyllida was attempting to memorize what it looked like and assumed her companions were doing the same.

After a few moments and further exploration, it seemed clear that there weren't any other tracks or markings. As they turned to climb back into the Daimler, it occurred to Phyllida to wonder whether the motorcar was even drivable after such a close call.

To her relief Bradford started the engine with no problem and soon they were continuing their route back to Mallowan Hall.

When the Daimler came to a halt outside the garage, Phyllida became aware of warring sensations of apprehension and anticipation. She dismissed both of these feelings with mental abruptness; for heaven's sake, she was simply arriving home as she had done so many times in the past. She should not allow tonight's arrival to be such cause for consternation and confusion.

Elton was opening the door for her almost before Bradford had turned off the engine. Phyllida climbed out and intended to head into the house just as she normally would do—with Elton on her heels, most assuredly—before Bradford could find a reason to delay her.

At least this time he didn't have Myrtle to use as a tool.

But to her surprise, he merely said, "Good night, Mrs. Bright. Elton."

Phyllida closed her mouth and marched into the house without a backward glance. Apparently the man found no reason to want to speak privately to her, which was absolutely fine with her.

"Mrs. Bright," said Elton as she entered the house. "Are you certain you're not hurt? That cut looks a bad one."

"I'm quite fine," she replied, forcing herself to sound firm but unaffected. "You might wish to cut a chunk of ice from the block to put on your bump, however. You're developing quite a handsome bruise. Wrap it in a towel."

"Yes, ma'am," he said, sounding pleased. Perhaps it was the word "handsome" that had delighted him.

Phyllida hurried off before the young man could attempt to engage her further. She had plenty of things to think about and preferred to conduct such contemplation in the privacy of her apartment.

Stilton and Rye were appalled by the state of her bloodstained clothing and the cut on her forehead. Both gave her wide-eyed looks of surprise and assessment. Rye even bestirred himself to come close enough to sniff at her experimentally, and, in doing so, allowed her to pat him on the head. Phyllida responded to their concern by providing them each with one of the tiny catnip treats Mrs. Puffley baked specially for them as a reward for their sympathy, then began to divest herself of her stained garments.

She donned her favorite robe, a Chinese-style dressing gown of black silk embroidered with red and white lotus blossoms. She was just finished washing her face—somehow she had acquired blood streaks on her cheek and one on her chin; she could only imagine what Fred Stiller had thought of that—when she heard a quiet tapping on the window of her bedchamber.

She forced herself to turn slowly. She had half expected something of this nature to occur, for she'd known that Bradford wouldn't retire for the night without further admonishing her over the events of the evening.

She went to the window and slid it up and open. A warm summer breeze wafted into the room and Bradford rested his elbows on the sill. Due to the position of the window and the ground below, the bottom of the opening was just below his chest.

"Mine or yours?" he asked quietly, and the sly, sultry smile he wore sent a pleasant little shiver through her belly.

She hesitated only a moment, giving him her own version of the same smile. "Your place would be more prudent, but mine would be far more comfortable."

"Prudence it is, my dear," he said, and before she quite realized what he was about, he offered his hand.

She allowed him to help her through the window—likely a provocative sight, with her having to climb over the sill whilst wearing the silky, shifting robe—unable to keep from grinning. "I haven't sneaked out of a window to meet a man in . . . well, *quite* some time," she murmured as he helped ease her to the ground.

He took his time doing so, and his hands went to several locations that weren't strictly necessary in order to assist her, but she didn't mind one bit.

"I suppose I should be glad to hear it," he said.

She looked around and felt confident that no one could see or hear them. Dobble's bedroom window was next to hers. It was closed and the room beyond was pitch dark. The maids were asleep four floors above in the attic, so they couldn't see anything, and the male servants were on the other side of the house in their sleeping quarters on the lower level. The near wall of the downstairs had no windows, for the house was built into the side of a small incline.

"I never thought how convenient my bedroom window was for having an assignation," she commented as they started toward the garage.

"I certainly did," he replied.

She glanced at him, but he was concentrating on navigating them to the garage whilst staying in the shadows, just in case someone had ventured out of their beds to use the outhouse. But they saw and heard no one.

"I must say, it took you quite long enough," she said quietly as he opened the side door to the garage.

The large, dark space which had once been a stable yawned in front of them, empty of all motor vehicles except the Daimler. The only illumination was a small electric light near the far left corner, where there was a hall leading to his apartment.

"I wanted to give you enough time to extricate yourself from Elton." She could hear the grin in his voice. "I didn't realize I'd find you in such dishabille, Mrs. Bright. I wonder what I would have found had I waited a bit longer before broaching the window."

"You'd have found me in bed, fast asleep," she replied a bit tartly. "I hadn't needed *that* much time to extricate myself from Elton, as you put it."

"Even so, surely you would have heard me tapping the window

over the sounds of your snoring," he said, his large hand sliding down the back of her dressing robe.

"I don't snore," she retorted.

"I should rather like to find that out for myself," he replied in a low, deep voice very close to her ear.

His hand felt good, sliding over the sensual material, up and down her spine . . . and lower . . . as she leaned against him. He smelled lightly of cigar and whisky, and his lips were doing delightful things along the side of her throat. But after a moment, she reluctantly stepped away from temptation. They did have important matters to discuss.

"Bradford, I sincerely thank you for your quick reactions and excellent driving skills," she said, starting to make her way through the garage toward the light. He followed. "We all could have been injured much worse than we were."

"Are you truly not hurt? I wasn't about to fight through Elton's mollycoddling to find out for myself."

"Just a bruise where I crashed into your shoulder. It's hard as a rock, Bradford, really," she said, then stopped to look up at him. "You're not hurt?"

"Not at all," he replied. "Except where your equally hard head bumped me." He rubbed his shoulder.

"Very well," she said, walking again. "Now that we have that out of the way, what did you learn during the card game?"

Phyllida had had only one previous occasion to venture into Bradford's private space in the garage, and that was during a thunderstorm when Agatha had insisted she "check on" Bradford. The apartment consisted of a small bedroom with a tiny sitting area that also had a compact sink as well as a small gas burner. There was a little desk at which, presumably, he managed any vehicle-related correspondence.

"Not as much as one would hope," he said, making no comment about the fact that she was leading the way. He went on to recount in great detail the conversation that had occurred during the card game. By the time he was finished, Phyllida felt as if she had actually been there herself. "I'm afraid I didn't learn anything very helpful, Mrs. Bright. Perhaps you should have been there after all."

He pulled a chain and a small overhead light came on, and there was his small living space. The bed was made (inexpertly, but at least the coverings and pillow were in place) and a pair of boots sat on the floor next to a small wardrobe, which was closed. A jacket hung from a peg on the wall, with a clean shirt moored next to it. The rug on the floor was swept and neatly aligned, and the curtains had been drawn. There was a small mirror atop a dresser, along with a comb, shaving equipment, and small pots of grooming products.

So he *did* know how to use hair pomade.

The compact desk with its chair was pushed up next to the single window in the room. A small lamp sat on another table next to the bed and he reached to turn it on.

Phyllida glanced at the bed and decided it was best to take a seat in the desk chair . . . at least for now. They had things to discuss.

"Hmm. Yes. Well, I've come to the conclusion that the more important thing is to focus my attention on the deaths that could be the murder Miss Ethel witnessed. Other than trying to identify the motorcar that ran her over, it's rather difficult to determine who from the dinner party might have doubled back to do the deed.

"According to Genevra, Ethel told her she'd seen the murder late last summer. Her bicycle was in the shop, so she was walking about quite a bit. Unfortunately, she didn't have any other details, for, as is characteristic of her, Genevra didn't really listen to what her sister told her."

"And so you have some candidates for the witnessed murder, Mrs. Bright?"

Bradford stripped off his coat and hung it over the back of a chair. Beneath he was wearing a shirt, and he pushed aside his suspenders to leave them dangling from his trousers. The shirt was partly unbuttoned and she could see the curve of an undershirt beneath it, along with a thatch of dark hair. This sight left

Phyllida momentarily distracted and a bit warm, but she quickly recovered.

"Indeed. There are three sudden deaths that I've been made aware of. Ralph Greenhouse, who died from a bee sting whilst in his motor. Ellie Mayhew, who drove into a stone wall—but I'm inclined to disregard that incident as a potential murder, based on Fred Stiller's assessment."

"Even after tonight's incident?" Bradford asked. "The same sort of tactic could have been used to induce her to drive into a wall."

"That is quite true," Phyllida replied, "and she surely wasn't as experienced a driver as you. However, I don't see how an event like that could have been witnessed and only realized later to be a murder. Remember, we are investigating something Miss Ethel saw. I'm certain if she saw Ellie Mayhew drive into a stone wall after being overtaken by another motorcar, she would have reported it immediately—and been there to assist Miss Mayhew, and we would have known about it. Everyone would have known about it."

"I cannot fault that logic, Mrs. Bright, but I wanted to point out the similarity to tonight's events," he replied smoothly. His eyes were dark and lit with a bit of humor from where he sprawled on the bed.

"Quite so, and well done, Bradford. It's instructive to review all possibilities. Now, if I may proceed with the third death of which I've been made aware: Mr. Arthur Grainger, who was found dead in his bed. He'd been healthy otherwise and was only fifty-five.

"Beyond those three untimely deaths, there is the fact that a young man named Clement Dowdy—a delivery man—seems to have disappeared. Perhaps run off to London. Perhaps not.

"All of these occurrences happened during the time period in question—sometime between July and September. It would be helpful to speak with Fred Stiller again to find out when Ethel Blastwick's bicycle was in for repairs. I should have asked him tonight," she said, quite exasperated with herself.

Bradford grunted thoughtfully from where he'd settled on the bed. He was partially reclined, leaning against the wall where the pillow was located, his legs extended long in front of him. "And if Miss Ethel did see something—"

"*If?*"

He shrugged. "One must be suspicious about all things in a murder investigation. People lie all the time for many reasons. What if Genevra is lying and it really *was* she—not her sister—who saw the murder?"

Phyllida glowered—she really disliked it when he interrupted her train of thought *and* when he made sense; and besides, *who* was the investigator here?—then flapped a hand at him. "I find that highly unlikely, mainly due to Genevra's nature. She would never have been able to keep such a thing a secret. Especially for so long, if it occurred last summer."

"I won't argue with that," he said agreeably. "I certainly got the impression from Avonlea and Crestworthy that Miss Genevra is the sort of person who could not keep a secret and who prefers to dominate a conversation. She might only have lied about her sister seeing the death once she realized that she would be the target for the killer."

"I suppose that is possible," Phyllida replied reluctantly. "I shall have to interrogate her further. And her father as well. In the meantime, let us further examine these deaths to determine whether any of them could have been a murder."

"In order for Ethel Blastwick to have seen a homicide, she would have had to have been present when it happened," Bradford said, quite unnecessarily, for Phyllida had already come to that conclusion. "Did she have access to Mr. Grainger's bedroom, for example? That seems unlikely."

"I was merely being thorough, Bradford," Phyllida told him. "Just as you were a moment ago. Mr. Grainger's death was likely not the murder Ethel witnessed, whether it was a murder or not. I shall have to do further investigation, but I cannot see how Ethel would have been in his bedroom—or even inside the house—to witness whatever might have happened.

"Even if it was poison, which is the obvious culprit for a healthy person being found unexpectedly dead, she would have had to have been in the house at the time—'she' being either one of the sisters," she added with emphasis. "I shall confirm with Dr. Blastwick and the housekeeper, as well as Genevra, whether they knew the Graingers or socialized with them."

Bradford made a noise that sounded a bit skeptical, but otherwise remained silent.

"Now, as for Ralph Greenhouse. His death is my prime suspect for the event witnessed by whichever Miss Blastwick it was. If someone had put bees into Mr. Greenhouse's motorcar and he drove off with them in the vehicle with him, he'd only need to be stung once or twice in order to have that fatal reaction. It wouldn't be difficult to put a jar or some other container of the insect in the motor, and perhaps that is what Ethel saw. Someone holding a very innocent looking jar of bees and then later when she learns what happened to Mr. Greenhouse, she is suspicious."

"Right, then," he said. "And as Miss Ethel was quite an outdoorsy type, she might have been out walking and saw someone capturing the bees."

"Yes," Phyllida said, rising from where she'd been sitting. "That could very easily have happened." She began to pace, the silk of her robe fluttering around her ankles. "And whom do we know who keeps bees? Wilfred Avonlea."

"Aye, that is quite true, Mrs. Bright, but as you are aware, Avonlea rode his bicycle to the Rollingbrokes' last night. He doesn't have a motorcar."

"Perhaps he borrowed one," Phyllida said rashly. "But I admit, it is unlikely he is the one who ran over Miss Ethel. Someone else could have collected bees to insert into Mr. Greenhouse's motorcar."

"Aye."

"Even Mr. Varney himself," Phyllida went on. "I must confirm the dates he made his house calls to Mrs. Greenhouse and compare them to the date of Mr. Greenhouse's death and see whether anything matches up. If Mr. Varney came to the house on the same day Mr. Greenhouse died, he could very well have put the jar of bees into the motorcar at that time."

"Right."

Phyllida was still pacing. "There was something else, however. Something else tickling the back of my mind. Something someone else said about... what *was* it now... condolences or a service or something..." She frowned as she spun to make her way back. "It might not be relevant, but the word *condolence* seems to stick in my mind... and condolence means a death has occurred..."

As she walked past, Bradford reached out and snatched her hand, easing her to a halt. "Perhaps if you cleared your mind for a bit, it might come to you."

She looked down at him, at the smirk he wore, and the question—and promise—in his dark eyes.

"I truly did miss you, Bradford," she said.

"I know you did," he replied, and gently tugged at her hand.

She allowed herself to be eased onto the bed in a slithery pool of silk. "I wasn't certain how—or whether, I mean to say—I was going to feel, when you returned..."

"And...?"

"I believe I'm going to prefer being here than scarpering about in a garden, hiding from windows," she replied.

"Excellent decision, my very prudent Mrs. Bright."

CHAPTER 13

THE NEXT MORNING, PHYLLIDA DISCOVERED SHE WAS IN A PARTICUlarly fine mood. There were certain advantages to having access to a private apartment rather than a garden bench, especially when that private apartment was lacking its unruly canine.

Phyllida had a busy morning planned. As Bradford had suggested, her mind *was* clearer now, and the rest of her felt quite pleasant and relaxed.

She had promised to visit John's surgery, and she also had decided it was time to call on Myrna Crestworthy. She'd finally remembered from whence the word "condolence" had stuck in her mind—Mr. Crestworthy's secretary had drowned only a week or so back in the swollen river, a fact which Phyllida had belatedly put together from Vera Rollingbroke's comment about offering condolences to the woman and the card-game conversation Bradford had recounted last night.

She was aware that the death of Rutherford Crestworthy's secretary was too recent to be the murder Ethel Blastwick had witnessed, but offering her—or, rather, Mrs. Christie's—condolences was the perfect excuse to call on Myrna Crestworthy. She knew Agatha would approve of the stratagem.

In addition, Phyllida felt it necessary to visit Vera Rollingbroke once more. She was still uncomfortably aware that mud and grass had been found up beneath the undersides of Sir Rolly's Bentley the morning after Ethel's death. That, along with the fact that she was certain the motor had been moved—along with Vera's and Sir Rolly's own admission they had been in bed together all the morning after, so he couldn't have driven it then. Much as she disliked the thought, Phyllida didn't feel as if she could remove Sir Rolly from her list of suspects without further investigation.

She was just finishing her morning tea and toast when the telephone rang.

"Mallowan Hall, Mrs. Bright speaking," she said crisply.

"Phyllida, dear, it's me," trilled Agatha from over the telephone line. "I just rang to find out if you've caught a killer yet, and to report back with my Hastings-like investigations for you."

"I'm so pleased you made it to the city, Mrs. Agatha," Phyllida said, using the more formal address in case Dobble was lurking (which he probably was). "Did the drive give you plenty of time to think about Poirot?"

"Indeed it did. I do believe I have him and the situation well in hand. And Max was delighted to see me unexpectedly. Now, I do have things to tell you."

"Already? Heavens, you've worked fast," Phyllida said.

"Well, as I told you, people do love to talk to a murder writer. And they want to be helpful. Anyhow, it wasn't very difficult at all. It seems that this Clement Dowdy is indeed back here in London, in Smithfield, having been incorporated into the family business of butchering. So he's certainly not your murder."

"Indeed. Thank you. That is quite helpful and certainly tends to narrow things down a bit." Phyllida went on to bring her up to date on everything except for the near motorcar accident last night. She decided to leave that for Bradford to discuss with Mr. Max; she wasn't certain whether there was any exterior damage to the Daimler or not. Aside from that, she didn't want to worry Agatha.

Then they caught up on a few household items, and Phyllida secured her employer's agreement that it would be most appropriate for her to drop off a basket of baked goods to the Crestworthy home as an offer of condolence over their loss, then rang off. When Phyllida turned from replacing the telephone, she discovered Mr. Dobble standing there with a frown.

"Good morning, Mr. Dobble," she said brightly. "I do hope you slept well last night."

His eyes narrowed. "I might have done if I hadn't heard all manner of strange noises outside the window last night."

Phyllida could not quite control the flush that raced up her throat. "Indeed? Well, I must say that I didn't hear a thing and slept quite soundly." *Once I got into my own bed.* "Did you pack up your little—or perhaps it is rather big and ungainly—secret yet? I'm certain Bradford will drive the crate over to the vicar's house for you. It would be rather difficult for you to manage on your bicycle."

Now it was the butler's moment to turn red. "I have no idea what you are going on about, Mrs. Bright. I suppose that's to be expected with all of the gallivanting you've been doing at all hours of the night; your mind has gone to pieces. If Mrs. Agatha knew what you were about—"

"Mrs. Agatha is quite aware of all of my gallivanting," Phyllida replied flatly. "Might I remind you that a woman was killed in a most horrible fashion and I am doing my best to bring the culprit to justice, whilst I see only complaining and crabbing from the likes of you, Mr. Dobble. And locking oneself away in one's pantry with one's little amusement is hardly conducive to managing one's staff, is it?"

Mr. Dobble was saved from having to reply by the ringing of the telephone. He leapt for the instrument despite the fact that Phyllida was within easy of reach of it.

She rolled her eyes and turned away once it was clear the call was nothing to which she needed to attend.

Not for the first time did she wish Mr. Dobble had decided to stay in London.

A short time later, she found Bradford waiting in the yard for her with the Daimler. The motorcar seemed unharmed from last night's attack.

"A ride into the village, Mrs. Bright?" he said, doffing his cap with an exaggerated flourish and a bow.

She didn't bother to comment on how he'd known to be waiting; she merely replied, "I suppose you're driving in to collect

Myrtle. Yes, I would appreciate a ride. I have to visit Dr. Bhatt this morning."

If anyone was observing, they would see or hear nothing out of the ordinary between the chauffeur and the housekeeper. Only Phyllida heard his low, "You're looking exceedingly well-rested this morning, my ever-so-prudent Mrs. Bright," before he closed the passenger side door behind her.

"Oh, Mrs. Bright! Mrs. Bright!" Opal came tearing out of the house, a little hat clutched in her hand. "Only, could I please ride with you into the village? Mrs. Puffley has given me permission to visit me mam whilst Mr. Bradford is collecting Myrtle. That way I can hold her safely in me lap on the way home," she added, beaming up at the driver.

"Aye, and that's a fine and welcome idea, Opal," replied Bradford, whisking open one of the rear doors. "Myrtle will be happy not to be jostled about on her ride home."

Phyllida smiled at Opal and agreed that it was very nice of Mrs. Puffley to allow her to be gone for a short time. With the young maid in the motorcar, she wouldn't be able to speak freely with Bradford . . . but they'd done quite a bit of free speaking—among other things—last night.

She left Opal and Bradford to their tasks, with the plan to ring back at Mallowan Hall if she needed a ride back. She didn't mind walking on such a fine day if there was no other option.

Dr. Bhatt had a well-appointed office and surgery at one end of the main street that wound through town, following the river.

"Good morning, Phyllida," he said when she came in. "You look particularly well this morning. Would you like some tea while we speak? I brought a special blend back with me from India. It's particularly good with a bit of milk and honey."

She could smell the unusual cinnamony, spicy scent and was intrigued. She accepted and they were soon seated in his office, where she immediately launched into her questions.

"Were you able to think of any unexpected or sudden deaths that happened last summer? I'm aware of Ralph Greenhouse and Ellie Mayhew, as well as Arthur Grainger. Are there any others?"

He lifted his thick, dark brows and smiled beneath his glorious mustache. "My, you have been busy. Yes, those were the three I had thought of."

"Was there anything strange about Ellie Mayhew's death? I understand she drove into a stone wall. I mean to say, I assume you were called to the scene, being the only physician in the area."

"Yes, yes, of course," he replied. If he was put off by her directness he didn't show it. "And, no, there was nothing strange. She drove into a stone wall. Likely died almost immediately; she was thrown very hard into the windshield. Conjecture is that she swerved to avoid something—an animal most likely."

Phyllida was nodding. "Yes, that was my assessment too. But one must be thorough. And Arthur Grainger? Were you attending him as well?"

"He was a patient of mine, yes, and I was treating him for a mild cardiac arrhythmia. It was not serious, and otherwise, he was healthy."

Phyllida sipped her tea. He'd added milk and some honey to it, and it was the most unusual tea she'd ever had. Aromatic and spicy with cinnamon and anise and other spices she couldn't identify. She found it quite delicious. "How do you think he died, then?"

He set his own teacup down, his long, dark fingers curled around the vessel. "I was unable to find a specific cause of death. It wasn't arsenic or cyanide or even nicotine—none of the easily available poisons you might be thinking of, Phyllida. He showed no evidence of being poisoned either. No trauma or other indications."

Phyllida's mind settled on a thought that had been wispy until crystallizing at this very moment. "What is the drug used by veterinarians—the one they employ to euthanize a bad horse or an old cow? Is that not also lethal to humans?"

John paused for a moment, tilting his head in a very Poirot-like manner. "An interesting thought," he replied slowly. "I've not heard of pentobarbitone—that's the name of it—used as a murder weapon but I suppose it would work in a high enough dose. It has lately become useful in human medicine for anesthetic purposes.

"But, as I said, I didn't see any sign of foul play. I believe Grainger simply died in his sleep, perhaps of an aneurysm or something of that nature. It does happen. There was nothing suspicious about his death, and," he added with a little twinkle in his eye, "although I thought about it quite stridently, I could not fathom a motive for anyone to want to do away with him. He had no money to squabble over. He had only a sister who lived with him and took care of the household. He rarely left the house or grounds; spending all of his time whittling wood in his shed when he wasn't working in his garden. They lived a simple life, he and his sister."

"Did the Graingers have any animals that might require a visit from a veterinarian?" Phyllida asked. "A dog, a cow, a horse?"

"I don't recall seeing any animals during my visit."

"What about Ethel and Genevra? Did either of them ever visit Mr. Grainger or his sister?"

"Not that I'm aware of. The Graingers are much older than the Blastwick sisters; there would be no reason for them to be socially engaged. But I suppose you could ask Mrs. Wallace—that's Grainger's sister. She's long widowed."

"Yes, I shall do that. I don't suppose you have the dates of these deaths?"

"Of course. I knew you would ask." He smiled and offered a piece of paper. On it, written in his painfully neat penmanship, were the dates:

> *Grainger—29 June*
> *Greenhouse—15 Aug*
> *Mayhew—26 Oct*

She *hmm*ed to herself. The only death that appeared during the time frame Genevra indicated was Ralph Greenhouse. But perhaps Genevra was wrong about the time frame. Phyllida needed to speak with Fred Stiller about when Ethel's bicycle had been in the shop.

"Thank you, John," she said, tucking the paper into her pocketbook. Then she paused and set it back on the table. She extracted the note she'd made yesterday about the dates Mr. Varney had made house calls to the Greenhouse residence.

One of them jumped out at her: *14 August.*
Very interesting.

Phyllida slipped the two papers into her handbag and took another sip of tea. "This *is* quite good, John. What sort of blend is it?"

"We call it *masala chai.* It's a type of Assam tea mixed with spices, most from my homeland. In India, it is often brewed with hot milk instead of water. Here, I simply add milk to it after I've already brewed it with water. I suppose that is due to the influence of you English," he said with a smile. "Always adding milk and sugar to your tea. Now, did you have any other questions I could answer?"

"I know there is to be a postmortem, but did you have occasion to look closely at Ethel Blastwick's body?" Phyllida asked after a moment of hesitation. It seemed rather crude and disrespectful to speak of examining the dead, naked body of a woman killed so brutally, but she knew it could be important. "What I should like to know is whether there was any sort of unusual bruising or marking on the front of her. We surmise she was struck from the front by the motorcar. Perhaps the grille or bumper left markings that could be helpful in identifying it."

John set his cup down slowly. His dark eyes danced. "You are reading my mind, Phyllida. I intended to tell you about the bruising. Sadly, I'm not certain Inspector Cork fully understands the importance of it. I can hardly account for it myself, but since I have been writing detective stories about a doctor who solves murders, I have become more interested in the postmortem aspect of the crime. The clues left on or in the body, so to speak.

"In fact, I made a rather long detour in order to stop in Paris on my return from India so that I could attend a lecture from Thomas Jackson, an American pathologist who has studied there under Alexandre Lacassagne, who was the—ah, forgive me, Phyllida. That is not what you asked me, is it?" He appeared slightly abashed. "I simply find it all so fascinating." His eyes gleamed with enthusiasm.

"Quite so. Am I to understand that this Dr. Jackson is an expert on postmortem examinations?"

"Indeed. He was trained by the man who is responsible for many of the advances in the science of it all, beginning over fifty years ago—this Alexandre Lacassagne, who died nearly a decade ago. Dr. Jackson currently works for La Sûreté—that is what they call Scotland Yard in Paris," he added, although Phyllida was already quite aware of what La Sûreté was. "There are so many things to be learned by minutely examining the body! I had no concept until after this lecture."

"Ah, the physical clues," Phyllida murmured with a smile. "The sort of thing Hastings would appreciate, no?"

John, who was almost as much an aficionado of Agatha's works as Phyllida was, grinned. "Precisely. And one must admit, there are times when the physical clues are just as important as the psychology of the crime, correct?"

"They certainly can help point one in the proper direction. Now, tell me about poor Ethel's bruising. Am I to gather it is important?"

"I believe so. You were correct in saying she was initially struck from the front, and there were two things I noticed about the marks left by what must have been that initial force. First, and most interesting, a small but deep penetration in the chest—something thrust through her left breast and into the pleural cavity."

"A puncture wound." Phyllida was suddenly quite fascinated with the idea of postmortem clues. Having been a nurse during the war, she had seen her fair share of injuries on bodies both alive and dead, and so was not the least bit squeamish. "Caused by something sharp on the motorcar itself, then."

"Precisely! I am certain it was something on the vehicle, for the rest of the impact left only bruising and mild lacerations. Some sort of ornamentation."

Phyllida set down her teacup a little carelessly, so fascinated by this idea. "Something on the vehicle that protrudes or was sharp enough to cause a puncture."

"I believe so," he replied, smiling back at her.

"A vehicle with a projecting sort of hood ornament—or at least a sharp one that would puncture a person," Phyllida said slowly as she tried to recall which of the suspects' vehicles sported hood ornaments that met that description. "But the bumper would strike first, would it not?" she said, thinking of the rounded front of nearly every motorcar she knew.

The bumper protruded further than the headlamps, and the headlamps were mounted well in front of the grille. Any hood ornament would be positioned on top of the hood, often acting as a radiator cap—which Phyllida knew from having to gingerly remove the running-lady ornament on a Crossley once when its radiator overheated.

"Yes, but the impact from the bumper would have been below her knees—which, in this case, left open fractures of her tibia and fibula—and thus would have sent her flying forward into the front of the motorcar where something jabbed into her. The other bit of interest was the bruising from the headlamp. There is only one circular bruise, suggesting the vehicle has only two headlamps instead of three or four. However, if there is a third headlamp, it would be too close to the bumper to have left a separate, explicit bruise, I believe."

"Why that is quite, quite important information," Phyllida said. The Bentley had two headlights, with a third, smaller one near the bumper. The Bugatti had four, but the top two were larger and the bottom two were small and recessed behind the bumper. "Thank you very much, John. I truly do appreciate it."

He set down his teacup and looked at her with sudden purpose in his expression. Phyllida tensed a little. "There is something else I wish to speak with you about."

She nodded. She suspected she knew what was coming, and she did not relish having to put him off—gently and firmly, of course. "Go on."

"We have been friends for a time, and, I believe, we have become quite close in this friendship. I enjoy your company immensely, Phyllida, and I am not certain how deep your feelings for me . . . might . . . go." He eyed her carefully.

She braced herself, keeping a steady, benign smile in place, but said nothing.

"And so I wanted to tell you myself, before anyone else heard about it and told you . . . I'm getting married."

Phyllida's teacup rattled slightly on its saucer. "Why, John, that's *wonderful!*" she said with sincere pleasure and a modicum of relief as she set down the cup. "I'm so very happy for you!"

"I thought . . . I'd hoped you'd feel that way," he replied. His gaze, which had been filled with hesitancy and question, became soft and warm.

"Is she someone from back home, then? From India?"

"Oh, no. Not at all," he said, smiling. "She's Miss Emily Hartparker from Wenville Heath. I met her when I was treating her elderly mother—who passed away shortly after—and . . . well, Phyllida, I must say, although I have great regard for you—truly *great* regard—I must admit I now believe in what is called love at first sight. It was the same for both of us, Emily and me." He had the sort of sappy expression that Elton often wore when he was looking at Phyllida.

"John, I could not be happier for you. Truly! I cannot wait to meet Miss Hartparker. I am certain we shall be great friends." She reached over and clasped his hand with hers, both relieved and immensely delighted about the situation. "She must be a lovely, kind, and intelligent woman to have captured your heart."

He flushed a little beneath his brown skin. "That is very kind of you to say. We intend to be married at her church in Wenville Heath within the next two months. She . . . traveled with me to India so she could meet my family." He appeared a little embarrassed by this admission. "We . . . well, the truth is, we actually were married in India, in my traditional Hindu faith. But we will be married here in the C.O.E. as well, and I hope you will attend."

"Of course I will attend," she replied. "I wouldn't miss it for anything. Please tell Miss Hartparker that if she needs any assistance with her planning or her move to Listleigh, I would be most pleased to help."

He heaved a sigh. "I'm so grateful for your acceptance of this . . .

in so many ways. Thank you, Phyllida." He lifted her hand to kiss the back of it. "You are a great friend. Now, I do hope you can find poor Ethel Blastwick's murderer."

"With all of this information you've given me, I am certain I can," Phyllida replied, rising. Her mind had already returned to reviewing the various motorcars that had been at Wilding Hall the night of the dinner party.

At least one of them had a hood ornament that would leave a puncture wound in a woman's chest.

CHAPTER 14

Myrna Crestworthy did not like the days when her staff had their day out. It made everything so much more difficult—such as getting meals, or when someone rang at the front door, which, to her dismay, had just happened. The door knocker had thudded quite loudly so she could not ignore it.

Certainly, the staff had left breakfast for her—toast, scones, tea, jams and jellies, soft-boiled eggs—but she much preferred a hot meal first thing in the morning. And with the maids gone, and Mrs. Dunbury off visiting her cousin of all things, and Mr. Tums off on *his* day out, that left Myrna to answer the door on her own.

She really ought to speak to Rutherford about adding a footman to the staff, and she wouldn't allow him to be off on the same days that the butler and maids were. Normally, she was out for her bridge luncheon on Fridays and so it didn't matter that they were all out, but bridge had been cancelled this week because Lorelei Prescott had gone unexpectedly to London.

She sighed. She supposed she had no choice but to see who was there. It wasn't even noon, for heaven's sake, and although it was early for callers, one had to answer the door, she supposed, even if they didn't want to.

She certainly hadn't expected it when that inspector with the ratty mustache arrived to inform them of Bentley Gillam's death. The policeman was still wet over the front of his clothing from them dragging the man out of the river! Imagine not changing one's clothing before going off to advise a person that their secretary had drowned!

Rutherford hadn't seemed to mind about the wet clothing when he got the news about his secretary, but Myrna thought it quite unpleasant that the man was dripping in her foyer. If they'd had a footman, he could have been mopping it all up!

She tsked and shook her head as the knocker thudded once more, then cast the massive wooden door a perturbed look. If only there was someone else who could open it. Cook was in the kitchen, but Myrna knew better than to call for her. That woman never left the kitchen but for her bed, and she had a mood about her anyway. Myrna didn't want to upset her, for they were hosting Sir Rolly and Vera for dinner tonight and she didn't quite trust that Cook would have the temperament to be on her best behavior if she bothered her to answer the door.

Myrna sighed. She was going to have to do for herself. *And*, depending who it was, she would have to offer tea and pour it as well.

Blast it. Why had Lorelei gone out of town and canceled bridge anyhow? If Myrna was at her card game, she wouldn't have to answer the door.

Rutherford had gone off to the office—if he'd been here, *he* could have been the one to answer the door and make excuses. And then he'd surely agree to hiring a footman. It wasn't as if they couldn't afford it. Father had left them loads, and the business was still doing gangbusters even in these economic times. It was hard to find good staff, and when a person did, they found the staff didn't want to work. Having days out and half days out and then *evenings* out seemed excessive.

Myrna grumbled to herself but now that the knocker had thudded for a third time, she knew she had no choice.

She opened the door to see someone she was not expecting in the least. "Oh, why, hello." She was momentarily shocked into speechlessness, then collected herself and greeted the visitor more appropriately.

"May I come in? I have something to speak with you about. It's rather important."

"Of course," Myrna said, thinking that she absolutely did not want anyone coming in right now and that she wished she had left to go somewhere before this person arrived.

She went to ring for tea as they settled in the parlor, but remembered too late that there was no one to bring it. She decided then and there that never again would Friday be a day out for the butler *and* the housemaids when her luncheon was cancelled. Especially when her housekeeper was off visiting a cousin—even if the cousin *was* dying!

And besides, Mary was probably at Heathers's sweet shop, mooning over the Heathers boy like she always was. She could miss a Friday one week, couldn't she? And so could Annie, come to think of it.

"One moment whilst I get a tray and teacups from the dining room," Myrna said when she realized her visitor was waiting patiently for the tea she'd stupidly offered. She was feeling very out of sorts over the situation. Especially with this person who'd arrived. She hardly knew them! Why would they be calling? The last time she'd seen them had been at Wilding Hall for Vera's little dinner party. *That* had ended quite strangely, hadn't it? That ridiculous game.

"Of course. Take your time." The guest smiled warmly at her. "A cup of tea would be quite nice."

Myrna calmed her fluttery nerves—she wasn't certain why she was feeling so out of sorts this morning. Perhaps it was due to Rutherford. He'd been a bit strange lately, hadn't he. A bit distant and even short with her. He never used to be that way.

It could have been because of Mr. Gillam going and getting himself drowned. Rutherford had been taking on quite a bit of extra work with his secretary being gone. Myrna didn't know why he hadn't hired a new one yet. Surely he had *someone* in the wings who could take on the job?

Still feeling frazzled, she arranged cups and a teapot on the tray, then added a creamer and a small sugar dish. Goodness, it was heavier than she expected. She certainly wasn't used to doing for herself. She hoped she wouldn't drop it.

"Here we are," she said, setting the tray down with the sort of messy, clinking rattle she'd never permit with her housemaids. "The staff is all off today, of all things, so I have to pour for us."

"I know," replied her visitor. "That was why I'd come. I thought you would prefer to have this meeting in private, without anyone knowing."

"Oh." Myrna felt confused about this statement. What on earth could they mean? "Right, then, of course." She managed to pour for the guest without splashing more than a couple of drops, even though for some reason her hand was a bit shaky. And the teapot was far heavier than she'd realized—and awkward too.

When she at last had her own tea poured, she looked expectantly at her companion. "You said you had something to tell me?"

He gave her an odd sort of look and said, "Yes, I do."

CHAPTER 15

Phyllida left Dr. Bhatt's surgery with a slightly lighter step and made her way down the street in the opposite direction of Panson's Bakery. She didn't want to be caught up in a conversation with Mrs. Panson, but even more importantly, she was intent on finding Fred Stiller's bicycle shop. She also wanted to stop into Mr. Heathers's tobacco shop in hopes of discovering where his motorcar was parked so she could take a look at it. Now that she knew what to look for, she felt even more motivated.

She'd walked only a few paces when she heard someone calling her name.

"Mrs. Bright. Is that you, Mrs. Bright?"

She turned to see Mrs. Gilbody, the Blastwicks' housekeeper, coming toward her. She was dressed in a drab gray frock with a black hat and black gloves. Her face was drawn and her eyes dull with fatigue. She carried an empty market bag.

"Oh, Mrs. Bright. I don't suppose you have any news?" she asked, obviously restraining herself from reaching to clasp Phyllida's arm.

"Good morning, Mrs. Gilbody. Why don't we sit on the bench in the park, under the tree. We can speak there." As much as she preferred not to be delayed from her tasks, Phyllida simply couldn't brush off the woman. Instead, she took her arm and led her away.

Mrs. Gilbody was clearly in need of a listening ear and some compassion. Servants grieved just as their employers did when there was a loss in the household, but they were still expected to carry on with their duties as if nothing had happened. Phyllida knew how difficult that could be.

"Oh, thank you, Mrs. Bright, thank you. You're so kind. It's only that I haven't had anyone to talk to. This is the first time I've left the house since—since we found out.

"It's so frightfully sad and lonely out at the cottage. People have been calling, of course, but Miss Genevra and Dr. Blastwick haven't been up to seeing them, and so I've been sending them all away.

"I do miss Miss Ethel so much. She was such a warm and kind person." Mrs. Gilbody fished in her coat pocket, then withdrew a handkerchief. She dabbed at her eyes.

"Everything I've heard about Miss Ethel certainly indicates the same," Phyllida said soothingly as they took their places on the bench.

The seat overlooked a park too small for anything other than a brisk walk beneath a row of elms, or perhaps a small picnic beneath the largest of them. The river, which had been swollen from heavy rains a week ago, had settled back into its banks and flowed more gently just down an easy slope from their bench. It was a pretty and quiet view, and Phyllida hoped it would help to soothe Mrs. Gilbody.

"I'm so very sorry you're having such a difficult time," Phyllida said. "I can only imagine how difficult it must be to lose such a fine young woman so tragically."

"Yes, yes. I keep finding myself looking about for her, or expecting her to come in from traipsing about on the countryside, I do," Mrs. Gilbody said, blinking rapidly. "I even set her a place at dinner yesterday. The sweet lamb would often bring me wildflowers or a small cup of berries she picked during her rambles." She dabbed at her eyes again. "Have you learnt anything yet, Mrs. Bright? Do you know who's gone and done such a terrible thing?"

Phyllida had to shake her head in negation even as she closed a hand over Mrs. Gilbody's, squeezing it in sympathy. "My investigation is in progress, and please be assured I'm doing everything I can. I've several clues to chase up regarding the motorcar in question, along with some other leads. I promise that as soon as I know something, I shall tell you. How is Genevra getting on, the poor thing?"

Phyllida didn't know whether Mrs. Gilbody knew the truth about Ethel being the one to have seen the murder and not Genevra, and didn't think it was her place to mention it. At least, not at the moment. The poor woman didn't need anything further to upset her.

"She's been very quiet—for Miss Genevra, I mean to say, but she finally did sit outside for a short time yesterday. She thought she might go for a walk or even a drive today, she said. I think she is still quite in shock over it all."

"Quite understandable."

"I think she is especially upset because she and Miss Ethel had not been getting on well over the last few days," Mrs. Gilbody went on, clutching her handkerchief as she stared out over the river. "They never got on all that well anyhow, to be fair—and sad to say, two sisters you know—but I heard them arguing, I did, at least twice in the days before. Miss Ethel even raised her voice, and that was quite unusual. She rarely did, you see. She was such a quiet lamb.

"And I was that surprised, wasn't I, when Miss Ethel agreed to go to the dinner party at Wilding Hall. I thought for certain she would make her excuses. Miss Genevra must have convinced her. They did seem on better terms when they left."

"Do you know what they were arguing about?" Phyllida asked.

Mrs. Gilbody heaved a sigh. "I thought it was about a man, I did. But how it could be, I can't see. Miss Genevra, well, she has had her share of men over the years, and she did recently seem to be distracted like she gets when she's got a man on the line . . . but I don't see why she would be arguing with her sister about it all.

"Miss Ethel, why she was a shy thing, and much preferred her own company to anyone else's, and she didn't much care about what her sister did in that vein. Still, I . . . well, I suppose I got the impression there *was* a man at the center of it."

"What gave you that impression, can you recall?" Phyllida asked.

"It was something like . . . well, Mrs. Bright, I really do hate to tell tales, and I can't see how any of this would have to do with the person who—who killed Miss Ethel. I just don't see it. I don't see it at all."

Phyllida tamped back a bit of impatience. Clearly the woman was not a reader of detective novels, or she would know that a seemingly unimportant or unrelated bit of information could often be instrumental to solving a murder.

"Still, Mrs. Gilbody, it would be helpful if you could put your finger on why you thought a man might have something to do with the sisters' argument. Was it perhaps because the man involved was unsuitable? Because he was married or otherwise engaged?" she said, taking a logical stab at a reason, based on Genevra's sly provocative comments at the dinner party.

Mrs. Gilbody's expression turned to one of shock. "But . . . how could you have known that, Mrs. Bright?"

Phyllida merely looked at her, compassion and encouragement in her expression, and waited for more. It would be redundant to remind Mrs. Gilbody that she knew such a thing because she was an excellent investigator.

"Oh, you understand I couldn't say for certain, but I did get the impression that Miss Genevra . . . well, that she was perhaps . . . well, that she had become involved with a-a"—her voice dropped to a whisper—"*married* man, and that Miss Ethel did not approve. Of course she wouldn't approve. Who would? Anyhow, I only heard snatches of the conversation, of course, and I certainly wasn't about to eavesdrop . . . but sometimes one can't help but overhear, you see."

"Quite so," Phyllida said soothingly. "Our employers often completely forget about our presence, don't they?" It was, to paraphrase Ms. Austen, a truth universally acknowledged that any secret in a household was not at all a secret to its staff.

"Yes, yes, they do. And of course, I would never, *never* tell tales."

"Certainly not," Phyllida said firmly—whilst silently encouraging her to do just that.

"But . . . well, I did get the impression that Miss Genevra had got herself mixed up with an inappropriate man," Mrs. Gilbody said in a hushed voice. "And Miss Ethel was quite upset about it. But I don't know why she would be so upset, to be honest, Mrs. Bright. She and Miss Genevra were not that close and of course Miss Genevra is terribly shocked and sad over her sister's death, but it wasn't as if they were the type to share secrets and whatnot. They just didn't get on that well. They were so different."

"I see. That might even make it more difficult for Miss Genevra, having lost her sister," Phyllida said thoughtfully. "Losing someone with whom you might have been close with but weren't."

"I thought the same thing, I did," said Mrs. Gilbody, dabbing at her eyes again. "The poor dear. Now she'll never know what it's like to have a bosom sister."

"Did you hear anything in particular? Any phrases or parts of their exchange you might have discerned?" Phyllida asked.

Mrs. Gilbody looked away. "I'm not certain. It was difficult to make out what they were saying."

"But you heard something."

There was a long silence. Birds chirped. The river splashed and surged below. A motorcar rumbled along behind them. Phyllida remained silent.

At last, Mrs. Gilbody spoke. "Miss Ethel said something like, 'can't believe you would do such a thing,' and Miss Genevra said something I couldn't hear as first, but then she said, 'he'll never know.' And I heard Miss Ethel say, quite stridently, enough that I could clearly hear, 'it's all wrong, Genny! Only think how you would feel!'"

"Was there anything else?" Phyllida asked after another moment.

Mrs. Gilbody studied the hands twisting in her lap. "Later, another time, they were still arguing. That time I heard Miss Ethel say something like 'kill him.' And then, a bit later she went on, 'if you don't, I shall. I swear it, Genny.'" She looked up suddenly. "I didn't want to tell you because Miss Ethel, why she would never hurt anyone. I-I'm not even sure that's what I heard."

But sure enough to tell me now, Phyllida thought grimly. This was all interesting to be sure.

"This could all be quite helpful, Mrs. Gilbody," said Phyllida once she was quite certain the woman had told her all she could. "There is always the chance that the sisters were arguing about whether one ought to go to the police regarding the murder that was witnessed. 'If you don't, I shall' certainly sounds as if that could be the case."

"Oh. Why, I never thought of that. But . . . why would Miss Genevra's beau be involved?"

"It might have been two different arguments," Phyllida said.

"Why, I never thought of that."

"Do tell me, how is Dr. Blastwick? I'm sorry I didn't get to see him to express my condolences—and Mrs. Christie's as well. Do you think he would like a visit?" Phyllida asked.

"He is taking it very badly, Mrs. Bright. Very badly indeed. It was he who insisted on calling on you for help, you see, after I suggested it. He is beside himself, the poor man. To lose his wife only three years ago, and now a daughter—and so horribly." She shuddered. "I haven't told him the details about what happened—about what Miss Genevra said at the dinner party. At least he believes it was an accident.

"But he's hardly left his bedroom, poor man. Not even to go and putter around in his digging barrow, and he always did that every day, rain or shine. Hasn't eaten much either. And on top of it all, poor Jarvis has taken a turn. One wonders whether he knows what's happened."

It took Phyllida a moment to recall that Jarvis was the old, half-blind dog who'd been lying on the Blastwicks' hearth. "Does Mr. Varney visit often?" she asked.

"Mr. Varney? Why, no, never." Mrs. Gilbody seemed surprised and off-balanced by the question. "Although I do believe Miss Genevra has spoken to him about Jarvis. The poor thing has terrible arthritis. Can hardly make his way to the door anymore. Can't see or hear neither, to be fair. Spend a fair bit of time cleaning up after him, I do, poor thing."

"You say he's taken a turn?"

Mrs. Gilbody seemed surprised by this line of questioning, and even Phyllida wasn't certain why she was following it. It was just that a connection between Mr. Varney and the Blastwicks could somehow be important.

Or perhaps not important at all.

"Jarvis is nearly sixteen years old," Mrs. Gilbody said in a tone that seemed rather final to Phyllida.

And so she moved on to a different subject. "Do Dr. Blastwick or his daughters know the Graingers very well? Arthur Grainger?"

"Why . . . no, not at all. I've never heard any of them mention that family." Mrs. Gilbody frowned. "Are you speaking of the Arthur Grainger who died last year?"

Phyllida inclined her head.

"As I say, no, I don't think so." Now Mrs. Gilbody's air of listlessness suddenly became more interested. "You're looking for the murder, aren't you, Mrs. Bright? The one Miss Genevra saw, aren't you?"

So Genevra *hadn't* told Mrs. Gilbody the truth—and from the sound of it, she hadn't told her father either.

"It seems clear that *someone*—besides Ethel—was murdered," was all Phyllida said.

"That is quite smart thinking," said Mrs. Gilbody with an approval that had been lacking only a moment earlier. "That's why I suggested they telephone you straightaway to look into what happened. Not to rely on that blundering fool Cork. We know what you've done for us people in service, Mrs. Bright." She patted her arm. "I have great faith in you."

"I appreciate that very much, Mrs. Gilbody. Incidentally, do you recall when Miss Ethel had her bicycle in the shop last summer? It was around that time, it seems, that the—uh—death in question, the murder, was witnessed."

Mrs. Gilbody shook her head, dabbing at her eyes and, this time, her nose as well. "I'm sure I can't recall, Mrs. Bright. I don't pay any mind to that. Why, I'm sure I don't remember it at all."

"Very well," Phyllida said. She would just have to speak with

Fred Stiller about it. Hopefully he kept good records. "I do think I might stop by this afternoon and pay my respects to Dr. Blastwick and Genevra again." Phyllida rose. She had spent as much time as she could allow with the grieving housekeeper, and hoped that she'd given her a bit of relief.

"Thank you, Mrs. Bright. I do think I might just sit here for a while and think about it all. And perhaps say a little prayer of godspeed for dear Miss Ethel."

Phyllida patted her shoulder and wished her a good day, then continued on to her next task.

Heathers' Tobacconist was on the corner of the main road—which was called Ploughman's Close until it got into the village and then became known as Main Street, reverting back to Ploughman's Close as it left—and Dickleberry Way.

There were several customers inside, most of them young women of the late teen or early twenties variety. They were all clustered around the sweets counter, which was manned by a slender, very pretty blond chap who looked as if he were in his early twenties. He sported a slight flush and seemed a bit overwhelmed by the small mob of admirers who were ordering their sweets and sodas.

Phyllida was delighted to see the activity concentrated in that area, for it was Mr. Heathers with whom she wished to speak. He was standing by himself at the tobacco table appearing quite ignored. Not that he seemed to mind; he held a pencil and was poring over a large ledger.

The shop smelled faintly of spun sugar and more strongly of tobacco, with the latter aroma becoming more evident as Phyllida approached Mr. Heathers. It wasn't an unpleasant smell, to be sure, and there were a number of different varieties whose scents mingled together.

The counter was made of scarred wood that held decades of smoke scent, and behind Mr. Heathers was a small array of shelves. Glass jars, neatly labeled, offered a number of tobacco varieties. There were two small pottery bowls with what appeared to be samples of his wares sitting on the tabletop next to the ledger.

One of them smoldered quietly, its scent clearly meant to tantalize a potential customer. A small pile of cotton pouches took up another corner of the counter.

"Good morning, Mrs. Bright," Peter Heathers said, looking up when she approached. "Are you looking for a bit o' stuffing for your pipe?" he said, obviously in jest and with a kind smile.

"Not at all," she replied, just as pleasantly. "Although I must confess, the scent of a pipe always puts me in mind of my grandfather. He used to have one permanently in his hand, lit, too, of course—except when he was sleeping. But I daresay, he had had it smoldering on the bedside table nearby. However, I have never taken up the habit of smoking myself, pipe or cigarette."

Mr. Heathers chuckled. "Well, then, if you aren't here for tobacco, one can only suppose you're here on official business, Mrs. Bright. I rather thought I might have had the honor of you calling before now."

She was mildly taken aback by his forthrightness, but kept her smile in place. "Indeed. My apologies for leaving you hanging, Mr. Heathers." She eyed him closely. He didn't seem nervous or unsettled in the least. In fact, she detected the slightest light of humor in his eyes, for they crinkled deeply at the corners. "Since you have opened the subject, do you have anything of interest to tell me about the death of Ethel Blastwick?"

He shook his head. "Not really. A terrible tragedy. I understand it was *murder*—not an accident?"

"Yes. Someone deliberately rammed into her with their motorcar and then drove over her several times," she said, choosing a blunt description in the hopes of seeing what sort of reaction it would provoke.

He shuddered, his expression losing its pleasant smile. "How very monstrous." His eyes were sad. "Terrible way to die."

"Did you happen to see Ethel Blastwick as you were leaving Wilding Hall, Mr. Heathers? She apparently got out of the motorcar her sister was driving and decided to walk the rest of the way. Surely you would have passed her, since the Blastwick sisters were the first to leave after me."

"I saw Miss Ethel get out of the motorcar, for they stopped on the side in front of me. She seemed quite discomposed—at least, that was how it appeared to me, for they were a bit further up the road and it was dark, of course.

"When I drove past, I noticed that she was walking quite rapidly, as if angry. I—I didn't stop. Perhaps I should have done, but I wanted to get home.

"Mrs. Heathers is in Llandudno visiting her cousin, and Young Peter isn't always as good about closing up and putting out the lamps as he ought to be." He glanced over at his son, who still appeared harried and flushed as he filled the orders of the crowd of young women. "He gets distracted, you see."

"Quite," Phyllida replied. So that was why Mrs. Heathers hadn't been at the dinner party. She eyed Mr. Heathers. For a man several years over fifty, he wasn't unattractive. He still had a head of thick hair, though it was turning gray, and the crinkles at the corners of his green-brown eyes added to his handsomeness. Though his beard was grizzled, it was shaped nicely and fairly well trimmed. He was neither running to fat nor turning bony as men tended to do when they aged.

He was also married, and although the Heatherses weren't terribly wealthy, they were certainly comfortable with a successful shop.

Nonetheless, she didn't think he was the sort of man who would appeal to the gregarious and boisterous Genevra Blastwick. Sir Rolly or Mr. Crestworthy were more her type.

"And so you drove on past Ethel Blastwick?"

"Yes, of course. I motored home, parked behind the shop here—we live above, you see—and came in to find that Young Peter had once again left the lamp burning in the storeroom. That boy needs to get his head out of the clouds," Mr. Heathers said with an aggravated sidewise glance at the person in question. "All this attention ain't good for him. It's good for business, but not for him, if you see what I mean."

"Quite. May I look at your motorcar, Mr. Heathers?" Phyllida asked with a smile.

His eyebrows rose, then fell as comprehension dawned. "Do you think there's *blood* on my motor from running over a young woman? How distasteful," he said. "*Quite* a distasteful notion. But I've nothing to hide, Mrs. Bright, and even though you don't have any authority over me, you go right on out and take a gander at my motorcar." His gesture, which directed her into the back of the shop and presumably outside, was jerky.

"Thank you, Mr. Heathers, I shall." Phyllida paid his ire no mind. Murder investigators were never particularly well-liked by suspects. "Before I do that, is there anything else unusual you noticed about either Miss Blastwick, or anyone else for that matter, on the night of the dinner party?"

"Yes," he said. His lips had clamped together firmly now that he'd become offended. "But I don't feel as if I ought to say it after all, after you made all sorts of accusations."

"Mr. Heathers," she said in the same tone she used when calming the ruffled feathers of a housemaid. "I merely wish to eliminate you from suspicion—as I've done a number of others. It's a logical process, you see—not so very different from the marking up and adding and subtracting from your ledger there. One must go through the steps in order to find the sum total." She nodded to the heavy book on the counter.

He eyed her with lingering skepticism. "Perhaps."

"What is it you noticed, Mr. Heathers?"

He closed his ledger with a thump, then placed his hands on his hips. "It may be nothing at all, but I did notice Miss Blastwick—Miss Ethel Blastwick—speaking quite insistently to Mr. Varney. They were standing at the end of the corridor, away from everyone, and I got the impression it was meant to be a private conversation. As soon as she saw me, Miss Blastwick turned away. I think—well, I think she might have dashed away a tear from her eye. She seemed quite upset."

"When was this?" Phyllida asked.

"It was just after dinner, before we began to play that silly game of Miss Genevra's."

Phyllida nodded, *hmming* thoughtfully to herself. "Very well,

Mr. Heathers. Thank you very much for your candidness. I should like to see your motorcar now, if you don't mind. As I said, merely for elimination purposes."

He gave her a disgruntled look but gestured to the back nonetheless.

Phyllida let herself out the rear of the tobacco shop after navigating past crates and boxes in the storeroom. She found a narrow mews behind the little shop. A Crossley motorcar was parked there, none too neatly she noted. As if someone had been in a hurry.

She examined the front of it closely, eyeing the radiator cap which sported the familiar Crossley mascot. It was the figure of a running lady perched atop a winged wheel. The ornament did not protrude forward, but Phyllida felt a little shiver of interest when she looked at the outstretched arms of the female figure. They were straight, and the ends—the hands—were pointed, and sharp enough to puncture a person at great impact. But the outstretched arms projected to the sides, not the front, as if the woman was running over the top from front to back. Was it possible Ethel had fallen into the front of the vehicle on impact and was tossed to the side where a small metal hand stabbed her?

It *was* possible.

Phyllida extracted from her handbag the small magnifying glass she'd taken to carrying and examined the winged hood ornament. Surely there would be blood if it had struck a person—unless Mr. Heathers had cleaned it off, which Phyllida certainly would have done had *she* driven over someone with intent to kill. The metal ornament was dirty, especially in its crevices, but she saw nothing that appeared like blood.

She stood and stepped back, and noticed that the glass of one of the two large headlamps was cracked. If a person struck the lamp, the impact could certainly cause breakage. *Would that make the light dimmer?* she wondered as she crouched in front of the motor to look for grass and mud beneath it.

She saw the scuffed shoes appear from the corner of her eye and rose swiftly to her feet.

"Inspector Cork," she said without a hint of embarrassment.

"Mrs. Bright. I suppose you think you're investigating Ethel Blastwick's murder." His tone and demeanor exuded displeasure.

"I have been asked by the family to—"

"Oi, now. There's always an excuse, isn't there, Mrs. Bright? You had best not get in my way, then."

"I have no intention of 'getting in your way,' Inspector," she replied crisply. "In fact, it's more accurate to suggest you've gotten in *my* way by arriving just at the moment where I am examining this motorcar for possible evidence of a human impact."

His eyes jolted from her to the Crossley then back again. "Oi, so you've been talking to Dr. Bhatt, have ye," he said, still sounding none too pleased. "His fancy ideas about puncture wounds and headlamp bruises have you poking around at every motorcar in Listleigh, have they?"

"I can only surmise that your appearance here suggests the same," Phyllida replied smoothly and was rewarded when his unruly mustache quivered alarmingly. "Have you spoken to Genevra Blastwick? Did she tell you the truth about who saw the murder?"

His glower turned darker, his eyes appearing to protrude a trifle more than usual. "So she told you that, did she. Oi, a person might just as well go about telling everyone now. Impossible to catch the killer off-guard."

"If the killer knows that Genevra didn't see the murder, that makes them less likely to try and do away with her," Phyllida reminded him. "I'm certain you don't want a second murder on your hands, do you, Inspector? Although, it seems as if there already *is* another murder—whatever it was that Ethel Blastwick saw last summer. So, to be clear, I'm certain you don't want a *third* murder on your hands."

He made a sneering, scoffing sound but otherwise seemed to have no response to this logical comment.

Phyllida tucked the magnifying glass into her bag. "If you haven't done, Inspector, I suggest you look into the sudden death of Ralph Greenhouse and also that of Arthur Grainger. It is possible either one of them was the murder witnessed by Ethel Blastwick. Good day."

She sailed off, ignoring the noises of mute frustration following her.

She had intended to speak to Fred Stiller next, but Mr. Heathers's information about Ethel Blastwick and Mr. Varney's private conversation had her turning in the opposite direction in order to see the veterinarian.

She found Bradford and Opal just climbing into the Daimler, which was parked near Mr. Varney's office.

"Oi, there, Mrs. Bright. Are you wanting a ride back to Mallowan Hall now?" asked Bradford. He turned from where he'd been settling a blanket-cloaked Myrtle on Opal's lap.

"No, not quite yet, thank you, Bradford," she said. "I've several other things to follow up on." She listed off her schedule of stops and the people to whom she planned to speak. "I may just walk back. It's a pleasant day and the path along the river will take me past the Crestworthys' as well as the Blastwicks' and Wilding Hall. I believe I might also take a brief detour and walk by Professor Avonlea's cottage. It would be quite instructive to see whether he would have had the time to bicycle home after the dinner party and then somehow drive back to . . . er . . . eliminate Ethel Blastwick. Perhaps there is a motorcar he might have used. Anyhow, she had been walking for no more than twenty minutes, I estimate, from where she was found."

"As you like, Mrs. Bright," he replied. "If you want my opinion, I'd say, aye, he would have had the time. But one ought to check it out for oneself. You can always ring if you want me to bring my bicycle to try it out. And I can stow it in the back of the motor when I come to fetch you."

"Yes, thank you, Bradford. That's an excellent idea. Perhaps if you could meet me at either Wilding Hall or Professor Avonlea's with the bicycle?"

"Aye, that I'll do for sure, Mrs. B."

"Now you ought to get Myrtle home and settled soonest. I'm certain Mrs. Puffley and the maids will keep an eye on her." She glanced into the motor and saw that the bundle of fur was sleeping heavily in Opal's lap. The creature looked almost sweet and innocent in her repose, but Phyllida wasn't fooled. "She seems . . .

well, she seems quite fine. And I'm quite relieved to note it," she said quickly, resisting the strange urge to pat the creature in order to ensure she was just sleeping.

"Mr. Varney put the bandages on a bit more securely this time," Bradford explained. "All right, then, Mrs. Bright. I shall find you at one of your stops—Wilding Hall, or Avonlea's cottage. Or, did you say, the Crestworthys'?"

"Yes. That is an excellent plan." She waved him and Opal off and started up the walkway to the veterinary office.

"Good morning, Mrs. Bright," said Mrs. Buckwhile when she came in. "If you're here for that sweet little Myrtle, I'm afraid you've just missed her. That nice Mr. Bradford has collected her. She did very well last night, and Mr. Varney said he stitched her up even more careful this time."

"I just saw them outside," Phyllida replied. "Myrtle appears to be well on her way to recovery. Now, I was hoping to speak with Mr. Varney about a different matter."

Mrs. Buckwhile's posture changed. "About *the murder*?" Her voice dropped low on the last three syllables.

"Not precisely," Phyllida replied. "Is Mr. Varney available?" As she spoke, she realized she hadn't yet ascertained the type of motorcar the veterinarian drove. "Or did I pass him in that Crossley on the street?"

"No, no, Mr. Varney drives a Morris," said Mrs. Buckwhile, giving Phyllida the information she sought so smoothly it might have been the scene from a play. "It's a brand-new *Isis Tourer*—as he'll tell anyone who asks"—she rolled her eyes a bit—"as he's quite enamored with it. Gets all worked up if even a leaf falls on it. It's a shame he's not so concerned with all of the inventory and equipment here in the office! Misplaces things and refuses to put them back where they belong. And forget organizing the supplies!" She huffed in exasperation. "Anyhow, he's still in the back room after meeting with that Mr. Bradford."

"Indeed. Well, I shall just go on back to speak with him," Phyllida said, starting toward the door that led to the recesses of the suite. "It will only take a moment."

She moved so quickly and fluidly that Mrs. Buckwhile hadn't

been able to extricate herself from behind the desk in time to stop her, a fact Phyllida had been counting on.

She ignored Mrs. Buckwhile's insistent, "Mrs. Bright!" and kept going.

She spied her quarry through a window in the door of what appeared to be an examination room. "Mr. Varney," she said, slipping inside.

"Oh. Mrs. Bright. Goodness, you gave me a start." He picked up the pair of forceps he'd dropped onto an examination table. "Er . . . what can I do for you?"

"I should like to ask you a question about the dinner party the other night," she said.

His expression tensed and his brows drew together. "You're still going on with the investigation? Even after what happened last night?"

Phyllida paused. "What do you mean what happened last night?"

"Why, when he came in to collect Myrtle, Bradford mentioned you'd nearly been run off the road. I thought for certain that would deter you from any further investigations."

Phyllida set her teeth. She was going to have to have words with Bradford over his interference in her investigation. "Not at all. A killer is still on the loose. Now, could you please tell me what you and Miss Ethel Blastwick were speaking about privately at the dinner party?"

His eyes widened. "What Miss Ethel and I . . . why I hardly see how it would pertain to—to anything."

"Then you won't have any problem recounting your conversation to me," she said.

"Well, n-no, of course not. I suppose it doesn't matter at all now, as it's all been decided and—well. Anyhow, Miss Ethel and I were discussing what was to be done about their dog Jarvis."

Phyllida blinked. This was not at all what she had expected to hear (not that she'd had any palpable expectation at all, but it hadn't been this). "I see."

"Miss Genevra feels that it is time for Jarvis to—er—be set free in the dog meadow of eternity, if you will, and I couldn't disagree with her opinion. Unfortunately, Miss Ethel is . . . er, *was* . . . not prepared to say farewell to him as of yet. She was concerned not only for the loss of the dog, but also for their father, who is very attached to him."

"I see," Phyllida said again. And suddenly, several things fell into place in her head. Mrs. Gilbody's snatches of conversation made much more sense—"kill him" had most likely been referring to poor Jarvis—and the housekeeper would surely be relieved to hear the explanation. "Thank you, Mr. Varney. I do appreciate your time."

"Yes, of course. I—I do hope you find the culprit," he added soberly. "Miss Ethel was a very kind and soft-hearted young woman. She didn't deserve what someone did to her."

"No, she certainly didn't." Phyllida took her leave, offering a pleasant "Good day" to Mrs. Buckwhile as she sailed out the door.

She made her way to Fred Stiller's bicycle shop only to discover that it was closed. A sign on the door said: TOOK MY BOY FISHING. BACK TOMORROW.

Despite her disappointment, she couldn't help grinning a little—for how could a person begrudge a beautiful day on the river or lake with a child?

Well, there was nothing for it. She would start her trek out of the village to the Crestworthy home, Wilding Hall, and Professor Avonlea's cottage. Perhaps she would be lucky and encounter Mr. Stiller and his son during her walk.

Her first stop would be Wilding Hall.

Phyllida's smile ebbed. It was time to speak frankly to Vera about the Bugatti: its sharp hood ornament, the grass and mud beneath it, and the fact that someone had driven it after the dinner party.

CHAPTER 16

"Oh, Phyllida! What a pleasant surprise. Do come in," said Vera when she caught sight of her in the foyer.

Mr. Whalley had answered Phyllida's knock, of course, but his mistress had appeared almost immediately.

"Why, where's your motorcar, Phyllida?" Vera asked, peering through the entrance as Mr. Whalley began to close the door.

"I am on foot today," Phyllida said, bracing herself for possible unpleasantness ahead. "Chasing up some clues. Could we speak privately?"

"You *walked?* Why on earth—but of course we can speak." Vera must have recognized the soberness in Phyllida's expression. "I was only taking a break from one more edit over my stories before I send them to the editor at *The Queen.* You look parched, darling. I'll ring for tea and let Rolly know you're here."

"Vera," Phyllida said, touching the woman's arm to stop her. "Just you and I, please."

"O-of course." Vera's blue eyes went wide. "No tea?"

"Tea would be lovely. It is a trifle warm out there today," Phyllida said, realizing the irony of her statement. But a cup of tea was always in order, especially when one had to brace oneself for difficult conversations.

"Whalley, please have tea brought in. And something for Mrs. Bright to eat as well. She must be famished after such a long trek."

Phyllida didn't allay her hostess's concerns; it had been a mere two miles from the village on a relatively flat and winding path that made its way through a small woods and over a flower-strewn meadow. Hardly strenuous for a person in her condition, but she was feeling a bit peckish.

"What is it?" Vera asked as soon as the parlor door closed behind them. "I can see that something is wrong. Did you find them, Phyllida? Did you find who did it?"

"Not yet," she replied as they took their seats. "But I have some questions."

"Yes, of course. Do go on, Phyllida."

"When I arrived at the dinner party, I noticed all of the motorcars lined up—very straight, in order of the guests' arrival," Phyllida went on. "I was the last to arrive and I . . ." Her thoughts trailed off and she hesitated as she remembered the arrival and her attention sliding over the motorcars, one by one. She collected herself even as the wisp of a thought filtered through her mind, seeing the row of vehicles shining in the early evening sunshine. "I mean to say, I noticed Sir Rolly's motorcar. His is the Bugatti, is it not?"

"Yes, of course," replied Vera, watching her closely. "He absolutely adores that thing."

"I noticed it because . . . well, I noticed it particularly because one summer I had occasion to become quite familiar with a similar model." Phyllida went on, a faint smile curving her mouth—and one that was reflected briefly in Vera's expression as well. Then the smiles faded. "What I mean to say is, I noticed the motorcar and I noticed where it was parked. It, too, was precisely lined up with the other motorcars that had arrived for the dinner."

"Ye-ess . . ." Vera sounded uncertain. "Phyllida . . . you're not suggesting . . ."

She held up a hand. "Please, allow me to finish my thought."

For the first time since Vera had come to visit her at Mallowan Hall, Phyllida was acutely aware of the difference in their classes and the repercussions that could be had should she misstep or make a mistake. It surprised her that, in these last few days, she'd almost come to think of Vera Rollingbroke as a friend—and that she would dislike losing that camaraderie.

Still. She would be on the side of right and justice.

"When I called yesterday morning, I noticed that the Bugatti had been moved—only slightly, but moved nonetheless—from where it had been parked the night before. *And*"—Phyllida held Vera's gaze with her own—"that there was mud and grass in the undercarriage, such as might collect should one drive off the road. There's one more thing," she said quickly as Vera drew in a breath to speak. "Ethel Blastwick had a sort of puncture wound in her chest from the . . . er . . . the impact of the motorcar that ran her over. The hood ornament on the Bugatti has sharp, pointed wings on it."

A long moment of silence reigned as her companion stared at her.

A knock came at the door and Vera called, "Come," in an absent and automatic voice as she continued to stare at Phyllida.

Mr. Whalley came in, wheeling a two-tier cart laden with food and drink that Phyllida suddenly suspected she would not have the chance in which to partake. She was particularly disappointed when she noticed thin cucumber, watercress, and butter sandwiches—a particular favorite of hers.

The two of them sat in a strained silence as the butler prepared their tea—a silence broken only by Phyllida's directive that she took her tea black and with two lumps—and poured it. After what seemed like a decade, he finally took his leave.

Well-trained servant that he was, he closed the door tightly behind him. Well-trained servant that he was, he would surely listen at said door in testament to that universally acknowledged truth that servants knew all secrets.

"You suspect Rolly's motorcar was used to run down Ethel Blastwick," Vera said at last. Her voice shook a little.

"I should very much like to eliminate it from suspicion," Phyllida replied evenly, even as she appreciated—and supported—the fine splitting of hairs suggested by her hostess.

"As would *I*," Vera replied flatly.

"Quite," Phyllida said quietly, and with great emotion. She hoped it was enough to demonstrate her own discomfort with this situation.

Vera heaved a great sigh and settled back into her seat, holding her cup and saucer close to her chest. She eyed her friend with a temerity Phyllida hadn't expected from a woman who could be amazingly scattered and superficial. Perhaps she had misjudged her. Or perhaps Vera Rollingbroke, like many women, knew when it was permissible to be easy and giddy and flighty, and when it was important to be sober and thoughtful.

"It wasn't Rolly," she said firmly. "He wouldn't have had the time, Phyllida, or the inclination. I am telling you that without a bit of doubt in my mind. He and I were together—*quite* together, if you get my meaning—from the time he came inside after seeing Rutherford and the professor off, until the time Inspector Cork arrived the next morning to tell us—to tell us what happened."

She leaned forward a bit, her eyes steady on Phyllida's. "The man wasn't about to slip out of bed to go off into the night. He had no thoughts about anything other than me," she added with an air of confidence and complacency. "Surely you know of what I speak."

"Quite," Phyllida replied. "But—"

"And he wouldn't have had time before he came inside to me," Vera went on firmly.

"You did mention that it seemed 'forever' that you waited for him to come inside," Phyllida reminded her.

"Yes, of course I did. I had all sorts of visions of him lurking in the shadows, canoodling with Genevra Blastwick whilst I waited inside for him to reappear," Vera said. "I was certain that was what was keeping him—but it was only the professor, who liked to talk. He wasn't *that* long in coming. It was only that it *felt* like it because I was quite upset and—and suspicious."

"Quite so. I can understand that," Phyllida replied in a neutral tone.

"But the motor was *moved* you say," Vera said. "I don't doubt you, Phyllida. If you say it was, I'm certain it was. I didn't move it—I dislike driving that thing; it's far too large *and* too fast. Besides, it needn't be said, need it, that I wasn't leaving Rolly's side any more than he was leaving mine."

"But who else could have moved it?" Phyllida asked reasonably. "Surely—"

"My husband is rather a forgetful sort. He does tend to misplace things—including, on occasion, the key to his motor. Sometimes he even leaves it in the automobile. I've spoken to him about it, but . . ."

Phyllida sighed internally. A convenient explanation. Somewhat reasonable, but also exceedingly convenient for explaining away a questionable situation. "So anyone could have found the key and used it to drive his motorcar."

"It's a *Bugatti*," said Vera drily. "Who wouldn't want to drive it? Except for me, of course, although I did drive it once when Rolly first got it. It was . . . it was rather like attempting to control a panther with one's hands. One felt like it could simply leap off onto a tear, all on its own. And it purrs like a cat too."

"Quite so. I see," Phyllida replied. She was wholly unconvinced, but she also had no clear rebuttal to her hostess's position.

"I shall do some investigating," Vera said. "I shall ask Rolly—"

The door opened at that moment. "You'll ask Rolly what, darling?" said the man himself, striding into the parlor. His round face was bright with pleasure and interest and a faint waft of woodsy cologne accompanied him. "Why, Mrs. Bright. Pleasure to see you again. Now, what is it you're wanting to ask me, old thing?" He leaned over to kiss Vera.

"I was just wondering if you'd noticed anything different about your motorcar since the dinner party." Phyllida spoke before Vera could say anything. "I noticed it when I came for the dinner party. It's quite a distinctive vehicle."

"Righto. Had it shipped in from Italy, you know. Cost buckets more than it should have but it drives like a dream. Lost the key to it, I did, and thought I was going to have to send for another one—and God knows how long that would take for it to get here from *Rome*." He shook his head in jovial exasperation. "But then I found the dratted thing and the problem was solved. I won't have to be taking off in your little ride, now will I, old bean."

Vera looked at Phyllida, one fine eyebrow arching just a bit.

"When did you lose your key, Sir Rolly?" asked Phyllida.

He looked startled then said, "Well, I suppose I realized it was missing yesterday after luncheon. After that inspector came through, telling us about what happened to Miss Ethel, poor thing. Thought I left it in the car, you see, but it wasn't there when I went to look."

"When did you find it, darling?" asked Vera. "Where was it?"

Phyllida was grateful Vera had stepped in; she didn't want to take the chance of aggravating Sir Rolly by interrogating him. She used the opportunity to take one of the cucumber and watercress sandwiches and bite into it. Delicious: crisp and fresh.

"Damnedest thing. The key was in the grass, wouldn't you know. Must've dropped out of my pocket, see." He shook his head. "Should take better care of my things, shouldn't I? My mother used to always say the same to me: 'Rolly, dear, I vow you'd lose a ten-pound note if someone sewed it to your forehead,' she'd say. Here I am, forty-three, and I ain't changed a bit, have I?" He chuckled.

Vera patted his hand. "And I wouldn't have it any other way." She looked at Phyllida. "Does that satisfy you, then?"

"It doesn't answer who moved the motorcar," she replied. "Sir Rolly, did you notice that your Bugatti had been moved? Is there anyone else who drives it? A chauffeur or the footman? He's new, isn't he?"

"Definitely not," Sir Rolly replied. "Only me. They know better than to get behind the wheel of that motorcar. Last time I allowed someone else to drive my Bugatti, they made a ding in it! Said a rock flew up and chipped it, but I can't account for that at all. But now you mention it, I noticed the driver's wheel was a bit off from the way I park it. Like to leave it straight up, you see." His affable expression suddenly grew thunderous. "Who was driving my motorcar?"

"That is what I intend to find out," Phyllida said.

"Do you really think it was used to kill Ethel Blastwick?" Vera said, her voice rising to a slightly higher pitch. "Oh, Rolly, it's simply *untenable*. First we have a murderer in my murder writing club, then we have a murderer at our dinner party, and now it seems the murderer has been driving *your motorcar*! I simply don't know *what* is happening."

"What's this?" Sir Rolly looked between the two of them, his stormy expression unabated. "What are you saying?"

Phyllida quickly explained. "So you see, we need to find out who drove your motorcar."

Then all at once, a thought struck her. She sat up sharply, catching her breath.

What if someone had used the Bugatti in order to hide their own motorcar's identity as the murder weapon?

What if that person left the dinner party with everyone else, *then came back*, got the Bugatti, and then drove off to find Ethel?

That would make sense as to why poor Ethel was driven over from the opposite direction in which she was walking. The killer drove past, saw her, then turned around and came back—and then kept on going in order to return the motorcar to its rightful place at Wilding Hall.

"Phyllida?" Vera said.

Phyllida opened her mouth to speak, then closed it.

The idea was too new, too flimsy, too nebulous for her to talk about. She shook her head.

"I think that's all I need to ask you for now. But, Sir Rolly, anything you can remember about when you last saw your key or whether anyone from the dinner party expressed any particular interest in the Bugatti would be helpful. Please ring me if you think of anything."

She rose, eyeing the cucumber sandwiches ruefully. She'd managed two, but they were small. But, unlike Inspector Cork and Constable Greensticks, she didn't have time to sit and chat and take tea.

She had more suspects to interview.

It was during her walk to Professor Avonlea's cottage that it occurred to Phyllida *he* would be the perfect suspect to have doubled back to "borrow" the Bugatti.

He had been the last one to leave, according to Sir Rolly and Mr. Crestworthy—although the three of them had been talking together. Avonlea was on a bicycle and didn't even own a motorcar.

And he owned bees—a fact which became even more obvious

as Phyllida approached the small, thatched-roof cottage. She was coming up from behind it, as the route from Wilding Hall had required her to take a path off Ploughman's Close around the small cemetery to the back of the professor's small parcel of property.

As she drew nearer, Phyllida kept a prudent distance from the two large beehives, which were surrounded by activity. A large, messy garden spilling with wildflowers, herbs, and other flowering plants was the recipient of more of that activity. From a distance, the blossoms appeared to be alive, covered as they were by hundreds of honeybees bouncing gracefully from one bloom to the next.

Phyllida started along the gravel walkway that arced off from the main path, veering toward the cottage. She was just close enough to one of the hives to hear the buzz of the bees when she heard another sound: a human scream.

CHAPTER 17

*T*HE SCREAM HAD COME FROM INSIDE THE COTTAGE, AND PHYLLIDA bolted toward the closest door—the one in the back, which opened into a small, well-groomed rose garden with a table and two chairs.

It had been a single scream, shrill and high-pitched, and could have been the sort of reaction one might have to unexpectedly seeing a mouse or snake. But that didn't keep Phyllida from running up to make certain. When she got to the door and yanked it open, she immediately saw that the incident was nothing so benign as a disturbed critter.

A tiny woman in her late fifties stood in the kitchen, gasping, wheezing, and sobbing whilst holding a hand to her aproned chest. She was looking down at the floor, where a man's body lay sprawled on the worn wooden planks.

It took only a glance for Phyllida to confirm the worst: It was Wilfred Avonlea who lay there.

The woman was startled out of her strangled hysterics by Phyllida's appearance. "Oh my heavens. Oh my good heavens. Is he dead? Is he dead? He can't be dead! I was only just here! He was only just here! He can't be dead!" She went on in variations of that theme as Phyllida knelt next to Professor Avonlea.

His body still held a bit of heat, but there was no pulse, no warm breath emitting from his nose or mouth. His hand was limp. There was no telltale blue around the mouth or nose, nor the signs of vomit or other emissions consistent with poison.

Still . . .

"Telephone to Dr. Bhatt's surgery immediately," she told the woman who was, presumably, Professor Avonlea's housekeeper or daily maid, "and also to the constable's office."

"Is he dead? He isn't dead. He can't be dead, can he? Good heavens, I simply can't—"

"If you would make the telephone calls *now*," Phyllida said sharply. The next step would be to slap the hysteria out of the woman with a well-placed blow to the cheek, but she would prefer not to descend to such extremes.

The woman, whose name remained unknown to Phyllida, seemed to snap out of her circular hysterics and tottered out of the room, presumably to utilize the telephone.

In the meanwhile, Phyllida did a quick but thorough examination of the professor. When she discovered a minute, rather messy puncture wound, relatively fresh—for there was a bit of blood, still bright red but dry—on the side of his neck, she hissed with satisfaction.

She could hear the muted voice of the housekeeper making the required telephone calls as she dug into her pocketbook to retrieve the magnifying glass.

No sign of a bee's stinger in the injury, she noted with satisfaction. That would surely be the first suggestion Inspector Cork would have upon being confronted by a puncture wound in the skin of a man who kept honeybees. While that might be a logical predisposition under other circumstances, in this case Phyllida suspected Professor Avonlea's death was the result of foul play via injection.

But she needed to be certain, so she examined the area around Avonlea minutely—including in the folds of his clothing—looking for the dead honeybee that would have resulted when it removed its barbed stinger from its victim. She knew that in doing so, the apian would destroy itself, and if Professor Avonlea had been stung, there should be a second, entomological corpse.

There wasn't.

She broadened her search to the table where the professor had obviously been sitting with a book and a stack of newspapers. There was a cup of very milky tea half gone and cold, along with a jar of honey with a dipper in it and a small plate containing only a few crumbs. A pipe, which had burned out sitting in its place, still emitted the scent of Professor Avonlea's tobacco blend. His pince-nez rested on the table. He'd been sitting here, enjoying his tea, and, by the looks of it, reading a battered copy of *Odysseus* along with the *Times*.

She narrowed her eyes, looking around, trying to imagine how it had unfolded.

If someone had come to the front door, the professor would have gone to greet them there, and then if he invited them in, surely it would have been into a front parlor, not back to the kitchen. That was most likely, unless the visitor was a close friend or intimate.

And if he invited them in, even here to the kitchen, there would be a chair pulled up, and a second cup and saucer . . .

Phyllida looked around. There was a single chair, not quite pushed in to the table, but not completely pulled out as if someone had been sitting there. She noted dishes by the sink that had been washed and put on a rack to dry. A plate, flatware, a cup and saucer—all of which likely had been from the professor's breakfast.

So it appeared he hadn't invited a guest to sit down and partake.

If the guest came from the back door, as Phyllida had done, the scenario might be different.

She liked the idea that the visitor had come from the rear of the cottage—via the same path she had, walking along the river and around the cemetery. That meant whoever it was wouldn't be seen from the road or passed by in a motorcar. And if he or she had come with the purpose of murder—which one could readily conclude, given the scene at her feet—then it was to their benefit not to be noticed.

She ran through it in her mind: The visitor appeared at the kitchen window and was invited in by the professor, who rose to open the door. They spoke for a moment then perhaps he gestured for the person to take a seat as he turned to get a cup and saucer for tea.

Perhaps he was walking over to the cabinet to fetch the cup when the killer struck from behind—jamming a hypodermic into Professor Avonlea's neck, and quickly pushing the plunger.

But what poison would work so quickly and efficiently? Cyanide for certain, but there was no froth around the mouth and when she sniffed the wound, she smelled no bitter almond scent. Arsenic would take hours after ingestion or injection, and there would be signs of distress. Nicotine was quick also, but it was difficult to ascertain whether there was the smell of tobacco near the wound, given the professor's love for his pipe.

Pentobarbitone.

A little shiver scuttled over the back of Phyllida's shoulders. She had no proof, no real reason to think it might be, but it was possible. The fact that Mr. Varney and his veterinary practice hovered at the periphery of this entire case might not be coincidental.

Just then, the housekeeper tottered in from the front of the cottage.

"I did it," she said, and Phyllida took that to mean she'd made the required telephone calls and not that she'd jabbed her employer with a needle.

"Thank you very much, Mrs., erm . . . ?"

"Waltz. Mrs. Waltz. I know who you are, I do, Mrs. Bright." The woman, who was barely five feet tall and looked as if she'd blow away in a strong wind if she wasn't secured to the ground, nodded meaningfully at her. "You're that detective housekeeper person for that lady murder writer, you are. How did you know he–he w-would be here like this? How could this happen? I only just—"

Phyllida held up a hand and eased the little woman to the chair that hadn't been quite pushed into the table. "Why don't you take a seat, Mrs. Waltz. It's quite a shock, isn't it? But I'm here and we are going to find out what happened to Professor Avonlea."

"Someone murdered him, didn't they?" said Mrs. Waltz, sounding a trifle stronger. "He was strong as an ox and healthy as a horse, he was, and I won't be letting *anyone* say he just died on his own." Her pale blue eyes flashed.

"I tend to agree with you, Mrs. Waltz. Could you tell me when you last saw the professor?"

"Why, it was this morning of course. I always come in by ten o'clock, and I make him a little late breakfast—he can manage his coffee, you see, and stoke up his own stove. But I cook him a luncheon, and then on Wednesdays—that's today—I go on in to the village to pick up the laundry and a fresh loaf of bread."

"And what time did you leave to do that today?"

"Why, it must have been half past one, wasn't it?"

Phyllida nodded encouragingly. "And you fetched the laundry and the bread . . . and then you returned, when?"

"Well, today I was longer than usual because I got to talking to Mrs. Panson about it all, you see, and—"

"What time did you return, Mrs. Waltz?" Phyllida interrupted. "Was there anyone here or anyone leaving when you returned?"

"No, no one was here at all. I mean to say, except for the professor." She looked down at the figure on the floor and her face crumpled.

Phyllida silently berated herself for not having the foresight to remove the poor woman from the scene. She handed Mrs. Waltz a handkerchief from her pocketbook. "Did you pass anyone on the road in a motorcar, either when you were leaving or returning?"

"Why, I'm not certain about that. I—I might have. I wasn't really paying attention, now, was I?" She sniffled and wiped her eyes.

"Quite understandable. Was Professor Avonlea expecting anyone today?"

"No, not that he told me. I don't think so. He doesn't really like to have visitors, you see. He only just likes to potter about with his books and his bees. His roses too, you know. He dines out whenever he can."

"Did he go anywhere today or take any telephone calls whilst you were here?"

"Why, yes, he did go for a bit of a ramble this morning, he did.

But he was back before I left at half one. He often did, you see, take a little walk before luncheon. He seemed rather satisfied with himself when he returned, I remember thinking."

"Did Professor Avonlea know Mr. and Mrs. Greenhouse very well?"

"Greenhouse? Why . . . I can't think whether he did. He never mentioned anything to me about them. Do you mean poor Ralph Greenhouse who died last summer? Terrible thing, those bee stings. And to be trapped in the motorcar with them!" Mrs. Waltz shook her head. "The professor was always so careful when he went around them, you know. The bees, I mean."

"He didn't know Mrs. Greenhouse?" Phyllida pressed.

"Why . . . I'm certain he probably knew her to say hallo on the street, but he wasn't friendly in that way anyhow," she said. "He'd as soon not speak to anyone if he didn't have to. That's why he walked along the river and in the woods, you see. And Mrs. Greenhouse . . . well, she's not quite the type to want to talk about books or bees, if you know what I mean. Now, her dog and cats, well, she could talk a century and still go on. When her dog was killed— terrible accident, you know—well, it was more of a tragedy than when Mr. Greenhouse died, I'm sure."

"What about Mr. Varney? Did the professor have any pets or animals that he would have treated?" Phyllida asked.

"Only an old cat that kept away the mice," Mrs. Waltz replied. "Scotty, he was called. Anyhow, the cat died over the winter. Old age. He was a good mouser, he was. The professor talked about getting another cat, but . . ." Her voice trailed off as she blinked rapidly. "Poor Professor."

Phyllida gave the woman a moment to pull herself together, then she asked, "Is there anyone you can think of who might have wanted to harm the professor? Anyone you know with whom he might have had a disagreement or an argument?"

"No, I can't. Not at all. He was—well, he was a crotchety old man, but he had a heart of cotton underneath it all, he did. Always gave me an extra day off around Christmas, he did, *and* a new fine pair of kid gloves. Every year. So very soft, they were."

Mrs. Waltz nodded vigorously. "You're going to find who did this, aren't you, Mrs. Bright?"

"I certainly intend to do so."

Just then someone pounded on the front door.

Inspector Cork, right on cue.

Phyllida never particularly enjoyed her encounters with Inspector Cork, and the one following the discovery of Wilfred Avonlea's murder was no exception. It was filled with remonstrations for her to leave the investigating to the police, and how unsurprising it was that *she* should be present at yet another murder, and perhaps one ought to take a closer look at *her* since that sort of thing kept happening.

She dismissed Inspector Cork's aggravated comments for being nothing more than that—exasperation because he hadn't the first idea how to go about solving these murders.

Phyllida took her leave as soon as possible, leaving the inspector to finish his examination of the scene—after she had assured him that it hadn't been a bee sting she'd found on the professor's neck. Dr. Bhatt arrived just as she was finishing her lecture to the inspector, and she had no doubt the physician would confirm her conclusions. She had a moment to suggest to him that the cause of death could be an injection of pentobarbitone, and then went on her way.

Bradford hadn't made his appearance by then either, but Phyllida knew he was astute enough to realize that with Avonlea dead, there was no sense in looking at the possibility of him using someone's motorcar.

It also meant that the man who'd started to solidify as Phyllida's strongest suspect was no longer a suspect.

But there had to be a reason the killer wanted him out of the way, didn't there? What did he know? What had he seen or heard?

More importantly, if he knew who the killer was, why would he let them into his kitchen?

That was the most troubling question, and it accompanied Phyllida as she walked along the road. Despite all of the wisps of ideas and the maelstrom of thoughts that bounded through her mind, she found herself continuing to enjoy the mild summer's day. Even the few clouds in the distance that suggested an evening rain didn't lessen her enjoyment.

But the rumble of a motorcar from behind had her edging to the side of the road, looking warily over her shoulder, preparing to leap aside at the last minute. But it was a familiar vehicle, and when the Daimler pulled up next to her, she smiled.

"Avonlea, was it?" Bradford said when she came up to the window he'd rolled down. Obviously he'd been to the cottage already. He shook his head. "Poor bloke."

"Yes. And I was just becoming comfortable with the thought that he'd left the dinner party on his bicycle, saw Ethel Blastwick, then went back and borrowed Sir Rolly's Bugatti to do the deed. And now—well, obviously it wasn't him."

"Borrowed a Bugatti?" The chauffeur's brows lifted in sardonic amusement.

She gave a quick explanation to which he nodded in comprehension.

"But someone else might have taken off in that motorcar," he said. "Especially if they saw the key lying there or noticed it in the ignition. It would be quite the temptation."

"Yes, it's possible." She sighed. "It seemed logical that Professor Avonlea was the culprit in this entire mess. After all, he had the bees that could have killed Ralph Greenhouse."

Bradford nodded again. "Aye, he did at that. So now what, Inspector Bright? Climb in, why don't you, and I'll drop you where you like."

"Thank you," she said primly, even though she felt a rush of pleasure when he smiled at her like that, his eyes warm and crinkling at the corners. To think that when they first met, he'd been so surly and disgruntled all of the time.

Of course, that might have had to do with the fact that she'd practically accused him of murder . . .

Then she saw the crate partly wedged into the boot of the Daimler, with the hatch tied down over it since the box wouldn't quite fit.

"Is that Dobble's?" she asked as she climbed into the passenger seat.

He nodded. "I'm taking it to the vicar."

"Do you know what's in it?" she asked.

He gave her a sidewise look and grinned. "Do you mean to say *you* don't know, my intrepid investigator?"

She pursed her lips. "I have a strong suspicion," she lied.

He chuckled as the Daimler eased forward along the road. "Where is it I'm taking you, then, Inspector Bright?" Clearly he wasn't going to tell her what was in the crate.

Fine. She would find out all on her own. "To the Crestworthys', if you please."

They drove in silence for a moment, then Bradford spoke. "Whoever offed the professor must have had a reason. He must have known or seen something."

"Precisely my thought, but I must admit, I'm at a bit of a loss. Whatever it was, he certainly didn't tell me. Of course, I never had the chance to actually interrogate the man, drat it," she grumbled. "We only spoke briefly after the card game last night. And of course, I saw him at the dinner party. Are you certain he didn't say anything that would be helpful?"

"Not that I remember, but I'll think about it again," he replied.

"Did you know that Fred Stiller took his son fishing today instead of opening his bicycle shop?" she said.

"Well, no, I didn't, but that sounds a fine idea."

"It does, but it rather stymies my investigation. I wanted to ask him about when Ethel Blastwick had her bicycle in for repairs. I feel as if this entire situation rests on that information—which would help to narrow down when the murder she witnessed took place. When I checked the dates of the three deaths in question, they were all quite spread out. One in June, one in August, and one in October."

"Well, now, Mrs. Bright, perhaps if you looked by the little fishing spot on the river near Kell's Curve you might find Fred and you could ask him. He has the sort of memory where he'd probably know straightaway."

"Thank you for that suggestion," she said, feeling more relieved. "I shall do that."

"Might I comment on how particularly well rested you look today, Mrs. Bright?" His attention was still on the road, but his eyes crinkled at the corners again and a smile twitched his lips.

"Well rested? After a mere three hours of sleep? Surely you jest," she said. "Nonetheless, I am certainly feeling quite . . . relaxed."

"Relaxation, as you call it, looks rather well on you, Mrs. Bright. It was a very prudent choice—my place, I mean," he said. "Shall I begin referring to you as my dear Miss Prudence?"

She rolled her eyes. "Prudence is a terrible name, Bradford. It sounds so . . . restrictive and as if one is wound up tightly, like a spring. Which I am not." She ignored the scoffing sound he made and went on. "To that end, Dobble did comment that he'd heard some sort of strange noises outside the window."

"Did he now?" Bradford's grin grew wider. "Do you think he suspects what caused those noises?"

"I should hope *not*," she replied. "I simply could not tolerate him looking down his nose at my—my—well, my sneaking around. Oh, the snide comments he would make. And if the *maids* found out . . . !" She shuddered.

Bradford remained silent, although his smile lingered.

"You don't think they know, do you?" she said. "Of course they don't know. They haven't the slightest idea. And I do think that in order to throw them off the scent—"

"What scent?"

"*Any* scent that—well, that there might be . . . well, Bradford, cease playing the ingenue! You know to what I'm referring." He was chuckling heartily by now and she sniffed in aggravation. "What I'm trying to say is, in order to keep them from suspecting, I do think it's best if we kept up appearances. What I mean to say is, we ought to remain as before."

"By 'as before,' do you mean one of us snipping and sniping about dog hair and canine drool and whatnot?"

"No, I meant one of us being sardonic and surly," she retorted, even as she fought to keep from laughing. One of the best things about being as experienced and mature as she was, was the ability to adapt and laugh at oneself. "And here we are."

The Daimler eased to a stop in the front drive of the Crestworthy home. A large sign hanging on the stone wall surrounding the grounds read CRESTWORTHY MANOR.

It was a large place, and would certainly be considered an estate by anyone, with its sprawling gardens and a vast expanse of lawn. A shiny Bentley sat in the drive. It was not the same one she'd seen at the dinner party, so the Crestworthys must own two of them. Phyllida clicked her tongue thoughtfully. They were certainly quite well-off.

She had a feeling one of her niggling suspicions was correct, but whether or how it played into the grand puzzle, she wasn't yet certain.

"Thank you, Bradford," she said in her prim voice because she knew it would elicit a smile from him. For some reason, he found it amusing when she was prim, proper, and—apparently—prudent.

"Do you want that I should come for you after taking the crate to the vicar's?" He'd started to lean over to kiss her, but stopped himself in time.

Phyllida smiled in recognition of his restraint and patted his hand instead. "That would be most convenient. If I am not here, I should be at either the Blastwicks' cottage or along the river looking for Mr. Stiller."

"Very well, Mrs. Bright. Good luck with your investigations."

Phyllida approached the Crestworthy home thoughtfully. Should she go to the rear and speak with the cook and other servants, or should she attempt to be invited in as a guest to speak with Myrna Crestworthy? That was one of the conundrums of being in this strange predicament, working as she was between the different strata of class.

Phyllida decided on the bold move (she was, after all, not the shy or retiring sort, and this was a matter of murder) and climbed the steps to the front door. She'd barely dropped the knocker when the door swung open.

"Yes?" The butler, whose name Phyllida did not know, was tall enough that she had to look up at him, but not nearly as tall—or skeletal—as Mr. Dobble. He was certainly dressed as well as the butler at Mallowan Hall—in a very correct gray suit and black tie that was just out of style enough that he wouldn't be mistaken for one of the upper class.

"Phyllida Bright to see Mrs. Crestworthy," she said. "On behalf of Mrs. Agatha Christie, with condolences for the recent loss in the household."

The butler's expression faltered for an instant, but he recovered quickly. "Mrs. Bright. If you'd come in, I shall see whether Mrs. Crestworthy is at home." As he stepped back to allow her entry, he said in a lower voice, "It's a right honor to meet you, Mrs. Bright."

She looked at him in surprise and smiled. "Likewise, Mr. . . . ?"

"Tums." He flashed her a very brief smile, then returned to the implacable demeanor of Proper Butler. He was a handsome man with brown skin, likely in his forties, with patrician features including a sharp jawline and a slender nose. His hair was cut very close to a well-shaped scalp and he was clean-shaven about the face. She had a brief but sincere moment of regret that he wasn't the butler at Mallowan Hall. "This way, please, ma'am."

He took her to a lovely parlor festooned in blue brocade with dark gold accents. The pillow-strewn sofa appeared quite comfortable and Phyllida was just lowering herself onto it when Mr. Tums spoke.

"Er . . . Mrs. Bright, would I be remiss in asking whether you are here on one of your murder investigations?" His voice was low, for the door was still open to the foyer and there could be heard in the distance the sounds of activity—maids, most likely, going about their business.

"That I am," she replied with a smile.

"Oh, thank heavens," he said with great emotion. "It's only that I thought it had all been swept under the rug, you see. I do hope you can set it all to rights soonest. I have great faith in you." He gave her a brief bow, then slipped out of the room, presumably to notify Mrs. Crestworthy of her arrival.

Although Phyllida was mildly taken aback at his vehemence over a murder that had certainly not been swept under the rug, she didn't have much time to contemplate it, for the parlor door opened only a few moments after he left. A parlourmaid came in with a tray laden with tea, scones, and deviled eggs.

Phyllida was delighted, for the two flimsy cucumber sandwiches she'd had at Wilding Hall had long been forgotten. She was also slightly surprised by the fact that a tray had been delivered before the mistress of the house had been present to order it, but she decided that must simply be the rules of the household—or something left to the butler's discretion, which in this case, was to her benefit.

"Mrs. Bright, is it really you?" said the parlourmaid as she curtsied—*curtsied*, to Phyllida!—after setting down the tray. "Oh, Mr. Tums said as how it was, and I insisted on being the one to bring in the tea so's I could meet you."

Phyllida managed to keep her reaction to the slight lifting of one eyebrow. "And it's my pleasure to meet you as well, then. What is your name?"

"Only, it's Briony, ma'am. I mean to say, that's me real name. The master and mistress call me Mary, here, of course, because that's always the name of the first parlourmaid, but I am Briony."

"Briony is a lovely name. Thank you very much for the tea," Phyllida replied, a little mystified by the welcome she was receiving from the staff here at Crestworthy Manor.

"Are you going to find out what happened, truly?" Briony asked, clasping her hands in front of her chest.

"I certainly intend to do so," Phyllida replied. "Did you know Miss Blastwick?" she asked, wondering whether there was some connection to the death of the young woman other than the dinner party attendees. Perhaps some of the staff here had known her well.

"Miss Blastwick?" Briony seemed confused.

"Miss Ethel Blastwick. The woman who was killed two days ago," Phyllida replied, even more mystified.

"Oh, right, then. I heard about that, poor thing. Terrible way to go, wasn't it?" Briony bobbed another sort of curtsy. "Well, I must be off. Mr. Tums is kind enough, but he still don't like it when we dawdle, and Mrs. Dunbury ain't come back from visiting her cousin yet.

"It was our day out, see, all of us this morning, because Mrs. Crestworthy is always out to an early luncheon on Wednesday. But Mrs. Crestworthy was not very happy when we all returned from our morning out. Seems she had a visitor and she had to answer the door *herself.*" Briony nodded, bobbed, then scampered out of the room before Phyllida could further react.

She stared at the door for a moment, caught up in an uncharacteristic moment of uncertainty. Then, being a pragmatist, she decided she might just as well apply herself to the tea tray since it had been brought for her.

She was well into her first cuppa and had tasted a sultana-dotted scone and enjoyed a deviled egg when the parlor door opened again.

It was Mr. Tums.

"Mrs. Bright, I'm very sorry to inform you that Mrs. Crestworthy is not at home at the moment." His voice suggested something very different from the words he'd spoken. In fact, Phyllida was quite versed in translating the vernacular of downstairs people, and she understood that Mrs. Crestworthy was, in fact, home, but did not wish to be disturbed.

"Of course. I do hope everything is all right," she said, rising.

"She has had a very difficult morning," Mr. Tums told her, obviously realizing she'd read the true meaning in his words. "I believe she got some rather difficult news. I—I heard her on the telephone to London. Quite agitated she was."

"I'm so very sorry to hear that," Phyllida said as she started out of the parlor. "I do hope she'll feel better soon. And please give her the condolences of Mrs. Christie over the loss of Mr. Crestworthy's secretary. Unfortunately, Mrs. Christie is in London at the moment, and she only just learned of Mr. and Mrs. Crestworthy's loss yesterday."

"You will find out what truly happened to him, won't you?" Mr. Tums said in a low, fierce voice as she followed him into the hallway. "To Bentley?"

Phyllida stopped short. "Are you speaking of the secretary? The one who drowned?" A little prickle skittered over her shoulders, turning into a great shiver of comprehension.

"Indeed I am. Isn't that why you're here? To look into his death?" Mr. Tums seemed as taken aback as Phyllida was.

"I am now," she murmured, looking up at him. "You think there was something suspicious about his death."

"I *know* there was, Mrs. Bright. You see, Bentley Gillam was terribly afraid of water and he couldn't swim. He *never* would have gone near the river. It's impossible that he drowned in an accident."

CHAPTER 18

"Perhaps he simply got too close to the edge and fell in," Phyllida said. "The river was rather swollen from the rains in the last fortnight."

Mr. Tums was shaking his head. "I don't believe it for one minute. And neither do the rest of us. We all knew him quite well, you see, because he lived here. The downstairs people, I mean to say. We liked him, even though he was the master's secretary, and one of the parlourmaids was quite sweet on him and it seemed he returned the affection.

"He didn't put on airs, and he was an earnest, jolly sort of chap. He ate with us most of the time downstairs, you know. I tell you, Mrs. Bright, there is something strange about his death. I think someone murdered him."

"Why would someone want to murder Mr. Crestworthy's secretary? What was his name?"

"Bentley Gillam. And I don't know. That's why I haven't said anything to the police yet. We none of us can think of any reason anyone would want to do away with him, but we just don't believe it happened the way they said."

"What did they say happened?" Phyllida asked, assuming he meant the police investigators.

"That someone saw him floating in the river and called for help. They pulled him out, but he was already dead. Looked like he'd been carried downstream and got caught up in a tree branch or he might have gone farther." Mr. Tums wore a miserable expression. "Poor chap. That inspector said he must have fallen in, but I don't believe it. I simply *don't* believe it. He never went near the river at all. Bentley wasn't the sort of chap who liked walking about or fishing or any such thing. He didn't spend much time in the outdoors. He liked to sit in a chair and read a book, he did, and he didn't like to cycle either."

Phyllida nodded. "I see. Do you or does someone else in the household know what he was doing on the day he died? What would take him from the house to the river?"

Mr. Tums seemed relieved that she was taking this new inquiry seriously. "That's just it—it's only that he mentioned he had a very difficult meeting that afternoon and he was rather upset about it all. And he hoped that it would end up all right. But he was determined to do the right thing, 'come hell or high water' he said." Mr. Tums grimaced.

"Did he give any indication of whom he was meeting or where?"

"No. But the parlourmaid he was sweet on—Linda—er, I mean to say, Anna is what we call her—said he left on foot instead of a bicycle and went round the back of the house, not the front. Which seemed quite odd. If he was doing a meeting in the village or at the factory office, he would leave from the front."

"Very interesting. Now, what is behind the house?"

"It's the walking path that leads along the river and around the cemetery and into the village."

"So he was clearly going to the proximity of the river," Phyllida said.

"Yes." The butler appeared miserable. "But that didn't mean he would go *near* it."

"Quite. Very well, I shall see what I can discover. In the meantime, do you know why Mrs. Crestworthy was upset about her visitor today? Do you know who it was?"

"She didn't say, but apparently she had *two* visitors." Mr. Tums appeared rather ill at ease. "It was, apparently, quite an undertaking for her to answer the door twice."

Phyllida made a *hmm*ing sound but otherwise didn't speak. There was more and she just had to wait.

"I believe," Mr. Tums said slowly, as if working through the process of giving himself permission to speak, "I mean to say, I got the impression that she was telephoning her solicitor in London over the bad news she received this morning."

Phyllida *hmm*ed again, with just a bit more encouragement for him to go on.

"I—I am quite certain I heard the word 'divorce,'" he said quietly. His expression was pained, for it was clearly outside of the norm for him to share such private details of the household. Phyllida was quite certain the only reason he did so was because of who she was.

"I see. And what, in your estimation, would give Mrs. Crestworthy cause to divorce her husband? I presume that this was prompted by whatever information she received from her callers today."

Mr. Tums battled within for a moment then at last he spoke so quietly she could hardly hear him. "Infidelity."

Phyllida nodded in satisfaction. "That was my suspicion as well, Mr. Tums. Thank you for confirming it. I do appreciate everything you've told me, and you may rest assured I will keep your counsel confidential." She started for the door, then paused. "Should anyone call or ring here looking for me, please let him know that I am going to walk that path behind the house Mr. Gillam took, and then I will be on my way to Ivygate Cottage and Kell's Corner on the river."

"Very good, Mrs. Bright," replied Mr. Tums, his expression turning slightly more optimistic. "I will tell the other downstairs people that you are on the case. *Thank you.*" He was far too proper to take her hand in emphasis, but it wasn't necessary. His gratitude shone in his face.

The path that led away from Crestworthy Manor and toward the river was a charming and pleasant walk. The formal gardens gave way to a small lea dotted with daisies, poppies, and other wildflowers, and a fringe of forest edged the estate's parcel.

When the path forked, requiring Phyllida to make a decision on which direction, she chose the left, western, route. That would lead her to Kell's Corner and also behind Ivygate Cottage, the other two locations she intended to visit. Then the path would curve around to a side road with a narrow bridge that crossed into Listleigh on the far west side. The other direction would have taken her directly to Listleigh, and she suspected that if Bentley Gillam's destination had been the village, he would have left from the front of the manor house.

The walking trail followed the basic path of the river, and Phyllida could hear its gentle rumbling in the distance. She caught sight of the sparkle of water between trees at different spots along the way until all at once, her route came much closer to the riverbank. There were trees along the edge, but they didn't grow as thickly, and there were patches of grass and meadow along the way.

She had no idea where Mr. Gillam was going for his meeting, and since it had happened well over a week ago, she knew there wouldn't be any remnants left behind from whatever the rendezvous. But she wanted to walk the path anyway, to give her little gray cells a chance to work.

There were a number of spots along the riverbank where a person might stand to fish, or a group or couple might arrange for a picnic under a large, solitary tree. Even from where she walked, Phyllida could see that the riverbank sloped gently to the water. It would be difficult for someone to accidentally fall in and be in water deep enough to drown them.

She reminded herself that when Bentley Gillam died, however, the river had swelled its banks a bit more and had rushed faster and stronger. Surely that was a factor in his death—whether it was accidental or murder.

After a time, the path curved away from the river and meandered through fields and small wooded copses. Phyllida had walked this way before, but not recently, and not with murder on her mind. It wasn't long before she caught sight of the back of Ivygate Cottage.

She'd gone farther than she realized, but now she cut across the small clearing that led to the house. Although there wasn't a wide trail, she could see that someone—Ethel—had walked this way regularly, beginning to create a footpath.

At the cottage, she approached the rear where, as in most cases, the kitchen was located. Mrs. Gilbody was inside and invited her in when she called out.

"Oh, Mrs. Bright! How nice to see you again. I must apologize for this morning," said the housekeeper. "I was simply feeling so very down about it all."

"Quite understandable," Phyllida replied, coming through the door into a small kitchen that still boasted a coal stove and gas lamps. "Am I to understand you're feeling a trifle better?"

"Yes, just a bit. I've learned there will be services for poor Ethel the day after tomorrow. Poor Dr. Blastwick simply couldn't be roused to make a decision until today, even though the vicar called several times. Poor man. He and Miss Genevra have taken to using sleeping draughts every night, and some during the day. But they don't seem to be helping much, if you ask me."

"Is Dr. Blastwick available? I should very much like to give him my condolences. And of course, I'd like to see Genevra as well."

"Miss Genevra is out, and glad I am for it," Mrs. Gilbody said rather stoutly. "After seeing her mope about and staying in her room half the day since it all happened, it's good for her to have fresh air, it is. She was gone when I returned from the village, and I've not seen her since."

Phyllida felt a little wave of apprehension trickle over her shoulders. "That's several hours she's been out," she commented.

Mrs. Gilbody paused, her eyes suddenly wide with concern. "You don't think she's in any danger, do you? I mean to say, not in broad daylight?"

"Professor Avonlea was just found dead in his kitchen," Phyllida told her bluntly. "Do you have any idea where she might have gone?"

Mrs. Gilbody's expression turned even more terrified. "Not at all. No. She didn't say, and I left before she did."

"Perhaps Dr. Blastwick knows," Phyllida said. "Would you see if he's willing to speak with me?"

"Yes, yes, of course." Mrs. Gilbody fled the kitchen, spurred by fear and worry.

Phyllida was overcome by a sudden and overwhelming rush of dread. There was something she was missing, something she'd overlooked . . . she felt that something was very wrong. Something was going to happen.

She was beginning to think she knew what had happened and why, and the very idea made her want to be ill.

For once in her life, she hoped the direction her thoughts were going was incorrect.

So overwrought was she, Phyllida very nearly succumbed to the urge to pace, but instead came gingerly out of the kitchen into the short hall that led to the front of the house where she'd sat with Genevra . . . good heavens, was it only yesterday they'd sat in the parlor and a teary, grieving Genevra confessed that she *hadn't* been the one to see the murder? That she was the cause of her sister's death?

Phyllida heard the murmur of Mrs. Gilbody and the lower, crustier response from Dr. Blastwick.

"I've gone into the parlor," Phyllida called and was rewarded by the sounds of shuffling feet coming closer.

"I'll bring you in a nice cup of tea with plenty of sugar and milk, Dr. Blastwick," Mrs. Gilbody was saying as she helped the gentleman make his way into the room.

He moved as if he were ancient, but Dr. Blastwick hardly looked older than fifty. Phyllida had occasion to meet him only once before, but she didn't recall him appearing so fragile.

Grief could do that to a person, she knew.

"Dr. Blastwick, I'm so very sorry for your loss," she said as the man settled himself unsteadily into an armchair. Jarvis, who'd been lying on the hearth, heaved to his paws and tottered over to lie on his master's slippers. Phyllida, who'd been the recipient of such an action from Myrtle, understood it to be a show of affection rather than a burden.

"Mrs. Bright. Thank you so much for coming." Dr. Blastwick's voice was stronger than his appearance. His hair was messily combed down, with tufts sticking up in the back. He hadn't shaved for some time. He was wearing a dressing coat and slippers. "I appreciate what you're doing to help us find out what happened to Ethel. Who—whoever did such a thing . . ." His voice died off and he looked away, blinking rapidly.

Phyllida's throat burned and her eyes dampened in the face of such grief. "Ethel was a lovely woman. I'm so very sorry that she was taken from you so monstrously, and especially whilst she was so young. I'm doing everything I can to find out who did such a wicked thing."

"Thank you. Thank you so very much. Sh-she didn't want me to bother you with it," said Dr. Blastwick. "Genny, I mean. She thought we ought to let the police handle it all. But Mrs. Gilbody assured me you wouldn't mind, that you would help, and so I telephoned up to Mallowan Hall for you. Gen was angry at first, but she came round, and I was very grateful when I learned you called and spoke to her. I'm sorry I wasn't feeling up to speaking with you," he went on. "I—I hardly know what day it is." He passed a hand over his bristly face. "Excuse my appearance, Mrs. Bright."

"Not at all," she said, resisting the urge to reach over to pat his arm. Instead, she infused her gaze with sympathy. "Do you happen to know where Genevra went this morning? Where she might be now?"

His eyes widened. "Why are you asking? What do you think has happened?"

She shook her head, trying to keep her voice soothing. She hoped and prayed she was wrong and that Dr. Blastwick wasn't to face even more tragedy. "Did you see her before she left? Did she say where she was going?"

He shook his head. "No, I don't think so. I've—I've been having trouble sleeping, you see, and I hardly know what day it is. I do remember Genny bringing me a cup of tea, and telling me she loved me and she was so sorry about Ethel, but I don't know when that was. If it was today, or yesterday. It's . . . it's all so very musty in my head. I'm—I'm sorry."

"Please don't apologize, Dr. Blastwick. But I think I'd best take my leave. I believe it's important to find Genevra," Phyllida said, standing just as Mrs. Gilbody came into the parlor with a tray.

There was far more food on it than Phyllida suspected Dr. Blastwick would partake of—if any—but she sympathized with Mrs. Gilbody's intent. The poor man needed some sustenance. Perhaps he would find something appetizing among the variety.

"Oh, Mrs. Bright, you're leaving?"

"Yes. I think it's best if I try to find Genevra. It—it would make me feel better, I think," Phyllida said, still unable to suppress a growing feeling of dread.

She beckoned for Mrs. Gilbody to follow her out of the parlor. She had one more question to ask the woman.

"Can you remember when Ethel's bicycle was being repaired? I believe it was last summer sometime," Phyllida said.

Mrs. Gilbody seemed quite perplexed by this question, but she screwed up her face in fierce contemplation. "I'm sorry, Mrs. Bright, but I can't remember it at all. Her bicycle was new last summer as the doctor got it for her birthday."

Phyllida felt a spike of interest. "When was Ethel's birthday?"

"In late May. The twentieth. But I don't recall it going in for any repairs. It was new, see."

Phyllida nodded. She hadn't expected to have an answer, but she'd had to ask. "Very well. Thank you, Mrs. Gilbody."

She left Ivygate Cottage from the front because it was closer and because she wanted to check the garage. The door was open and the motorcar was gone.

So Genevra wasn't on foot, wherever she was. Phyllida hesitated for a moment—she despised feeling torn and indecisive—then started toward the rear of the cottage to the footpath from which she'd come. If Genevra had gone into Listleigh or any of the other locations Phyllida suspected she might have gone, the path would be faster to get there on foot rather than walking along Ploughman's Close.

Aside from that, she still hoped to speak to Fred Stiller. She needed to clarify the timing of Ethel's bicycle repair, once and for all. That information would confirm or deny her suspicions about what had happened to Ethel Blastwick and why.

Phyllida walked far more quickly now than she had before. She had the feeling there was no time to waste, that things were going to be happening very soon. They might already have done.

But when she came around the bend in the footpath that revealed Kell's Corner—a curve in the river with a sloping bank and a large willow that spilled its branches near the water—she was chagrined to find no one there. Fred Stiller had obviously packed up and he and his son had gone home for the day.

With a sigh, she continued on the footpath. The trail would take her to a small side road that led into the village and she could hunt Mr. Stiller down at the bicycle shop, or badger someone into telling her where he lived so she could speak to him there.

For the first time, she wished she had a bicycle to ride. Despite the hassle of managing a skirt and Mary Jane heels on such a vehicle with its greasy chain—not to mention what might happen to her hat and hair—Phyllida felt she would prefer the speed and efficiency of such a conveyance today.

Nonetheless, she hurried along, that sense of urgency nearly causing her to trip over a rock in the center of the trail because she was peering ahead through the trees in hopes of catching a glimpse of Stiller and his son along the way. Perhaps they had only just left and she could still catch up with him.

The footpath merged with the small side road a half mile from the river and the narrow bridge that spanned it on the west side of Listleigh. She strode quickly down the lane, listening for any sound of a motorcar coming up from behind while peering ahead for signs of the Stillers.

Only once was she required to move aside for a motor, but it was no one she knew or was expecting (she'd rather hoped it might be Bradford in the Daimler come to fetch her; he ought to be along anytime) and it rumbled carefully past with the driver giving her a friendly wave.

The narrow bridge that spanned the river was just ahead, and beyond she could see glimpses of the village rooftops to the right. Just as Phyllida got to the foot of the bridge, she saw a man and a young boy walking on the other side. They were heading into town after a day of fishing, poles slung over their shoulders, and a hamper, along with a line of fish, dangling between them.

"Mr. Stiller!" she called, waving as she started over the bridge.

He turned and stopped. When he recognized her, he waved and, leaving the poles, hamper, and their catch with his son, began to walk toward her.

"Mr. Stiller, I need to speak with you," Phyllida said when they met at the village side of the bridge. She wasn't out of breath, but it was close. She didn't like to be seen out of breath or in any disarray.

"Oi, then, Mrs. Bright, what can I do for you?" He smiled, his face sunburned despite the hat he wore. He smelled faintly of fish and summer day.

"Ethel Blastwick had a bicycle."

"Aye, that she did. Bought it from me shop a year ago May," he said with a smile, confirming precisely what Bradford had told Phyllida about his memory. "Her father did, I mean to say. Right nice beauty of a cycle, it was. A forest-green BSA Regency," he said with reverence. "Sleek little number."

"She had it in for repairs sometime last summer. In August perhaps, or maybe October?" Phyllida said. "Can you remember when it was—or could you look it up for me?"

His expression sobered. "Does this have to do with what happened to her, Mrs. Bright?"

"Yes it does. And your answer will be quite consequential to what happened. When did she have the bicycle in for repairs?"

Mr. Stiller scratched his nose, then pushed up the brim of his hat a bit so that his fire-engine-red hair sprang out from beneath. "Well, you see, Mrs. Bright, she never did. That bicycle was a beaut, as I said, and she run like a dream when I sold it to Dr. Blastwick.

I haven't seen that bicycle in me shop since she rode it out the door last May."

Phyllida's heart sank. "You're quite certain of this?"

"As certain as I'm standing here, Mrs. Bright."

"And there's no other shop she might have taken it to?" she asked, heedless of the proprieties of grammar in her agitation.

Fred Stiller gave her a look of comprehension. "No, Mrs. Bright. Why would she, if she got it from me and I'm the closest one?"

She nodded. "Thank you, Mr. Stiller."

"Fred, please, Mrs. Bright," he said, likely unaware of the irony.

"Fred, then. Thank you. Have a good evening." She smiled and watched as he loped off to join his equally bright-headed son, who looked to be about ten years old and exhausted—yet elated—after a long day of fishing.

She stood there for a moment, feeling weary beyond her age. She wished Bradford were here.

And then she immediately discarded the thought.

And then it stubbornly and forcefully returned, heedless of her prudent, independent-minded, battered heart. If Bradford were here, she could at least touch someone and feel the strength from them.

Sometimes it was impossible being strong and in control and always, always right.

She turned and began to walk back over the bridge. The river churned and swirled gently below. The same river that had claimed the life of a young man who, she now believed, had been purposely silenced.

She was barely halfway over the river when the motorcar appeared. It came seemingly from out of nowhere and it surged onto the bridge.

Phyllida froze for a moment, spinning to face the vehicle as it roared toward her. It was a terrible moment of déja vu.

She could run, but she would never outrun the motorcar and make it across the bridge in time. The span was too narrow for her to dodge; there was nowhere for her to go.

Nowhere but over the side of the bridge.

As the Hispano-Suiza, with its sharp-beaked stork mascot mounted proudly on the hood, flew toward her, Phyllida launched herself over the side of the bridge.

She heard a shout, felt the heat of the motorcar and the blast of its energy as it roared past, and felt herself falling, flailing, tumbling . . . and then she plunged underwater.

CHAPTER 19

THE RIVER WAS A COLD, TERRIBLE SHOCK. BUBBLES SHOT PAST HER face, water filled her ears and stung her eyes as she plunged deep into the shadowy depths.

Phyllida fought to the surface with difficulty; she had fallen far and fast, and had touched the bottom with her feet. Some water had gone up her nose, stinging and sharp, and she fought to keep from choking as she kicked to send herself back up.

At last she burst free, up from the rushing water as her lungs burned from the effort of holding in her breath. She spewed it out, gasping as more water splashed into her face and nose, and fought not to cough or choke, fought to keep her nose and mouth free of the waves.

The river might not be as full and fast as it was two weeks ago, but it had a current and she was stupefied by shock, and it had been some time since she'd been swimming.

She fought back the panic and tried to move her arms and legs in the way she knew, struggling to catch her breath as the water splashed and churned and tossed her about.

There were shouts; she heard them, but she couldn't tell from where they were coming. It sounded like her name, but she couldn't find the source. She was fighting to keep her face above the water as the trees and bushes on the riverbank trundled past as easily as if she were on a little skiff.

All at once someone grabbed her, yanking, dragging her away. For an instant, she almost panicked and clutched wildly at whatever or whoever it was, then she somehow calmed herself and relaxed as hands—several of them; strong, capable—maneuvered her toward the shore.

It was a blur of movement, tugs, shouts, water, fog, a great rushing in her ears, until finally she was staggering toward the shore, dripping, her clothes sagging heavily over her body. Someone was holding her up on either side.

By now she recognized her rescuers: Fred Stiller and, perhaps not so miraculously, Bradford.

She wanted to collapse when her feet touched the riverbank, but she refused to allow herself. Instead, she used the closest tree to prop herself up as there was a flurry of activity around her, voices talking—lecturing her about being foolish (that was Bradford)—asking if she was all right (Fred Stiller). Someone wrapped her in a coat. It smelled like Bradford.

"I'm fine," she said once she'd assured herself that she wasn't about to empty her stomach of river water in front of everyone. Her knees were trembling and someone, warm and solid, was standing behind her so she could lean against him without looking as if she was doing so. Bradford.

"I'm fine," she said again. "It was a nice day for a swim," she managed, trying for some levity.

"Blimey, Phyllida," was all Bradford said.

"Thank you," she said, looking at him and then Fred Stiller. Fred's son stood there, wide-eyed, gap-mouthed, still holding the line of trout or bass or whatever it was they'd caught.

"I saw the motorcar," Fred said. "I heard it first. And then I saw it. It just—it just came right at you. It didn't stop. It wasn't slowing down. I couldn't get there in time. I shouted and—"

"Thank you," Phyllida said. "I can swim, thank goodness."

"Not in a bloody river," Bradford snapped.

"It certainly wasn't my plan when I left the house today," she retorted, then had to clamp her teeth together to keep them from chattering. "Bradford," she said, placing a hand on his arm. It was warm and solid, and she really wanted to surge into him and have those strong, warm arms come around her.

But she couldn't.

She started to speak, then words failed her. She hated what she knew. Hated that she was going to have to do what she was going to do.

"Who was it?" he asked in a slightly gentler voice. "You know who it was this time, don't you." It wasn't a question.

She looked at him. "It was a Hispano-Suiza."

His face stilled with comprehension. "The stork mascot. You never mentioned that there was a Hispano-Suiza at the dinner party."

Phyllida looked away. "It never occurred to me that Genevra Blastwick had been driving the vehicle that killed her sister. It never occurred to me, that is, until today. I'd been following up the wrong . . ."

She shook her head sharply and stepped away from Bradford's solid support. "We've got no time to lose. We've got to find her. We've got to find her before it's too late."

"Phyllida, you're soaking and shivering, and—"

"We have to find her," she said flatly.

"Blimey, Phyllida, I've never met a more stubborn woman in all my bloody life," Bradford said as he spun away.

For a moment, she thought he was leaving; then she realized he was going to get the Daimler. It was parked not far from where she'd been retrieved from the river.

Apparently, she hadn't been carried nearly as far along as it had felt during those infinitesimally long . . . and yet, shotgun-quick . . . minutes.

"Mrs. Bright?" Fred said.

"Please do call me Phyllida," she said. "I feel as if someone is going to save my life, he ought to be able to be familiar with me, don't you think?"

"Aye, of course, but if you could just take one minute, I'm certain Sally, me wife, would give you a dry frock. And—and some shoes. It's only just round the corner, and, honestly, ma'am," he said, making her feel like his mother for some reason, "she'd as like to skin me hide if she found out I let you go on like that."

"There's no 'letting' Mrs. Bright do anything," said Bradford, who'd turned back from the Daimler. "She'll do as she damned well pleases, but I do think even Mrs. Bright will see the sense in your suggestion. It will take only a few minutes, Phyllida," he said sharply when she thought about arguing.

She acquiesced, mostly, she told herself, so that poor Fred Stiller wouldn't get a lambasting from his wife—who sounded very sensible, and in fact, turned out to be quite so.

It was only a few minutes after all, and not only did Phyllida get a fresh and clean-smelling frock and a pair of shoes that were slightly too large, she was also the recipient of a vacuum flask of hot tea. She was rather glad to have had a few moments in front of a mirror, for she did look quite a fright. Her face was streaked with dirt and mud. Her hat was long gone and her hair, quite wavy and curly when it was dry, hung like coiling rat tails nearly to her shoulders. She was able to comb it out then bundle it up in a wrap to sop up some of the water, which would help to keep the shoulders and back of her dry frock from getting wet again.

But she didn't want to waste any more time, and soon enough, Phyllida was ushering Bradford out the door to where he'd brought the Daimler while she was changing.

"Where are we going?" he asked.

"I think . . . I think . . ." Phyllida closed her eyes for a moment. Her brain was a whirlwind of thoughts and fears and worries. "I think . . . to Ivygate Cottage."

Bradford cast her a surprised look, but said nothing more. He reached over and closed his hand over her colder one and squeezed.

And then he drove.

CHAPTER 20

Phyllida held herself in a tight, tense position, hardly daring to breathe during the short drive over the bridge where she'd nearly been killed, down the lane, and to the side road that led to Ivygate Cottage.

She didn't take a full breath until she saw the Hispano-Suiza sitting in the drive, and then she exhaled forcefully.

One of her fears had not come to pass.

But there were others that she would need to face.

She climbed out of the motorcar and hurried to the front door without waiting for Bradford. She knocked and called loudly, ready to let herself in if necessary. Mrs. Gilbody arrived rather quickly with a harried and surprised look on her face.

When she saw who it was, Mrs. Gilbody relaxed. "Oh, Mrs. Bright, she's back! Miss Genevra has returned! She's here and she's safe. Please, come in."

It took all of Phyllida's composure not to push past the housekeeper and rush in to find Genevra. "Where is she?" she managed to ask in a steady voice. Her heart pounded in her ears. "And where is Dr. Blastwick?"

"Why, my goodness, I said she was safe, didn't I," Mrs. Gilbody said, taken aback by Phyllida's vehemence. "And she and the doctor are sitting out yonder, back near the river, having a little bit of a picnic, they are. First time I've seen him willing to—"

Phyllida brushed past her and fairly dashed through the house, down the short hall, into the kitchen, and then out the rear door. She could hear Mrs. Gilbody squawking her shock and affront behind her and left Bradford to soothe. He was much better at that sort of thing than Phyllida was.

She pelted across the small yard to the footpath she'd used only an hour or so ago.

It wasn't difficult to find them. The two Blastwicks were arranged under the low arch of an old maple, sitting on a blanket. Food and drink items were spread out in front of them. The river tumbled gently beyond, its blue sparkling in the late afternoon sun.

"Why, Mrs. Bright," said Dr. Blastwick, who was facing in her direction. He tried to haul himself to his feet, but couldn't quite manage it and sagged back down. He seemed even foggier than he'd been earlier, and Phyllida's throat dried.

Genevra turned and her eyes met Phyllida's from across the way. She didn't rise or speak. She merely watched as Phyllida drew near while handing a teacup to her father.

"Don't!" Phyllida said sharply. "Genevra, please don't do it. Dr. Blastwick, don't drink that—"

"It'll be much better," Genevra said, pressing the teacup into her bewildered father's hands. "For him. Drink it, Papa. Drink some more."

Phyllida launched herself forward and lunged for the cup Dr. Blastwick was holding. She knocked it out of his hand, and nearly bowled the man over.

"What on earth—" he gasped, trying to pull himself upright.

"The tea has poison in it. I'm not certain what. At first I thought it would be pentobarbitone, but . . . I was wrong about that."

"Only a sleeping draught," said Genevra in a flat, cold voice. She had made no effort to rise. "Plenty of it will put someone to sleep forever, won't it, Papa? That's how my mother did it, by the way," she said, looking at Phyllida with eyes as cold as her voice.

Phyllida nodded—she hadn't known that—then looked around to make certain there was nothing else Genevra had that could be used as a weapon. If it was only the drugs in the tea, then she could talk to her. Reason with her. She saw nothing but a small paring knife as part of the picnic supplies and decided to keep her eye on it.

"What is this? What is going on?" Dr. Blastwick said. He appeared shell-shocked as he looked wildly from his daughter to Phyllida.

"I didn't want him to know," Genevra said. "It's better, Mrs. Bright. Don't you think? It's *better* this way. He's suffered enough—"

"His current suffering is your fault, Genevra," Phyllida said as a shadow fell over her from behind. Bradford, and from the sounds of snuffling, Mrs. Gilbody as well.

"Mrs. Gilbody, Bradford, would you please help Dr. Blastwick into the house," Phyllida said, never taking her eyes off Genevra. "He's going to need . . . well, he's going to need his dog and some tender care. And I think you ought to call Dr. Bhatt. I believe Dr. Blastwick has been highly dosed with some sleeping draught. Hopefully it's not too late."

As her confused, slightly protesting father was helped to his feet, Genevra merely watched. Her eyes were rimmed with red, but they were cold. Her hands, which sat in her lap, were still and pale.

Once the others were out of earshot, she said, "I knew it was a mistake to call you in. I knew you'd figure it all out. I was so *angry* when I learned that Papa had telephoned you, even after I told him not to. I begged him not to. I . . . I knew it would end this way. And so when you came, I had to—I had to play the game."

"Tell me," was all Phyllida said.

Genevra heaved a sigh and looked into the distance. "It's rather complicated." She seemed disinclined to speak further.

"It started with your affair with Rutherford Crestworthy, didn't it?"

Genevra's eyelids fluttered and she looked down. "Yes, I suppose it did. It was only supposed to be a little romp, but I became rather attached to him. And he's got loads of money. We stayed at places like the Savoy and the Ritz when we met up in London, and over in Wenville Heath at a cunning little inn. Papa knew I loved the city and he never thought once about me going in for a visit.

"It was," she said with a fat, satisfied smile, "rather exciting to be at the dinner party with my lover sitting next to me, and his wife right there... and no one knowing the truth. Even whilst playing footsie with him as he touched my thigh during the dinner, I thought I played my part very well." She looked at Phyllida for confirmation.

"Other than your blatant announcement that you were involved with a married man," Phyllida said dryly. "But, I do concur, there was no outward evidence of your... connection."

Genevra seemed pleased by this admission. "Yes. It was all going very well. We enjoyed being together, and it was all right that he was still married. I knew that should he divorce that dried-up, foolish Myrna, he'd lose all of his money. It's her family's business, you see. She's rather controlling and certainly not the sort to look away from being a cuckold. She'd take it all and he'd be left destitute.

"I didn't want that, of course, and so I was content with the way things were. Ruthy bought me jewelry and took me to nice places... it was he who helped me afford the motorcar, if you can believe the irony."

"And then... Bentley Gillam found out."

Genevra's expression darkened. "Yes. We were so careful, but Bentley was Ruthy's secretary and he poked his nose into everything. He must have seen us or heard a telephone call or something..." She shrugged. "And he caught me one day in the village and told me that if I didn't 'walk away and leave Mr. Crestworthy alone'—that's just how he said it, in his prissy, Oxford voice—then *he'd* tell Mrs. Crestworthy what was going on. I knew what would happen then." She picked up her teacup and sipped.

When she caught Phyllida looking at her drink in speculation, Genevra smiled. "Not to worry. There wasn't enough to drug mine too. I had to pretend to take all of my doses and only give Papa half of his in order to have enough for him. I hid them away." She made a jerky gesture to the spilled teacup.

Phyllida tended to believe her. She thought she knew what Genevra had in mind. After all, Jarvis was still tottering about on all fours. That also meant that another of her fears had likely not come to pass. "And so you decided you had to silence Bentley Gillam."

Genevra looked off into the distance as she nodded. "It wasn't something I *wanted* to do, you see," she said. "But it needed to be done. Ruthy and I had a trip to Paris planned for next week—he was going for business, of course—and I didn't want anything to happen to change that. I've always wanted to go to Paris, and Papa would never take us.

"Instead, he spent all his time digging in that bloody barrow of his, spending money on tools and artifacts and foolish things like that instead of us. He changed after Mum died. I don't know . . . I don't know whether she did it purposely or whether it was a mistake."

Phyllida did not allow the stony heart she'd adopted for this moment to crack even a little, despite the sorrow in Genevra's eyes.

"How did you manage it, with Bentley Gillam? I have my suspicions, but I'd like to hear it from you."

A crafty smile replaced the sadness in Genevra's face. "I told him I wanted to meet with him to discuss the situation. I made it sound as if I was willing to pay him for his silence because I knew he'd be so outraged, he'd want to tell me to my face what a terrible person I was." Her voice faltered at that moment.

"It wasn't difficult. If there's one thing about Bentley, it's that he thought of himself as a gentleman and he could always be counted on doing the right thing. So we met—it wasn't far from here, actually—very near the river. I knew he was terrified of water and that he couldn't swim. We grew up together, you see, here in Listleigh.

"Anyhow, the timing was perfect because of the rains we'd had, so even if Bentley could have floundered to the shore during a normal time, the bigger river would make that difficult.

"I'd had it all prepared before he arrived. The riverbank edge was very muddy and slippery, and I added more water along the edge to make it even worse, and I made the incline steeper.

"When he arrived, he found me very upset because my hat had

just flown off and landed right at the edge of the river, on a branch. It wasn't even in the water, just over it. Perfectly positioned.

"Of course Bentley went to retrieve it for me—gentleman that he aspired to be. He slipped and fell, just as I had planned. He tumbled into the water, and the next thing I knew, he was floating away. All my troubles were floating away." She said this last part dreamily. "I watched it all . . . float . . . away."

Phyllida swallowed hard in order to hold back the vicious words she wanted to say. Instead, she spoke very calmly. "And if he hadn't fallen in?"

"I would have helped him if I'd had to. But I knew he would fall. It was very slippery. I nearly did myself when I was hanging up my hat, and I had a walking stick with me. I didn't have to do anything but watch." Her lips curved in a smile that faded suddenly, sharply. She looked up. "And then I saw Ethel." Her eyes went hard and her lips flattened. "She'd been out rambling, like she always was, and she was standing there."

"And so Ethel did see a murder."

Genevra gave a jerky shrug. "She wasn't certain what she'd seen. I thought quickly, I'll tell you, and I came up with a story that made sense.

"'Oh, thank God, Ethel,' I said, crying as I ran toward her. 'My hat fell in the river and h-he went to get it out, and he fell in. I tried to save him, but I couldn't.'"

"'He, who?' Ethel was looking out over the river. I said, sounding very upset, 'Bentley Gillam, the poor thing. He was such a gentleman. He tried to g-get my hat and he fell in.' Ethel sort of gasped and ran as fast as she could toward the river. I almost thought she was going to do the same thing as Bentley had done, and slip right in. It might have been better if she had," Genevra murmured. Her eyes were far away, staring into the distance as if she was trying to separate herself from the tale she was relaying.

Once again Phyllida had to clamp her jaw closed to keep from screaming at the girl. She saw from the corner of her eye that Bradford had returned and he stood back a distance. Watching, but allowing the two women to speak uninterrupted.

"I begged Ethel not to tell anyone what had happened. I pleaded with her: 'I couldn't save him—it happened so fast. There's nothing we can do, and—and I feel so terrible about it all. As if it was my fault. Please do say you'll keep it quiet, Ethel. I feel *so bad* about it all. I think I'll have nightmares.'

"I'm not sure how I convinced her, but she agreed not to tell what she'd seen. The damage was already done, and poor Bentley Gillam would be found eventually." Genevra brushed off her skirt. "We compromised and she made a telephone call to the constable's office, telling them she thought she'd seen someone fall into the river, but couldn't be certain. That was all we could do."

"And then . . . ?"

"And then about a week later she came and confronted me. She said she thought the whole situation had seemed strange and she realized afterward what seemed odd to her. That my hat hadn't been wet . . . and neither was I." Genevra grimaced. "She pointed out that if my hat had been in the water, it would have been wet. And, more damningly, that if I had tried to help Bentley when he fell in, *I* would have been wet—at least on my shoes and socks— and I hadn't been.

"Of course she was right, and I suppose she could tell by my reaction. She told me that if I didn't come clean and report what really happened, she would do it for me. I don't know whether she knew what I-I really did, or if she just suspected. Even so, she was going to report me. She didn't *care* that I was her sister!" Genevra's eyes filled with tears and fury. Her pretty face turned sharp and hard. "She would have turned me over to the police. It would have been manslaughter at best!"

Phyllida nodded. She didn't think she could find the words to speak at that moment. Fortunately, it seemed that Genevra, once started, had no intention of stopping.

"And so I asked her for a couple of days to think about it, and she agreed. She didn't want anything bad to happen to me, she *said,* so of course she understood why I needed the time. She'd figured out about me and Ruthy a while before that and I think she realized why I—why Bentley had to . . . go. Ethel wasn't happy about that either. My relationship with Ruthy. She said it was *wrong* and *unethical* and all of those old-fashioned ideas.

"But Ethel was *very* upset about Bentley." Genevra was playing with the hem of her frock now, where it had bunched up around her ankles where she was sitting on the blanket. "So you see, I didn't *intend* to kill her. Not at that time. I was trying to think of a way to convince her. To . . . make her see reason. It was on the way to the dinner party that she told me my time was up. She was done waiting and that if I didn't come clean, the next day she was going to do it for me.

"I'll be honest. It wasn't until we were eating dinner that I had the idea—about the game, I mean. A way to . . . well, to give someone a motive for . . ." She swallowed. "For getting rid of Ethel."

"So you purposely lied and said you'd seen a murder, knowing that was Ethel's truth and not yours."

"That's right, because if *she'd* seen a murder, then *she* was in danger from the murderer," Genevra said, spreading her hands for emphasis. "But everyone knows *Ethel* was the sort of person who would never say something like that in public—to announce that she'd seen a murder! And so I had to do it in order to . . . well, to open the topic. To put the idea out there, you see? And then when she turned up dead, everyone would run around in circles, looking for whoever had done the murder she saw. That's what *you* did." She arched a brow at Phyllida and it took every bit of control for Phyllida not to slap that look of superciliousness off the woman's face. She restrained herself with great effort, hardly remembering a time she'd been so furious, so filled with disgust and loathing for a person.

"Of course, Ethel didn't realize why I'd said such a thing during the game," Genevra went on. "She only thought I was teasing her about it all. Playing with her, poking at her. I liked to tease her, you see. That's part of the reason we don't—didn't—really get on."

"And that's why she got out of the motorcar and walked home," Phyllida said, pleased that her voice came out steady and neutral. Murder aside, Genevra Blastwick was not a very nice person. "You argued about it when you were driving away. Did you purposely upset her, rile her up, knowing she'd get out and walk?"

Genevra heaved a breath, a smile playing about her mouth. "I might have done. Ethel was not a sort of confrontational person, you see. And she was very predictable. I knew she'd get out and stomp home. I . . . I didn't know what I was going to do after. I truly didn't.

"It's just that I got so *angry* with her, trying to ruin my life, trying to play like she was so much better than me, that she had better morals than I did, that she was a better person! I—I didn't even really know what I was doing when I . . ." She heaved a shuddering breath. "I just was so angry. So, so angry."

Phyllida sat there for a moment. Her fingers were curled tightly in her lap, clenched together to keep them from lashing out at the monstrous person in front of her. She'd known she didn't care for Genevra Blastwick. She just hadn't realized it was because of who the woman was as a person, not simply because she was tiresome and impetuous.

"And so you drove over your sister. You rammed into her with your motorcar, ran over her, and then did it again and again . . ." Phyllida's voice choked off as nausea welled in her stomach. "*Your sister.*"

There was silence. The sounds of the river gurgling in the near distance and birds twittering filled the moment. Phyllida was conscious of Bradford, standing stony and silent, just beyond.

"I regretted it as soon as I realized what I'd done," Genevra said. Her voice was low and unsteady and Phyllida saw a teardrop plop down into the woman's lap. "I couldn't believe what I'd done. I just—I just didn't *think*. I just . . ." She looked up, eyes that had been slightly red-rimmed now rosy and glistening with tears. "I didn't lie when I told you it was my fault. That I'd killed Ethel. I was telling the truth then, you see."

Phyllida nodded. Yes, she realized that. She hadn't *wanted* to realize it, hadn't *wanted* to think that a person could do what Genevra had done to her own flesh and blood . . . and that was why it had taken her so long to understand what had happened.

She supposed she'd known, deep in her heart, from the first moment she spoke to Genevra that morning after. But it was such a monstrous thing, such a horrific thought, that she'd not allowed it to take form in her mind.

She hadn't looked in the garage at the motorcar she knew was in there. She hadn't told Bradford that there had been a Hispano-Suiza at the dinner party, parked *right next* to her own motorcar—the first one to leave after her own.

She swallowed hard. The nausea was insistent, and she was still a little shaky from her unexpected plunge in the river.

"And now . . . you were trying to do away with your own father too?" she managed to say.

Genevra shrugged, words failing her at last. Tears were falling more rapidly now and she couldn't lift her face. "He . . . he's suffered enough," she whispered. "I couldn't do this to him as well. Let him learn the truth. If h-he knew w-what I'd done . . . I thought . . ." She shrugged.

A sound behind had Phyllida turning to look toward the cottage. Inspector Cork and Constable Greensticks were striding across the yard toward them. Genevra took a shuddering breath and shifted, struggling to get to her feet. She canted to one side, stumbled, then bumped against the maple's trunk as she withdrew her hand from her pocket.

Phyllida saw a glint of something and the sharp movement too late. She cried out, lunging toward the girl . . . but it was already done.

The hypodermic needle had been shoved into Genevra's own thigh, and the plunger was all the way down.

Genevra caught her eye. "I couldn't . . . I didn't want to . . . go on." She sank back to the ground as the police approached.

"It's too late," Phyllida said, turning to Inspector Cork. Her words were brittle and her insides heavy. "She's injected herself with, I believe, pentobarbitone. It won't be long."

"Pento-what?" the inspector said.

Genevra was sitting on the ground, staring into space. She seemed to be showing no discomfort, no distress.

"You saved it for yourself, then. Not Myrna Crestworthy." Phyllida gestured to the hypodermic needle, which now lay innocently on the blanket.

"I . . . thought about it. I even stopped by to . . . visit her today. She knew." Genevra huffed a dark laugh. "She already knew . . . And so . . . I might have . . . might have done it then. But . . . if she died, that would be the end of the trip to Paris next week. Wouldn't it?"

Phyllida closed her eyes briefly and took a deep breath. It was a shame Genevra Blastwick would not face justice for her monstrousness.

She crouched next to the dying woman and said, "And Professor Avonlea. That wasn't you, was it?"

Genevra shook her head. A grimace crossed her expression. "Not me," she said. "I-I saw him leaving . . . Crest . . . worthy today, b-but . . . it wasn't me. I kn-knew he'd seen me . . . and Ruthy . . . that night, after the card game. In t-town. He was the one . . . told Myrna about it." Pain spasmed over her face and she shuddered, slumped . . . and was gone.

CHAPTER 21

*P*HYLLIDA MANAGED TO KEEP HERSELF TOGETHER THROUGH THE ENsuing explanations to the police (which she made as succinct as possible) and a wholly unnecessary "examination" by John Bhatt due to her unexpected dip in the river—accompanied by the assurances that Dr. Blastwick would be fine—but no sooner had the Daimler turned off the lane leading out of sight from Ivygate Cottage than she directed Bradford to pull over.

She erupted from the vehicle and promptly, violently, lost the contents of her stomach.

"Sorry about that," she muttered when she felt Bradford come up behind her. She was unpleasantly clammy and shaky, and suspected her face was sheet white.

"Blimey, Phyllida," he said for the third time that day, thrusting a handkerchief into her hand. The inflection on this occasion, however, was more of affection and exasperation than irritation or anger. He didn't wait for her to finishing wiping her mouth before enveloping her in the close, steadying embrace she'd desired earlier but would not allow herself to have in public.

They were still in public, standing here by the side of the road where anyone might happen by, she reminded herself, and reluctantly extracted herself from his strong, warm arms.

"Thank you, Bradford," she said, a little primly and a little shakily as she folded up the handkerchief. "Today has been most difficult."

"Just another day in the life of the great Inspector Bright," he said, injecting what he probably thought was a note of levity into the moment, even as he reached out to caress her cheek with the back of his hand. It was a gentle, welcome touch. "Back to Mallowan Hall, then?"

She was about to agree when another thought entered her mind. It was, after all, Wednesday, and there was one more mystery she wanted to put to rest. She was feeling a trifle better now that her stomach was no longer churning. "Perhaps we could make a stop at the vicarage first."

He gave her an odd look, but agreed.

By now, the sun had nearly set and twilight burned around them. The village was quiet and the only activity seemed to be a pair of patrons going into the Screaming Magpie.

Phyllida was feeling even more steady by the time they arrived at Mr. Billdop's vicarage, due in part to the remnants of the tea—still hot—remaining in the vacuum flask pressed on her by Sally Stiller.

"Why, Mrs. Bright," said Mr. Billdop when he opened the door to find her standing there. He wore a completely astonished expression that metamorphosed into one of chagrin and discomfiture. His cheeks turned pink and so did the tips of his ears.

Phyllida tucked away a small smile. So she'd been correct.

"If I may come in for just a moment, Mr. Billdop," she said, for she truly had a practical reason for being here. "I should like to speak with you about Dr. Blastwick and his daughters. There have been some . . . developments."

"Oh, my . . . well, Mrs. Bright, I-I don't . . . it's not really . . ."

"You might just as well let the blasted woman in," growled a voice from the depths of the cottage. "You won't get rid of her otherwise."

"Oh, goodness, Mr. Dobble, what a surprise to find you here," Phyllida said in a tone she didn't even attempt to infuse with consternation. There was no sense in playing along with such a farce.

The butler appeared, looming behind Mr. Billdop. His coat was missing and so was his tie. His waistcoat was unbuttoned as well. Phyllida had never seen him dressed so informally. He appeared almost human.

"Checkmate, then, Mrs. Bright," he groused, even though they both knew he and the vicar weren't playing chess tonight. Then he looked behind her and saw Bradford. "I might have suspected," Dobble added grimly as he and Mr. Billdop stepped back to allow them entrance.

"Never mind that, Mr. Dobble," Phyllida said. "I truly do wish to speak to Mr. Billdop. Something terrible has happened over at Ivygate Cottage. I suspect Dr. Blastwick is going to need some bracing up from his vicar, as well as other friends."

"Oh dear." Mr. Billdop's expression turned to one of genuine concern as he gestured for her to sit on a settee in the front room. "I suppose you've found out who killed Miss Ethel?"

As Phyllida launched into a description of what had happened, Mr. Billdop's face grew tighter and worried and even more concerned.

"How absolutely wicked," he said at last in a shaky voice. "And I am so very grateful that you came to me, Mrs. Bright. I shall go to Ivygate Cottage immediately to speak with Dr. Blastwick."

Phyllida patted his hand. "There's no need tonight, I think," she said. "He was dosed rather heavily with the sleeping draught and according to Dr. Bhatt should be left to rest overnight. But I am certain he will appreciate a visit tomorrow morning. He will have much grief to work through."

"Yes, yes, of course," replied Mr. Billdop. "I will certainly do that."

Phyllida rose from the settee. "Thank you," she said. "I'll take my leave and let you get on with your . . ." She peered into the depths of the small house and saw that the study was lit up.

Two steps in that direction solved the great mystery of what had been in Mr. Dobble's pantry.

It was a model train set. A very complicated and detailed train set, complete with realistically painted papier-mâché mountains and tunnels, small cottages and larger mansions, little motorcars, trees, ponds, meadows . . . and, of course, an electric model train with shiny blue cars and a red caboose. It looked like every young boy's dream—and, apparently, that of grown men as well.

"I do hope you enjoy the rest of your evening," she said, glancing at Mr. Dobble—whose expression had returned to its normal one of hauteur—and then Mr. Billdop.

"Well, Mrs. Bright," said Bradford as they drove away, "you've solved all of the mysteries . . . save one, I think."

"Which is?"

"That of who did away with Professor Avonlea," he said.

"Oh, I know who did that," she replied. "I shall have to advise Inspector Cork tomorrow. He rather has his hands full today, I thought. It was Mrs. Greenhouse."

"Was it now?" He sounded surprised, a fact which warmed her heart. She delighted in having one over on him, because he was quite often nearly as astute as she was.

"Yes, and before I explain, I must congratulate you on being correct," she said, feeling rather charitable now that everything was over. Not for Dr. Blastwick, for sure, but at least he could begin to heal once he learned the worst.

"Oi, what? Again? And what is it that I've done correct this time?" He reached over to close his fingers over her hand. "Lord, woman, your hand is *freezing*."

"The remnants of my unexpected swim, I suppose," she said. "My hair is still quite damp."

"Well, I can certainly think of an excellent way to warm you up, there, Mrs. Bright." She could hear his smile even though she wasn't looking at him. "But first, do tell me how I was right again, if you please."

"It was only that you said Genevra might be lying about seeing a murder—or about Ethel seeing a murder. She *was* lying. The entire time. Everything she told me was a lie. And that was how I realized the thing I most dreaded was true: She lied about Ethel's bicycle being repaired."

"Aye, indeed. One should never give too much detail in a lie. It tends to trip one up."

"Quite. Now, about poor Professor Avonlea," she said, ready to steer the conversation back to her own deductions and conclusions. "As I said, it was Mrs. Greenhouse who decided to silence him. I can only conjecture, but it seems quite obvious that somehow Professor Avonlea purposely or unknowingly provided her with the bees to arrange for the murder of her husband. I suspect she wanted to do away with him after he ran over her beloved pet dog. Perhaps she knew it wasn't an accident.

"And when I began poking about, asking questions about those unexpected deaths, Mrs. Greenhouse certainly heard about it—everyone in town knew about it and was talking about it—and I suspect she thought she'd best do away with the professor before he said something that incriminated her.

"I believe that Mrs. Greenhouse not only put the bees in her husband's motorcar, but also that she did not leave anything to chance. She injected him with pentobarbitone as well—a syringe of pentobarbitone which she received from Mr. Varney in order to, purportedly, euthanize one of her cats. She used the same method to kill Professor Avonlea. She may even have stolen more of the drug from Mr. Varney's office in order to make certain she had enough to kill the professor. I wouldn't be surprised if she'd intended to add the—er—window dressing of some dead bees into the professor's kitchen, but I suspect she might have been interrupted by Mrs. Waltz's return before she was able to do so."

Bradford whistled. "And Miss Genevra Blastwick was also in possession of the same lethal drug?"

Phyllida nodded grimly. "Yes. She had convinced Mr. Varney that it was time to end poor Jarvis's life. She did not do so, in favor of taking the coward's way out from justice. For a while, I feared that she intended to use it on Mrs. Crestworthy.

"At any rate, someone is going to have to speak to Mr. Varney about his propensity for allowing his patrons to euthanize their own pets," she went on in disgust. "He's quite lackadaisical about it all, as his housekeeper has indicated."

"That sort of drug ought to be locked up," Bradford said.

"I wholly agree. I suspect Mr. Varney might find himself in a bit of legal trouble in relation to that, which is rather a shame because I think he is quite a soft-hearted man after all. Perhaps that is why he preferred to allow his patrons to end their pets' lives on their own."

She heaved a sigh and settled back into the seat of the Daimler, but a shiver took her by surprise.

"There's a blanket in the back," Bradford said, reaching behind the seat to drag over the covering in question.

"Thank you. I suppose the chill is catching up with me again," she said.

"That was a very near thing today, Phyllida," he said, his eyes focused on the road where the headlight beams shined ahead. "I was very grateful to have arrived at just the nick of time."

"I would have made it to shore, I'm sure. I *was* swimming."

"It didn't look like it to me," he said flatly.

She brushed off his appraisal. "Fred Stiller was quite the hero too," she said, unable to suppress a shiver as she remembered the way the water had completely overtaken her senses . . . and the dark depths to which she'd plunged.

"I told him so," Bradford replied. "It's rather a good thing poor Elton didn't see you slogging out of the river, though, Mrs. Bright. The way your clothes clung to your figure—and what a figure it is!—would have made the poor bloke swoon."

She smiled at his return to her formal name. He really was quite a silly man. "Incidentally, Elton had the effrontery to invite me to the Screaming Magpie to have a sherry with him on the night of the card game."

"A *sherry*? You?" Bradford snorted. "What on earth was the poor bloke thinking?"

Phyllida chuckled and leaned against his solid arm and shoulder. She was finding that she rather liked these more honest and easy interactions with Bradford. "I did set him rather straight on my preferences when it comes to spirits, as well as the inappropriateness of his suggestion. I don't suppose he's quite got the message yet."

Bradford shrugged. "He will. Eventually."

She was quite pleased that he didn't suggest that *he* should handle it or say anything to the young man. He wouldn't meddle in that affair of hers, at least.

"I've been wondering," he said in a musing voice, "what two truths and what lie you might have shared during the game when it was your turn. Or were you planning to tell three lies, only to set everyone on their ear?"

"As a matter of fact, I was. Well done, Bradford."

"But if you were to tell two truths and a lie . . . what might they be?"

She stared into the darkness, smiling. Despite the terrible day, she could find some pleasure in the moment.

"All right, then. First . . . I was once an uninvited guest at No. 10 Downing Street. Second, I once liberated an item from the British Museum . . . after hours. Third, I've piloted an aeroplane."

He grunted quietly, but otherwise gave no suggestion of surprise. "Such wide and varied statements, aren't they?" he said thoughtfully. "Aye, then, well, I look forward to determining which one is the lie, Mrs. Bright. It should be rather an entertaining investigation."

She patted him on the arm. "But don't think it'll be a simple one."

He chuckled, low and quiet. "If there's one thing I know, Mrs. Bright, there's not a thing about you that's simple."

As the Daimler's headlights revealed the driveway leading to Mallowan Hall, Phyllida had occasion to be rather grateful that Mr. Dobble wasn't home at the moment.

That way he wouldn't hear any of the strange sounds that might come from her bedroom.

ACKNOWLEDGMENTS

I had the most delightful time writing Phyllida's fifth adventure, which was inspired by Agatha Christie's *Hallowe'en Party*. I hope you enjoy the developing relationships between Phyllida and her friends (especially Bradford and Myrtle) as much as I do.

Writing is a solitary event, but the publication of a book takes a village and then some. I owe all my gratitude for the team at Kensington Publishing Corp. for all the love and effort they've put into my dear Phyllida's adventures.

Since the beginning of this series, I've been blown away by the attention to detail, the creativity, the enthusiasm, and the sheer delight that has been evident for these books. *Thank you* from the bottom of my heart, especially to my incredibly patient and understanding agent, Maura Kye-Casella, along with my brilliant and equally patient editor, Wendy McCurdy, and her on-top-of-everything assistant, Sarah Selim. Larissa Ackerman, Sofia Szyfer, Vida Engstrand, and the entire publicity, marketing, and social media team are consistently hitting things out of the park. You all blow my mind, and I'm very grateful to you for your support for this series. Lou Malcangi and Chris Gibbs have gone above and beyond by conceiving and designing the most perfect covers ever. Dame Agatha would be proud to have herself presented between such gorgeous plates, and so would, I think, Phyllida—who'd appreciate the attention to detail and the vibrancy of these covers. Every time I get a new image for this series, I spend a good deal of time admiring all of the details and picking out the wonderful elements included in the illustrations.

I have many other people to thank, including my friends and family who must constantly listen to me discuss ways to off people and to find devious ways to present clues, all within a historical time frame. Thank you to everyone, including Darlene, Gary, Erin, Devon, MaryAlice, Kate, and my love, Steve.

I'm also greatly in debt to all of the independent bookstores and their wonderful staff who have supported the Phyllida Bright

Mystery series since its inception, including (but not only!) 2 Dandelions Bookshop, Bay Books, Inscribe Books, Fenton's Open Book, Schuler's Books, Murder by the Book, The Poisoned Pen, Gathering Volumes. There are so many more to list that I'd be here forever, listing each of them. Thank you also to libraries and librarians all over the country who have purchased for circulation and highlighted Phyllida and Co. in their mystery sections and in their book clubs. I appreciate each and every one of you who've hand-sold, recommended, loaned, or otherwise talked-up these books. Thank you for helping to keep reading alive, and for helping Phyllida to solve even more cases!

And thank *you*, Dear Reader, for picking up *Two Truths and a Murder*. I hope you enjoyed the read and perhaps have been inspired to take a perusal of Christie's original works, including the one that inspired this story.

I love to hear from readers and can be reached at my website, colleencambridge.com.